NEW GAME! 3 volume | Shotaro Tokuno

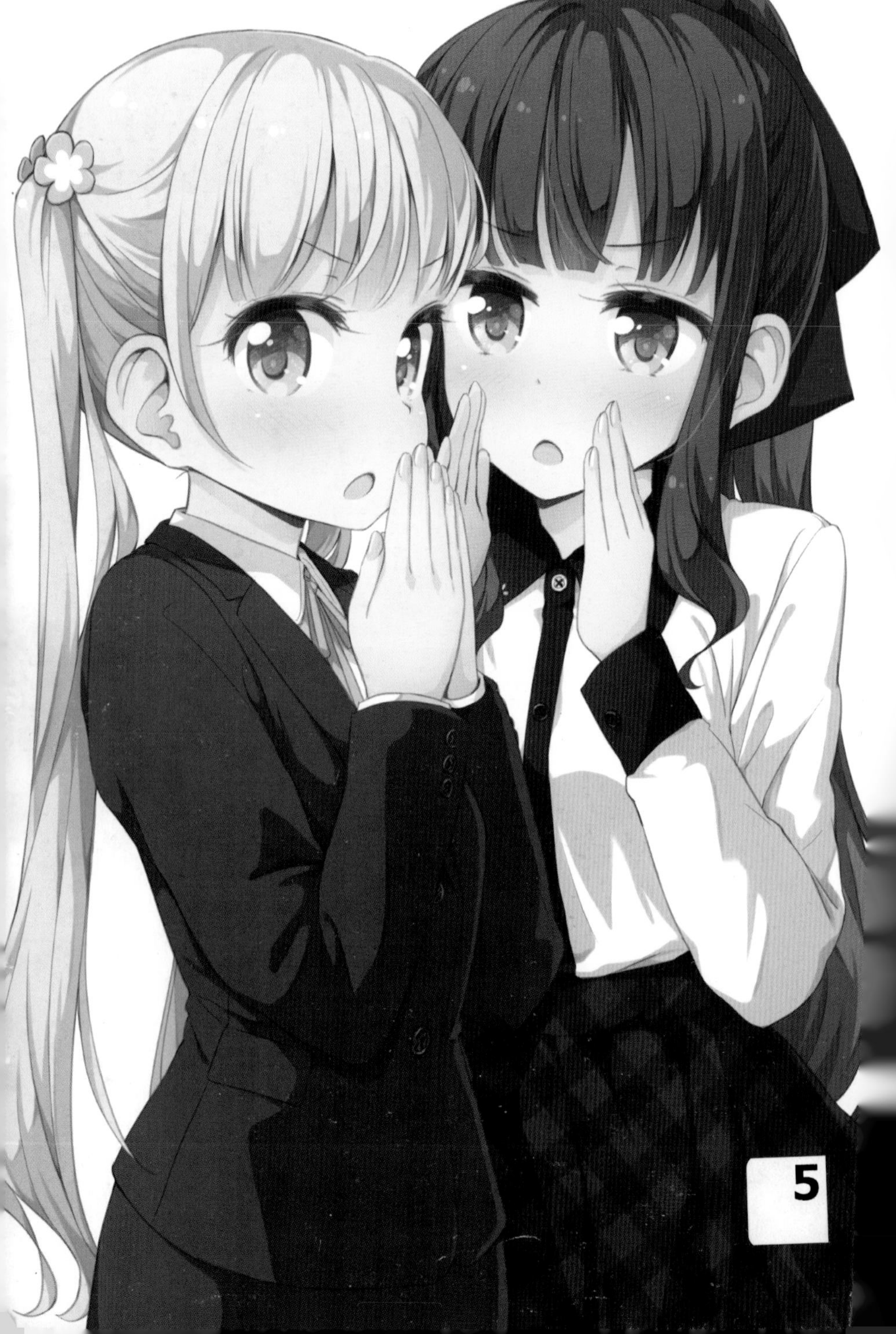
5

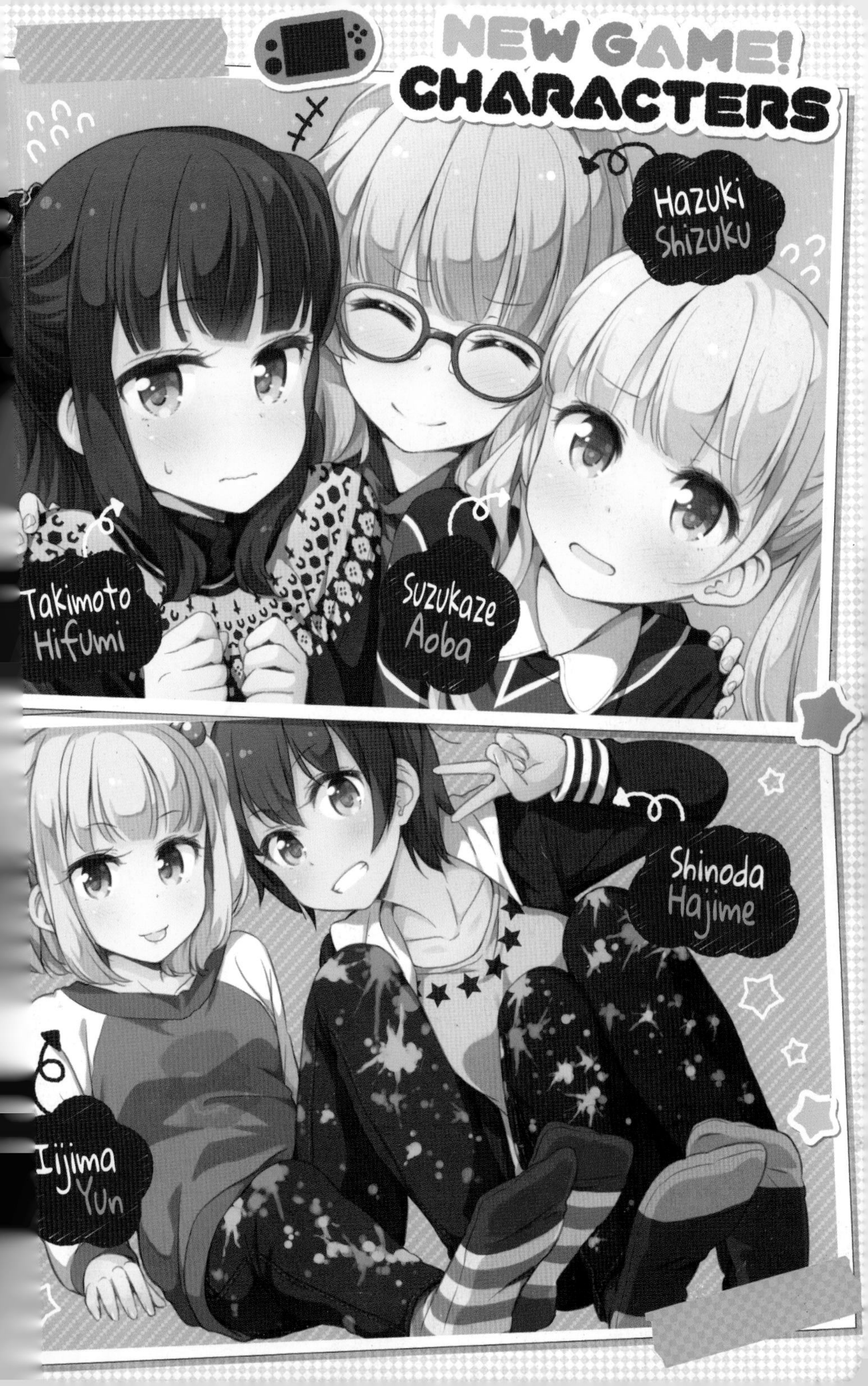
NEW GAME!
CHARACTERS
Hazuki Shizuku
Takimoto Hifumi
Suzukaze Aoba
Shinoda Hajime
Iijima Yun

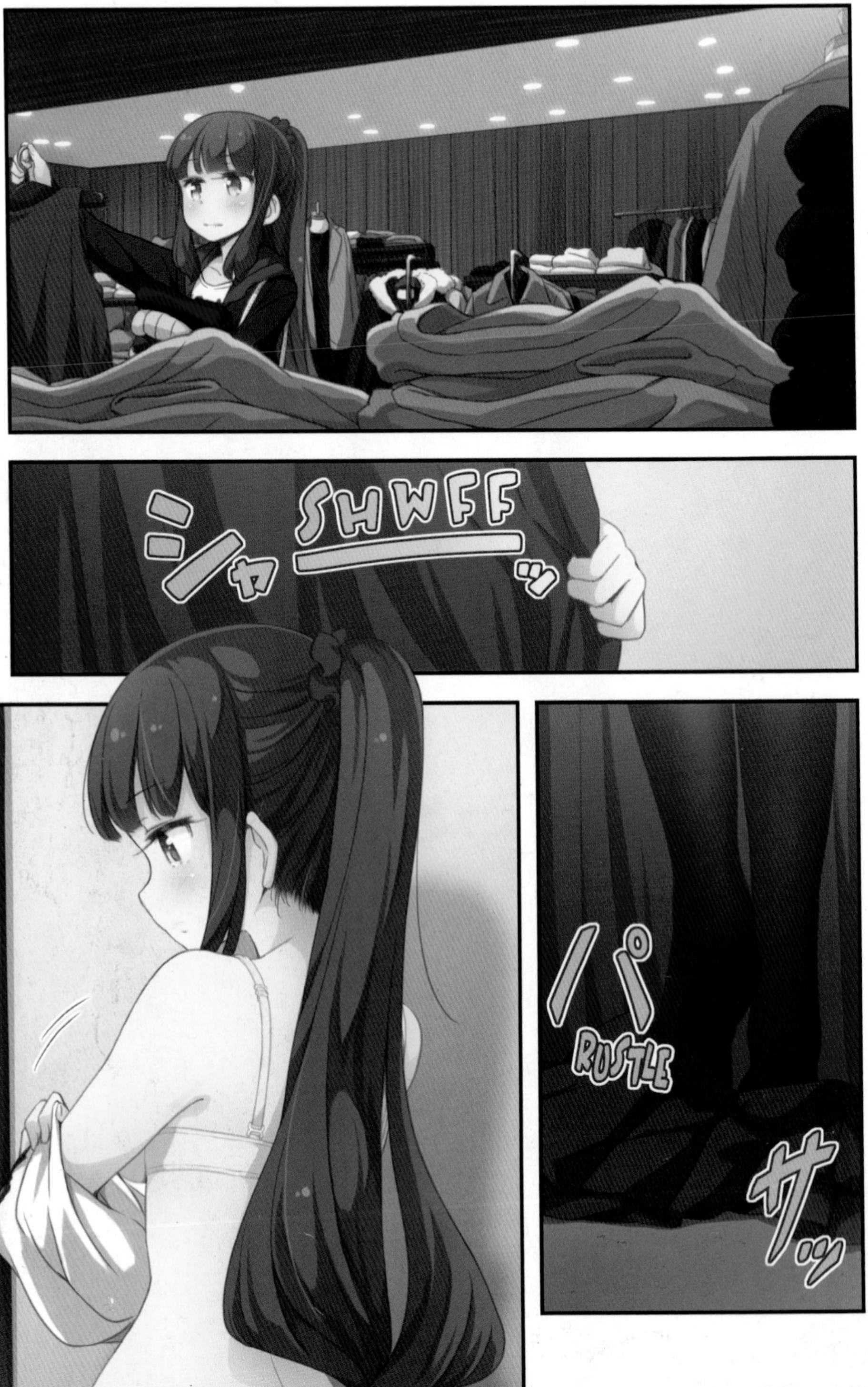

シャッ
SHWFF
パ
RUSTLE
サッ

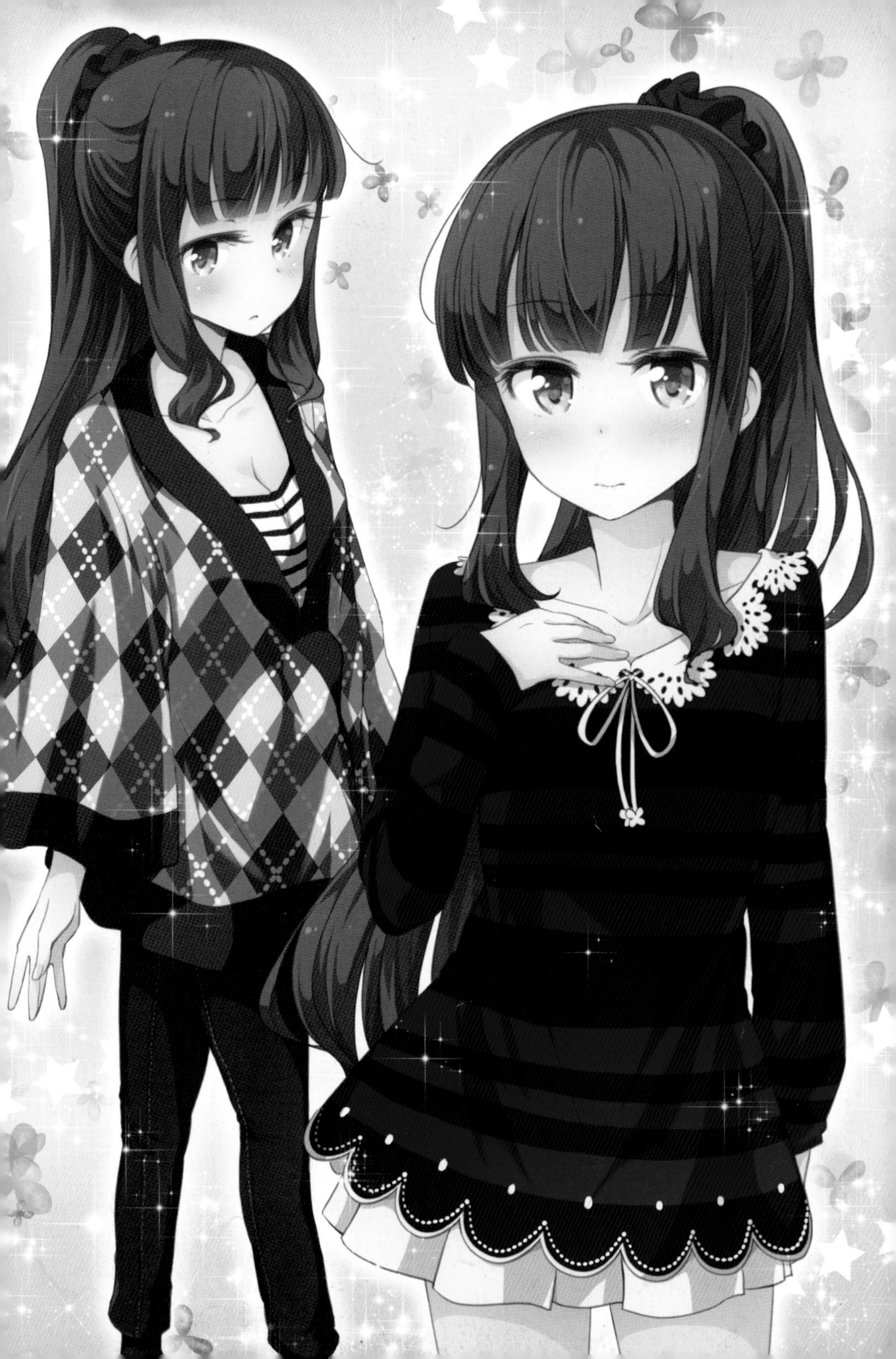

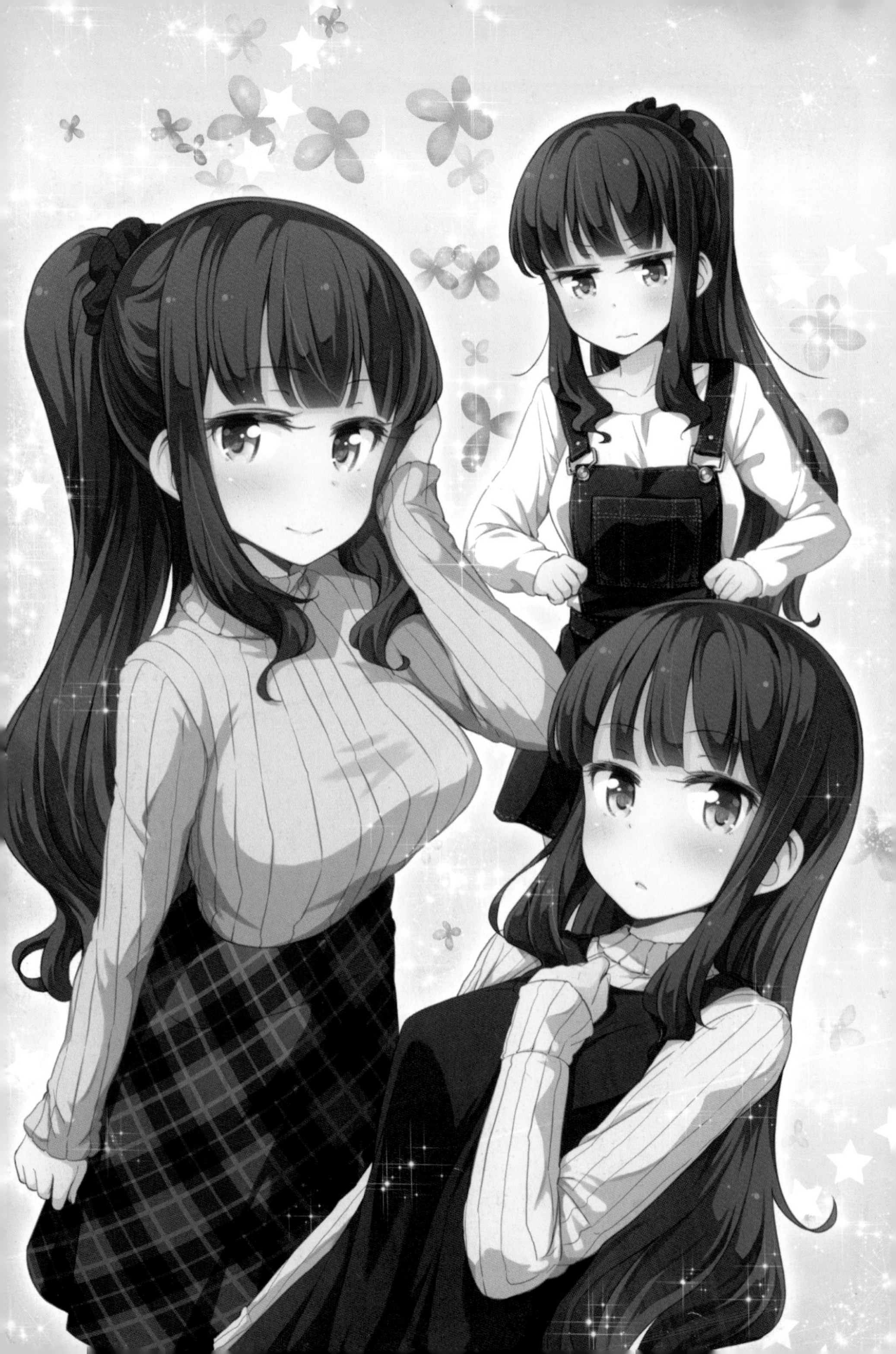

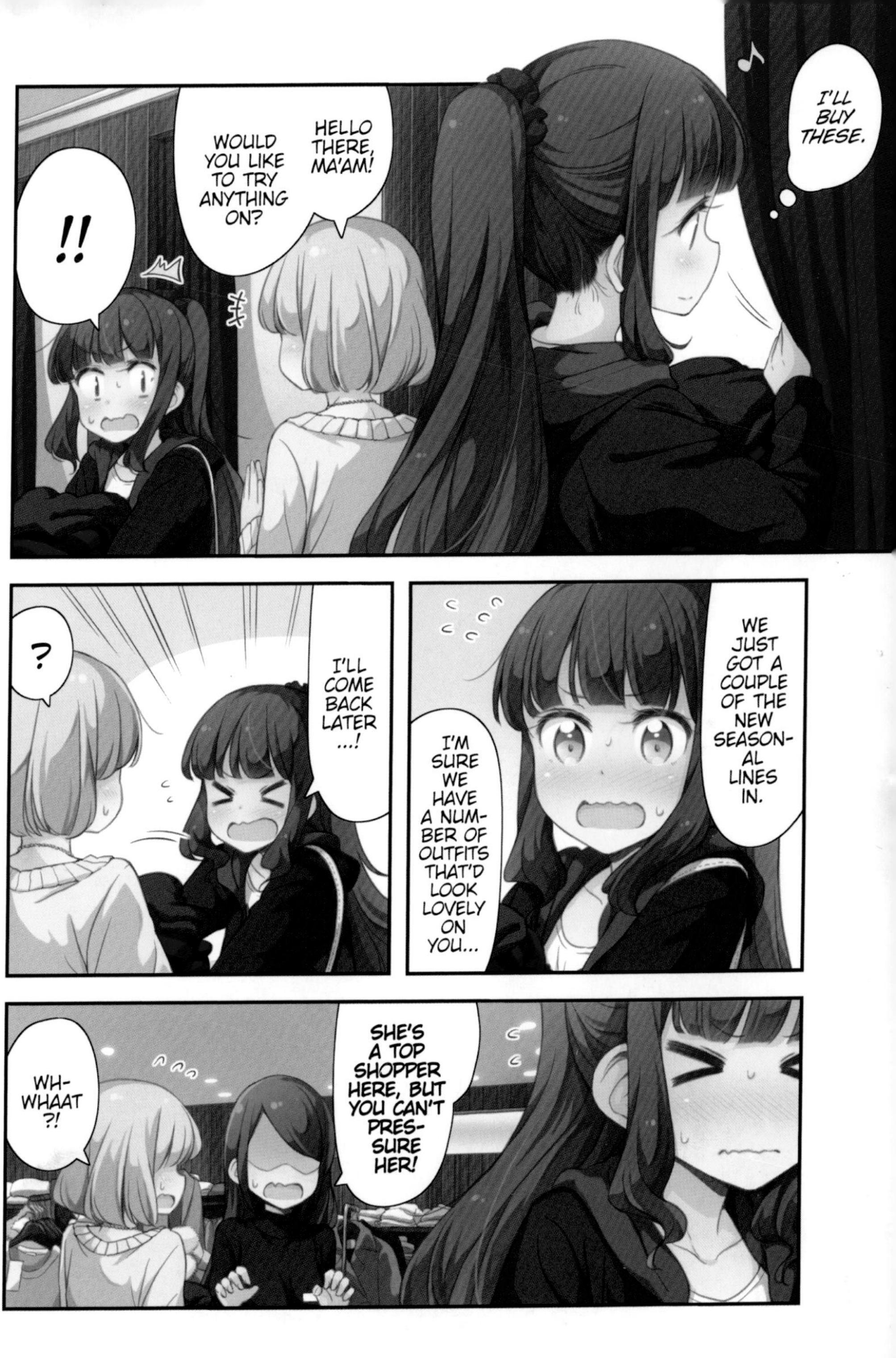
I'LL BUY THESE.
HELLO THERE, MA'AM!
WOULD YOU LIKE TO TRY ANYTHING ON?
!!
WE JUST GOT A COUPLE OF THE NEW SEASON-AL LINES IN.
I'M SURE WE HAVE A NUM-BER OF OUTFITS THAT'D LOOK LOVELY ON YOU...
I'LL COME BACK LATER ...!
?
SHE'S A TOP SHOPPER HERE, BUT YOU CAN'T PRES-SURE HER!
WH-WHAAT?!

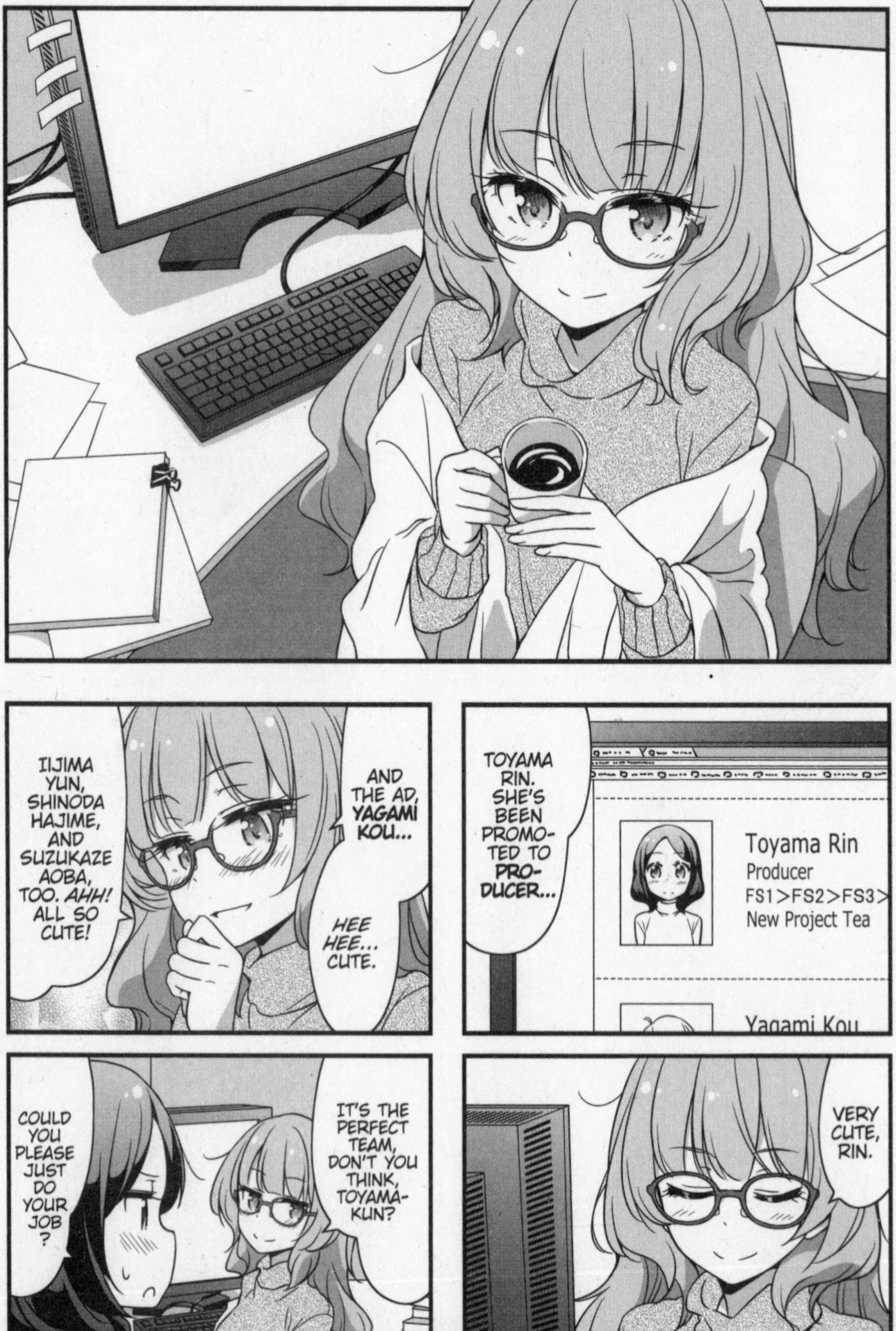
TOYAMA RIN. SHE'S BEEN PROMOTED TO **PRODUCER...**
Toyama Rin
Producer
FS1>FS2>FS3>
New Project Tea
Yagami Kou
AND THE AD, **YAGAMI KOU...**
IIJIMA YUN, SHINODA HAJIME, AND SUZUKAZE AOBA, TOO. *AHH!* ALL SO CUTE!
HEE HEE... CUTE.
VERY CUTE, RIN.
IT'S THE PERFECT TEAM, DON'T YOU THINK, TOYAMA-KUN?
COULD YOU PLEASE JUST DO YOUR JOB?

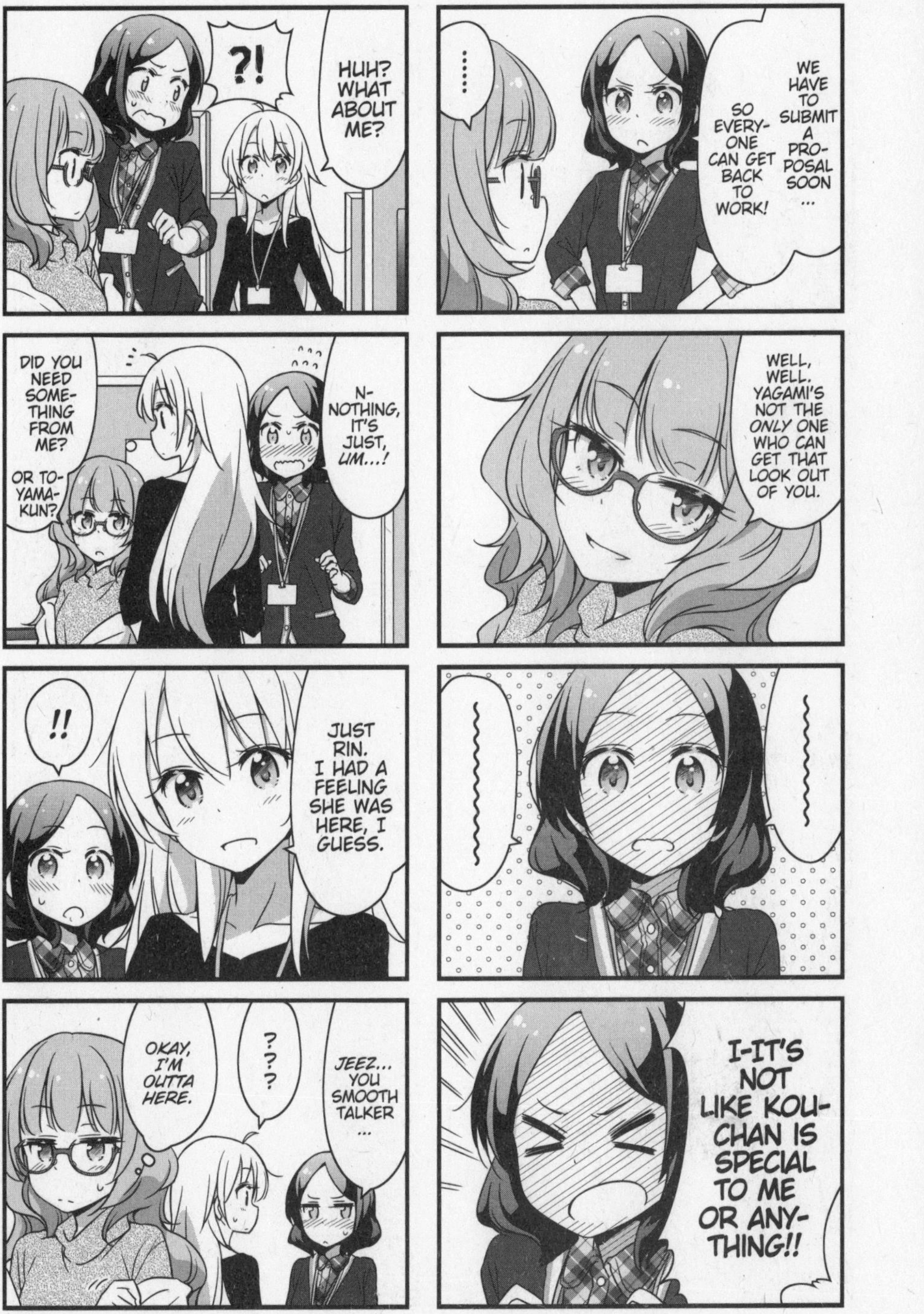

WE HAVE TO SUBMIT A PROPOSAL SOON ... SO EVERYONE CAN GET BACK TO WORK!
......
HUH? WHAT ABOUT ME?
?!
WELL, WELL. YAGAMI'S NOT THE *ONLY* ONE WHO CAN GET THAT LOOK OUT OF YOU.
N-NOTHING, IT'S JUST, *UM...!*
DID YOU NEED SOMETHING FROM ME?
OR TOYAMA-KUN?
JUST RIN. I HAD A FEELING SHE WAS HERE, I GUESS.
!!
I-IT'S NOT LIKE KOU-CHAN IS SPECIAL TO ME OR ANYTHING!!
JEEZ... YOU SMOOTH TALKER ...
???
OKAY, I'M OUTTA HERE.

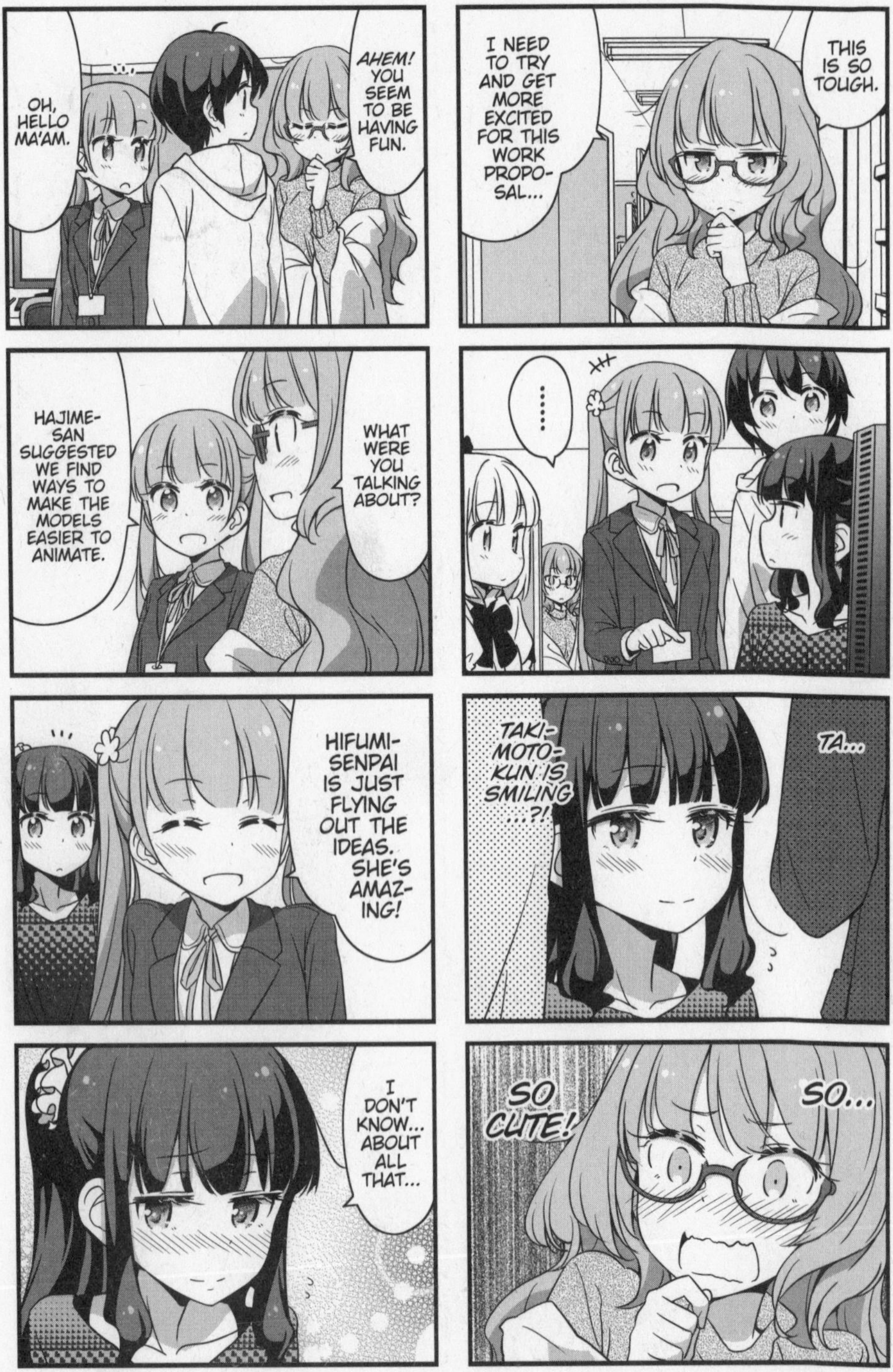
THIS IS SO TOUGH.
I NEED TO TRY AND GET MORE EXCITED FOR THIS WORK PROPOSAL...
AHEM! YOU SEEM TO BE HAVING FUN.
OH, HELLO MA'AM.
......
WHAT WERE YOU TALKING ABOUT?
HAJIME-SAN SUGGESTED WE FIND WAYS TO MAKE THE MODELS EASIER TO ANIMATE.
TA...
TAKI-MOTO-KUN IS SMILING...?!
HIFUMI-SENPAI IS JUST FLYING OUT THE IDEAS. SHE'S AMAZING!
SO...
SO CUTE!
I DON'T KNOW... ABOUT ALL THAT...

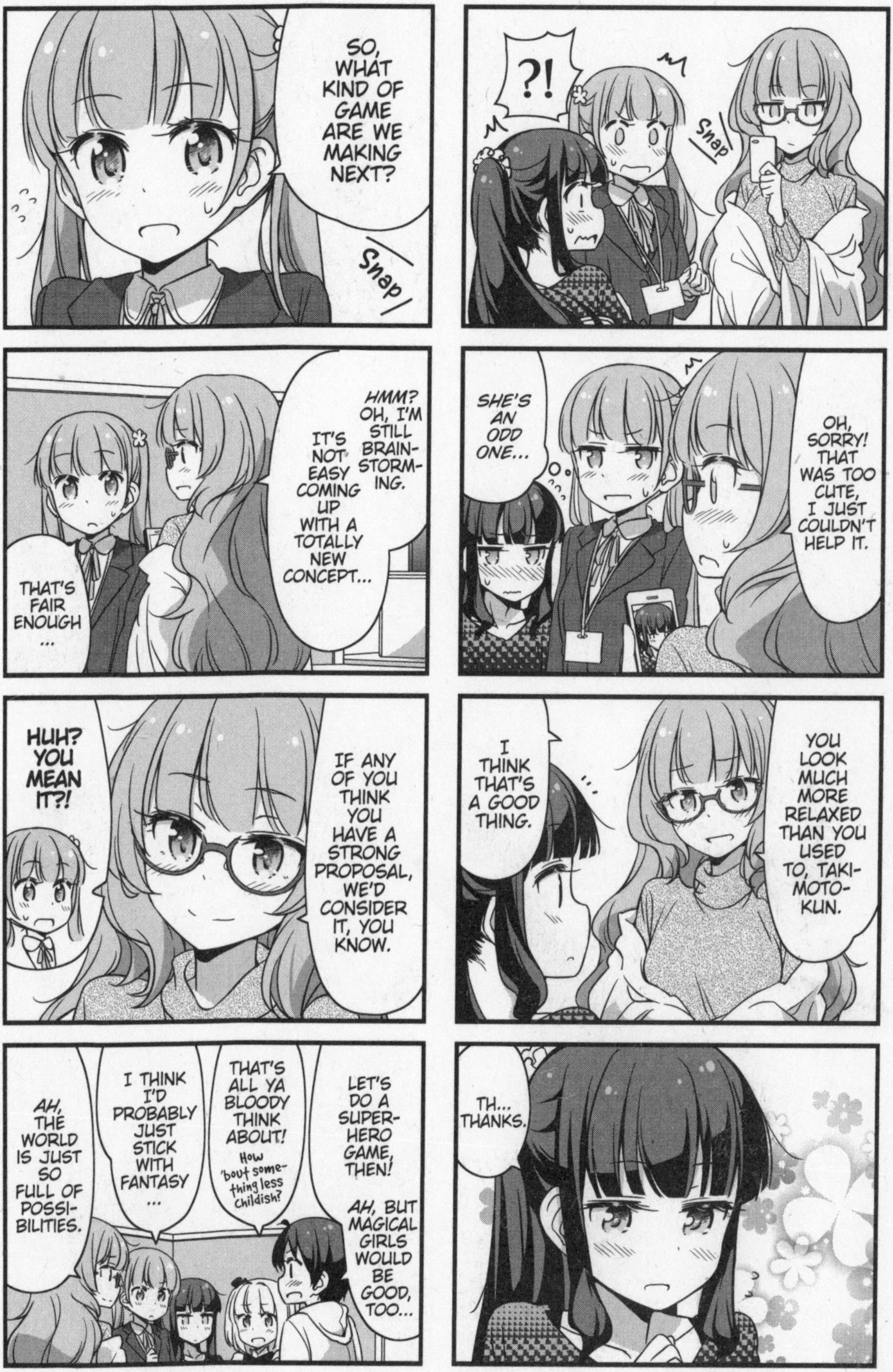
?!
Snap
SO, WHAT KIND OF GAME ARE WE MAKING NEXT?
Snap
OH, SORRY! THAT WAS TOO CUTE, I JUST COULDN'T HELP IT.
SHE'S AN ODD ONE...
HMM? OH, I'M STILL BRAIN-STORMING.
IT'S NOT EASY COMING UP WITH A TOTALLY NEW CONCEPT...
THAT'S FAIR ENOUGH...
YOU LOOK MUCH MORE RELAXED THAN YOU USED TO, TAKI-MOTO-KUN.
I THINK THAT'S A GOOD THING.
...
IF ANY OF YOU THINK YOU HAVE A STRONG PROPOSAL, WE'D CONSIDER IT, YOU KNOW.
HUH? YOU MEAN IT?!
TH... THANKS.
LET'S DO A SUPER-HERO GAME, THEN!
AH, BUT MAGICAL GIRLS WOULD BE GOOD, TOO...
THAT'S ALL YA BLOODY THINK ABOUT!
How 'bout some-thing less childish?
I THINK I'D PROBABLY JUST STICK WITH FANTASY...
AH, THE WORLD IS JUST SO FULL OF POSSI-BILITIES.

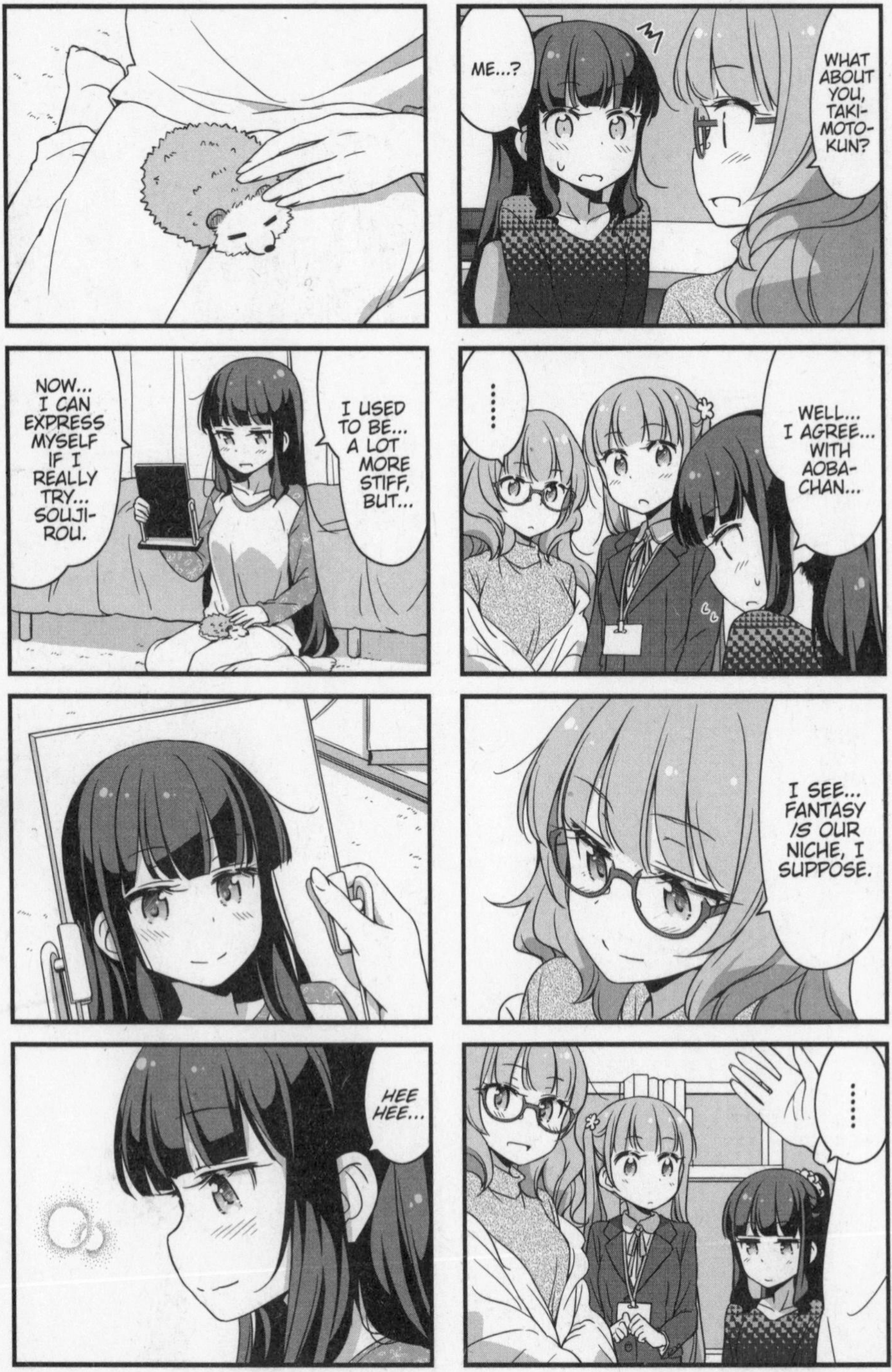
WHAT ABOUT YOU, TAKI-MOTO-KUN?
ME...?
WELL... I AGREE... WITH AOBA-CHAN...
......
I USED TO BE... A LOT MORE STIFF, BUT...
NOW... I CAN EXPRESS MYSELF IF I REALLY TRY... SOUJI-ROU.
I SEE... FANTASY IS OUR NICHE, I SUPPOSE.
......
HEE HEE...

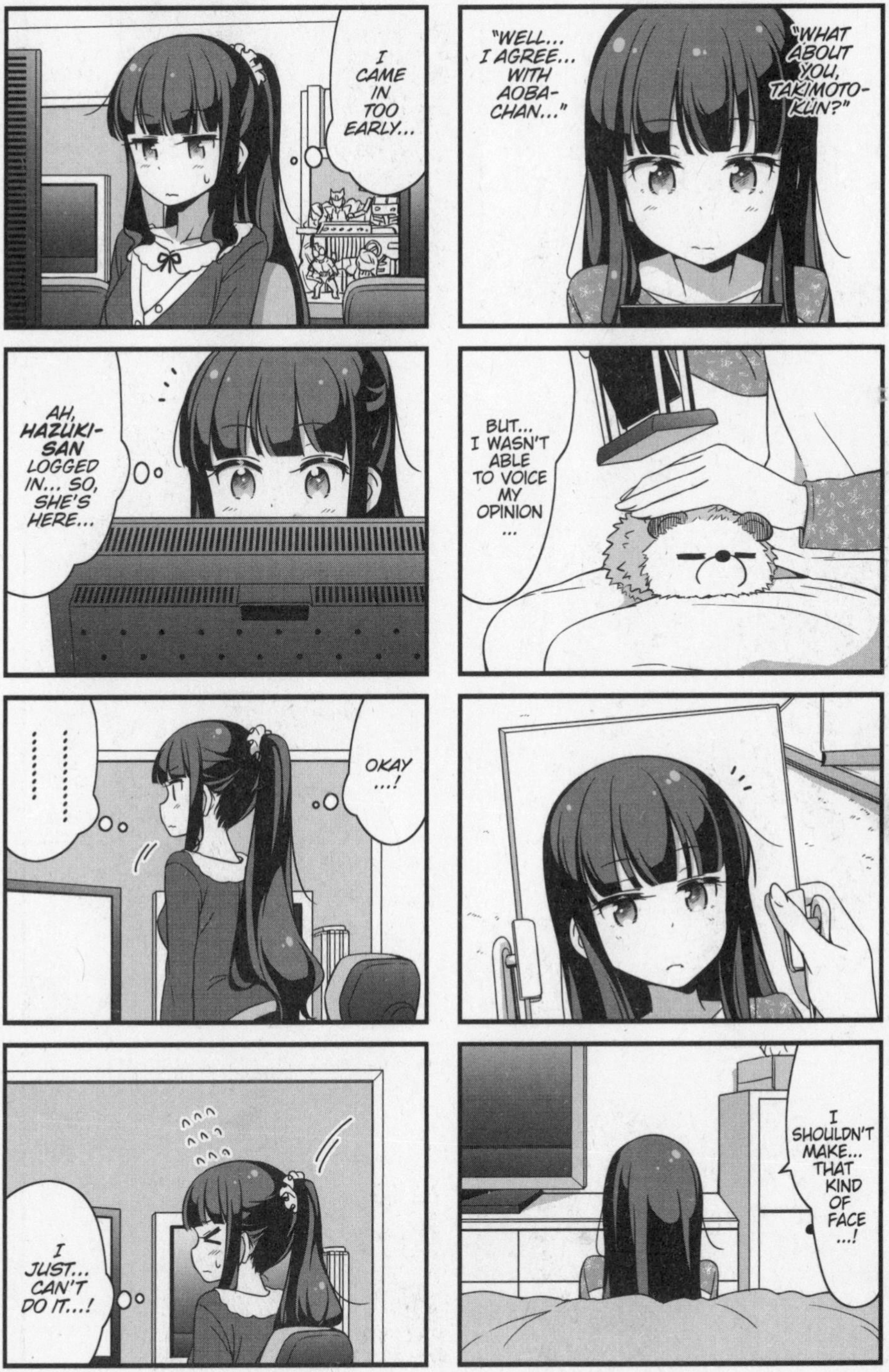
"WHAT ABOUT YOU, TAKIMOTO-KUN?"
"WELL... I AGREE... WITH AOBA-CHAN..."
BUT... I WASN'T ABLE TO VOICE MY OPINION ...
I SHOULDN'T MAKE... THAT KIND OF FACE ...!
I CAME IN TOO EARLY...
AH, HAZUKI-SAN LOGGED IN... SO, SHE'S HERE...
OKAY ...!
....
I JUST... CAN'T DO IT...!

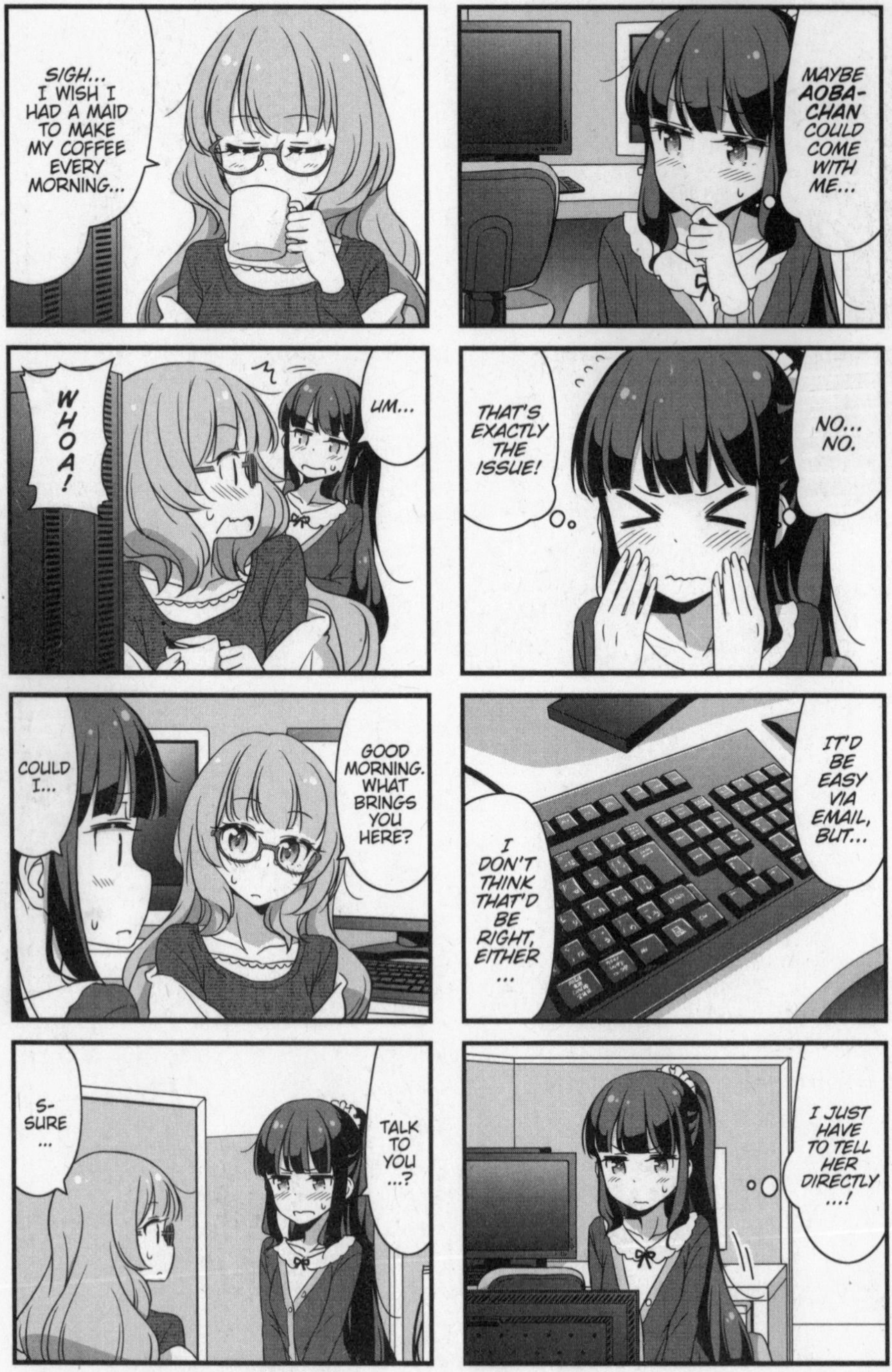
MAYBE AOBA-CHAN COULD COME WITH ME...
SIGH... I WISH I HAD A MAID TO MAKE MY COFFEE EVERY MORNING...
NO... NO.
THAT'S EXACTLY THE ISSUE!
UM...
WHOA!
IT'D BE EASY VIA EMAIL, BUT...
I DON'T THINK THAT'D BE RIGHT, EITHER ...
GOOD MORNING. WHAT BRINGS YOU HERE?
COULD I...
I JUST HAVE TO TELL HER DIRECTLY ...!
TALK TO YOU ...?
S-SURE ...

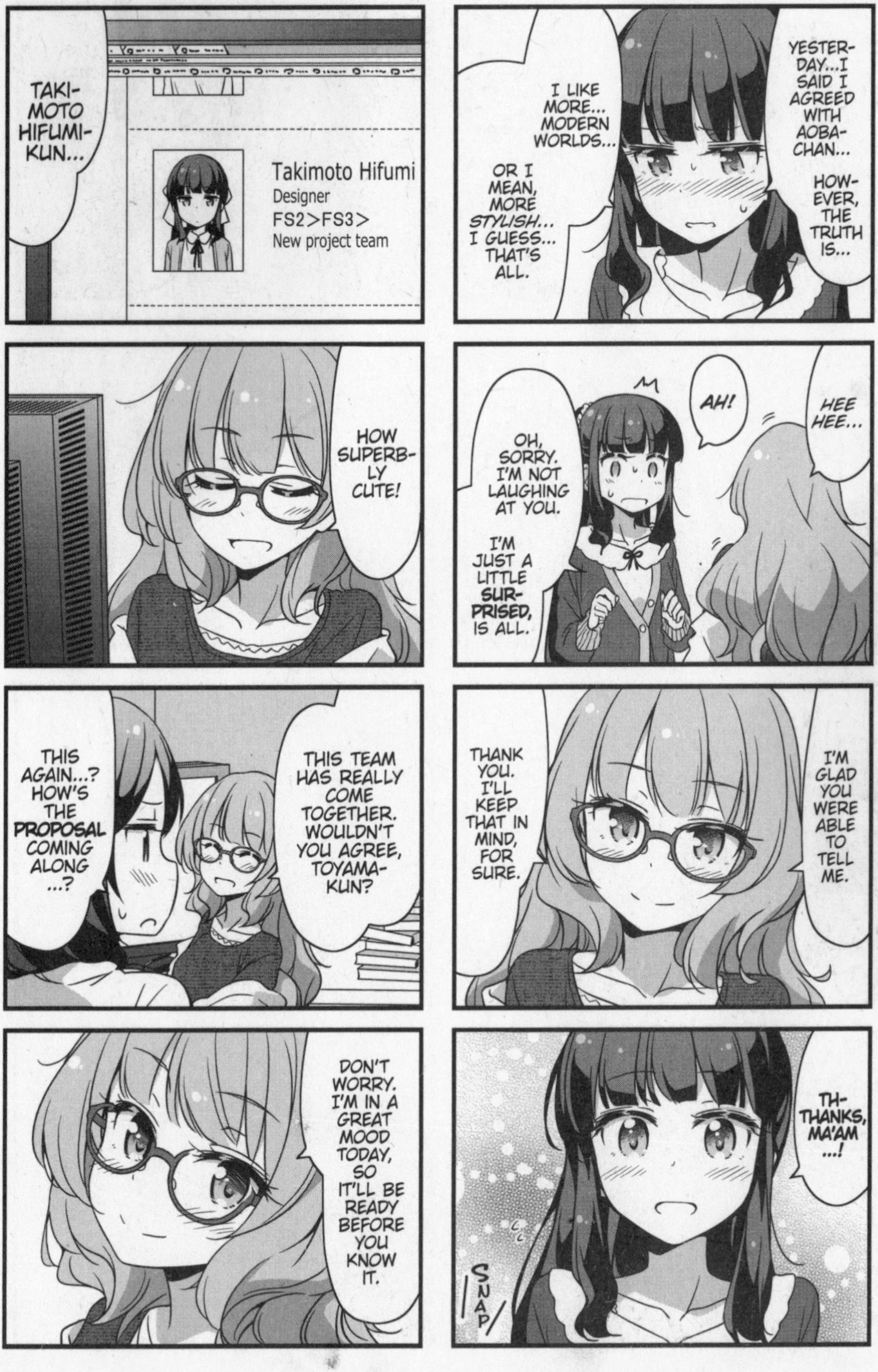
YESTERDAY...I SAID I AGREED WITH AOBA-CHAN... HOWEVER, THE TRUTH IS...
I LIKE MORE... MODERN WORLDS...
OR I MEAN, MORE *STYLISH*... I GUESS... THAT'S ALL.
TAKIMOTO HIFUMI-KUN...
Takimoto Hifumi
Designer
FS2>FS3>
New project team
HEE HEE...
AH!
OH, SORRY. I'M NOT LAUGHING AT YOU.
I'M JUST A LITTLE **SURPRISED**, IS ALL.
HOW SUPERBLY CUTE!
I'M GLAD YOU WERE ABLE TO TELL ME.
THANK YOU. I'LL KEEP THAT IN MIND, FOR SURE.
THIS TEAM HAS REALLY COME TOGETHER. WOULDN'T YOU AGREE, TOYAMA-KUN?
THIS AGAIN...? HOW'S THE **PROPOSAL** COMING ALONG...?
TH-THANKS, MA'AM...!
SNAP
DON'T WORRY. I'M IN A GREAT MOOD TODAY, SO IT'LL BE READY BEFORE YOU KNOW IT.

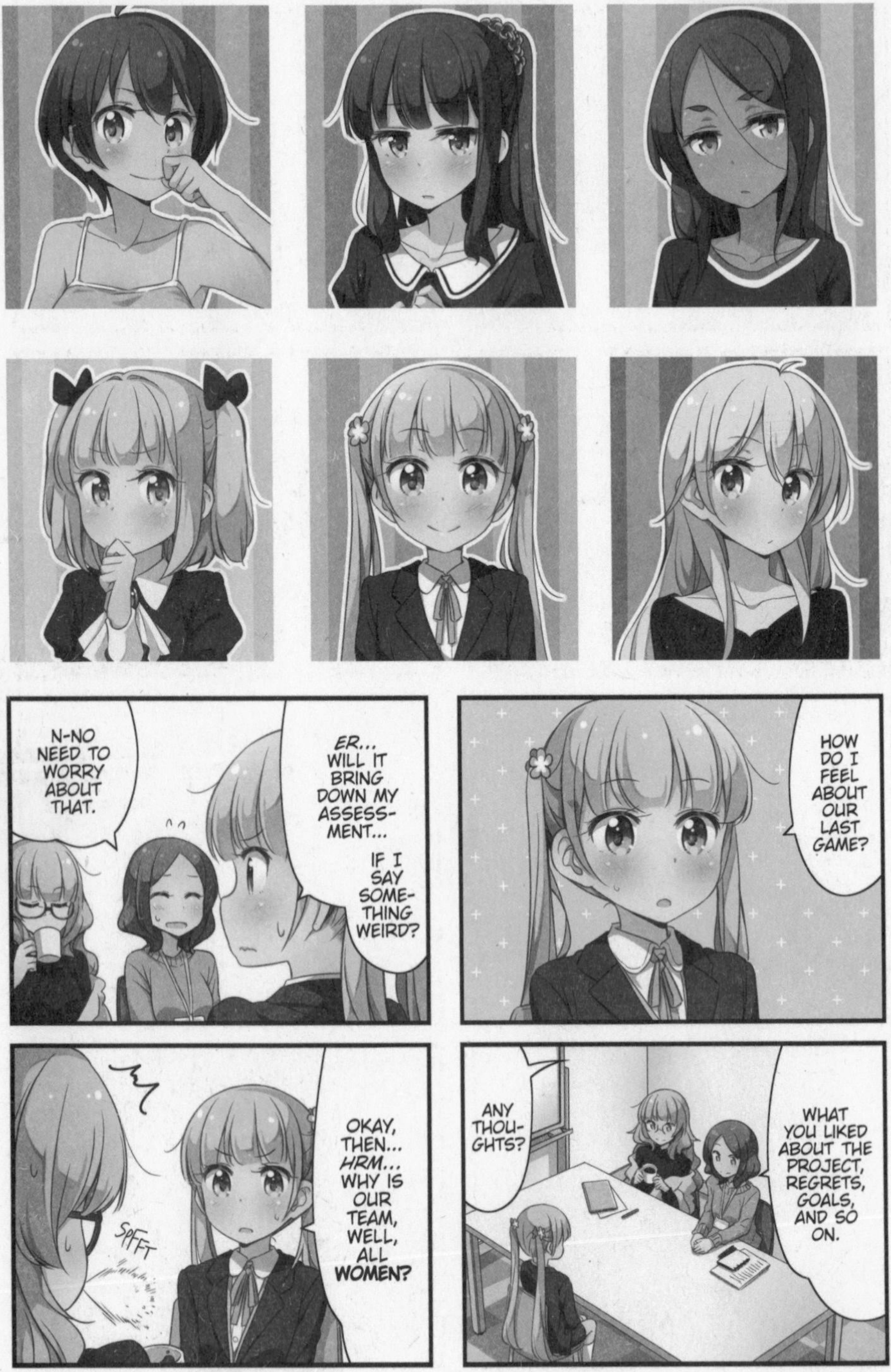

HOW DO I FEEL ABOUT OUR LAST GAME?
ER... WILL IT BRING DOWN MY ASSESSMENT...
IF I SAY SOMETHING WEIRD?
N-NO NEED TO WORRY ABOUT THAT.
WHAT YOU LIKED ABOUT THE PROJECT, REGRETS, GOALS, AND SO ON.
ANY THOUGHTS?
OKAY, THEN... *HRM*... WHY IS OUR TEAM, WELL, ALL **WOMEN**?
SPFFT

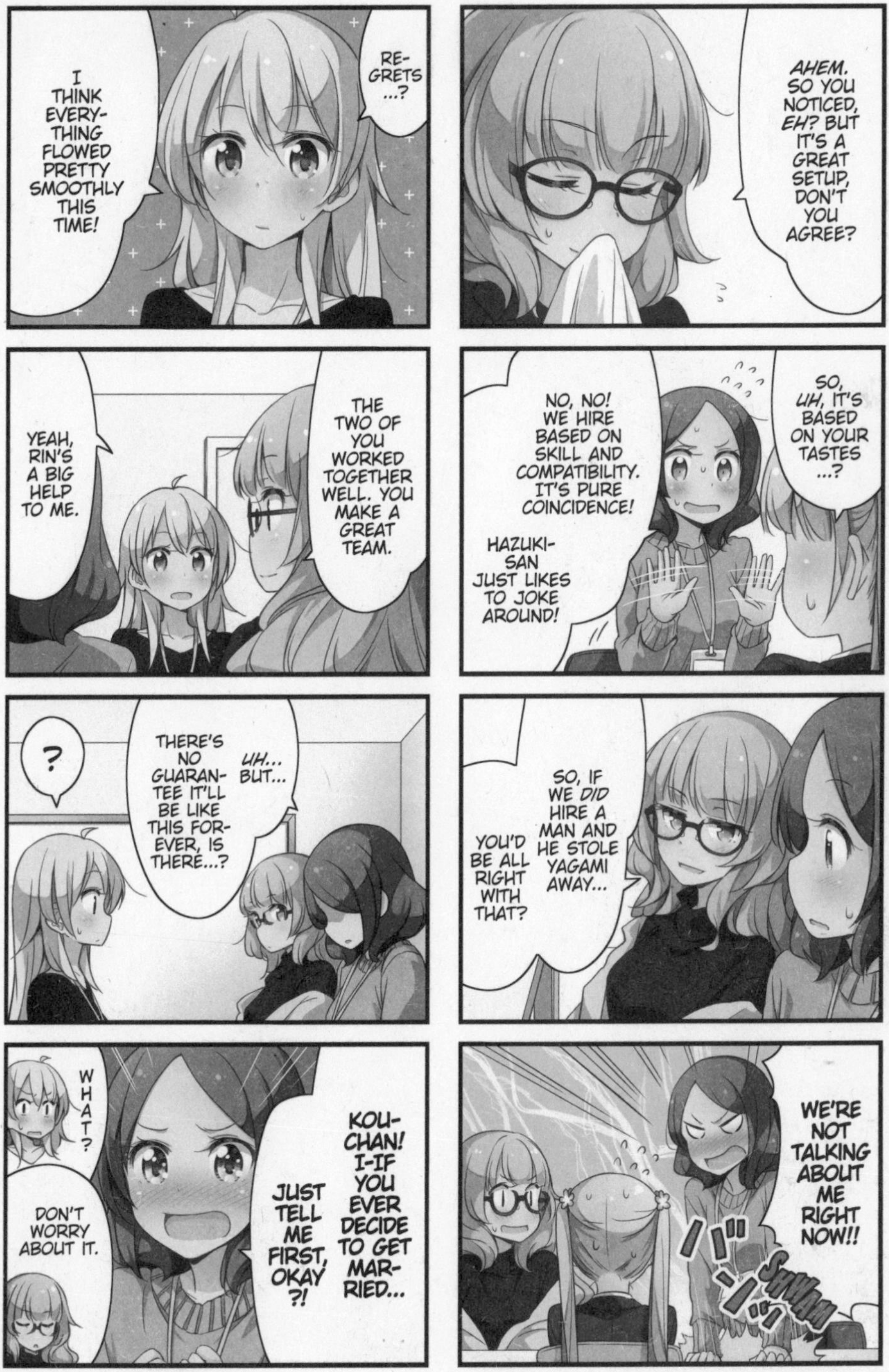
AHEM. SO YOU NOTICED, EH? BUT IT'S A GREAT SETUP, DON'T YOU AGREE?
REGRETS...?
I THINK EVERYTHING FLOWED PRETTY SMOOTHLY THIS TIME!
SO, UH, IT'S BASED ON YOUR TASTES...?
NO, NO! WE HIRE BASED ON SKILL AND COMPATIBILITY. IT'S PURE COINCIDENCE!
HAZUKI-SAN JUST LIKES TO JOKE AROUND!
THE TWO OF YOU WORKED TOGETHER WELL. YOU MAKE A GREAT TEAM.
YEAH, RIN'S A BIG HELP TO ME.
SO, IF WE DID HIRE A MAN AND HE STOLE YAGAMI AWAY...
YOU'D BE ALL RIGHT WITH THAT?
UH... BUT...
THERE'S NO GUARANTEE IT'LL BE LIKE THIS FOREVER, IS THERE...?
?
WE'RE NOT TALKING ABOUT ME RIGHT NOW!!
SHWAM
KOU-CHAN! I-IF YOU EVER DECIDE TO GET MARRIED...
JUST TELL ME FIRST, OKAY?!
WHAT?
DON'T WORRY ABOUT IT.

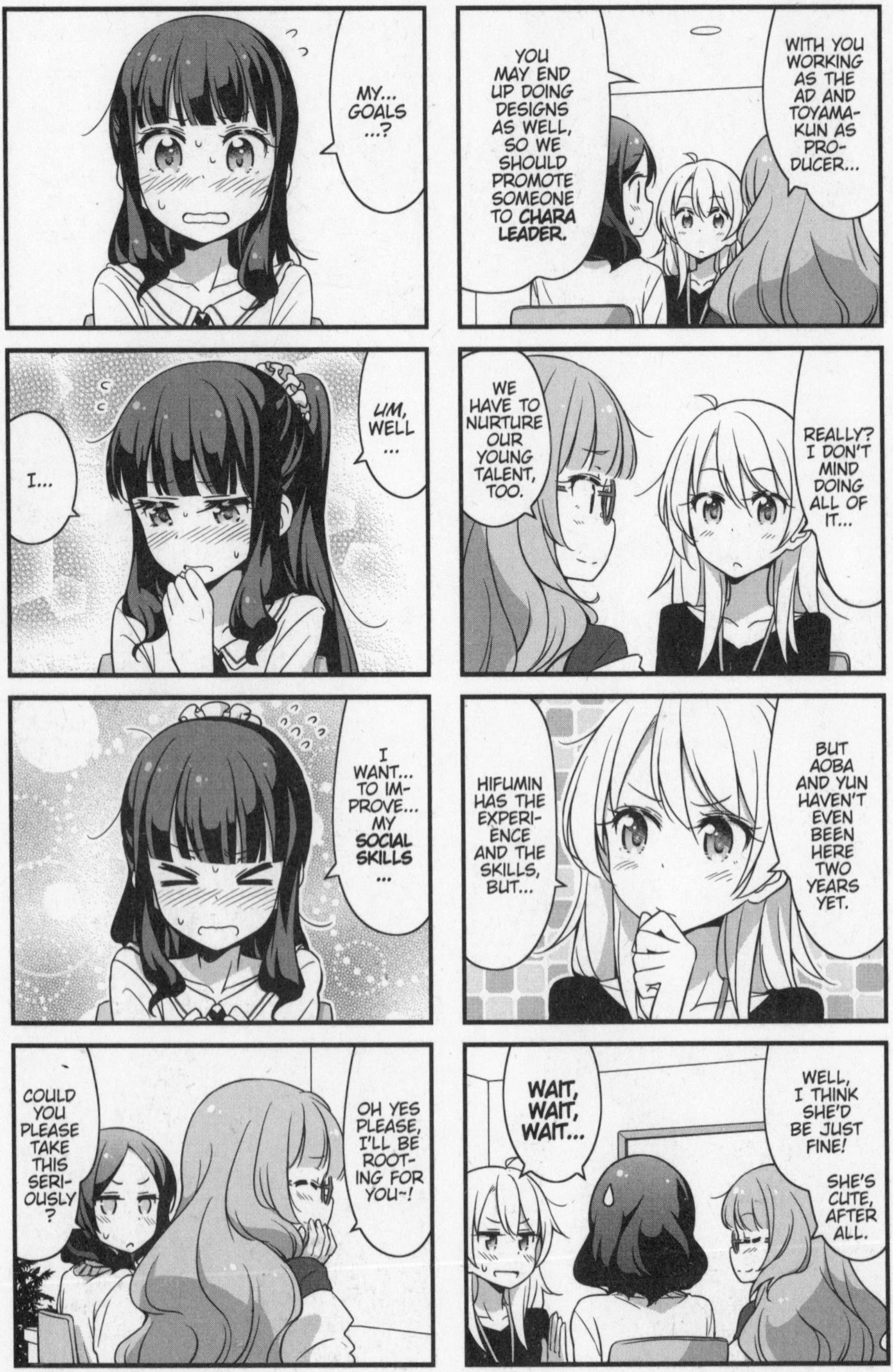
WITH YOU WORKING AS THE AD AND TOYAMA-KUN AS PRODUCER...
YOU MAY END UP DOING DESIGNS AS WELL, SO WE SHOULD PROMOTE SOMEONE TO **CHARA LEADER.**
MY... GOALS ...?
REALLY? I DON'T MIND DOING ALL OF IT...
WE HAVE TO NURTURE OUR YOUNG TALENT, TOO.
UM, WELL ...
I...
BUT AOBA AND YUN HAVEN'T EVEN BEEN HERE TWO YEARS YET.
HIFUMIN HAS THE EXPERIENCE AND THE SKILLS, BUT...
I WANT... TO IMPROVE... MY **SOCIAL SKILLS** ...
WELL, I THINK SHE'D BE JUST FINE!
SHE'S CUTE, AFTER ALL.
WAIT, WAIT, WAIT...
OH YES PLEASE, I'LL BE ROOTING FOR YOU~!
COULD YOU PLEASE TAKE THIS SERIOUSLY?

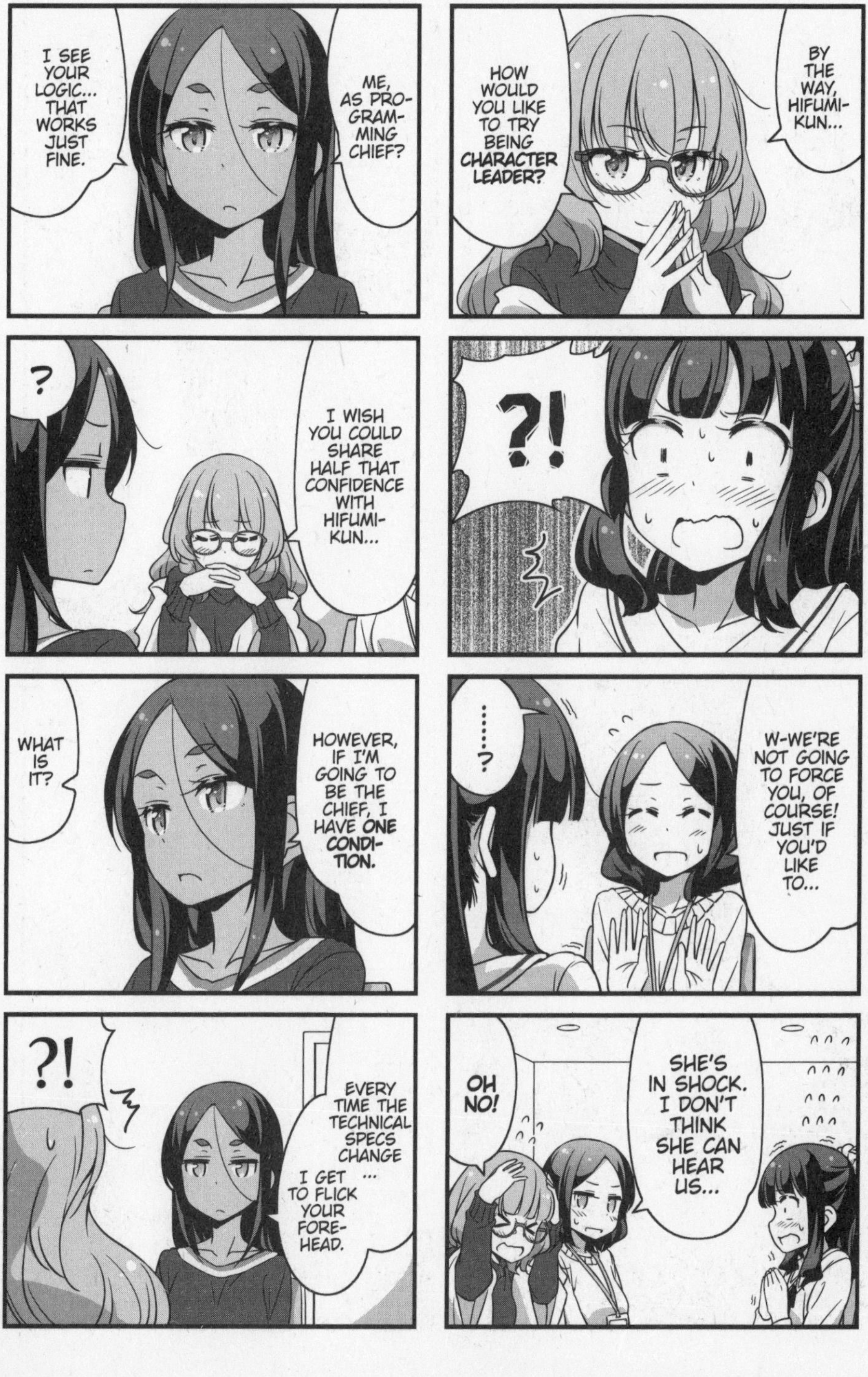
BY THE WAY, HIFUMI-KUN...
HOW WOULD YOU LIKE TO TRY BEING **CHARACTER LEADER?**
?!
W-WE'RE NOT GOING TO FORCE YOU, OF COURSE! JUST IF YOU'D LIKE TO...
......?
SHE'S IN SHOCK. I DON'T THINK SHE CAN HEAR US...
OH NO!
ME, AS PRO-GRAM-MING CHIEF?
I SEE YOUR LOGIC... THAT WORKS JUST FINE.
I WISH YOU COULD SHARE HALF THAT CONFIDENCE WITH HIFUMI-KUN...
?
HOWEVER, IF I'M GOING TO BE THE CHIEF, I HAVE **ONE CONDI-TION.**
WHAT IS IT?
EVERY TIME THE TECHNICAL SPECS CHANGE ...
I GET TO FLICK YOUR FORE-HEAD.
?!

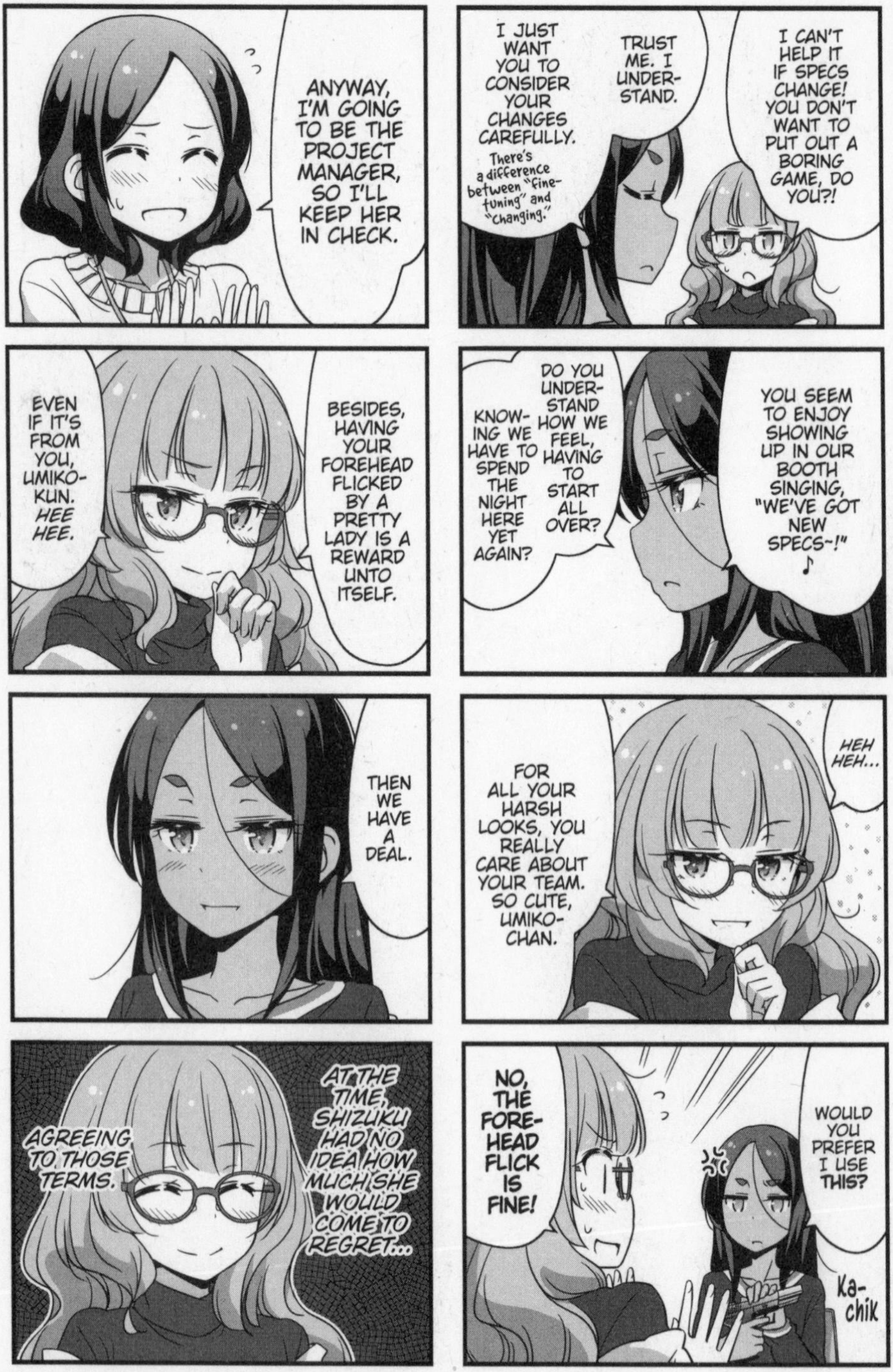
I CAN'T HELP IT IF SPECS CHANGE! YOU DON'T WANT TO PUT OUT A BORING GAME, DO YOU?!
TRUST ME. I UNDERSTAND.
I JUST WANT YOU TO CONSIDER YOUR CHANGES CAREFULLY.
There's a difference between "fine-tuning" and "changing."
ANYWAY, I'M GOING TO BE THE PROJECT MANAGER, SO I'LL KEEP HER IN CHECK.
YOU SEEM TO ENJOY SHOWING UP IN OUR BOOTH SINGING, "WE'VE GOT NEW SPECS~!" ♪
DO YOU UNDERSTAND HOW WE FEEL, HAVING TO START ALL OVER?
KNOWING WE HAVE TO SPEND THE NIGHT HERE YET AGAIN?
BESIDES, HAVING YOUR FOREHEAD FLICKED BY A PRETTY LADY IS A REWARD UNTO ITSELF.
EVEN IF IT'S FROM YOU, UMIKO-KUN. HEE HEE.
HEH HEH...
FOR ALL YOUR HARSH LOOKS, YOU REALLY CARE ABOUT YOUR TEAM. SO CUTE, UMIKO-CHAN.
THEN WE HAVE A DEAL.
WOULD YOU PREFER I USE THIS?
NO, THE FOREHEAD FLICK IS FINE!
Ka-chik
AT THE TIME, SHIZUKU HAD NO IDEA HOW MUCH SHE WOULD COME TO REGRET...
AGREEING TO THOSE TERMS.

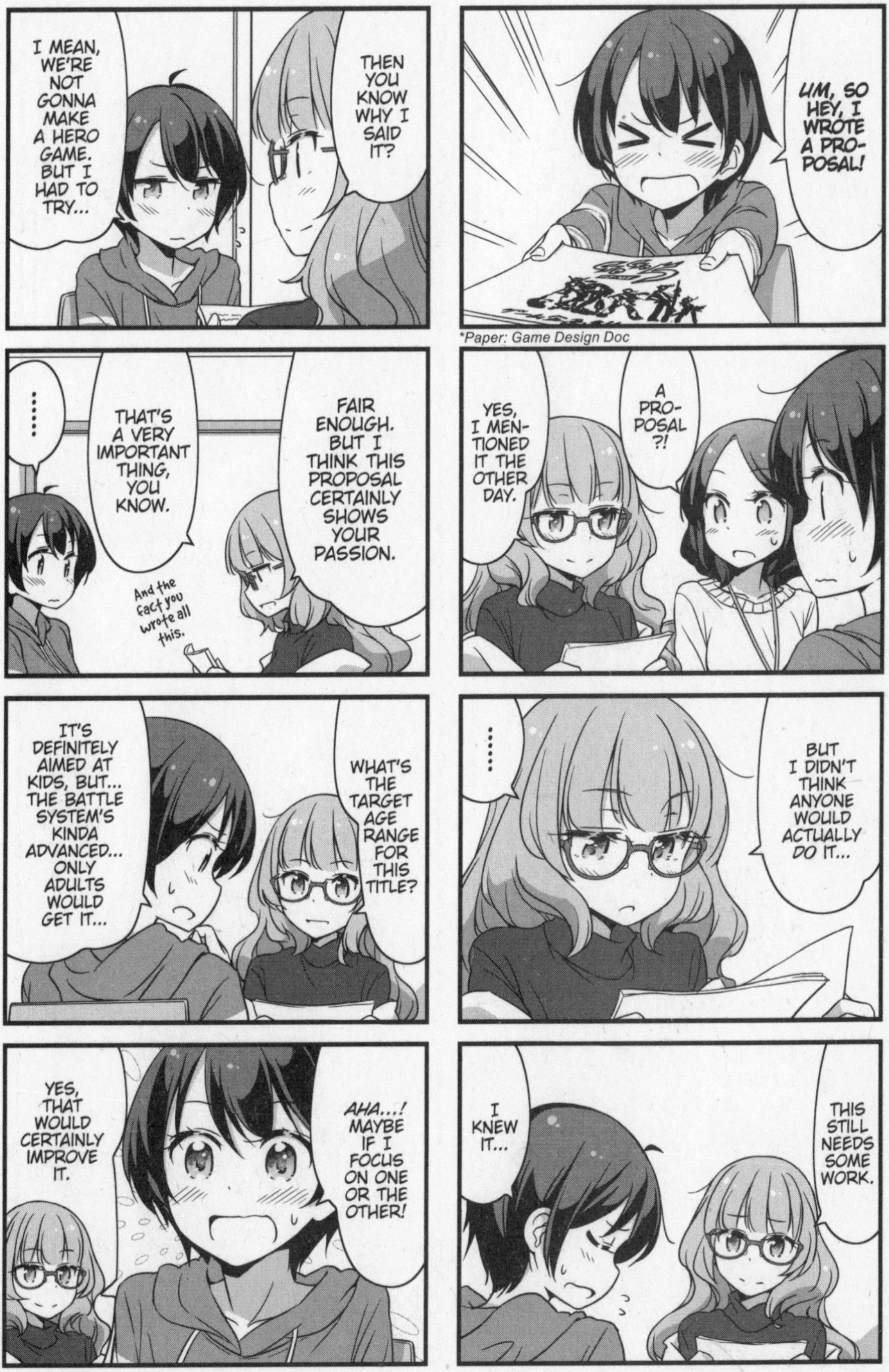
UM, SO HEY, I WROTE A PROPOSAL!
*Paper: Game Design Doc
A PROPOSAL?!
YES, I MENTIONED IT THE OTHER DAY.
BUT I DIDN'T THINK ANYONE WOULD ACTUALLY DO IT...
......
THIS STILL NEEDS SOME WORK.
I KNEW IT...
THEN YOU KNOW WHY I SAID IT?
I MEAN, WE'RE NOT GONNA MAKE A HERO GAME. BUT I HAD TO TRY...
FAIR ENOUGH. BUT I THINK THIS PROPOSAL CERTAINLY SHOWS YOUR PASSION.
And the fact you wrote all this.
THAT'S A VERY IMPORTANT THING, YOU KNOW.
......
WHAT'S THE TARGET AGE RANGE FOR THIS TITLE?
IT'S DEFINITELY AIMED AT KIDS, BUT... THE BATTLE SYSTEM'S KINDA ADVANCED... ONLY ADULTS WOULD GET IT...
AHA...! MAYBE IF I FOCUS ON ONE OR THE OTHER!
YES, THAT WOULD CERTAINLY IMPROVE IT.

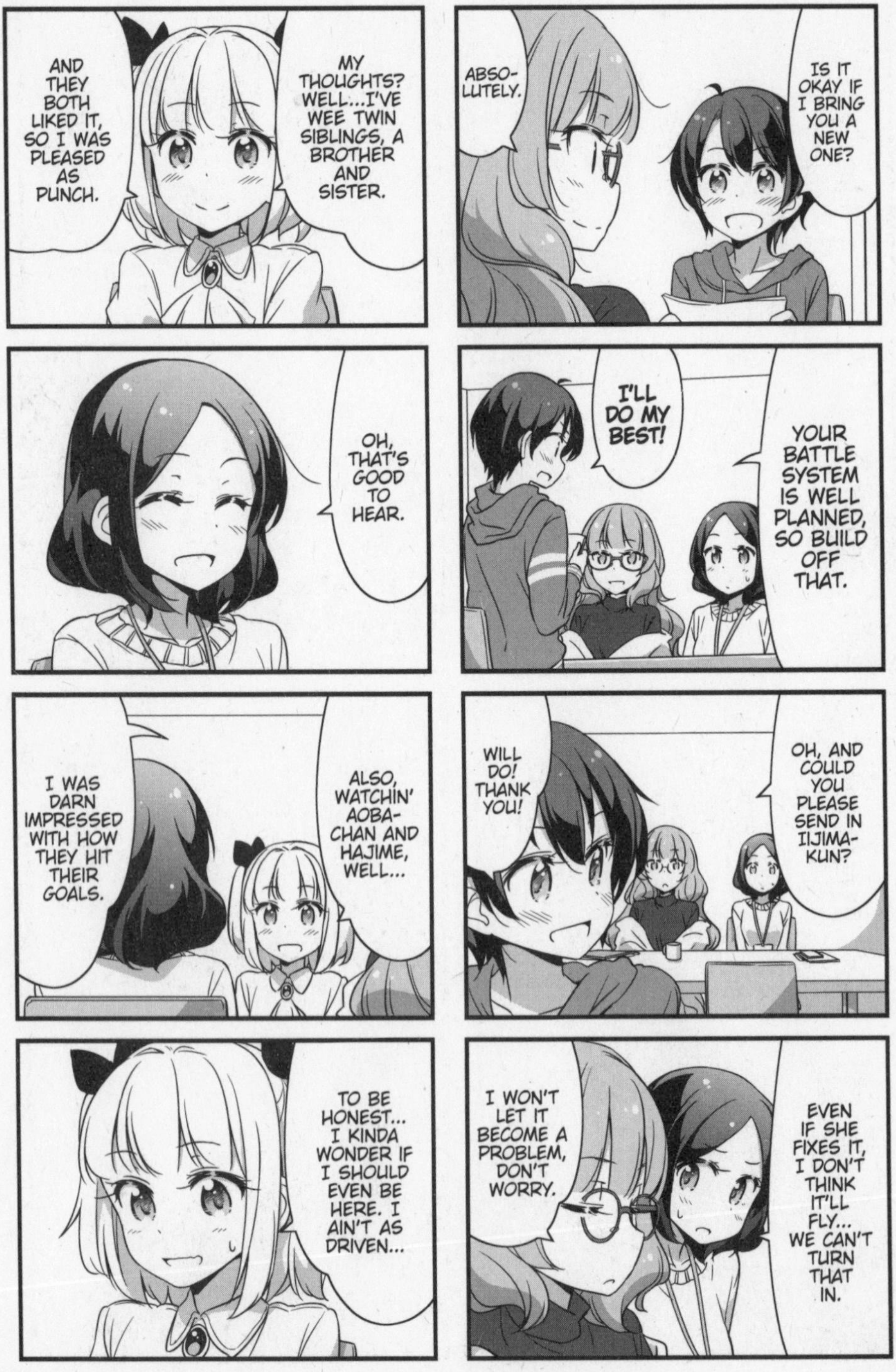
IS IT OKAY IF I BRING YOU A NEW ONE?
ABSO-LUTELY.
MY THOUGHTS? WELL...I'VE WEE TWIN SIBLINGS, A BROTHER AND SISTER.
AND THEY BOTH LIKED IT, SO I WAS PLEASED AS PUNCH.
YOUR BATTLE SYSTEM IS WELL PLANNED, SO BUILD OFF THAT.
I'LL DO MY BEST!
OH, THAT'S GOOD TO HEAR.
OH, AND COULD YOU PLEASE SEND IN IIJIMA-KUN?
WILL DO! THANK YOU!
ALSO, WATCHIN' AOBA-CHAN AND HAJIME, WELL...
I WAS DARN IMPRESSED WITH HOW THEY HIT THEIR GOALS.
EVEN IF SHE FIXES IT, I DON'T THINK IT'LL FLY... WE CAN'T TURN THAT IN.
I WON'T LET IT BECOME A PROBLEM, DON'T WORRY.
TO BE HONEST... I KINDA WONDER IF I SHOULD EVEN BE HERE. I AIN'T AS DRIVEN...

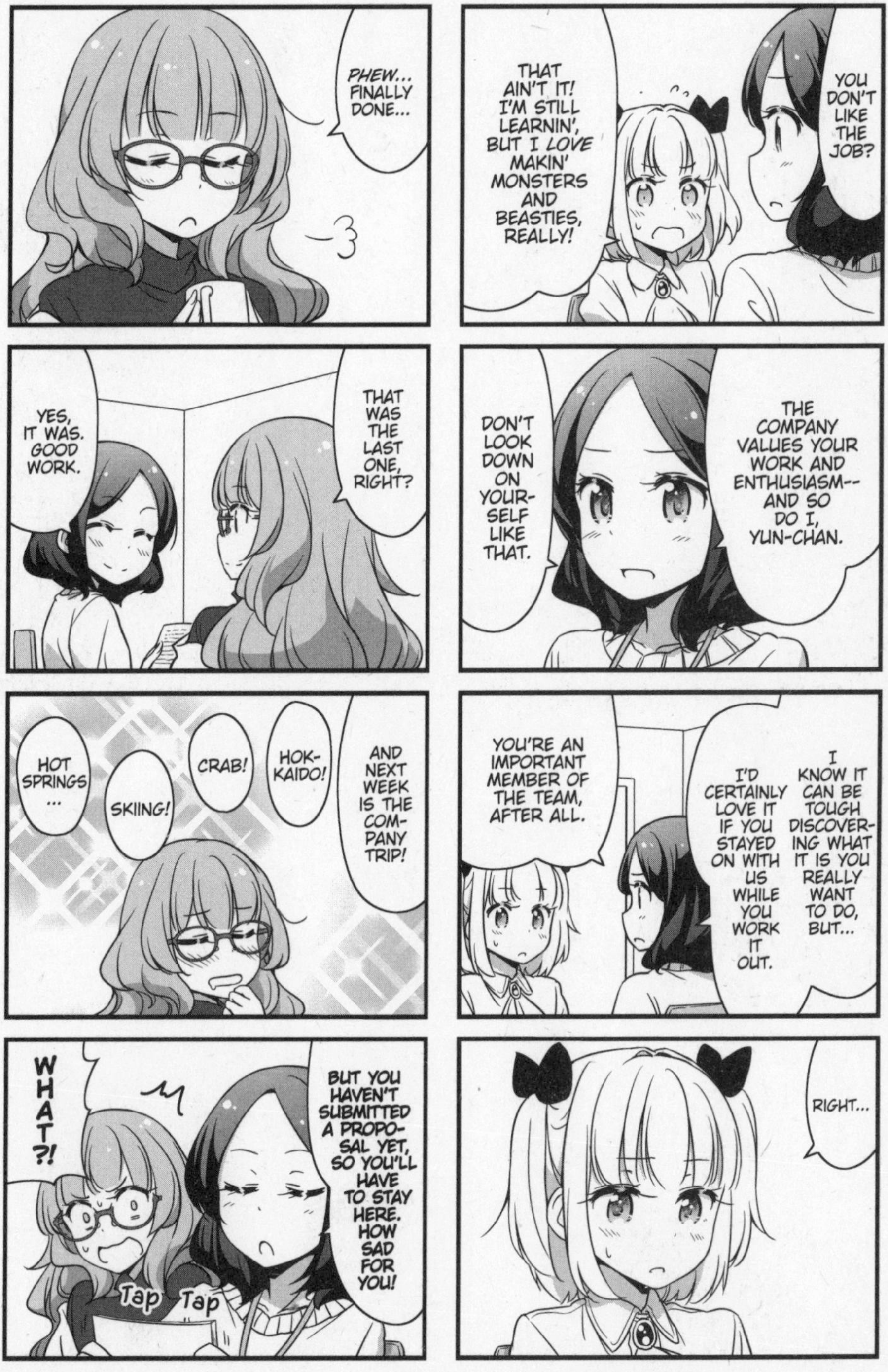
YOU DON'T LIKE THE JOB?
THAT AIN'T IT! I'M STILL LEARNIN', BUT I *LOVE* MAKIN' MONSTERS AND BEASTIES, REALLY!
THE COMPANY VALUES YOUR WORK AND ENTHUSIASM--AND SO DO I, YUN-CHAN.
DON'T LOOK DOWN ON YOURSELF LIKE THAT.
I KNOW IT CAN BE TOUGH DISCOVERING WHAT IT IS YOU REALLY WANT TO DO, BUT...
I'D CERTAINLY LOVE IT IF YOU STAYED ON WITH US WHILE YOU WORK IT OUT.
YOU'RE AN IMPORTANT MEMBER OF THE TEAM, AFTER ALL.
RIGHT...
PHEW... FINALLY DONE...
THAT WAS THE LAST ONE, RIGHT?
YES, IT WAS. GOOD WORK.
AND NEXT WEEK IS THE COMPANY TRIP!
HOKKAIDO!
CRAB!
SKIING!
HOT SPRINGS...
BUT YOU HAVEN'T SUBMITTED A PROPOSAL YET, SO YOU'LL HAVE TO STAY HERE. HOW SAD FOR YOU!
WHAT?!
Tap Tap

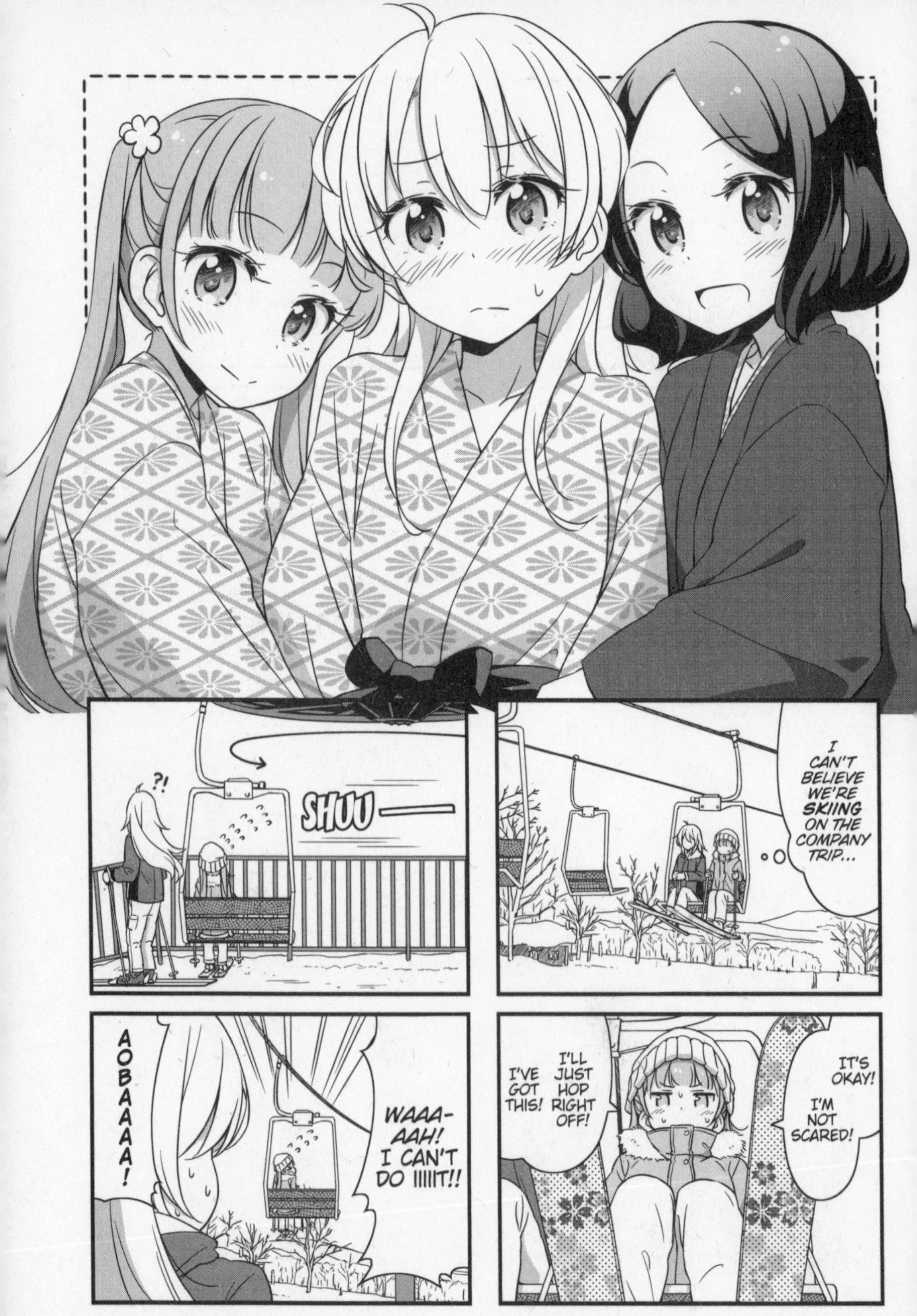
I CAN'T BELIEVE WE'RE SKIING ON THE COMPANY TRIP...
?!
SHUU
IT'S OKAY!
I'M NOT SCARED!
I'LL JUST HOP RIGHT OFF!
I'VE GOT THIS!
WAAA-AAH! I CAN'T DO IIIIIT!!
AOBAAAAA!

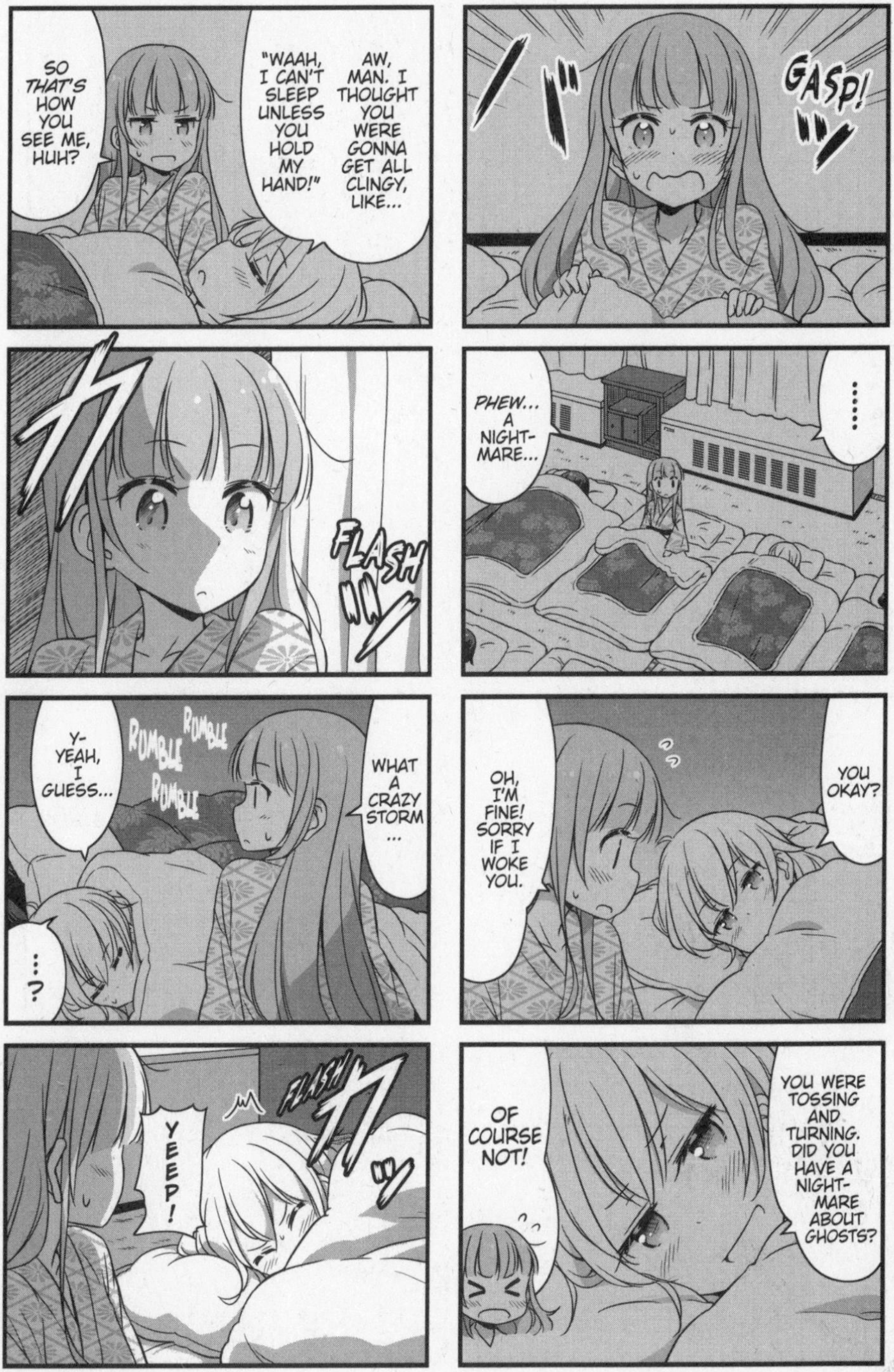
GASP!
AW, MAN. I THOUGHT YOU WERE GONNA GET ALL CLINGY, LIKE...
"WAAH, I CAN'T SLEEP UNLESS YOU HOLD MY HAND!"
SO THAT'S HOW YOU SEE ME, HUH?
......
PHEW... A NIGHT-MARE...
FLASH
YOU OKAY?
OH, I'M FINE! SORRY IF I WOKE YOU.
WHAT A CRAZY STORM ...
RUMBLE
RUMBLE
RUMBLE
Y-YEAH, I GUESS...
...?
YOU WERE TOSSING AND TURNING. DID YOU HAVE A NIGHT-MARE ABOUT GHOSTS?
OF COURSE NOT!
FLASH
YEEP!

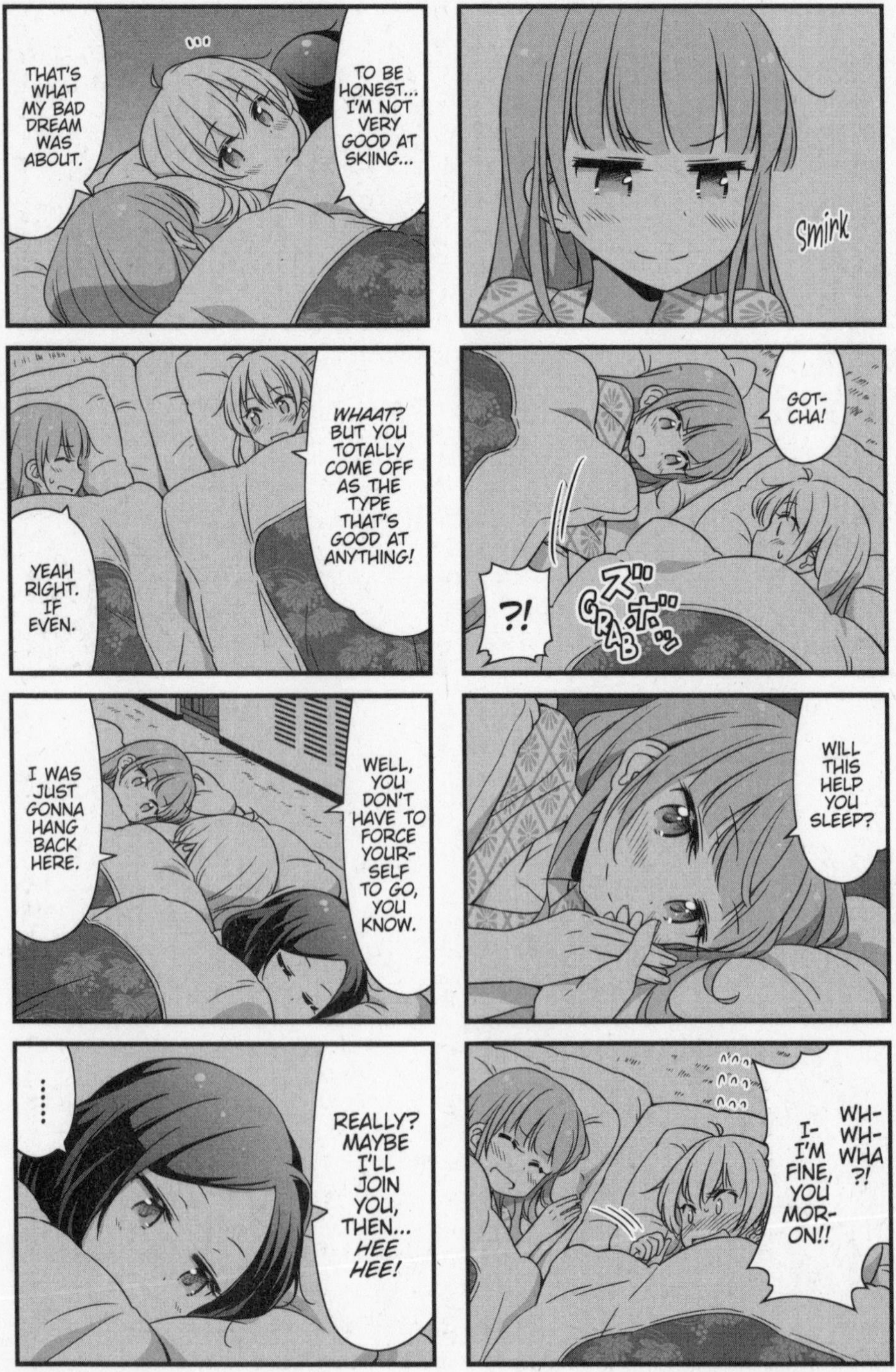

Smirk
GOT-CHA!
?!
ズボッ GRAB
WILL THIS HELP YOU SLEEP?
WH-WH-WHA?!
I-I'M FINE, YOU MOR-ON!!
...
TO BE HONEST... I'M NOT VERY GOOD AT SKIING...
THAT'S WHAT MY BAD DREAM WAS ABOUT.
WHAAT? BUT YOU TOTALLY COME OFF AS THE TYPE THAT'S GOOD AT ANYTHING!
YEAH RIGHT. IF EVEN.
WELL, YOU DON'T HAVE TO FORCE YOUR-SELF TO GO, YOU KNOW.
I WAS JUST GONNA HANG BACK HERE.
......
REALLY? MAYBE I'LL JOIN YOU, THEN... HEE HEE!

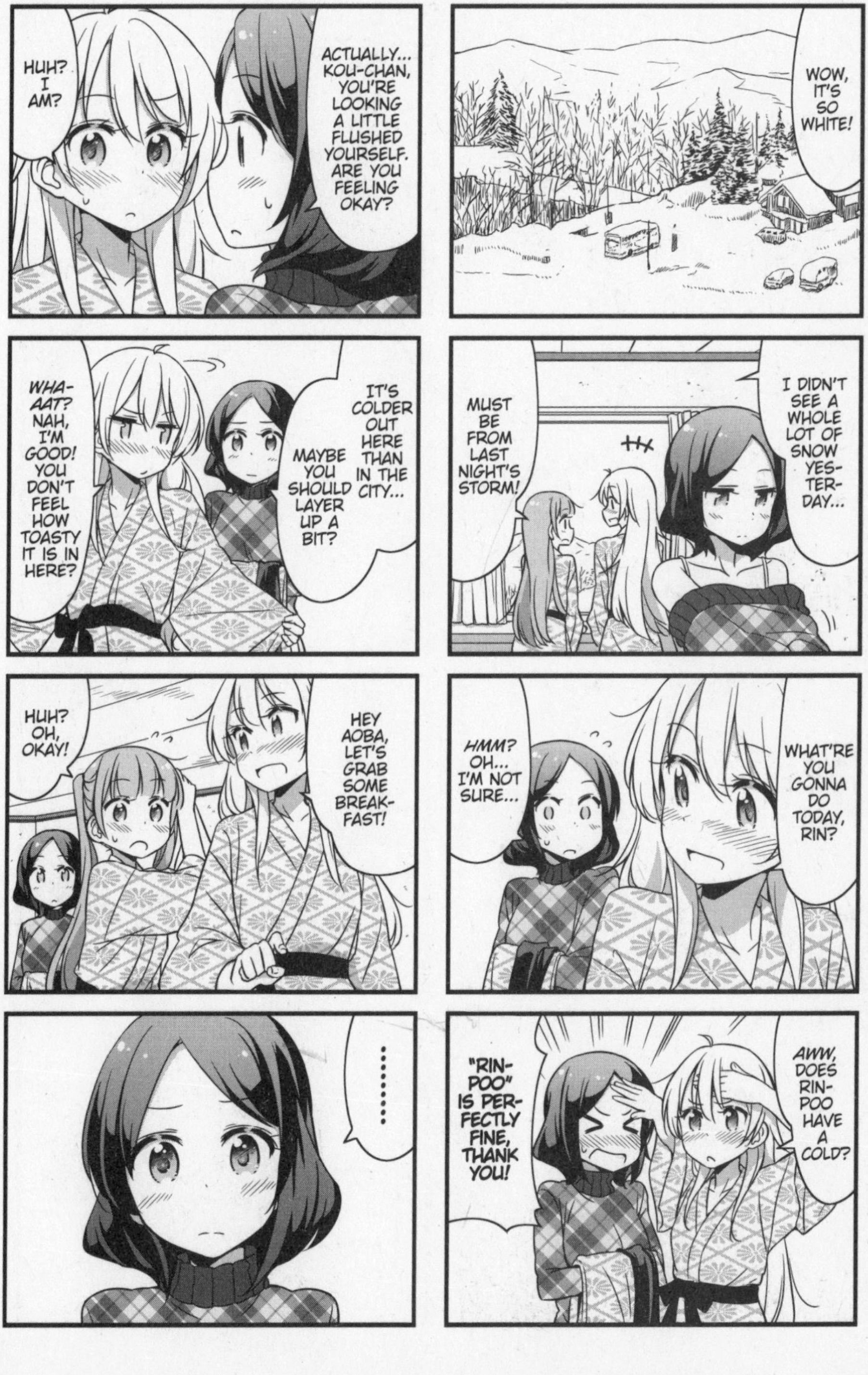
WOW, IT'S SO WHITE!
I DIDN'T SEE A WHOLE LOT OF SNOW YES-TER-DAY...
MUST BE FROM LAST NIGHT'S STORM!
WHAT'RE YOU GONNA DO TODAY, RIN?
HMM? OH... I'M NOT SURE...
AWW, DOES RIN-POO HAVE A COLD?
"RIN-POO" IS PER-FECTLY FINE, THANK YOU!
ACTUALLY... KOU-CHAN, YOU'RE LOOKING A LITTLE FLUSHED YOURSELF. ARE YOU FEELING OKAY?
HUH? I AM?
IT'S COLDER OUT HERE THAN IN THE CITY... MAYBE YOU SHOULD LAYER UP A BIT?
WHA-AAT? NAH, I'M GOOD! YOU DON'T FEEL HOW TOASTY IT IS IN HERE?
HEY AOBA, LET'S GRAB SOME BREAK-FAST!
HUH? OH, OKAY!
....

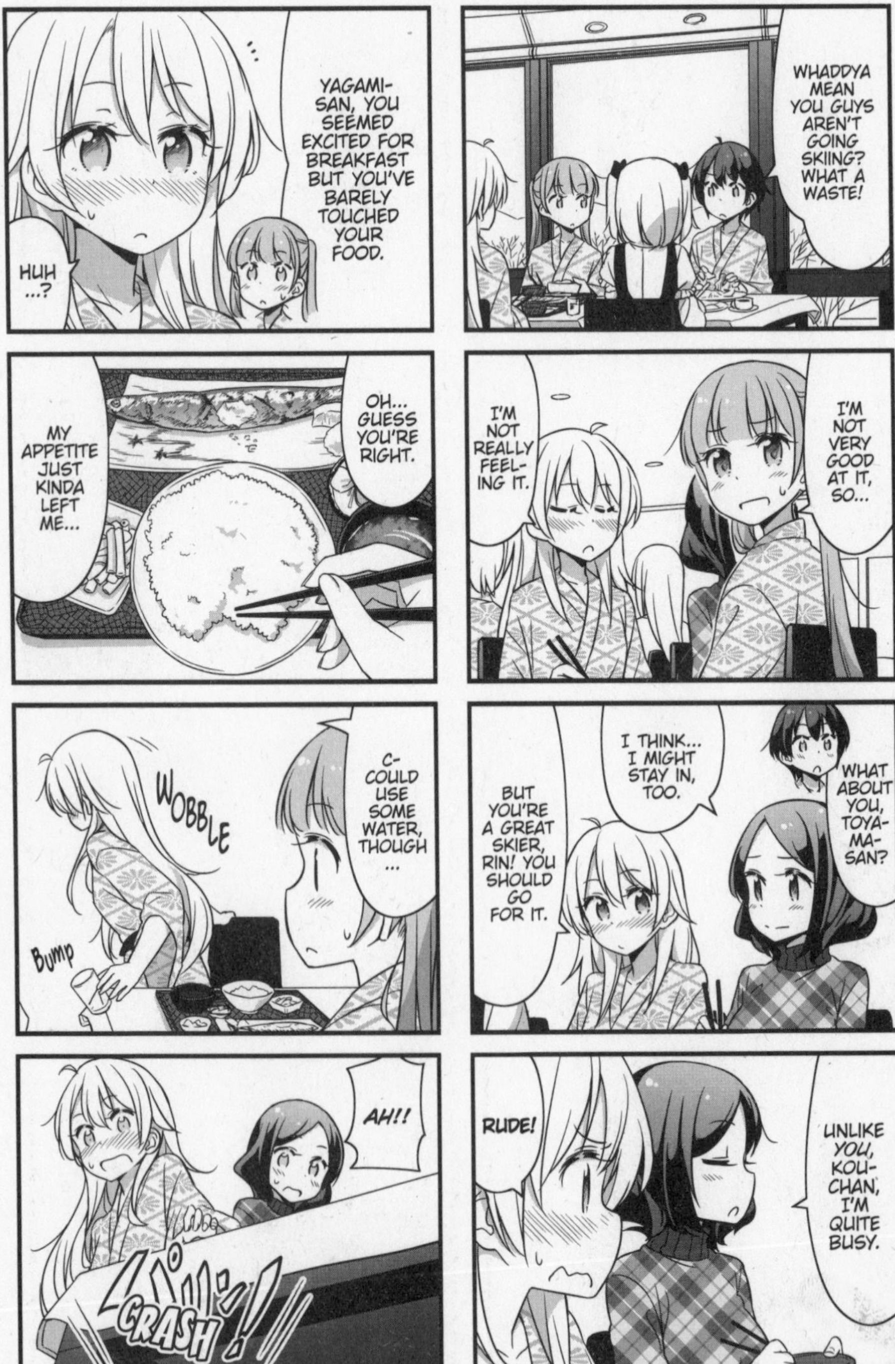
WHADDYA MEAN YOU GUYS AREN'T GOING SKIING? WHAT A WASTE!
I'M NOT VERY GOOD AT IT, SO...
I'M NOT REALLY FEEL-ING IT.
WHAT ABOUT YOU, TOYA-MA-SAN?
I THINK... I MIGHT STAY IN, TOO.
BUT YOU'RE A GREAT SKIER, RIN! YOU SHOULD GO FOR IT.
UNLIKE YOU, KOU-CHAN, I'M QUITE BUSY.
RUDE!
YAGAMI-SAN, YOU SEEMED EXCITED FOR BREAKFAST BUT YOU'VE BARELY TOUCHED YOUR FOOD.
HUH ...?
OH... GUESS YOU'RE RIGHT.
MY APPETITE JUST KINDA LEFT ME...
C-COULD USE SOME WATER, THOUGH ...
WOBBLE
Bump
AH!!
CRASH

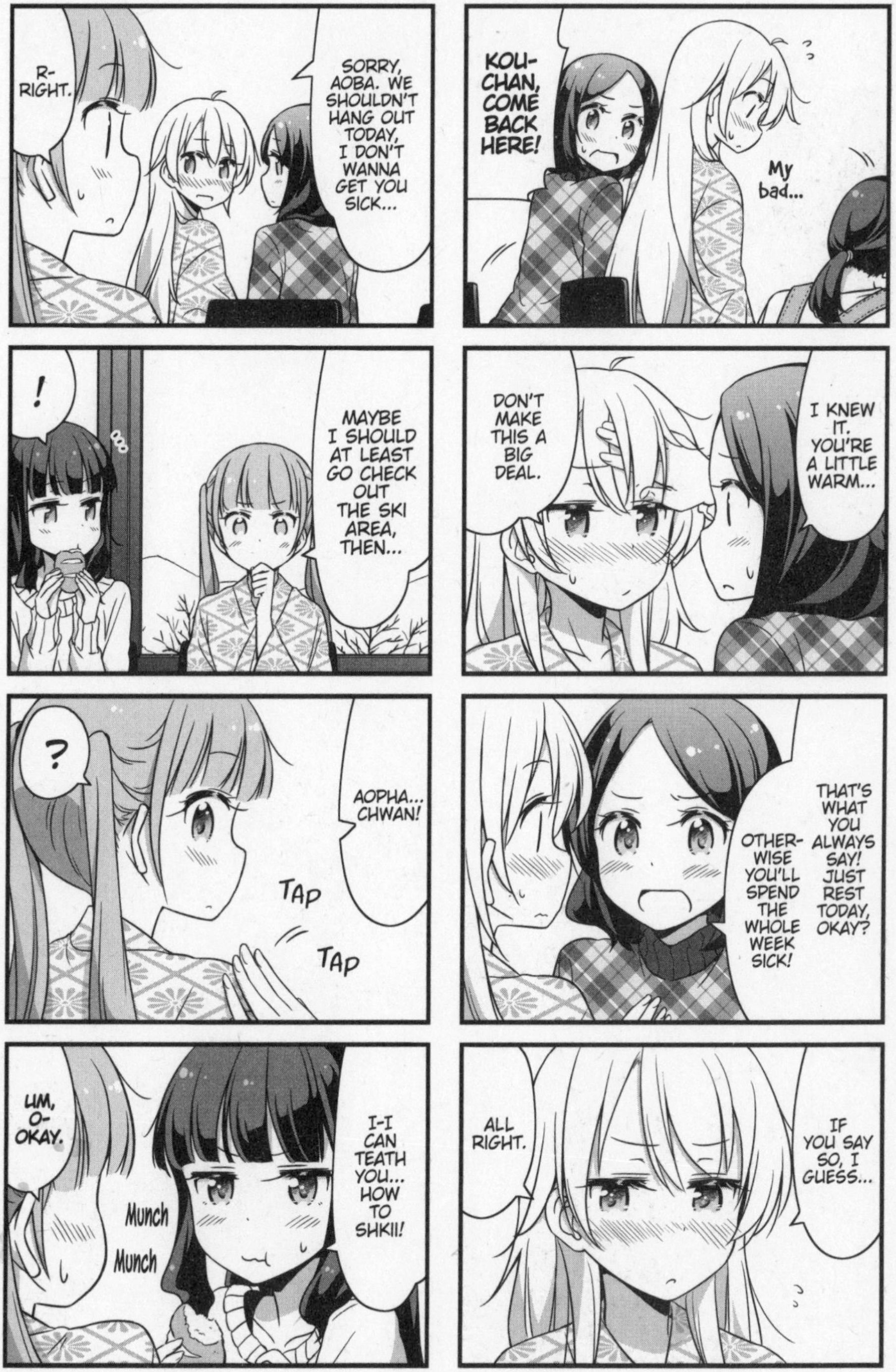
KOU-CHAN, COME BACK HERE!
My bad...
SORRY, AOBA. WE SHOULDN'T HANG OUT TODAY, I DON'T WANNA GET YOU SICK...
R-RIGHT.
I KNEW IT. YOU'RE A LITTLE WARM...
DON'T MAKE THIS A BIG DEAL.
MAYBE I SHOULD AT LEAST GO CHECK OUT THE SKI AREA, THEN...
!
THAT'S WHAT YOU ALWAYS SAY! JUST REST TODAY, OKAY?
OTHERWISE YOU'LL SPEND THE WHOLE WEEK SICK!
AOPHA... CHWAN!
TAP
TAP
?
IF YOU SAY SO, I GUESS...
ALL RIGHT.
I-I CAN TEATH YOU... HOW TO SHKII!
Munch
Munch
UM, O-OKAY.

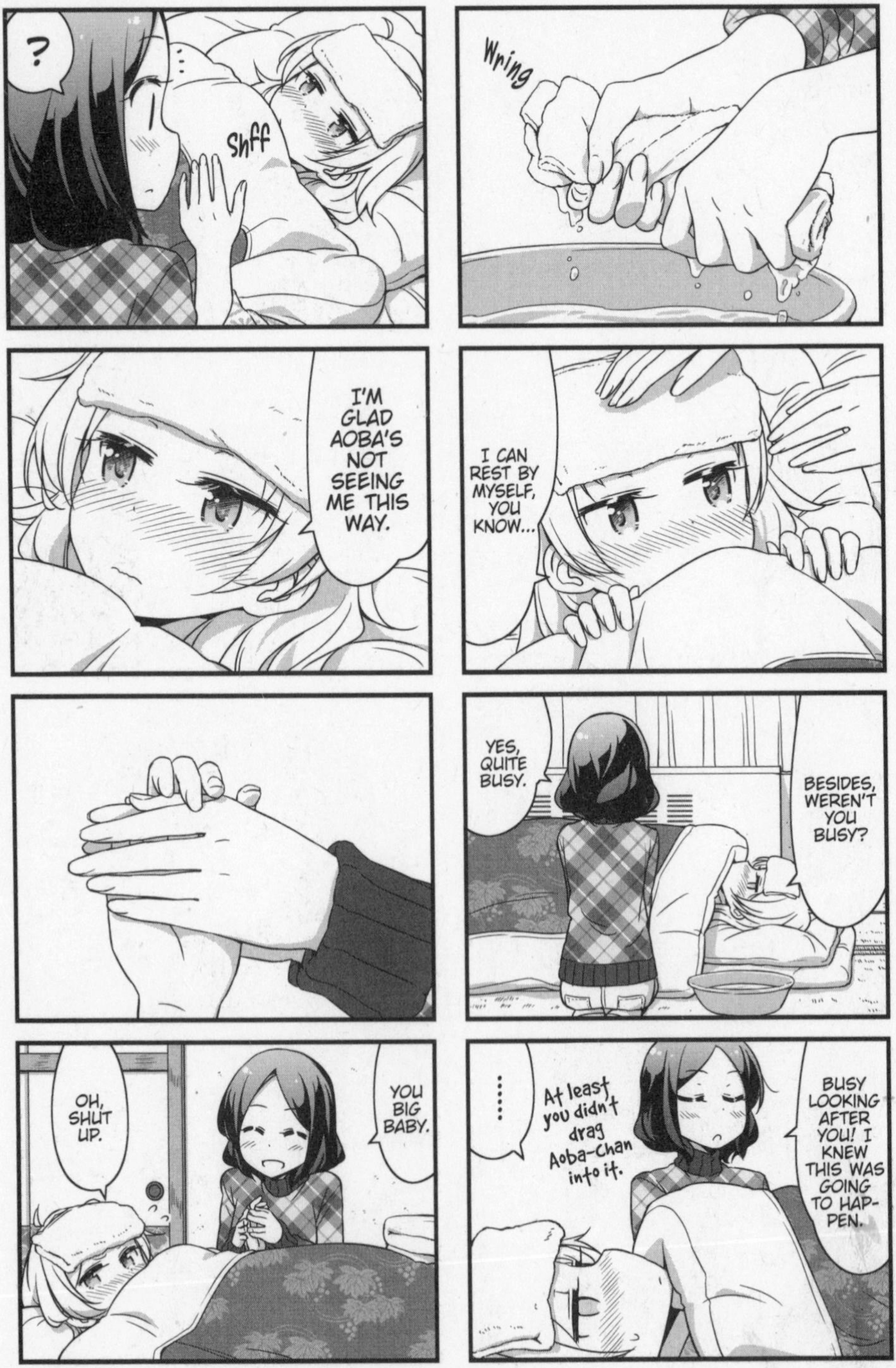
Wring
?
...
Shff
I CAN REST BY MYSELF, YOU KNOW...
I'M GLAD AOBA'S NOT SEEING ME THIS WAY.
BESIDES, WEREN'T YOU BUSY?
YES, QUITE BUSY.
BUSY LOOKING AFTER YOU! I KNEW THIS WAS GOING TO HAP-PEN.
At least you didn't drag Aoba-Chan into it.
......
YOU BIG BABY.
OH, SHUT UP.

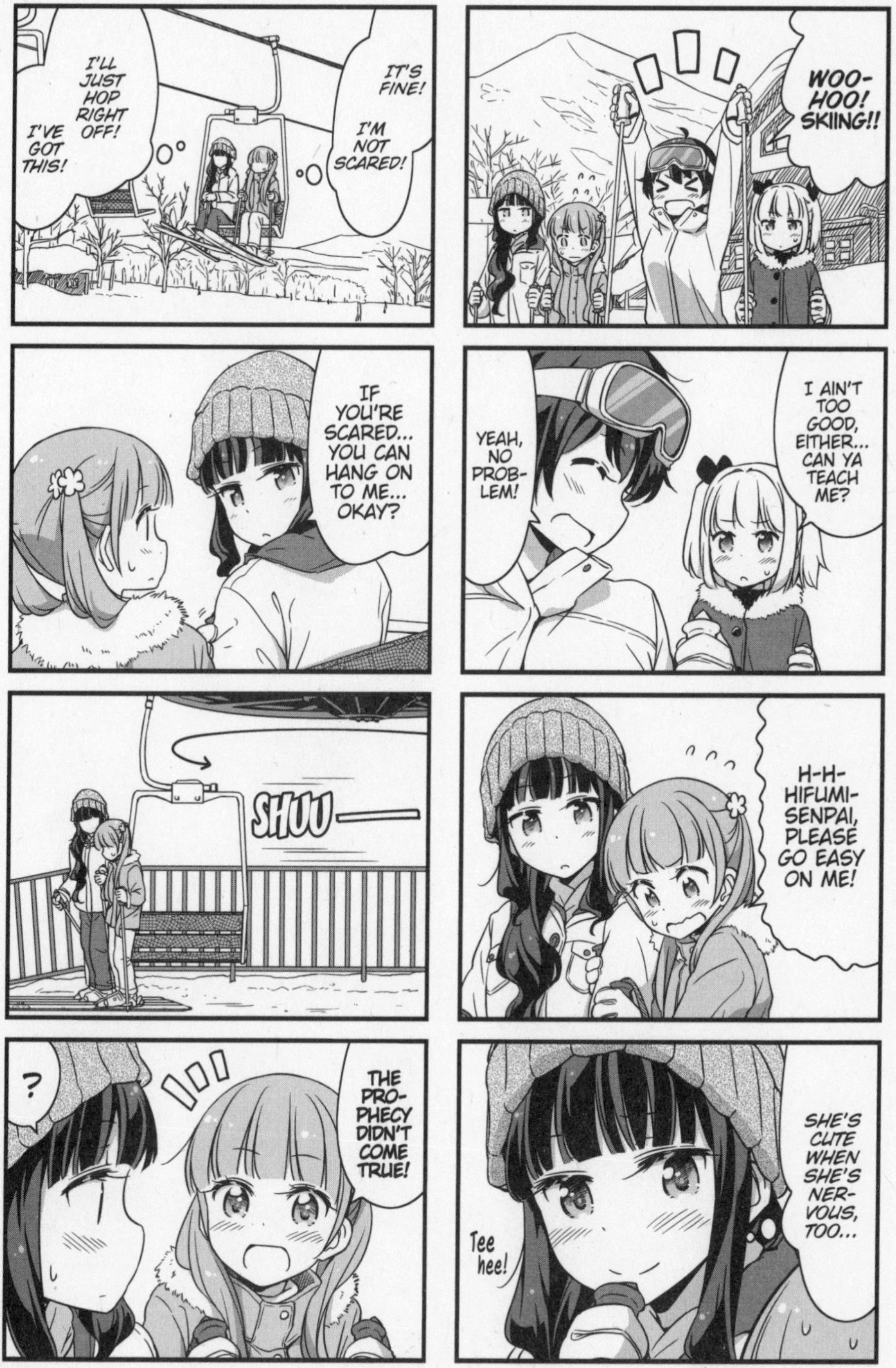
WOO-HOO! SKIING!!
IT'S FINE! I'M NOT SCARED!
I'LL JUST HOP RIGHT OFF! I'VE GOT THIS!
I AIN'T TOO GOOD, EITHER... CAN YA TEACH ME?
YEAH, NO PROB-LEM!
IF YOU'RE SCARED... YOU CAN HANG ON TO ME... OKAY?
H-H-HIFUMI-SENPAI, PLEASE GO EASY ON ME!
SHUU—
SHE'S CUTE WHEN SHE'S NER-VOUS, TOO...
Tee hee!
THE PRO-PHECY DIDN'T COME TRUE!
?

nEW GAME!

nEW GAME!

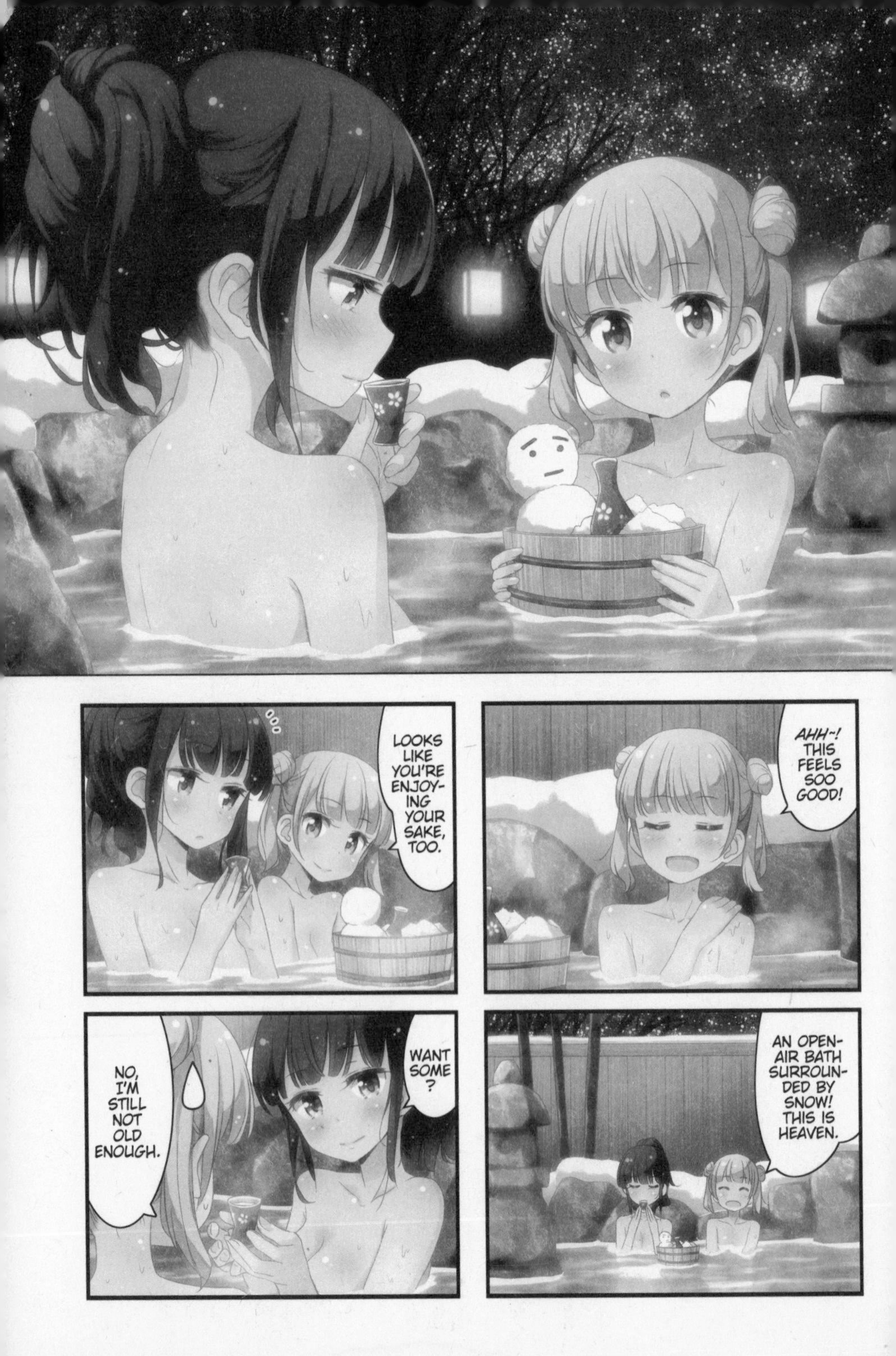
AHH~! THIS FEELS SOO GOOD!
LOOKS LIKE YOU'RE ENJOY-ING YOUR SAKE, TOO.
AN OPEN-AIR BATH SURROUN-DED BY SNOW! THIS IS HEAVEN.
WANT SOME?
NO, I'M STILL NOT OLD ENOUGH.

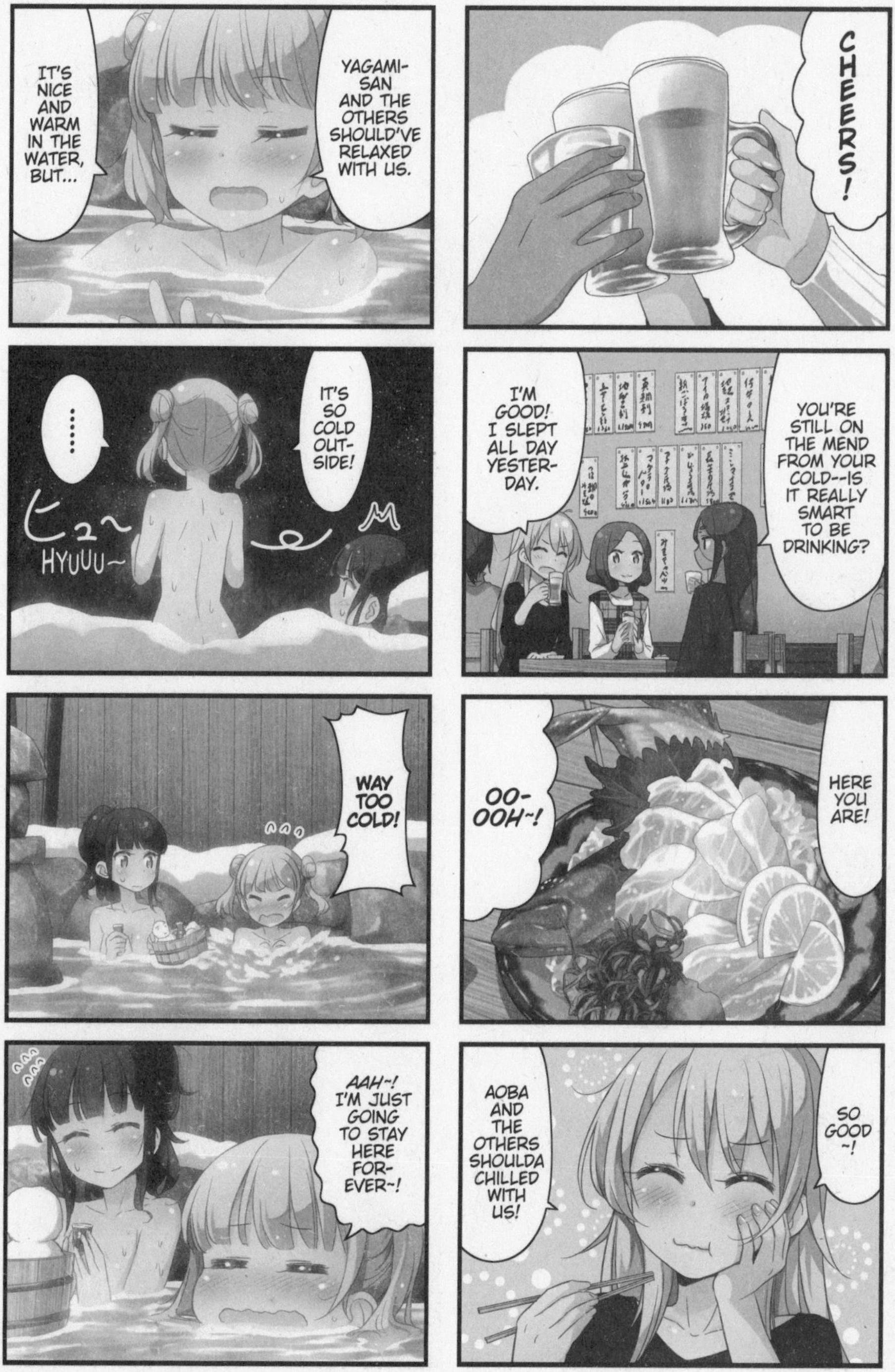
CHEERS!
YOU'RE STILL ON THE MEND FROM YOUR COLD--IS IT REALLY SMART TO BE DRINKING?
I'M GOOD! I SLEPT ALL DAY YESTER-DAY.
HERE YOU ARE!
OO-OOH~!
SO GOOD~!
AOBA AND THE OTHERS SHOULDA CHILLED WITH US!
YAGAMI-SAN AND THE OTHERS SHOULD'VE RELAXED WITH US.
IT'S NICE AND WARM IN THE WATER, BUT...
IT'S SO COLD OUT-SIDE!
......
HYUUU~
WAY TOO COLD!
AAH~! I'M JUST GOING TO STAY HERE FOR-EVER~!

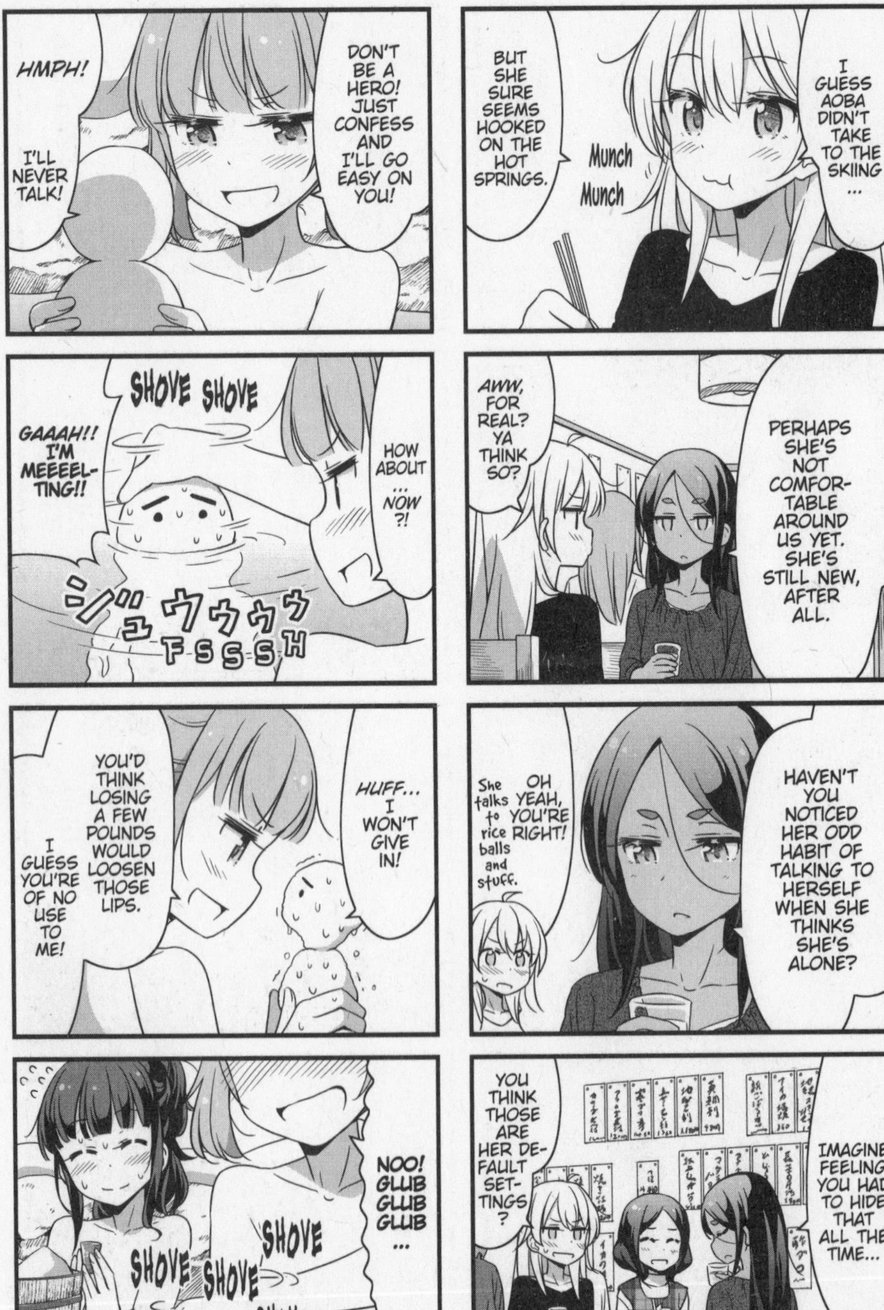
I GUESS AOBA DIDN'T TAKE TO THE SKIING ...
Munch
Munch
BUT SHE SURE SEEMS HOOKED ON THE HOT SPRINGS.
PERHAPS SHE'S NOT COMFORTABLE AROUND US YET. SHE'S STILL NEW, AFTER ALL.
AWW, FOR REAL? YA THINK SO?
HAVEN'T YOU NOTICED HER ODD HABIT OF TALKING TO HERSELF WHEN SHE THINKS SHE'S ALONE?
OH YEAH, YOU'RE RIGHT!
She talks to rice balls and stuff.
IMAGINE FEELING YOU HAD TO HIDE THAT ALL THE TIME...
YOU THINK THOSE ARE HER DEFAULT SETTINGS?
DON'T BE A HERO! JUST CONFESS AND I'LL GO EASY ON YOU!
HMPH!
I'LL NEVER TALK!
HOW ABOUT ... NOW ?!
SHOVE SHOVE
GAAAH!! I'M MEEEEL-TING!!
ジュウウウウ
FSSSH
HUFF... I WON'T GIVE IN!
YOU'D THINK LOSING A FEW POUNDS WOULD LOOSEN THOSE LIPS.
I GUESS YOU'RE OF NO USE TO ME!
NOO! GLUB GLUB GLUB ...
SHOVE
SHOVE
SHOVE
SHOVE

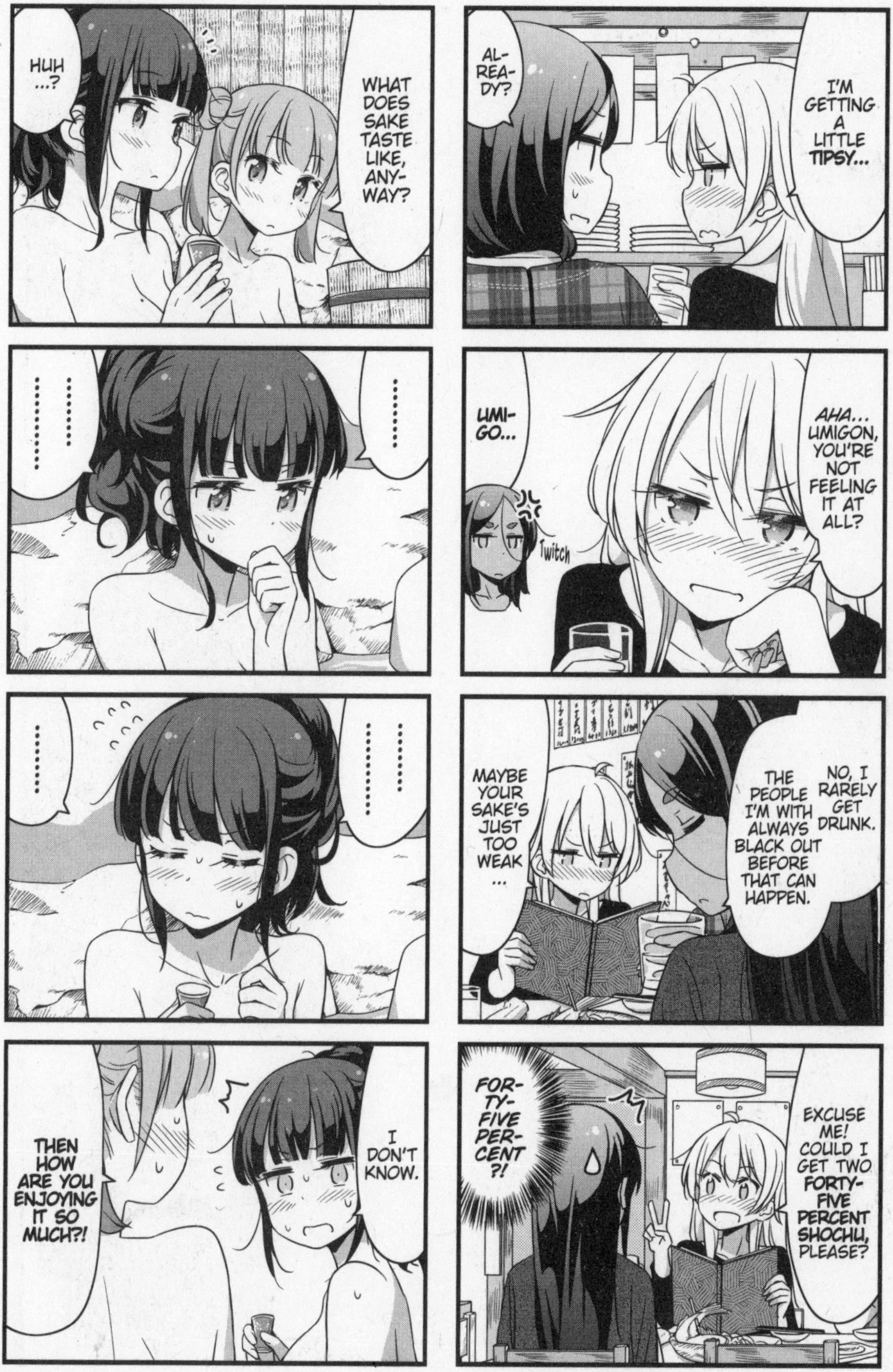
I'M GETTING A LITTLE TIPSY...
AL-READY?
AHA... UMIGON, YOU'RE NOT FEELING IT AT ALL?
UMI-GO...
Twitch
NO, I RARELY GET DRUNK.
THE PEOPLE I'M WITH ALWAYS BLACK OUT BEFORE THAT CAN HAPPEN.
MAYBE YOUR SAKE'S JUST TOO WEAK ...
EXCUSE ME! COULD I GET TWO FORTY-FIVE PERCENT SHOCHU, PLEASE?
FORTY-FIVE PERCENT?!
WHAT DOES SAKE TASTE LIKE, ANYWAY?
HUH ...?
....
....
....
....
....
I DON'T KNOW.
THEN HOW ARE YOU ENJOYING IT SO MUCH?!

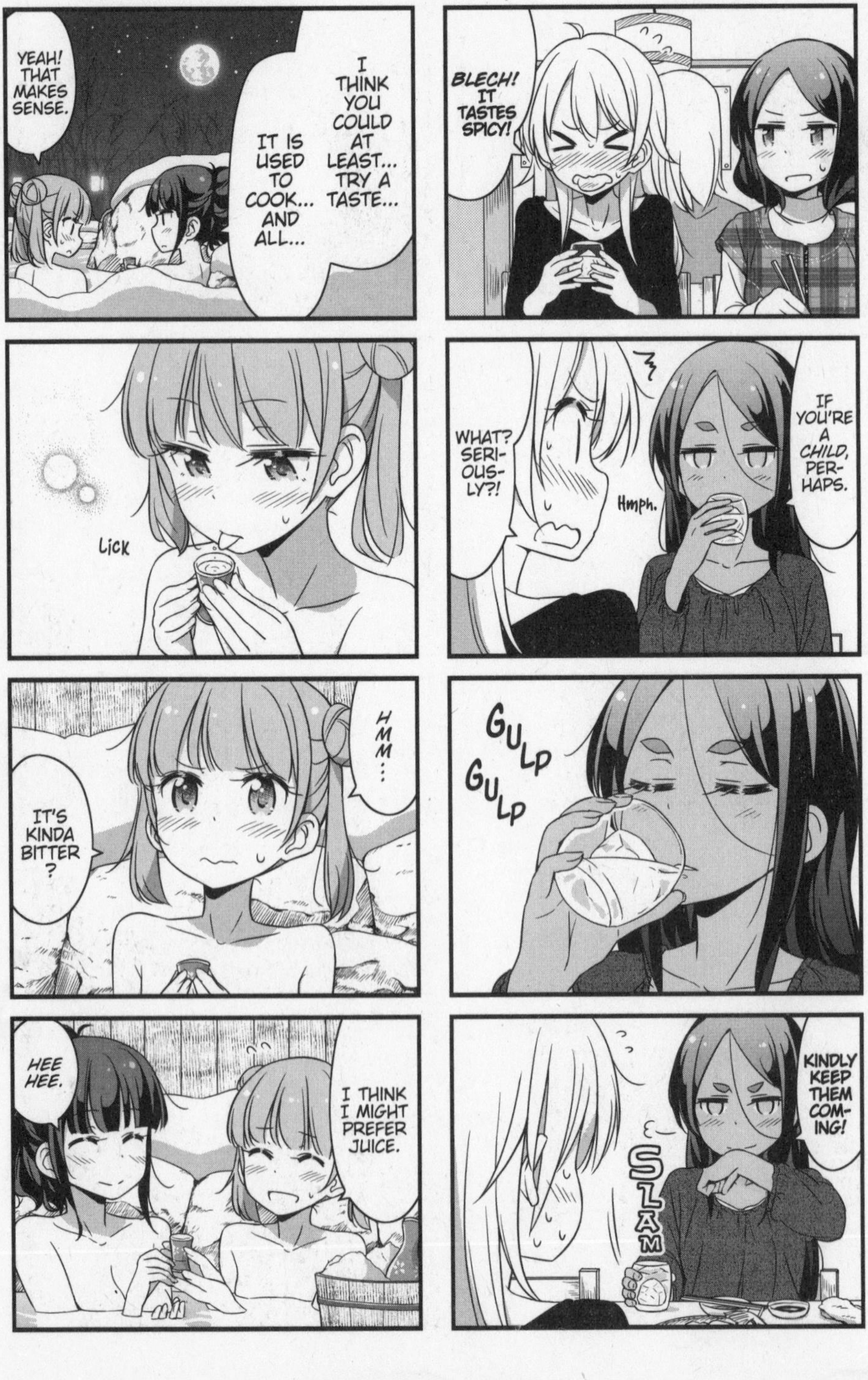
BLECH! IT TASTES SPICY!
IF YOU'RE A CHILD, PER-HAPS.
Hmph.
WHAT? SERI-OUS-LY?!
GULP GULP
KINDLY KEEP THEM COM-ING!
SLAM
I THINK YOU COULD AT LEAST... TRY A TASTE...
IT IS USED TO COOK... AND ALL...
YEAH! THAT MAKES SENSE.
Lick
HMM...
IT'S KINDA BITTER?
I THINK I MIGHT PREFER JUICE.
HEE HEE.

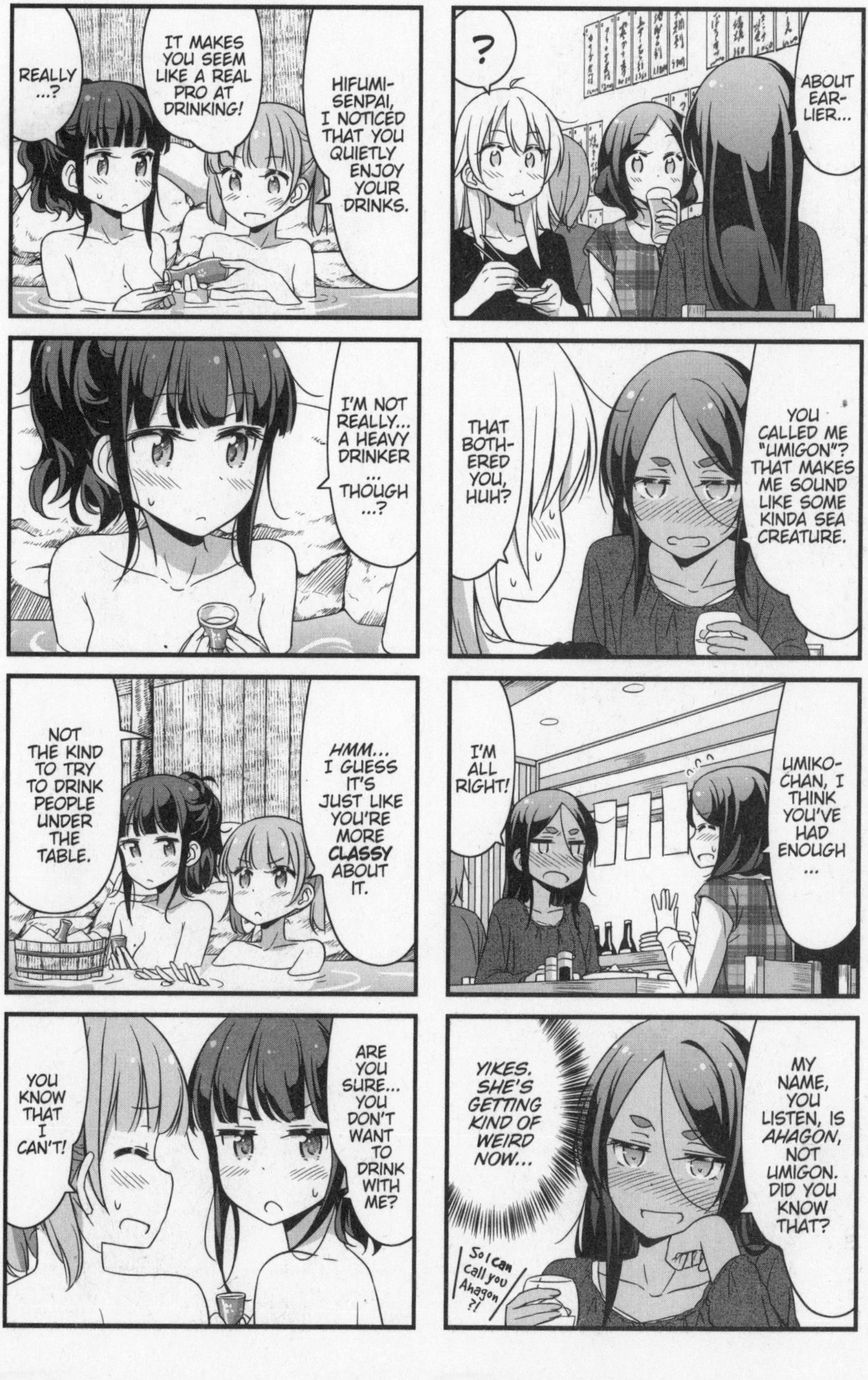
ABOUT EAR-LIER...
?
YOU CALLED ME "UMIGON"? THAT MAKES ME SOUND LIKE SOME KINDA SEA CREATURE.
THAT BOTHERED YOU, HUH?
UMIKO-CHAN, I THINK YOU'VE HAD ENOUGH...
I'M ALL RIGHT!
MY NAME, YOU LISTEN, IS AHAGON, NOT UMIGON. DID YOU KNOW THAT?
YIKES. SHE'S GETTING KIND OF WEIRD NOW...
So I can call you Ahagon?!
HIFUMI-SENPAI, I NOTICED THAT YOU QUIETLY ENJOY YOUR DRINKS.
IT MAKES YOU SEEM LIKE A REAL PRO AT DRINKING!
REALLY...?
I'M NOT REALLY... A HEAVY DRINKER... THOUGH...?
HMM... I GUESS IT'S JUST LIKE YOU'RE MORE CLASSY ABOUT IT.
NOT THE KIND TO TRY TO DRINK PEOPLE UNDER THE TABLE.
ARE YOU SURE... YOU DON'T WANT TO DRINK WITH ME?
YOU KNOW THAT I CAN'T!

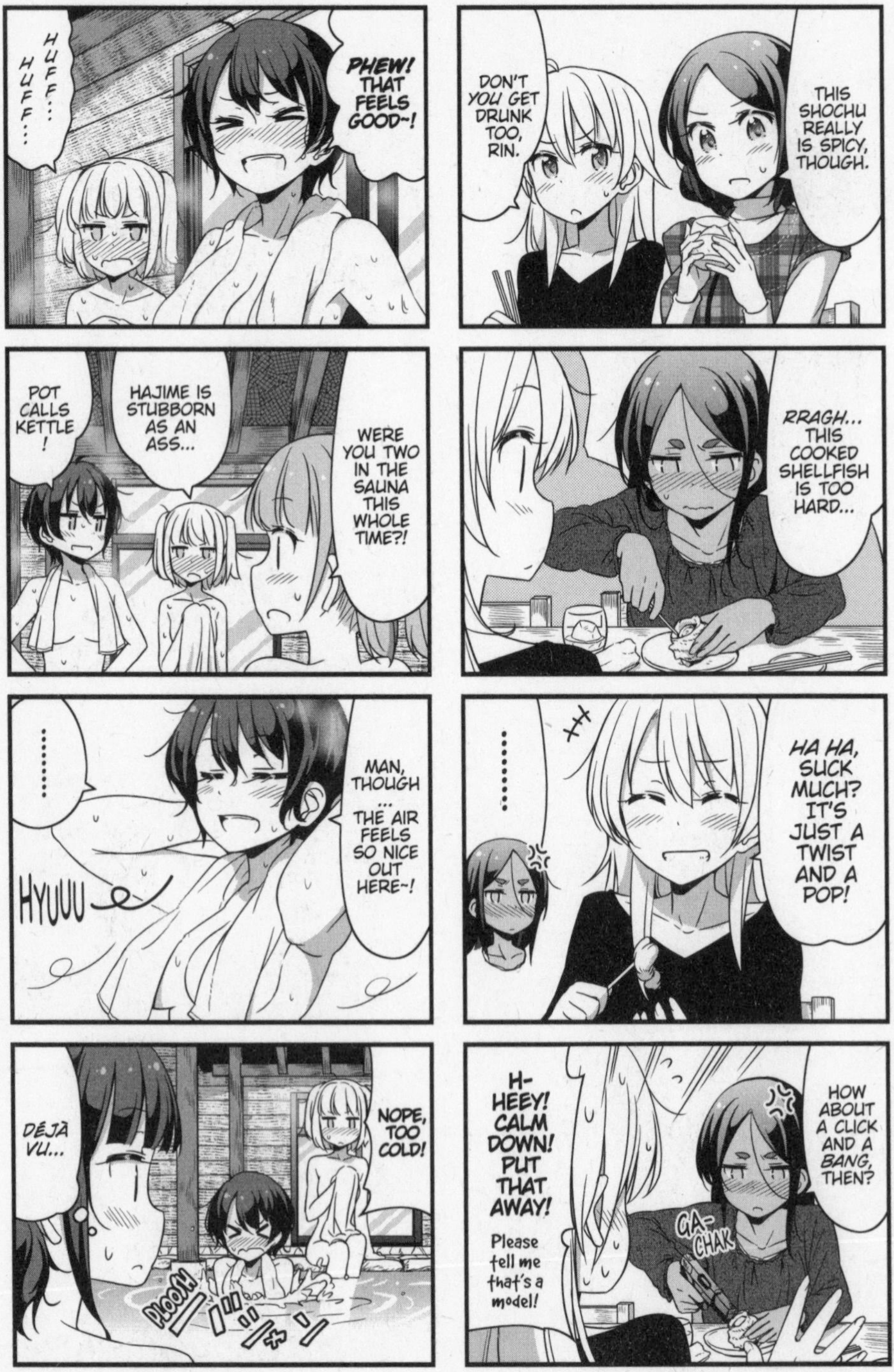
THIS SHOCHU REALLY IS SPICY, THOUGH.
DON'T YOU GET DRUNK TOO, RIN.
RRAGH... THIS COOKED SHELLFISH IS TOO HARD...
HA HA, SUCK MUCH? IT'S JUST A TWIST AND A POP!
....
HOW ABOUT A CLICK AND A BANG, THEN?
GA-CHAK
H-HEEY! CALM DOWN! PUT THAT AWAY!
Please tell me that's a model!
PHEW! THAT FEELS GOOD~!
HUFF... HUFF...
WERE YOU TWO IN THE SAUNA THIS WHOLE TIME?!
HAJIME IS STUBBORN AS AN ASS...
POT CALLS KETTLE!
MAN, THOUGH... THE AIR FEELS SO NICE OUT HERE~!
....
HYUUU
NOPE, TOO COLD!
DÉJÀ VU...

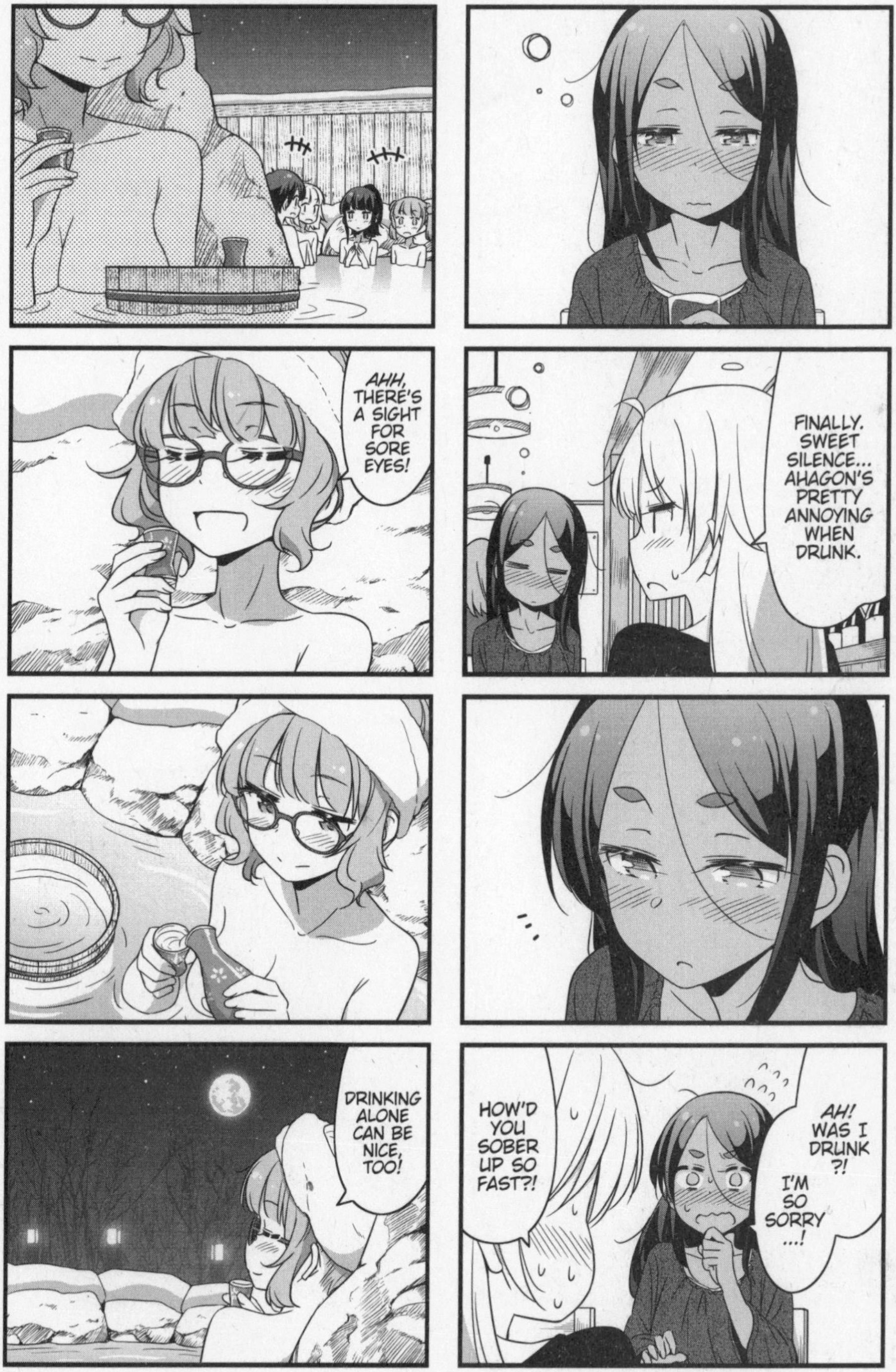
FINALLY. SWEET SILENCE... AHAGON'S PRETTY ANNOYING WHEN DRUNK.
AH! WAS I DRUNK?!
I'M SO SORRY...!
HOW'D YOU SOBER UP SO FAST?!
AHH, THERE'S A SIGHT FOR SORE EYES!
DRINKING ALONE CAN BE NICE, TOO!

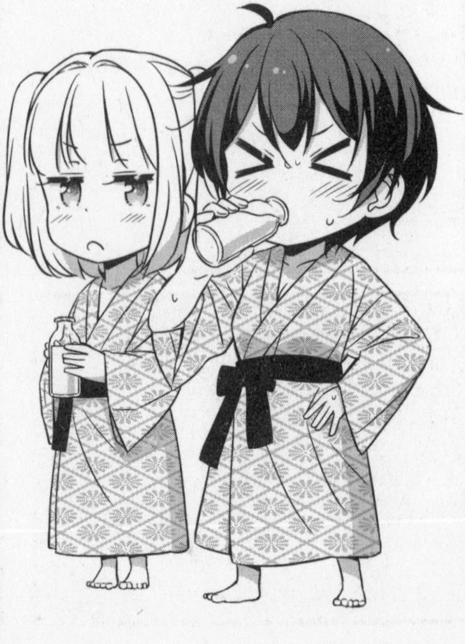

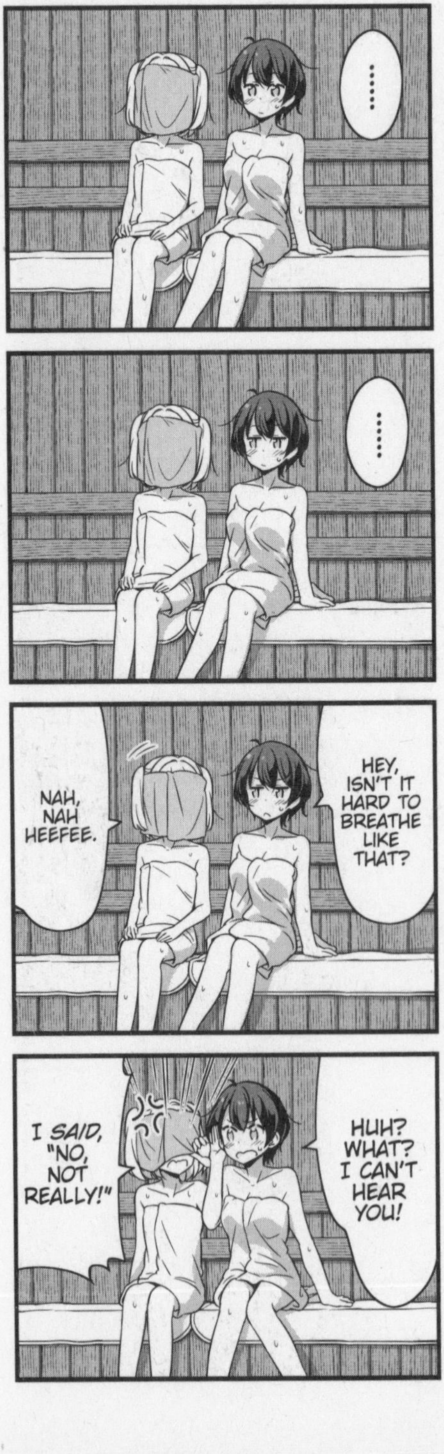
......
......
HEY, ISN'T IT HARD TO BREATHE LIKE THAT?
NAH, NAH HEEFEE.
HUH? WHAT? I CAN'T HEAR YOU!
I SAID, "NO, NOT REALLY!"

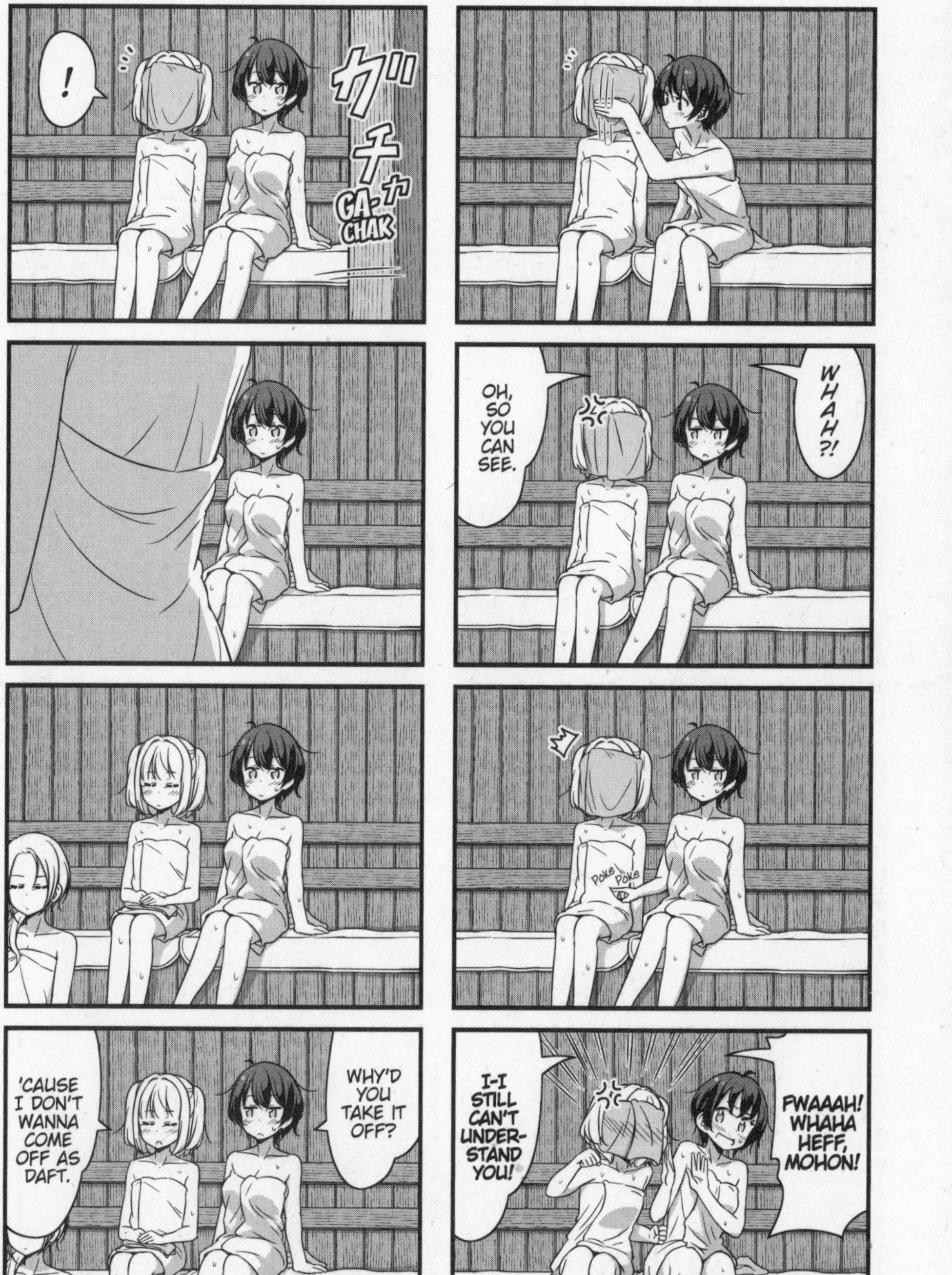
!
ガチャ
GA-CHAK
WHAH?!
OH, SO YOU CAN SEE.
Poke Poke
FWAAAH! WHAHA HEFF, MOHON!
I-I STILL CAN'T UNDER-STAND YOU!
WHY'D YOU TAKE IT OFF?
'CAUSE I DON'T WANNA COME OFF AS DAFT.

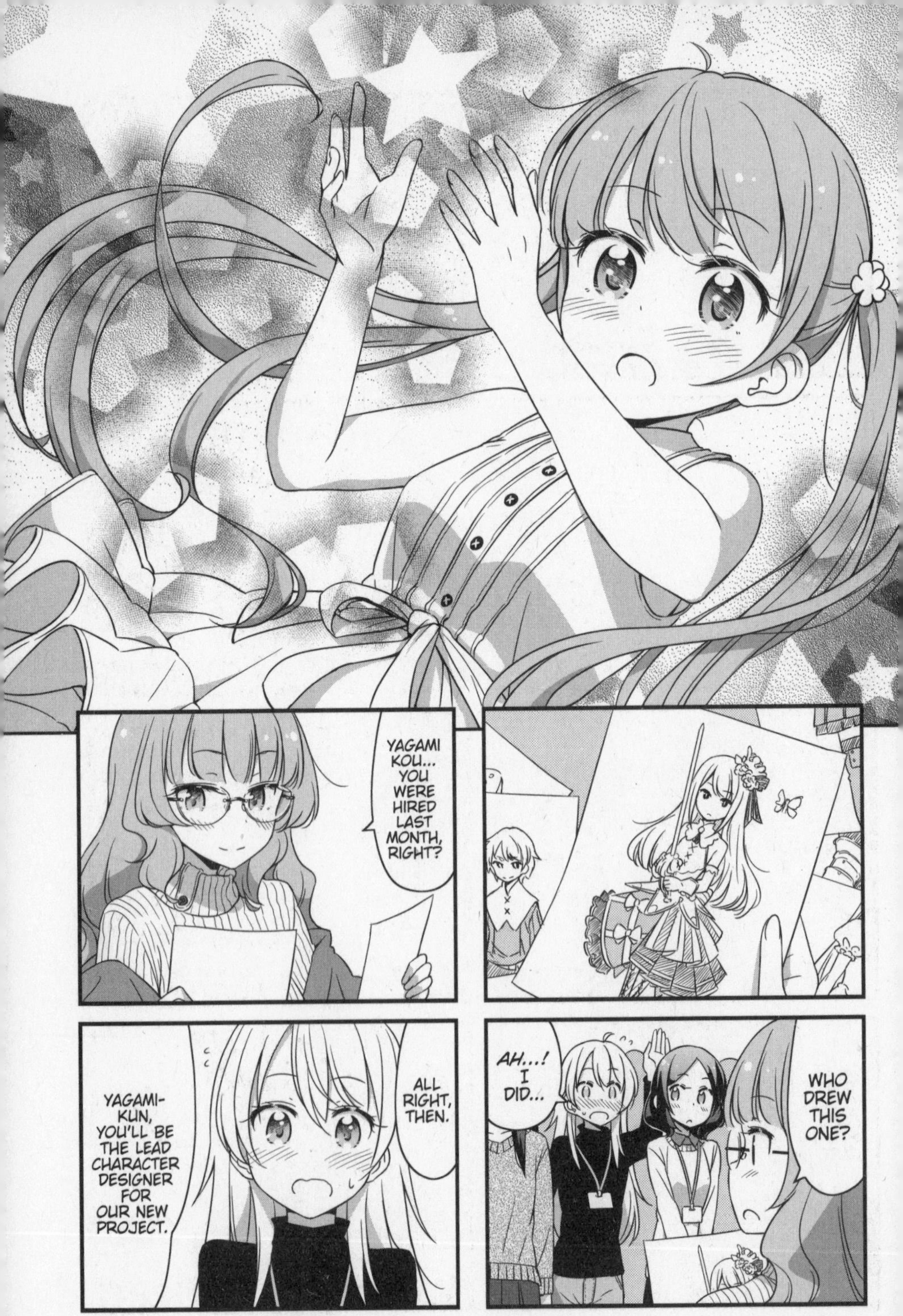
YAGAMI KOU... YOU WERE HIRED LAST MONTH, RIGHT?
WHO DREW THIS ONE?
AH...! I DID...
ALL RIGHT, THEN.
YAGAMI-KUN, YOU'LL BE THE LEAD CHARACTER DESIGNER FOR OUR NEW PROJECT.

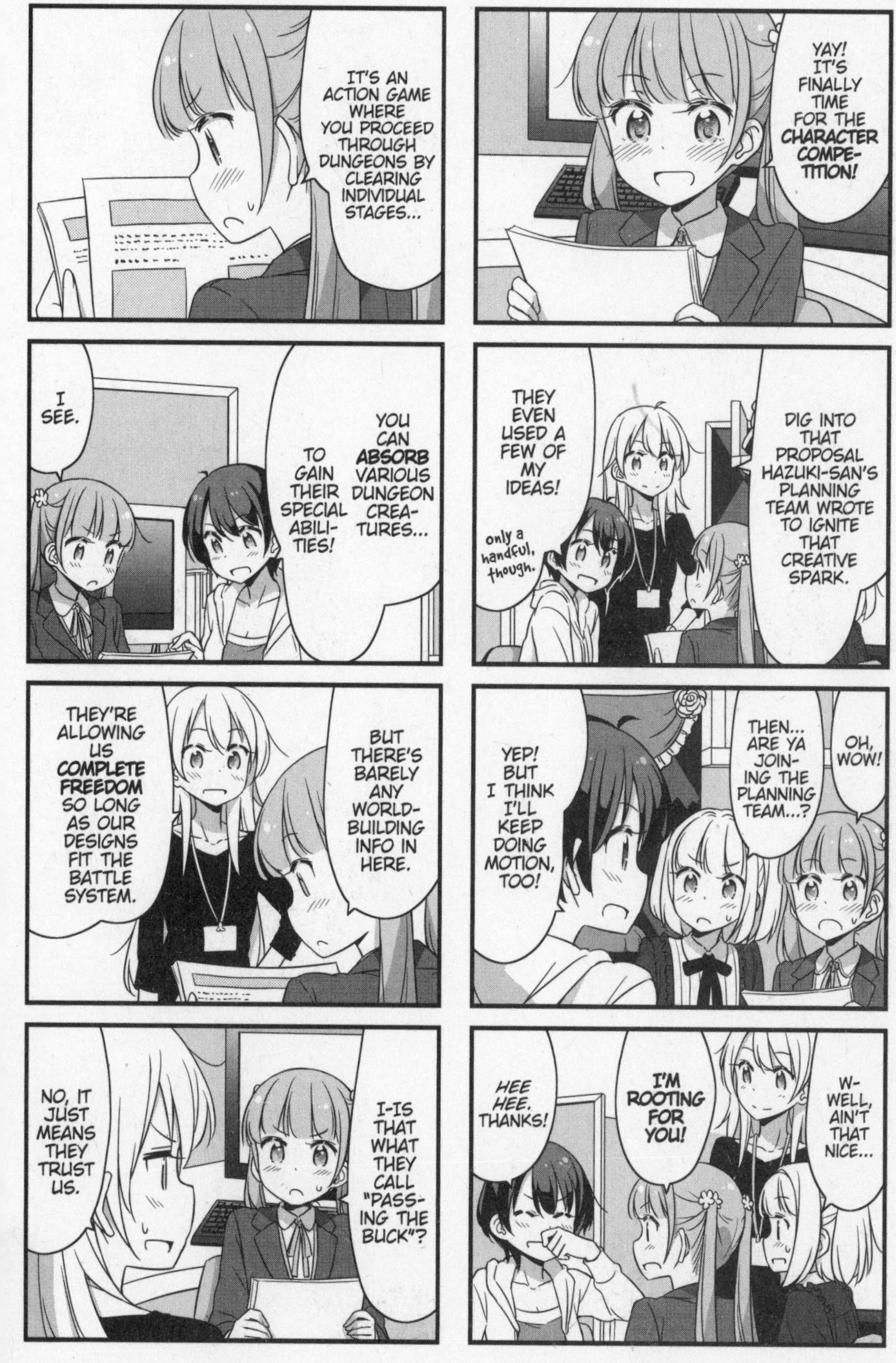
YAY! IT'S FINALLY TIME FOR THE CHARACTER COMPETITION!
IT'S AN ACTION GAME WHERE YOU PROCEED THROUGH DUNGEONS BY CLEARING INDIVIDUAL STAGES...
DIG INTO THAT PROPOSAL HAZUKI-SAN'S PLANNING TEAM WROTE TO IGNITE THAT CREATIVE SPARK.
THEY EVEN USED A FEW OF MY IDEAS!
only a handful, though.
YOU CAN ABSORB VARIOUS DUNGEON CREATURES...
TO GAIN THEIR SPECIAL ABILITIES!
I SEE.
OH, WOW!
THEN... ARE YA JOINING THE PLANNING TEAM...?
YEP! BUT I THINK I'LL KEEP DOING MOTION, TOO!
BUT THERE'S BARELY ANY WORLD-BUILDING INFO IN HERE.
THEY'RE ALLOWING US COMPLETE FREEDOM SO LONG AS OUR DESIGNS FIT THE BATTLE SYSTEM.
W-WELL, AIN'T THAT NICE...
I'M ROOTING FOR YOU!
HEE HEE, THANKS!
I-IS THAT WHAT THEY CALL "PASSING THE BUCK"?
NO, IT JUST MEANS THEY TRUST US.

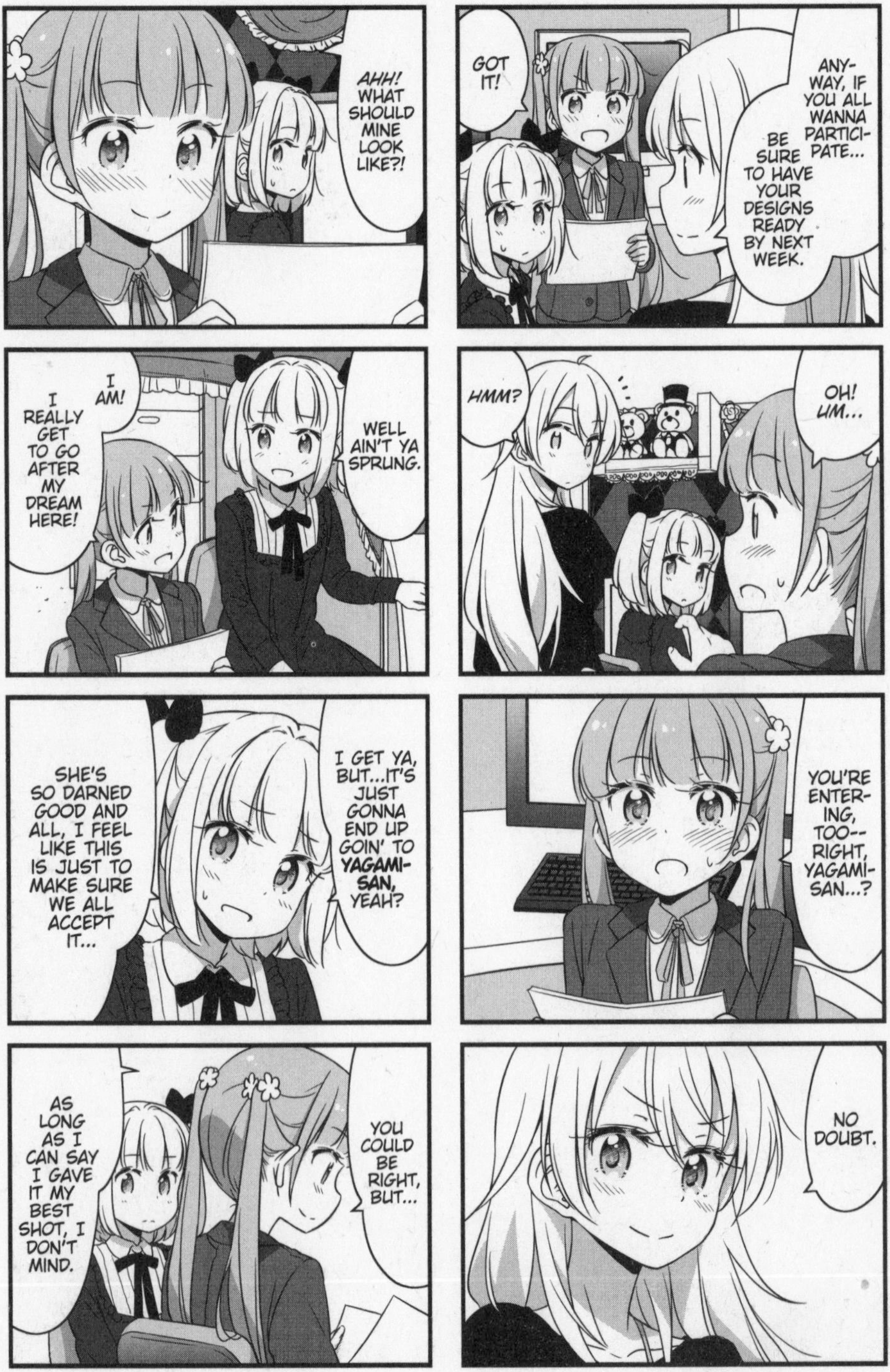
ANY-WAY, IF YOU ALL WANNA PARTICI-PATE...
BE SURE TO HAVE YOUR DESIGNS READY BY NEXT WEEK.
GOT IT!
OH! UM...
HMM?
YOU'RE ENTER-ING, TOO--RIGHT, YAGAMI-SAN...?
NO DOUBT.
AHH! WHAT SHOULD MINE LOOK LIKE?!
WELL AIN'T YA SPRUNG.
I AM!
I REALLY GET TO GO AFTER MY DREAM HERE!
I GET YA, BUT...IT'S JUST GONNA END UP GOIN' TO YAGAMI-SAN, YEAH?
SHE'S SO DARNED GOOD AND ALL, I FEEL LIKE THIS IS JUST TO MAKE SURE WE ALL ACCEPT IT...
YOU COULD BE RIGHT, BUT...
AS LONG AS I CAN SAY I GAVE IT MY BEST SHOT, I DON'T MIND.

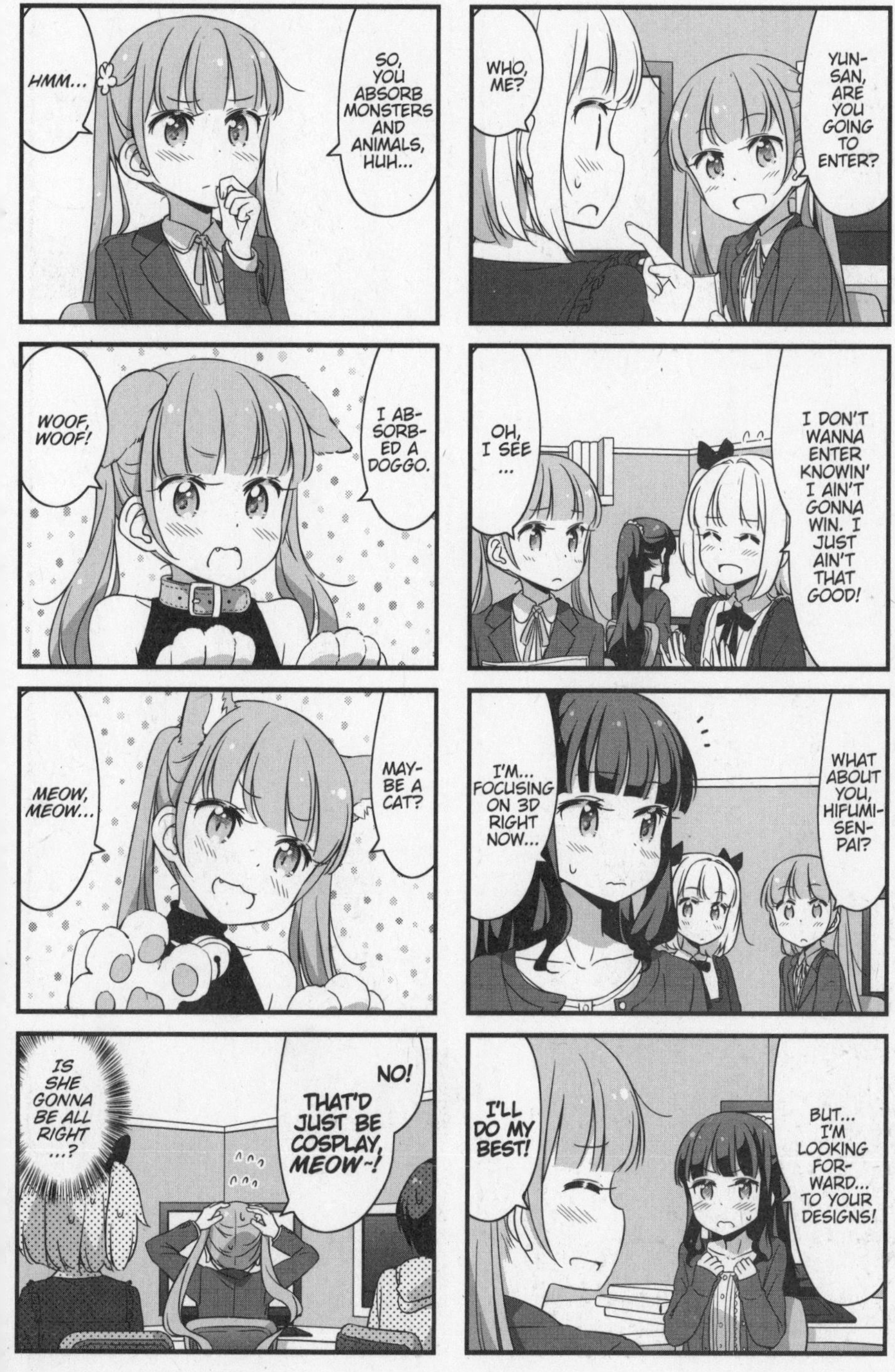
YUN-SAN, ARE YOU GOING TO ENTER?
WHO, ME?
I DON'T WANNA ENTER KNOWIN' I AIN'T GONNA WIN. I JUST AIN'T THAT GOOD!
OH, I SEE ...
WHAT ABOUT YOU, HIFUMI-SENPAI?
I'M... FOCUSING ON 3D RIGHT NOW...
BUT... I'M LOOKING FORWARD... TO YOUR DESIGNS!
I'LL DO MY BEST!
SO, YOU ABSORB MONSTERS AND ANIMALS, HUH...
HMM...
I ABSORBED A DOGGO.
WOOF, WOOF!
MAYBE A CAT?
MEOW, MEOW...
NO!
THAT'D JUST BE COSPLAY, MEOW~!
IS SHE GONNA BE ALL RIGHT ...?

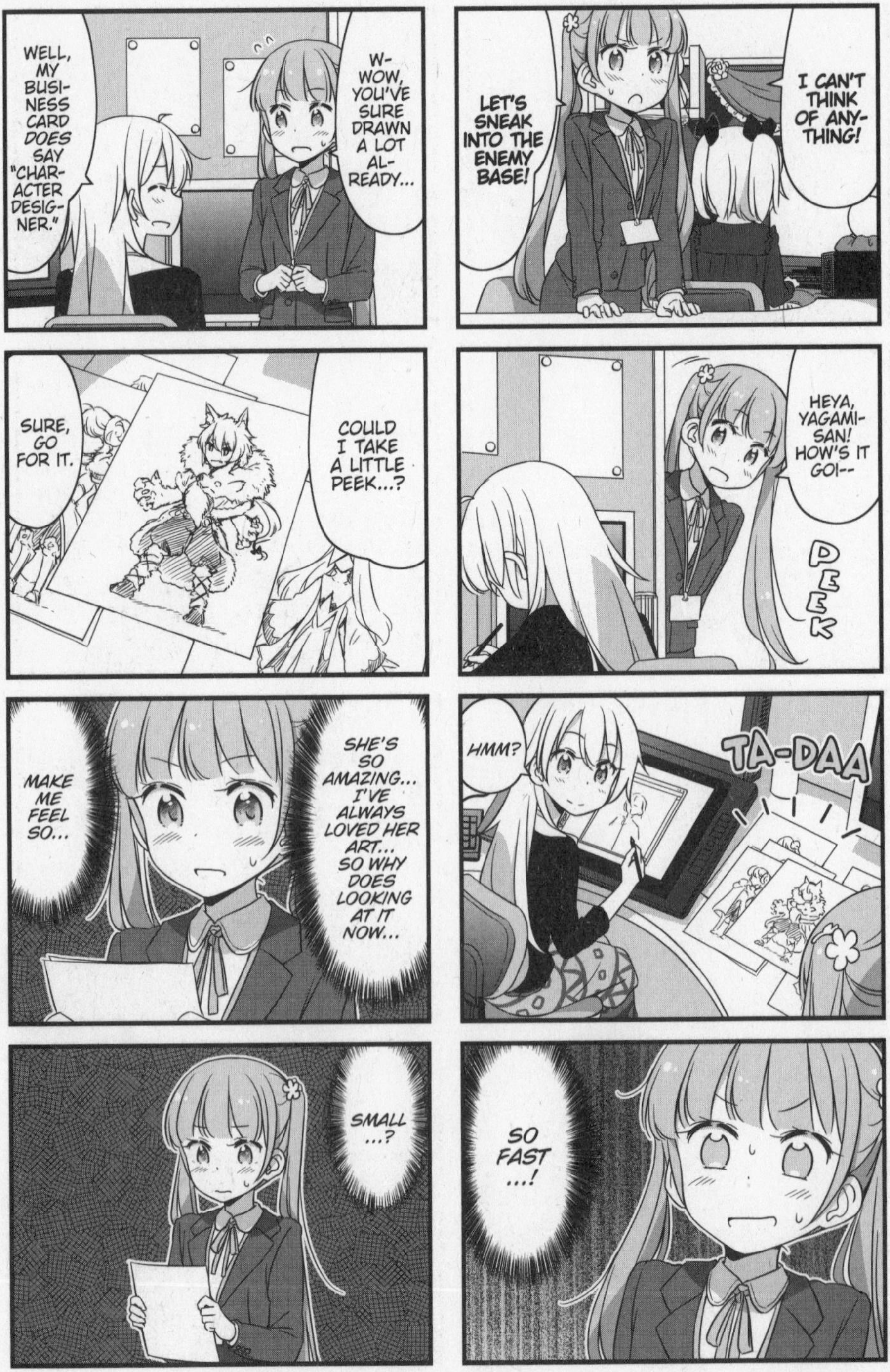
I CAN'T THINK OF ANY-THING!
LET'S SNEAK INTO THE ENEMY BASE!
HEYA, YAGAMI-SAN! HOW'S IT GOI--
PEEK
HMM?
TA-DAA
SO FAST ...!
W-WOW, YOU'VE SURE DRAWN A LOT AL-READY...
WELL, MY BUSI-NESS CARD DOES SAY "CHAR-ACTER DESIG-NER."
COULD I TAKE A LITTLE PEEK...?
SURE, GO FOR IT.
SHE'S SO AMAZING... I'VE ALWAYS LOVED HER ART... SO WHY DOES LOOKING AT IT NOW...
MAKE ME FEEL SO...
SMALL ...?

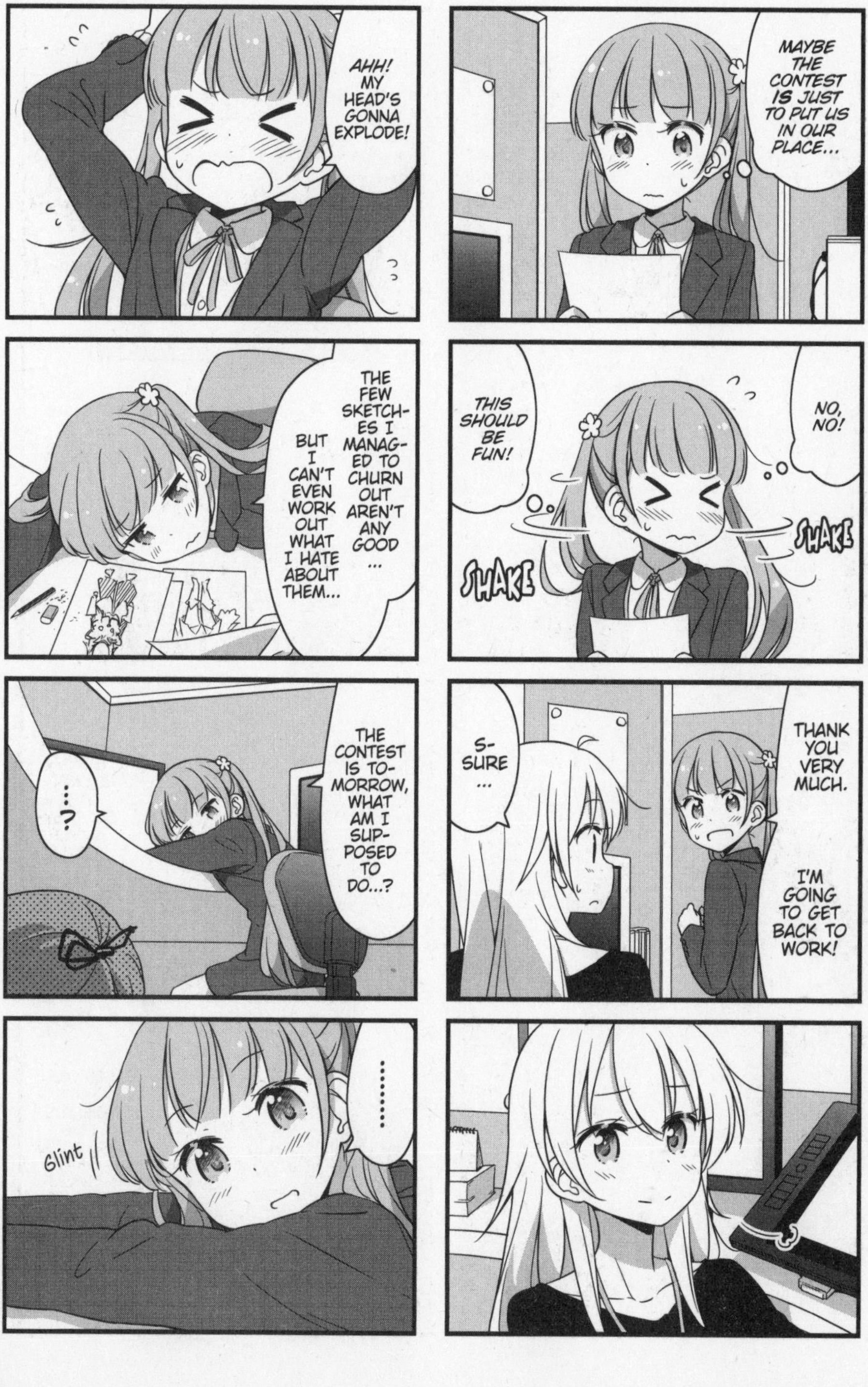
MAYBE THE CONTEST IS JUST TO PUT US IN OUR PLACE...
NO, NO!
THIS SHOULD BE FUN!
SHAKE
SHAKE
THANK YOU VERY MUCH.
I'M GOING TO GET BACK TO WORK!
S-SURE...
AHH! MY HEAD'S GONNA EXPLODE!
THE FEW SKETCHES I MANAGED TO CHURN OUT AREN'T ANY GOOD...
BUT I CAN'T EVEN WORK OUT WHAT I HATE ABOUT THEM...
THE CONTEST IS TOMORROW, WHAT AM I SUPPOSED TO DO...?
...?
......
Glint

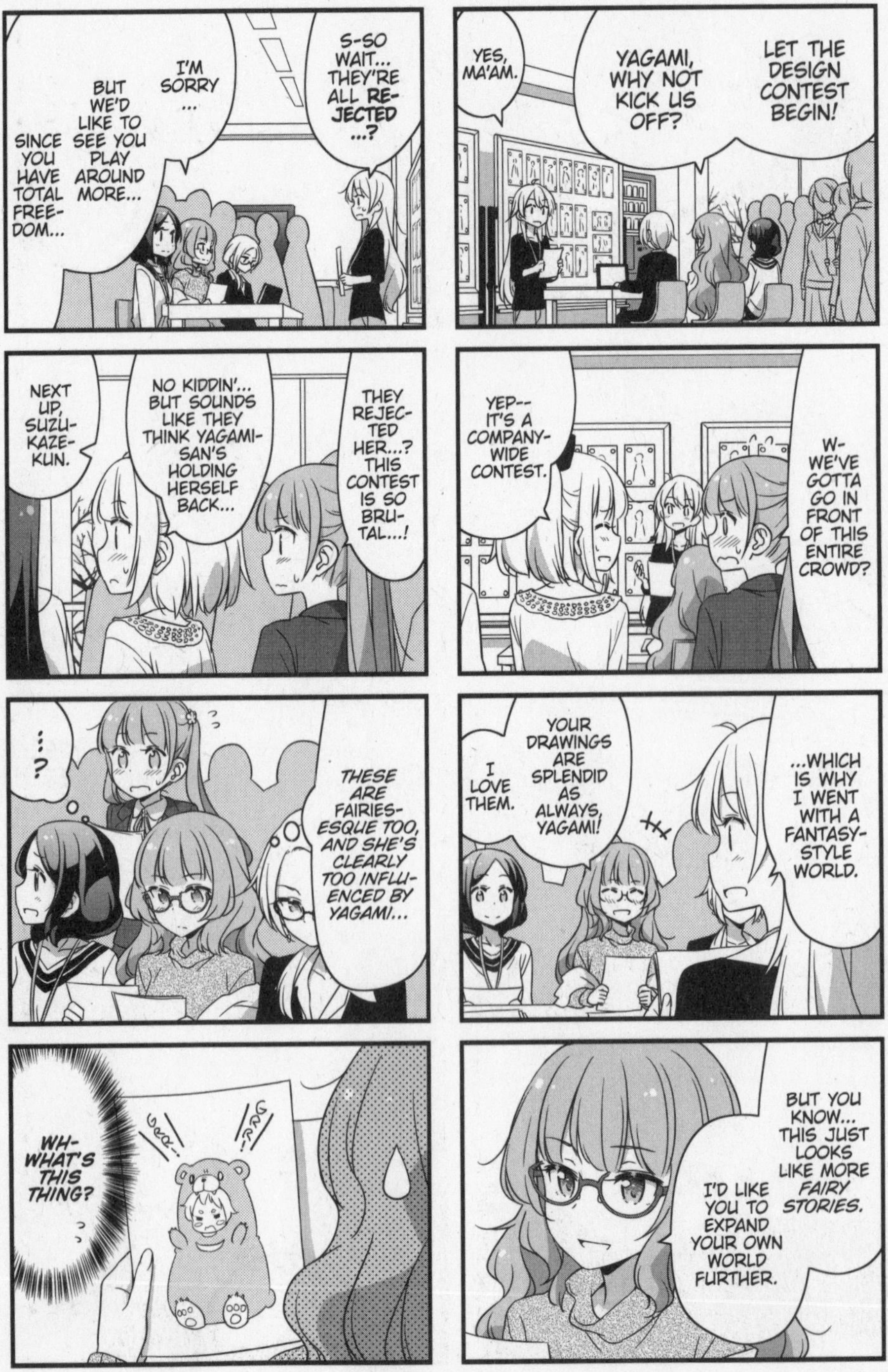
LET THE DESIGN CONTEST BEGIN!
YAGAMI, WHY NOT KICK US OFF?
YES, MA'AM.
W-WE'VE GOTTA GO IN FRONT OF THIS ENTIRE CROWD?
YEP-- IT'S A COMPANY-WIDE CONTEST.
...WHICH IS WHY I WENT WITH A FANTASY-STYLE WORLD.
YOUR DRAWINGS ARE SPLENDID AS ALWAYS, YAGAMI!
I LOVE THEM.
BUT YOU KNOW... THIS JUST LOOKS LIKE MORE *FAIRY STORIES.*
I'D LIKE YOU TO EXPAND YOUR OWN WORLD FURTHER.
S-SO WAIT... THEY'RE ALL **REJECTED**...?
I'M SORRY...
BUT WE'D LIKE TO SEE YOU PLAY AROUND MORE...
SINCE YOU HAVE TOTAL FREEDOM...
THEY REJECTED HER...? THIS CONTEST IS SO BRUTAL...!
NO KIDDIN'... BUT SOUNDS LIKE THEY THINK YAGAMI-SAN'S HOLDING HERSELF BACK...
NEXT UP, SUZUKAZE-KUN.
THESE ARE FAIRIES-ESQUE TOO, AND SHE'S CLEARLY TOO INFLUENCED BY YAGAMI...
...?
GRR...!
GRR...!
WH-WHAT'S THIS THING?

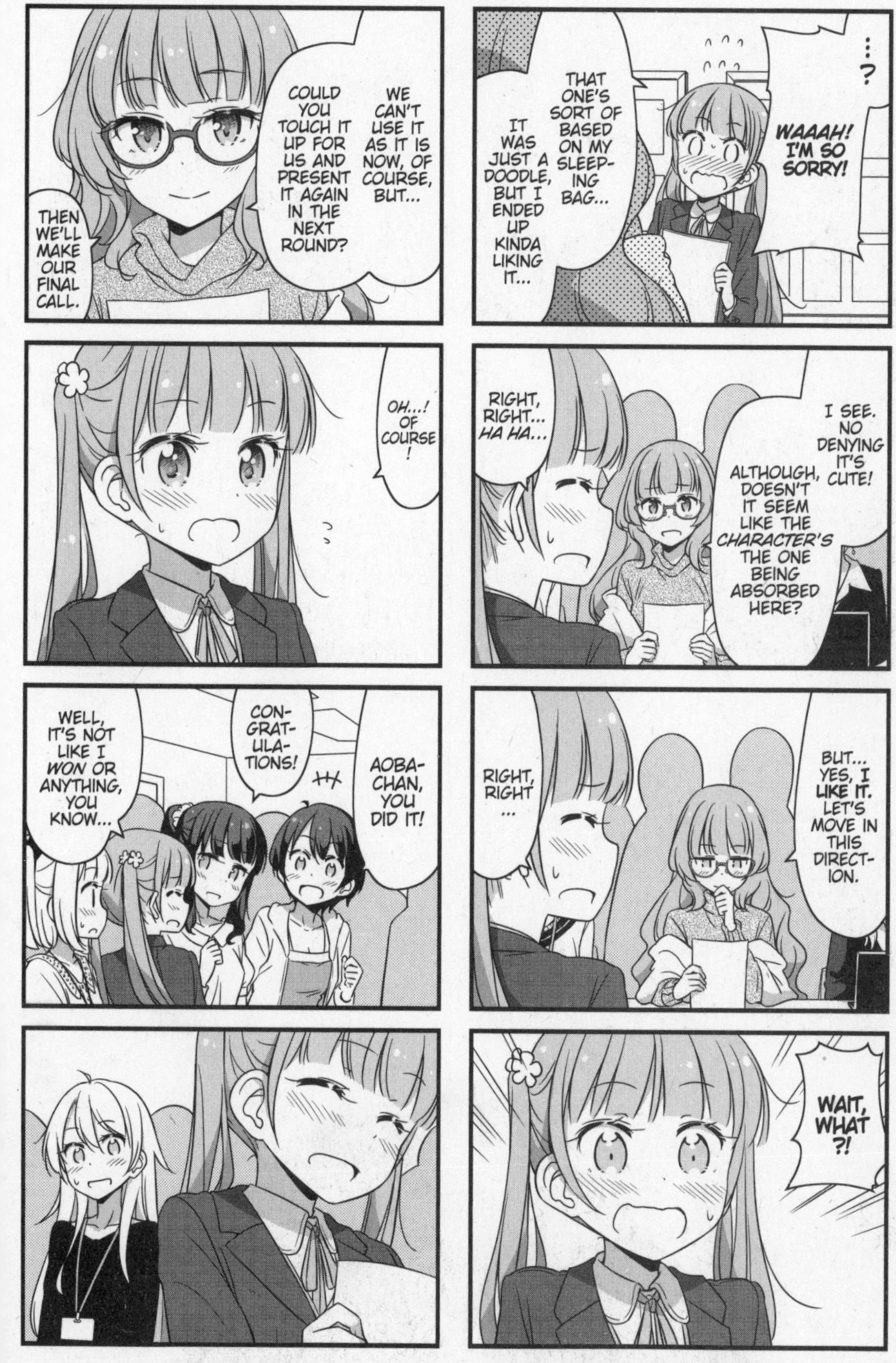
...?
WAAAH! I'M SO SORRY!
THAT ONE'S SORT OF BASED ON MY SLEEPING-BAG...
IT WAS JUST A DOODLE, BUT I ENDED UP KINDA LIKING IT...
I SEE. NO DENYING IT'S CUTE!
ALTHOUGH, DOESN'T IT SEEM LIKE THE *CHARACTER'S* THE ONE BEING ABSORBED HERE?
RIGHT, RIGHT... *HA HA*...
BUT... YES, I LIKE IT. LET'S MOVE IN THIS DIRECT-ION.
RIGHT, RIGHT ...
WAIT, WHAT?!
WE CAN'T USE IT AS IT IS NOW, OF COURSE, BUT...
COULD YOU TOUCH IT UP FOR US AND PRESENT IT AGAIN IN THE NEXT ROUND?
THEN WE'LL MAKE OUR FINAL CALL.
OH...! OF COURSE !
AOBA-CHAN, YOU DID IT!
CON-GRAT-ULA-TIONS!
WELL, IT'S NOT LIKE I *WON* OR ANYTHING, YOU KNOW...

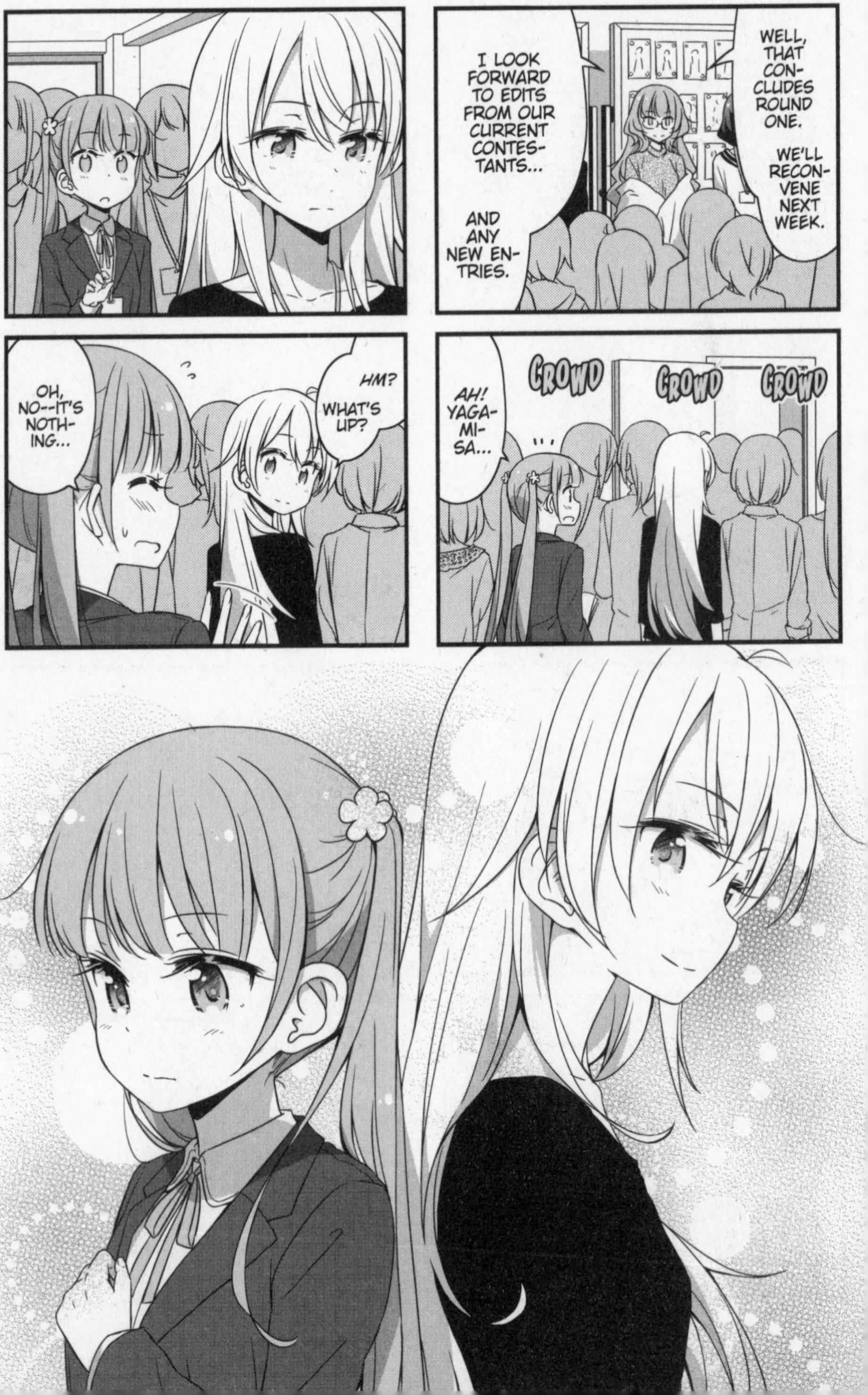
WELL, THAT CONCLUDES ROUND ONE.
WE'LL RECONVENE NEXT WEEK.
I LOOK FORWARD TO EDITS FROM OUR CURRENT CONTESTANTS...
AND ANY NEW ENTRIES.
CROWD
CROWD
CROWD
AH! YAGAMISA...
...
HM?
WHAT'S UP?
OH, NO--IT'S NOTHING...

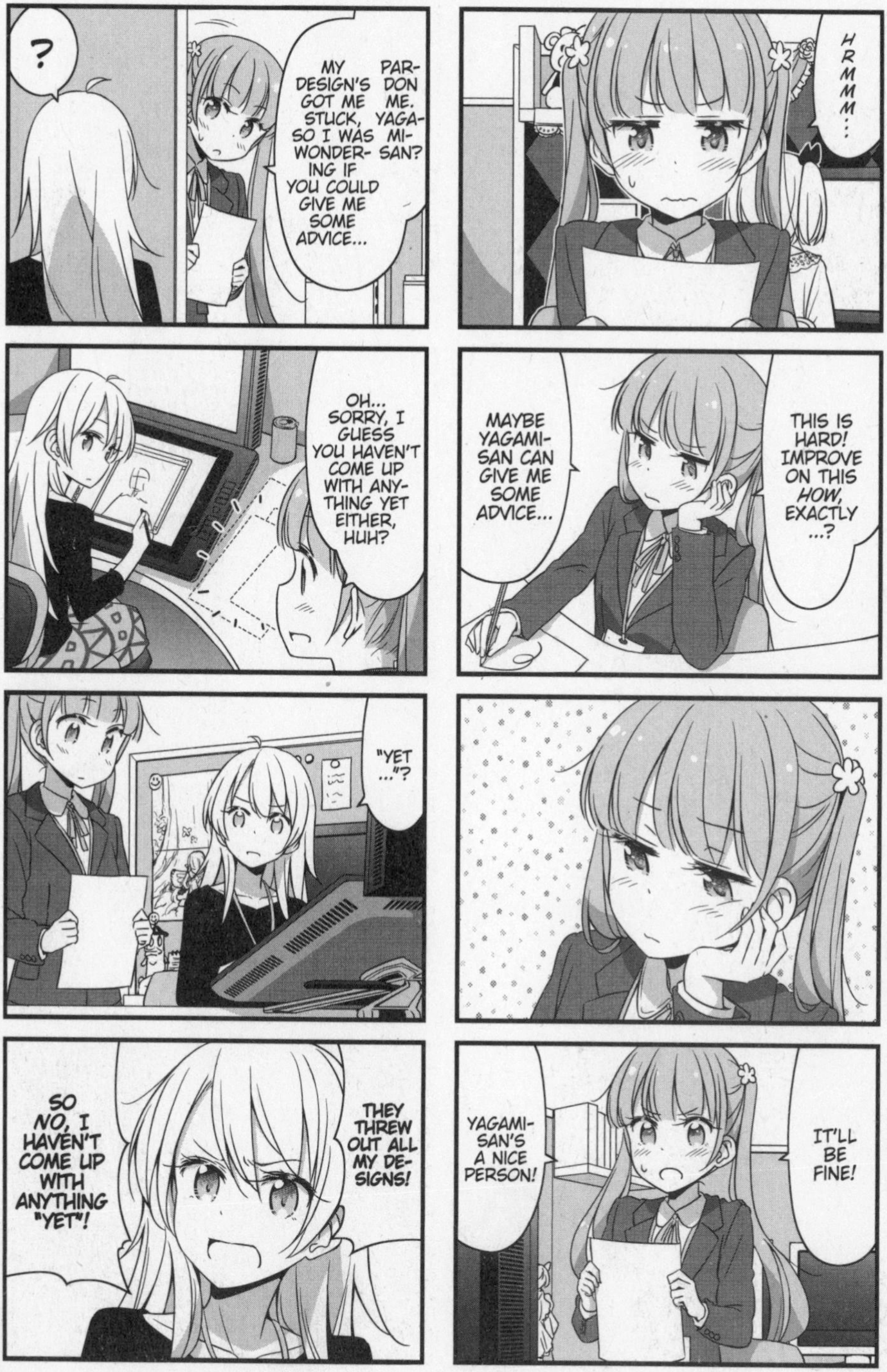
HRMMM...
THIS IS HARD! IMPROVE ON THIS *HOW*, EXACTLY ...?
MAYBE YAGAMI-SAN CAN GIVE ME SOME ADVICE...
IT'LL BE FINE!
YAGAMI-SAN'S A NICE PERSON!
?
PARDON ME. YAGAMI-SAN?
MY DESIGN'S GOT ME STUCK, SO I WAS WONDERING IF YOU COULD GIVE ME SOME ADVICE...
OH... SORRY, I GUESS YOU HAVEN'T COME UP WITH ANYTHING YET EITHER, HUH?
"YET ..."?
THEY THREW OUT ALL MY DESIGNS!
SO *NO*, I HAVEN'T COME UP WITH ANYTHING "YET"!

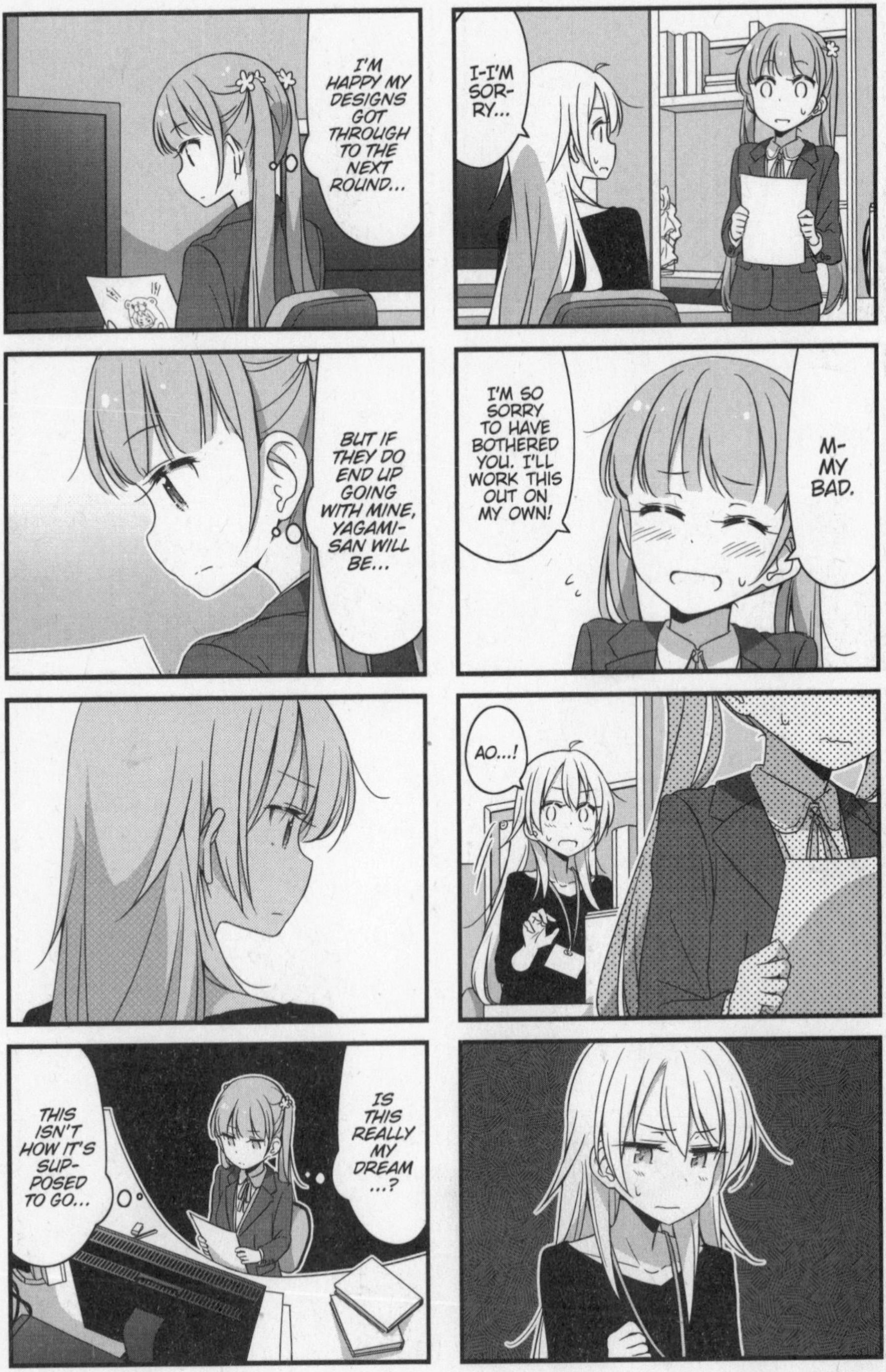
I-I'M SORRY...
I'M HAPPY MY DESIGNS GOT THROUGH TO THE NEXT ROUND...
M-MY BAD.
I'M SO SORRY TO HAVE BOTHERED YOU. I'LL WORK THIS OUT ON MY OWN!
BUT IF THEY DO END UP GOING WITH MINE, YAGAMI-SAN WILL BE...
AO...!
IS THIS REALLY MY DREAM ...?
THIS ISN'T HOW IT'S SUPPOSED TO GO...

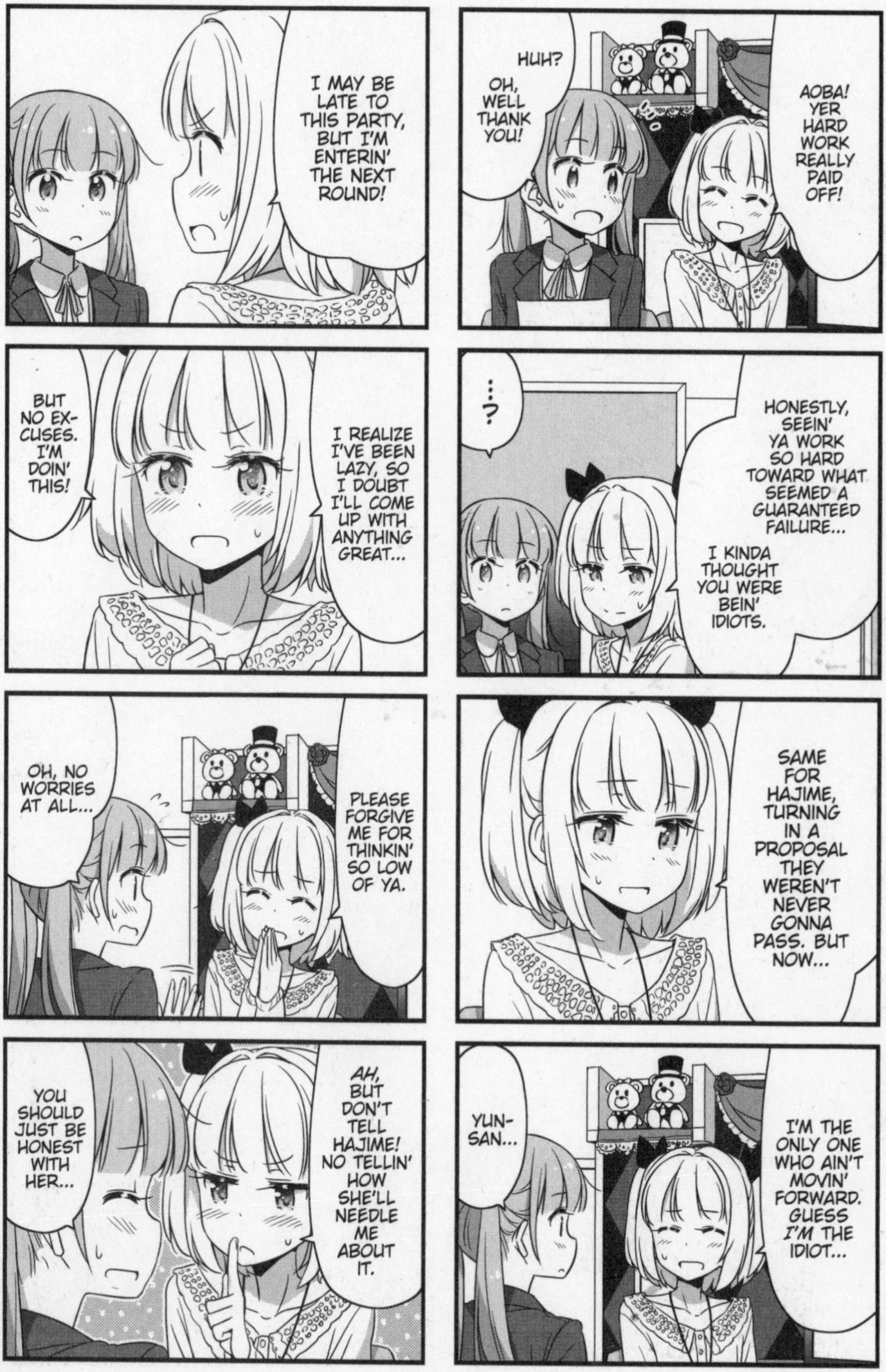
AOBA! YER HARD WORK REALLY PAID OFF!
HUH?
OH, WELL THANK YOU!
HONESTLY, SEEIN' YA WORK SO HARD TOWARD WHAT SEEMED A GUARANTEED FAILURE...
I KINDA THOUGHT YOU WERE BEIN' IDIOTS.
...?
SAME FOR HAJIME, TURNING IN A PROPOSAL THEY WEREN'T NEVER GONNA PASS. BUT NOW...
I'M THE ONLY ONE WHO AIN'T MOVIN' FORWARD. GUESS I'M THE IDIOT...
YUN-SAN...
I MAY BE LATE TO THIS PARTY, BUT I'M ENTERIN' THE NEXT ROUND!
I REALIZE I'VE BEEN LAZY, SO I DOUBT I'LL COME UP WITH ANYTHING GREAT...
BUT NO EXCUSES. I'M DOIN' THIS!
PLEASE FORGIVE ME FOR THINKIN' SO LOW OF YA.
OH, NO WORRIES AT ALL...
AH, BUT DON'T TELL HAJIME! NO TELLIN' HOW SHE'LL NEEDLE ME ABOUT IT.
YOU SHOULD JUST BE HONEST WITH HER...

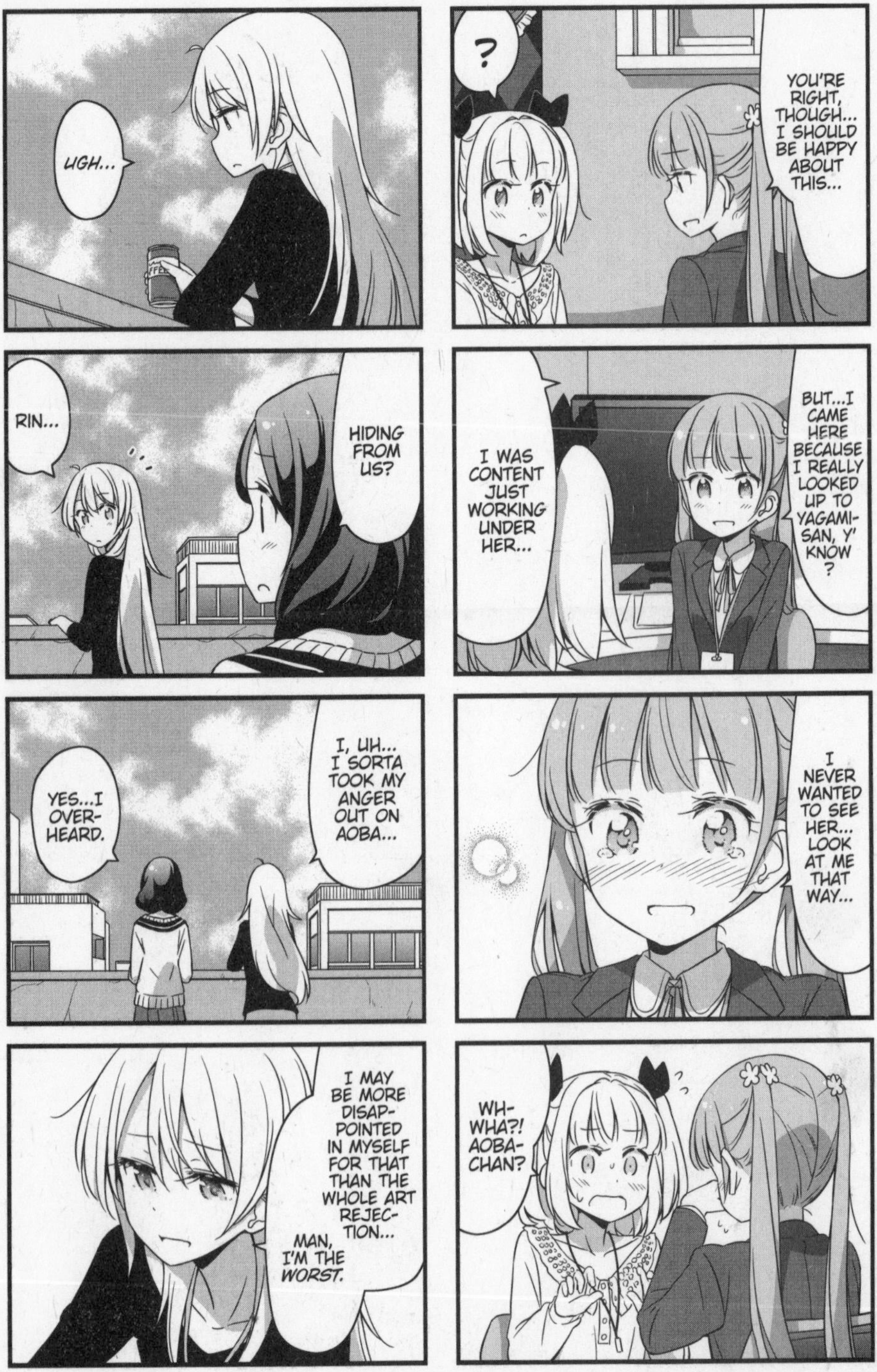
?
YOU'RE RIGHT, THOUGH... I SHOULD BE HAPPY ABOUT THIS...
UGH...
BUT...I CAME HERE BECAUSE I REALLY LOOKED UP TO YAGAMI-SAN, Y' KNOW?
I WAS CONTENT JUST WORKING UNDER HER...
HIDING FROM US?
RIN...
I NEVER WANTED TO SEE HER... LOOK AT ME THAT WAY...
I, UH... I SORTA TOOK MY ANGER OUT ON AOBA...
YES...I OVERHEARD.
WH-WHA?! AOBA-CHAN?
I MAY BE MORE DISAPPOINTED IN MYSELF FOR THAT THAN THE WHOLE ART REJECTION...
MAN, I'M THE *WORST*.

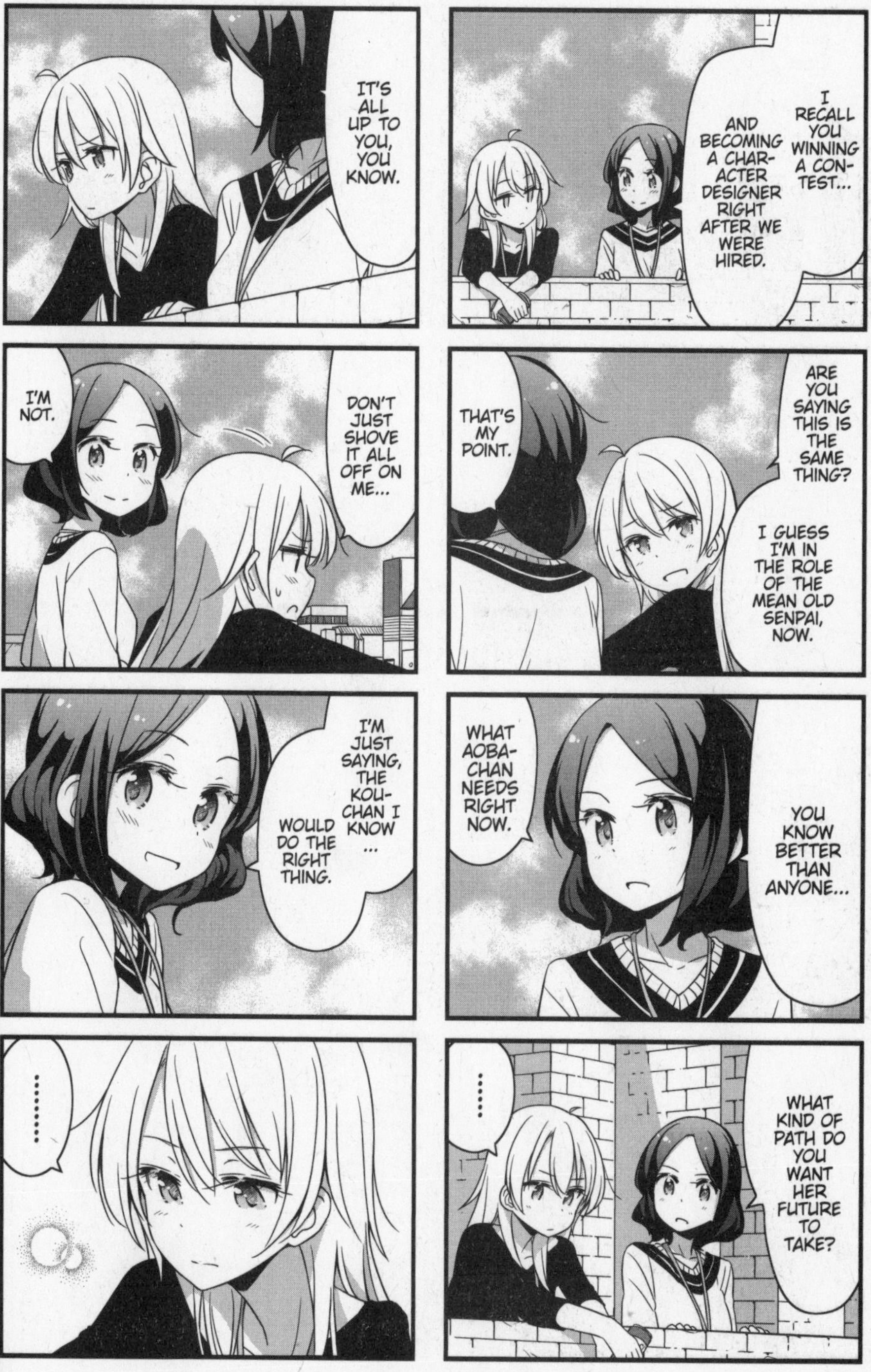
I RECALL YOU WINNING A CON-TEST...
AND BECOMING A CHAR-ACTER DESIGNER RIGHT AFTER WE WERE HIRED.
IT'S ALL UP TO YOU, YOU KNOW.
ARE YOU SAYING THIS IS THE SAME THING?
I GUESS I'M IN THE ROLE OF THE MEAN OLD SENPAI, NOW.
THAT'S MY POINT.
DON'T JUST SHOVE IT ALL OFF ON ME...
I'M NOT.
YOU KNOW BETTER THAN ANYONE...
WHAT AOBA-CHAN NEEDS RIGHT NOW.
I'M JUST SAYING, THE KOU-CHAN I KNOW ...
WOULD DO THE RIGHT THING.
WHAT KIND OF PATH DO YOU WANT HER FUTURE TO TAKE?
......
......

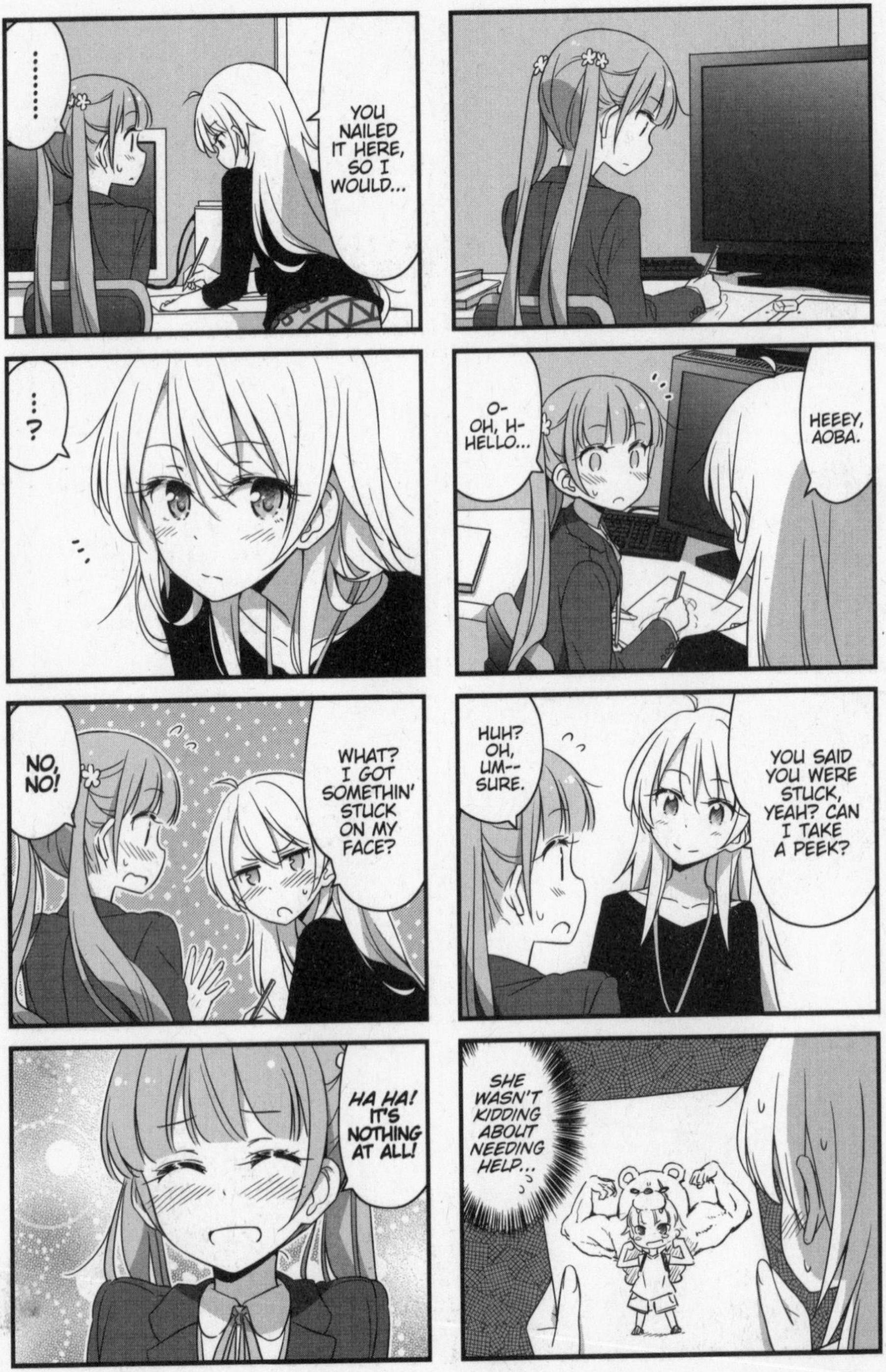
YOU NAILED IT HERE, SO I WOULD...
......
HEEEY, AOBA.
O- OH, H- HELLO...
...?
YOU SAID YOU WERE STUCK, YEAH? CAN I TAKE A PEEK?
HUH? OH, UM-- SURE.
WHAT? I GOT SOMETHIN' STUCK ON MY FACE?
NO, NO!
SHE WASN'T KIDDING ABOUT NEEDING HELP...
HA HA! IT'S NOTHING AT ALL!

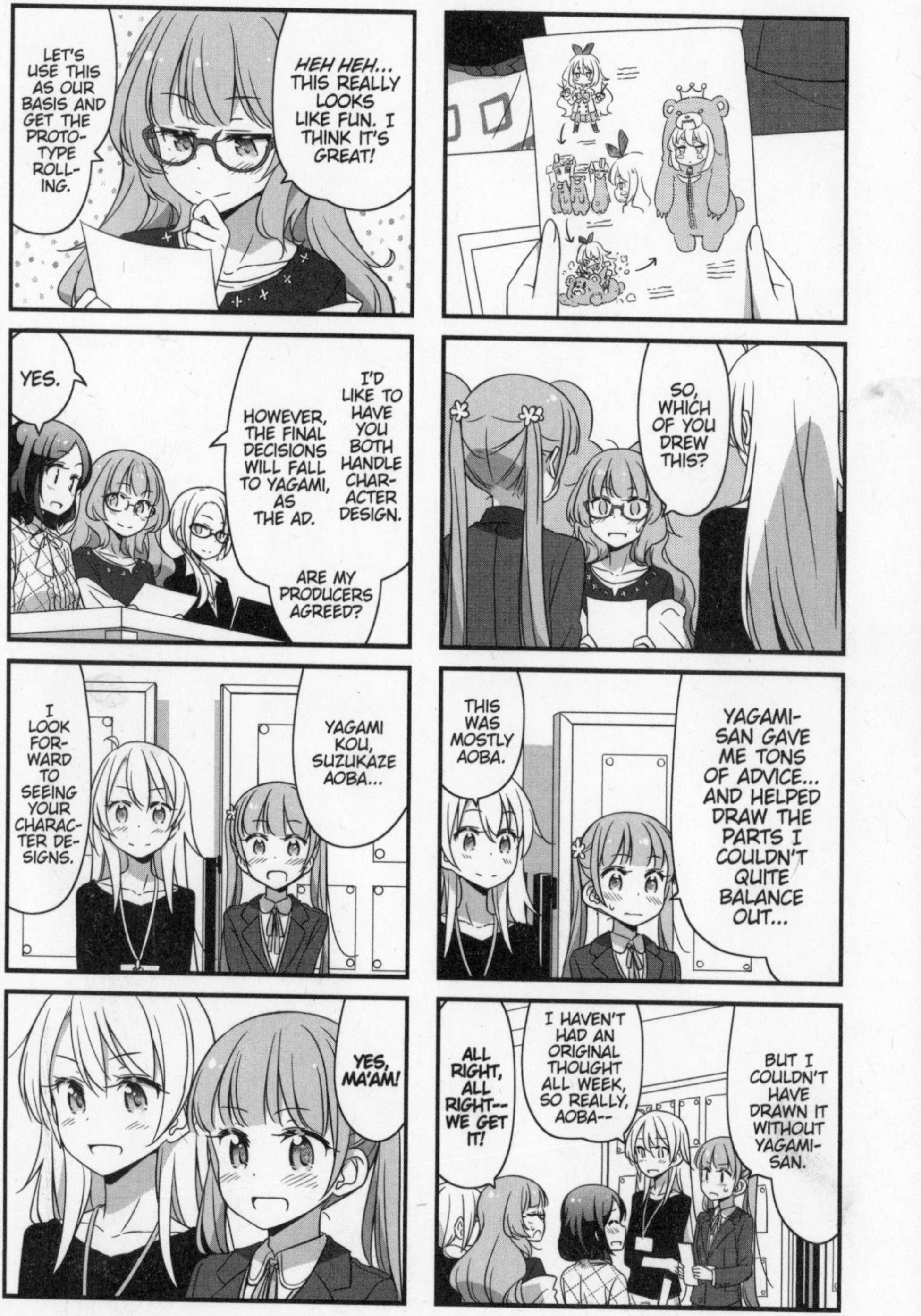
HEH HEH... THIS REALLY LOOKS LIKE FUN. I THINK IT'S GREAT!
LET'S USE THIS AS OUR BASIS AND GET THE PROTOTYPE ROLLING.
SO, WHICH OF YOU DREW THIS?
I'D LIKE TO HAVE YOU BOTH HANDLE CHARACTER DESIGN.
HOWEVER, THE FINAL DECISIONS WILL FALL TO YAGAMI, AS THE AD.
ARE MY PRODUCERS AGREED?
YES.
YAGAMI-SAN GAVE ME TONS OF ADVICE... AND HELPED DRAW THE PARTS I COULDN'T QUITE BALANCE OUT...
THIS WAS MOSTLY AOBA.
YAGAMI KOU, SUZUKAZE AOBA...
I LOOK FORWARD TO SEEING YOUR CHARACTER DESIGNS.
BUT I COULDN'T HAVE DRAWN IT WITHOUT YAGAMI-SAN.
I HAVEN'T HAD AN ORIGINAL THOUGHT ALL WEEK, SO REALLY, AOBA--
ALL RIGHT, ALL RIGHT-- WE GET IT!
YES, MA'AM!

NEW GAME!

NEW GAME!

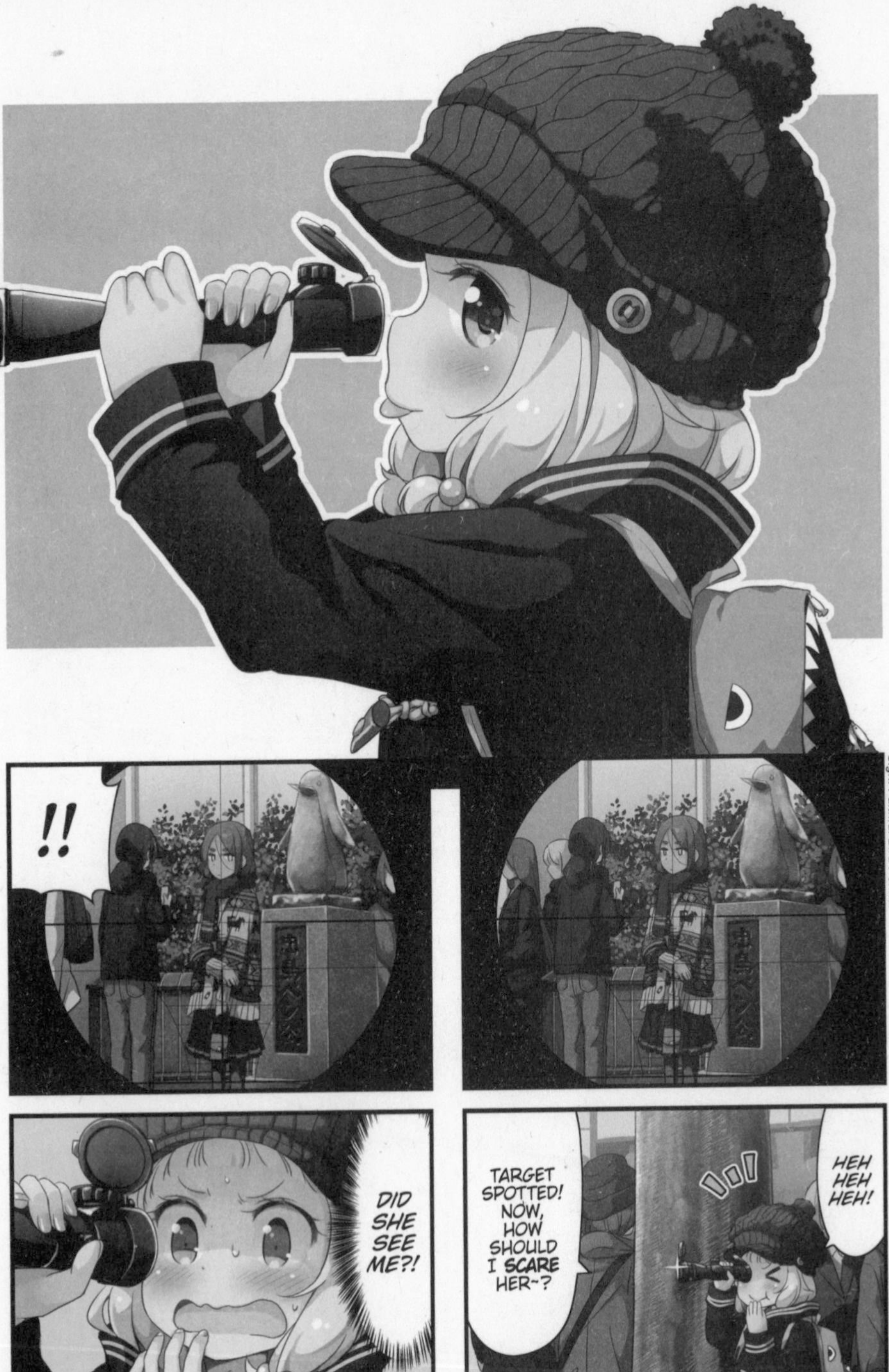
!!
HEH HEH HEH!
TARGET SPOTTED! NOW, HOW SHOULD I SCARE HER~?
DID SHE SEE ME?!

Sign: Faithful Bird Penko.

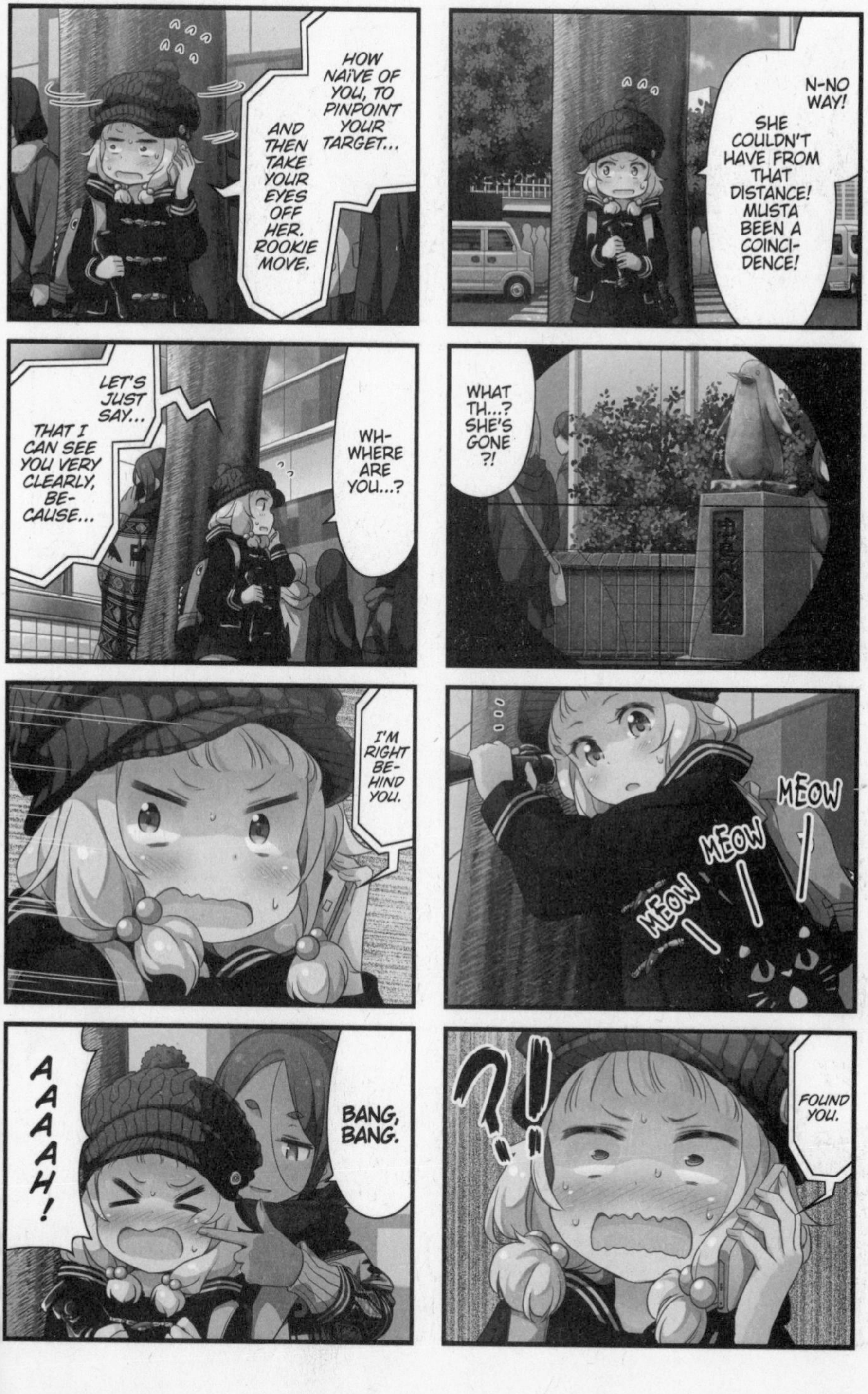
N-NO WAY!
SHE COULDN'T HAVE FROM THAT DISTANCE! MUSTA BEEN A COINCIDENCE!
HOW NAïVE OF YOU, TO PINPOINT YOUR TARGET...
AND THEN TAKE YOUR EYES OFF HER. ROOKIE MOVE.
WHAT TH...? SHE'S GONE?!
WH-WHERE ARE YOU...?
LET'S JUST SAY...
THAT I CAN SEE YOU VERY CLEARLY, BE-CAUSE...
MEOW
MEOW
MEOW
I'M RIGHT BE-HIND YOU.
?!
FOUND YOU.
BANG, BANG.
AAAAAH!

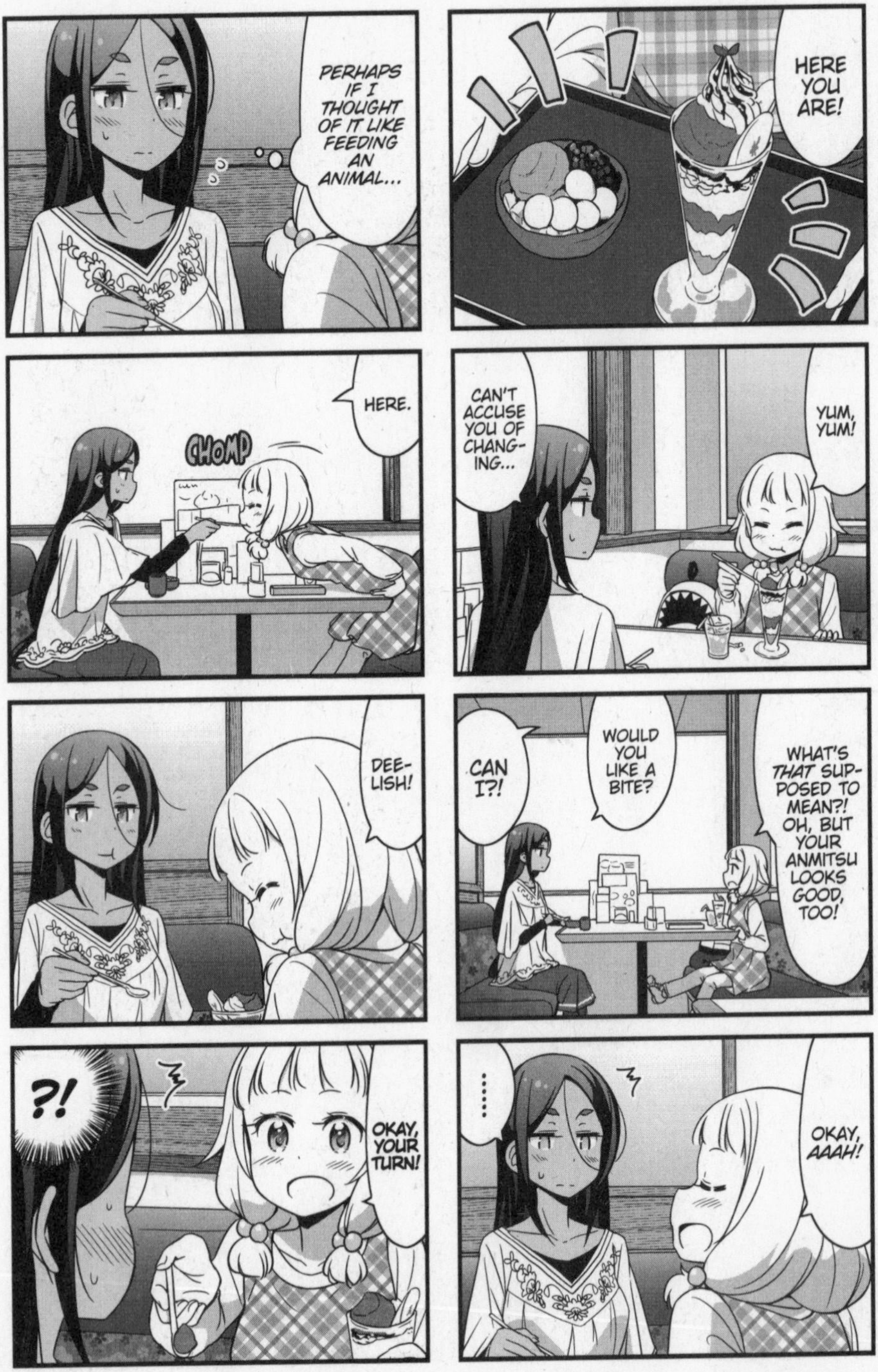
HERE YOU ARE!
PERHAPS IF I THOUGHT OF IT LIKE FEEDING AN ANIMAL...
YUM, YUM!
CAN'T ACCUSE YOU OF CHANG-ING...
HERE.
CHOMP
WHAT'S *THAT* SUP-POSED TO MEAN?! OH, BUT YOUR ANMITSU LOOKS GOOD, TOO!
WOULD YOU LIKE A BITE?
CAN I?!
DEE-LISH!
OKAY, AAAH!
......
OKAY, YOUR TURN!
?!

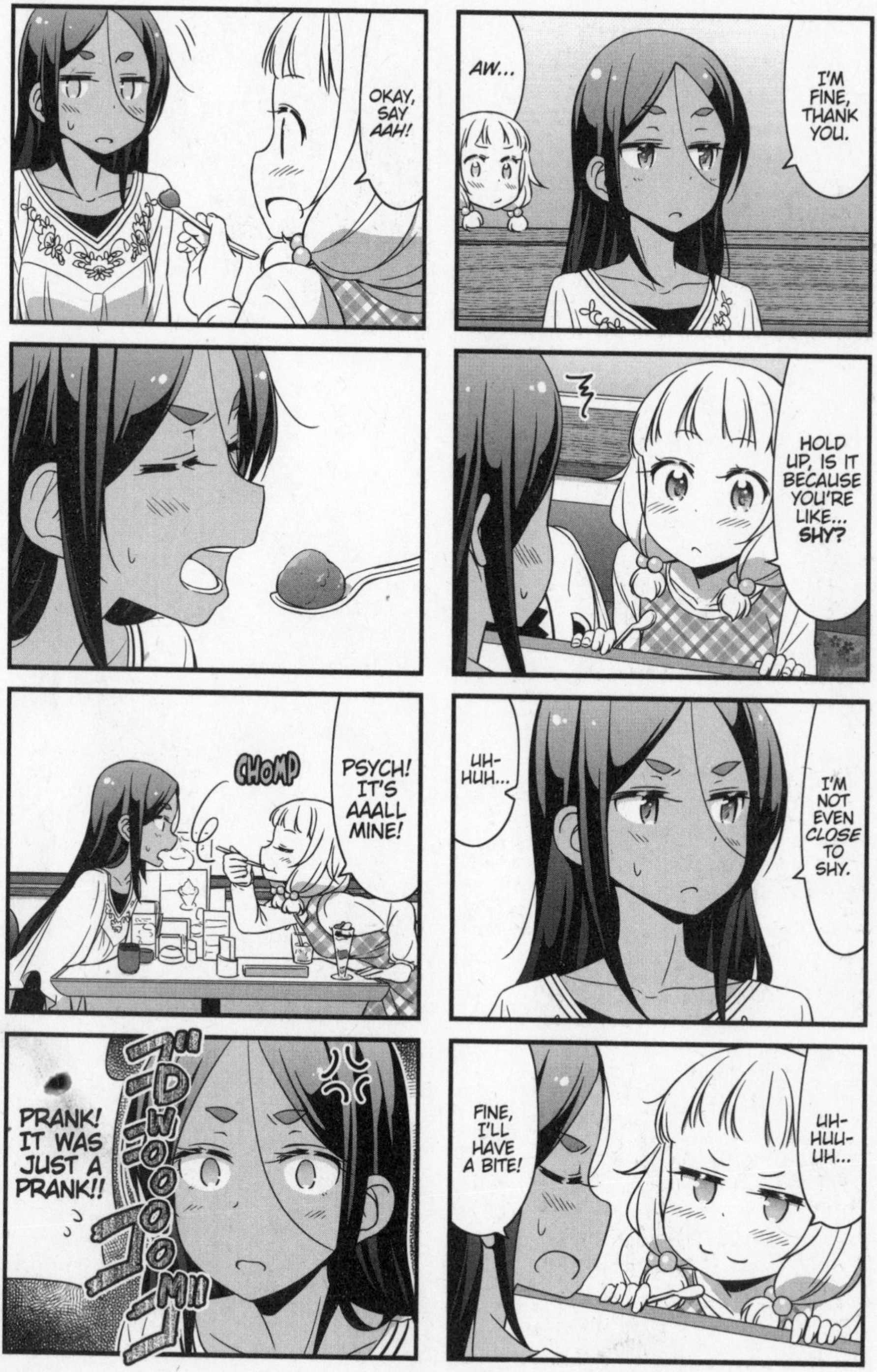
I'M FINE, THANK YOU.
AW...
HOLD UP, IS IT BECAUSE YOU'RE LIKE... SHY?
I'M NOT EVEN CLOSE TO SHY.
UH-HUH...
UH-HUUU-UH...
FINE, I'LL HAVE A BITE!
OKAY, SAY AAH!
PSYCH! IT'S AAALL MINE!
CHOMP
DWOOOOOM!!
PRANK! IT WAS JUST A PRANK!!

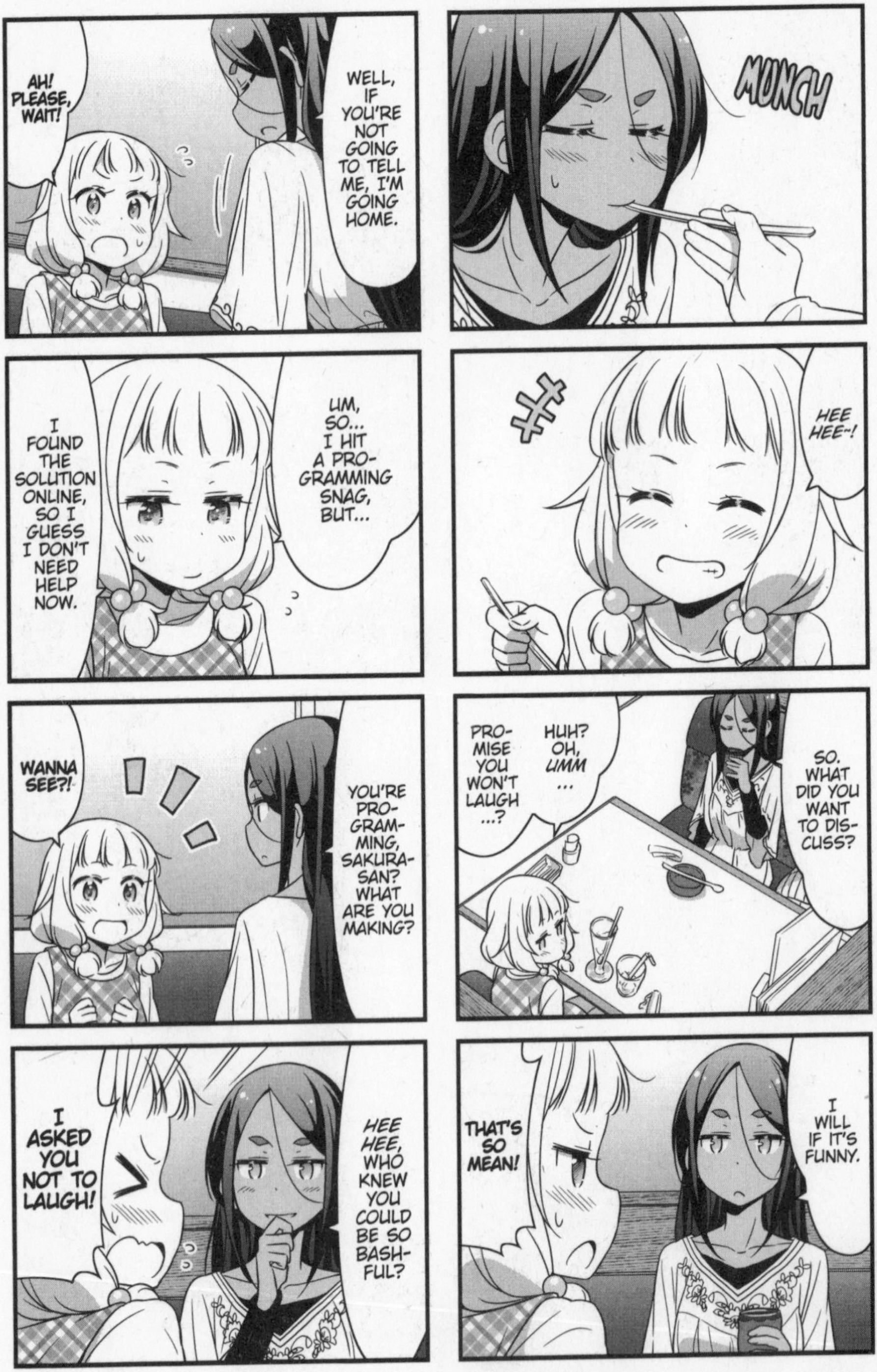
MUNCH
HEE HEE~!
SO. WHAT DID YOU WANT TO DISCUSS?
HUH? OH, UMM ...
PROMISE YOU WON'T LAUGH ...?
I WILL IF IT'S FUNNY.
THAT'S SO MEAN!
WELL, IF YOU'RE NOT GOING TO TELL ME, I'M GOING HOME.
AH! PLEASE, WAIT!
UM, SO... I HIT A PROGRAMMING SNAG, BUT...
I FOUND THE SOLUTION ONLINE, SO I GUESS I DON'T NEED HELP NOW.
YOU'RE PROGRAMMING, SAKURA-SAN? WHAT ARE YOU MAKING?
WANNA SEE?!
HEE HEE, WHO KNEW YOU COULD BE SO BASHFUL?
I ASKED YOU NOT TO LAUGH!

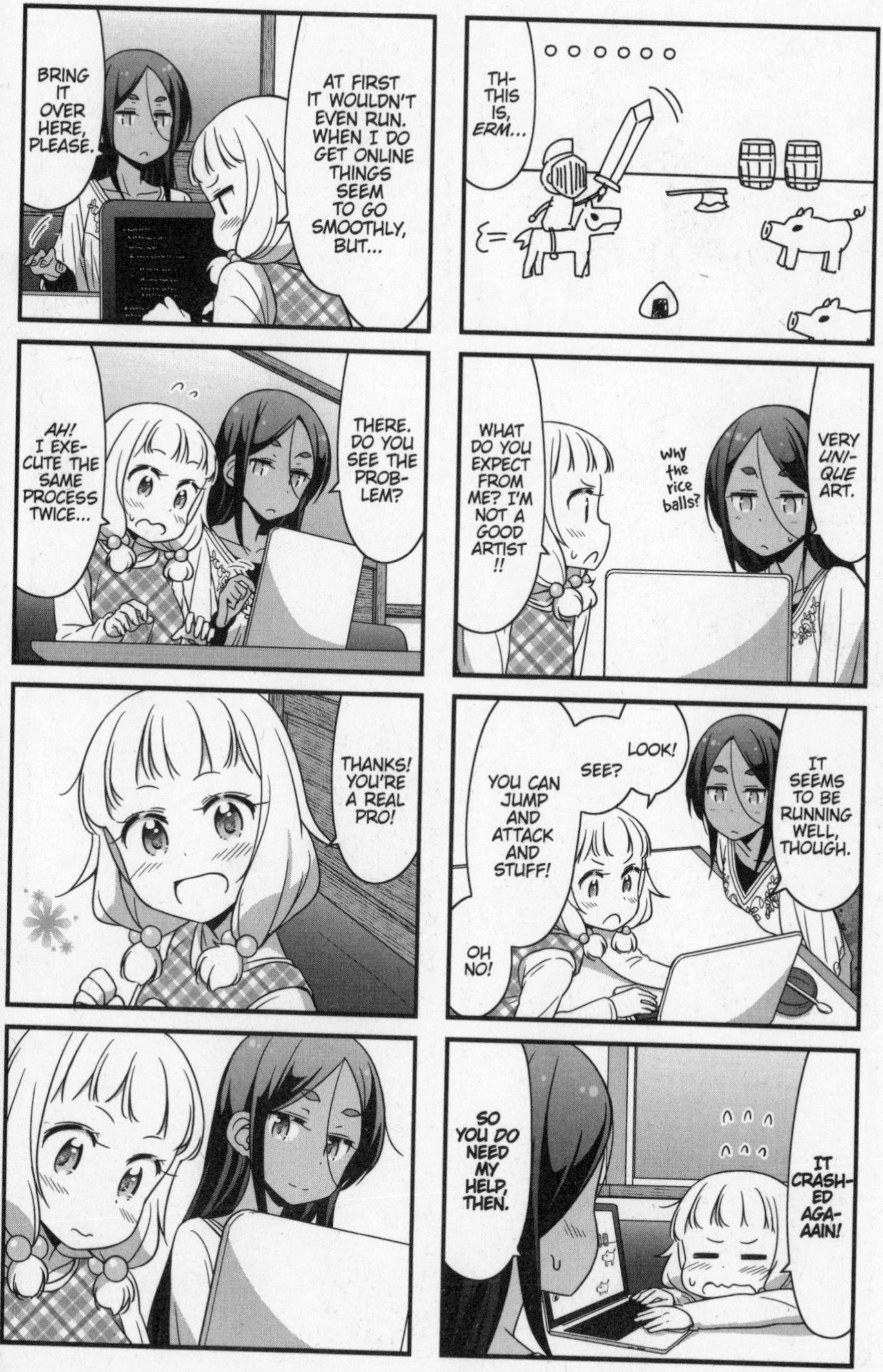

OOOOOO
TH-THIS IS, ERM...
VERY UNIQUE ART.
why the rice balls?
WHAT DO YOU EXPECT FROM ME? I'M NOT A GOOD ARTIST !!
IT SEEMS TO BE RUNNING WELL, THOUGH.
LOOK!
SEE?
YOU CAN JUMP AND ATTACK AND STUFF!
OH NO!
IT CRASHED AGA-AAIN!
SO YOU DO NEED MY HELP, THEN.
AT FIRST IT WOULDN'T EVEN RUN. WHEN I DO GET ONLINE THINGS SEEM TO GO SMOOTHLY, BUT...
BRING IT OVER HERE, PLEASE.
THERE. DO YOU SEE THE PROBLEM?
AH! I EXECUTE THE SAME PROCESS TWICE...
THANKS! YOU'RE A REAL PRO!

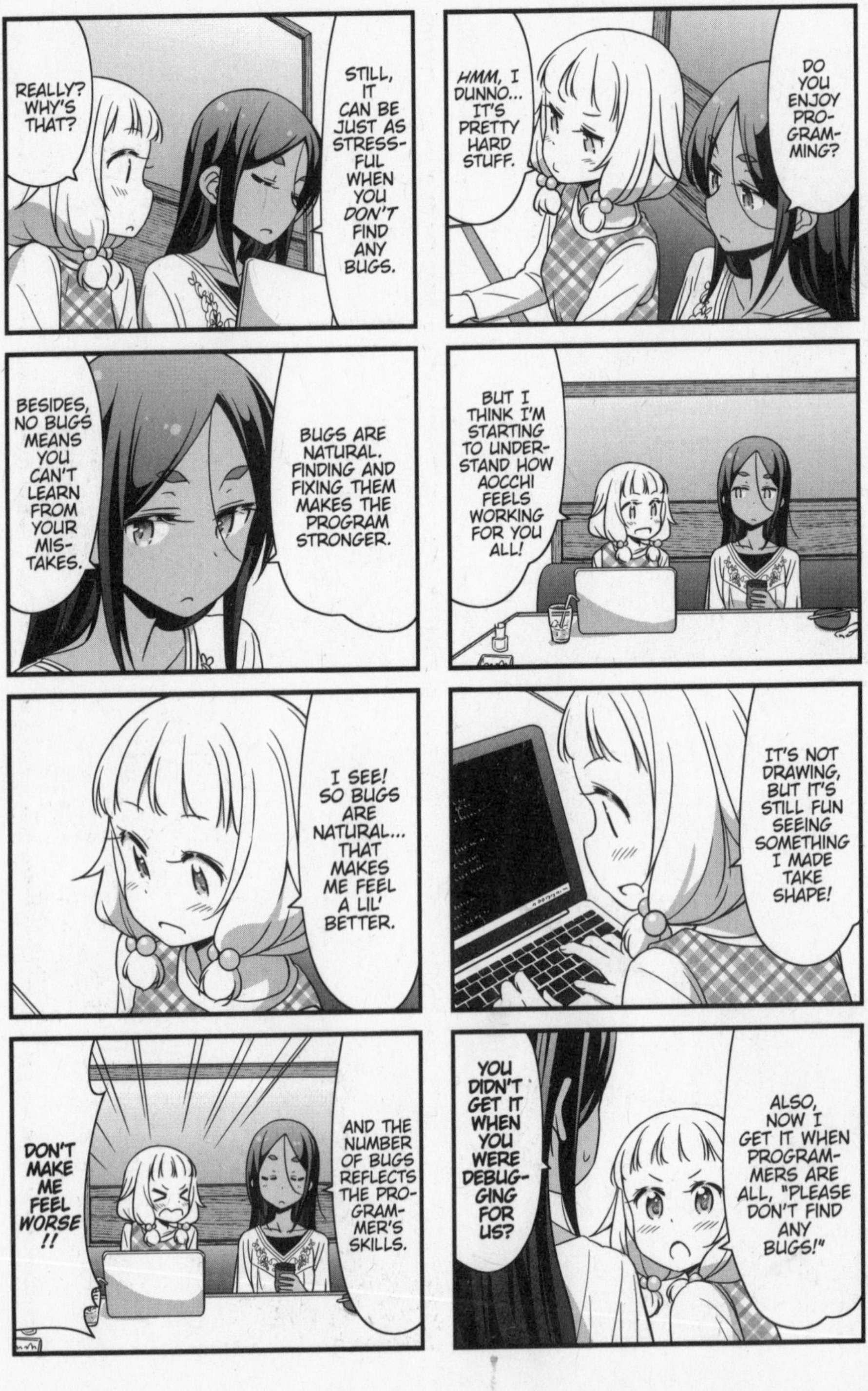
DO YOU ENJOY PROGRAMMING?
HMM, I DUNNO... IT'S PRETTY HARD STUFF.
BUT I THINK I'M STARTING TO UNDERSTAND HOW AOCCHI FEELS WORKING FOR YOU ALL!
IT'S NOT DRAWING, BUT IT'S STILL FUN SEEING SOMETHING I MADE TAKE SHAPE!
ALSO, NOW I GET IT WHEN PROGRAMMERS ARE ALL, "PLEASE DON'T FIND ANY BUGS!"
YOU DIDN'T GET IT WHEN YOU WERE DEBUGGING FOR US?
STILL, IT CAN BE JUST AS STRESSFUL WHEN YOU *DON'T* FIND ANY BUGS.
REALLY? WHY'S THAT?
BUGS ARE NATURAL. FINDING AND FIXING THEM MAKES THE PROGRAM STRONGER.
BESIDES, NO BUGS MEANS YOU CAN'T LEARN FROM YOUR MISTAKES.
I SEE! SO BUGS ARE NATURAL... THAT MAKES ME FEEL A LIL' BETTER.
AND THE NUMBER OF BUGS REFLECTS THE PROGRAMMER'S SKILLS.
DON'T MAKE ME FEEL *WORSE*!!

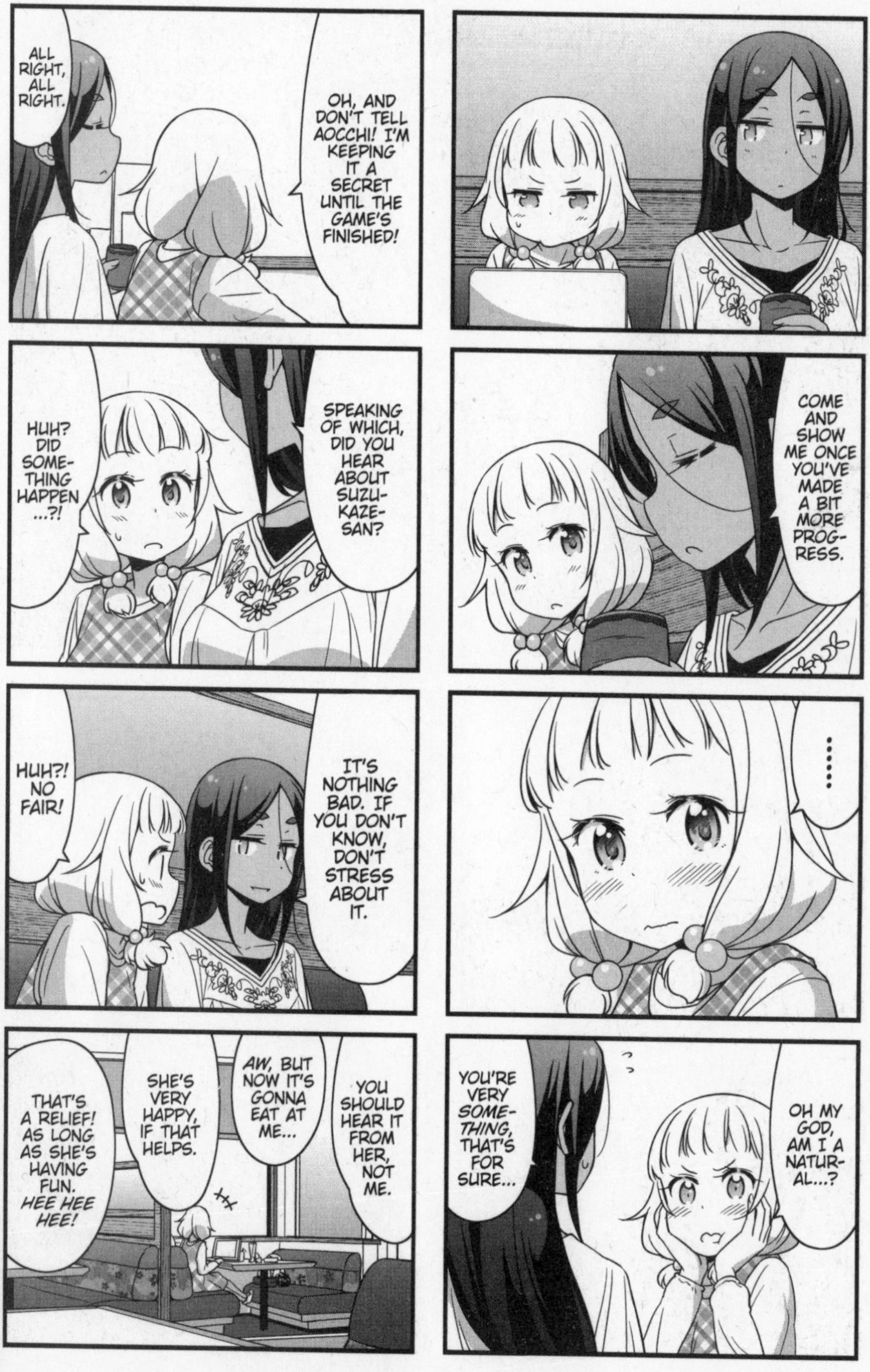
OH, AND DON'T TELL AOCCHI! I'M KEEPING IT A SECRET UNTIL THE GAME'S FINISHED!
ALL RIGHT, ALL RIGHT.
COME AND SHOW ME ONCE YOU'VE MADE A BIT MORE PROGRESS.
SPEAKING OF WHICH, DID YOU HEAR ABOUT SUZUKAZE-SAN?
HUH? DID SOMETHING HAPPEN...?!
......
IT'S NOTHING BAD. IF YOU DON'T KNOW, DON'T STRESS ABOUT IT.
HUH?! NO FAIR!
OH MY GOD, AM I A NATURAL...?
YOU'RE VERY *SOMETHING*, THAT'S FOR SURE...
YOU SHOULD HEAR IT FROM HER, NOT ME.
AW, BUT NOW IT'S GONNA EAT AT ME...
SHE'S VERY HAPPY, IF THAT HELPS.
THAT'S A RELIEF! AS LONG AS SHE'S HAVING FUN. *HEE HEE HEE!*

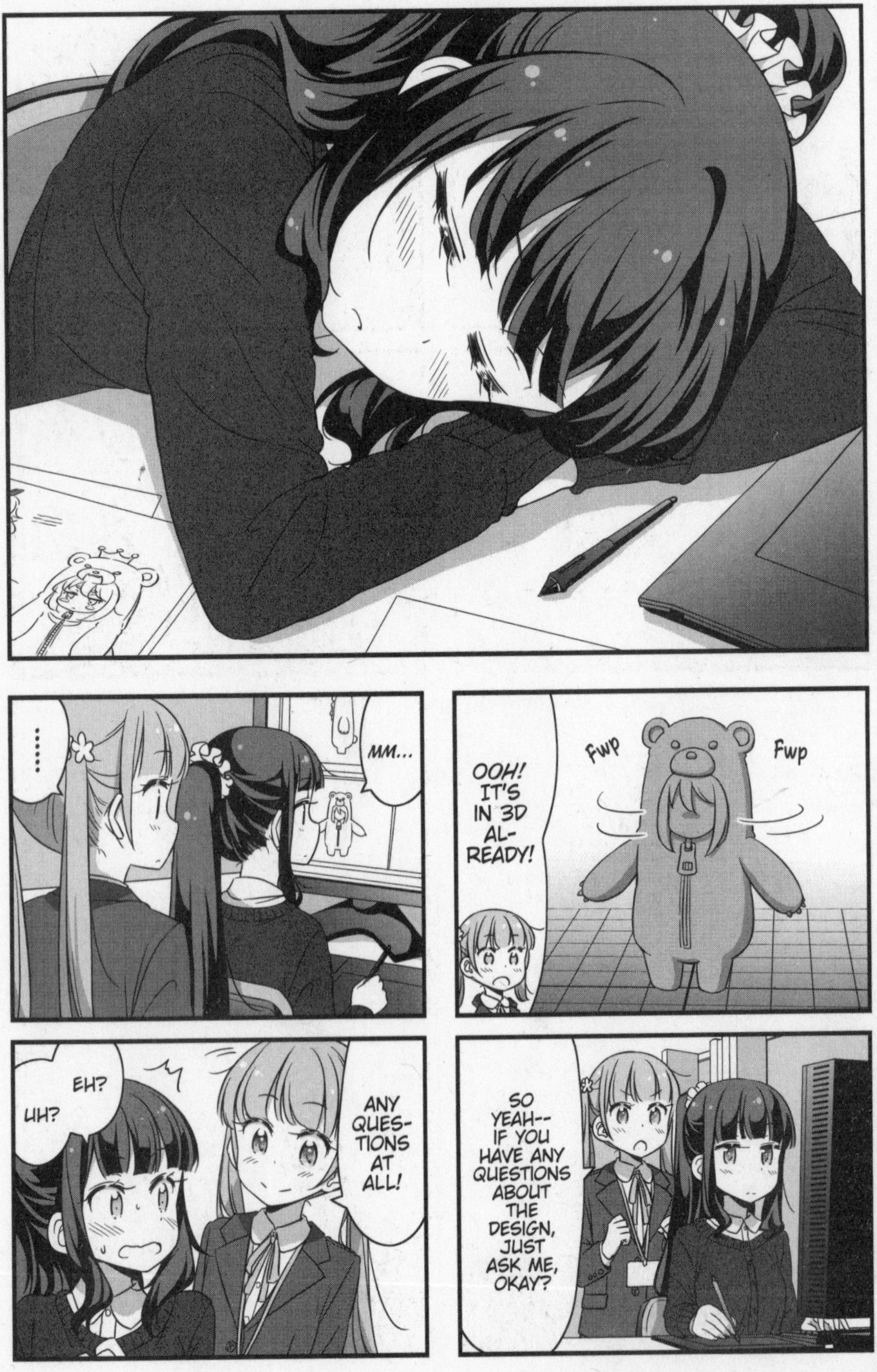
Fwp
Fwp
OOH! IT'S IN 3D AL-READY!
MM...
......
SO YEAH-- IF YOU HAVE ANY QUESTIONS ABOUT THE DESIGN, JUST ASK ME, OKAY?
ANY QUES-TIONS AT ALL!
EH?
UH?

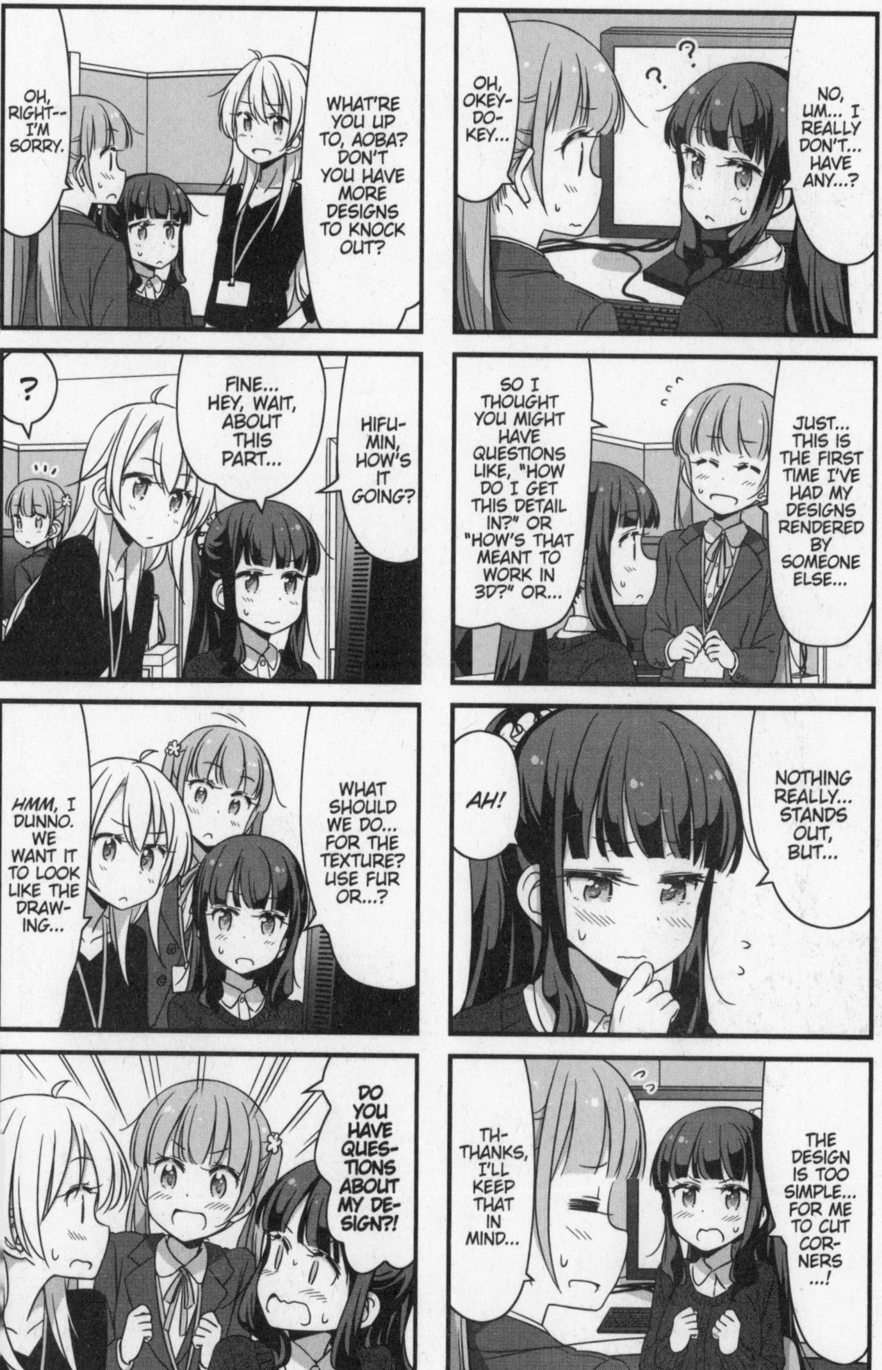
NO, UM... I REALLY DON'T... HAVE ANY...?
?
?
OH, OKEY-DOKEY...
JUST... THIS IS THE FIRST TIME I'VE HAD MY DESIGNS RENDERED BY SOMEONE ELSE...
SO I THOUGHT YOU MIGHT HAVE QUESTIONS LIKE, "HOW DO I GET THIS DETAIL IN?" OR "HOW'S THAT MEANT TO WORK IN 3D?" OR...
NOTHING REALLY... STANDS OUT, BUT...
AH!
THE DESIGN IS TOO SIMPLE... FOR ME TO CUT CORNERS ...!
TH-THANKS, I'LL KEEP THAT IN MIND...
WHAT'RE YOU UP TO, AOBA? DON'T YOU HAVE MORE DESIGNS TO KNOCK OUT?
OH, RIGHT-- I'M SORRY.
HIFU-MIN, HOW'S IT GOING?
FINE... HEY, WAIT, ABOUT THIS PART...
?
WHAT SHOULD WE DO... FOR THE TEXTURE? USE FUR OR...?
HMM, I DUNNO. WE WANT IT TO LOOK LIKE THE DRAW-ING...
DO YOU HAVE QUES-TIONS ABOUT MY DE-SIGN?!

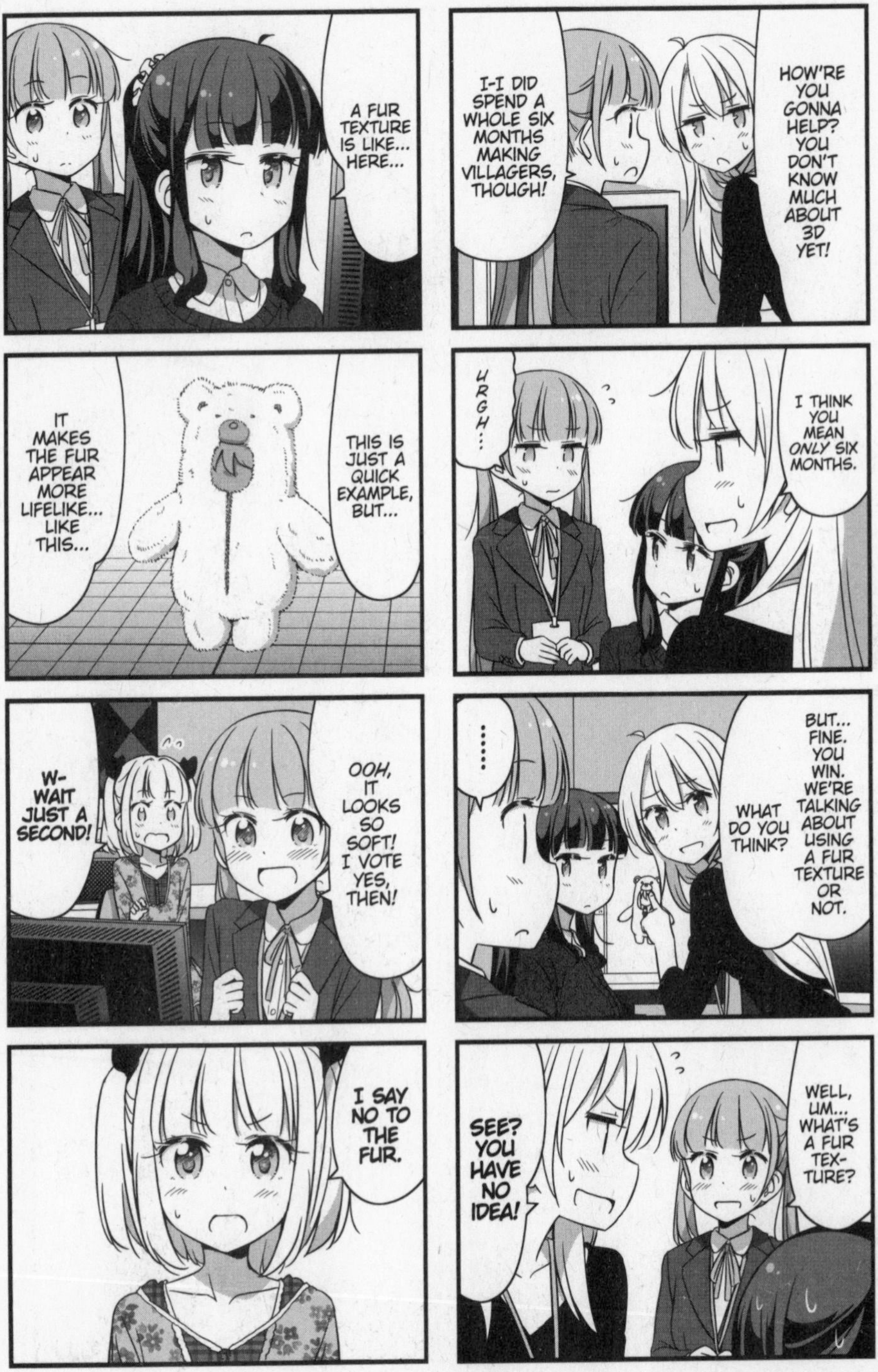
HOW'RE YOU GONNA HELP? YOU DON'T KNOW MUCH ABOUT 3D YET!
I-I DID SPEND A WHOLE SIX MONTHS MAKING VILLAGERS, THOUGH!
I THINK YOU MEAN *ONLY* SIX MONTHS.
URGH...
BUT... FINE. YOU WIN. WE'RE TALKING ABOUT USING A FUR TEXTURE OR NOT.
WHAT DO YOU THINK?
......
WELL, UM... WHAT'S A FUR TEX-TURE?
SEE? YOU HAVE NO IDEA!
A FUR TEXTURE IS LIKE... HERE...
THIS IS JUST A QUICK EXAMPLE, BUT...
IT MAKES THE FUR APPEAR MORE LIFELIKE... LIKE THIS...
OOH, IT LOOKS SO SOFT! I VOTE YES, THEN!
W-WAIT JUST A SECOND!
I SAY NO TO THE FUR.

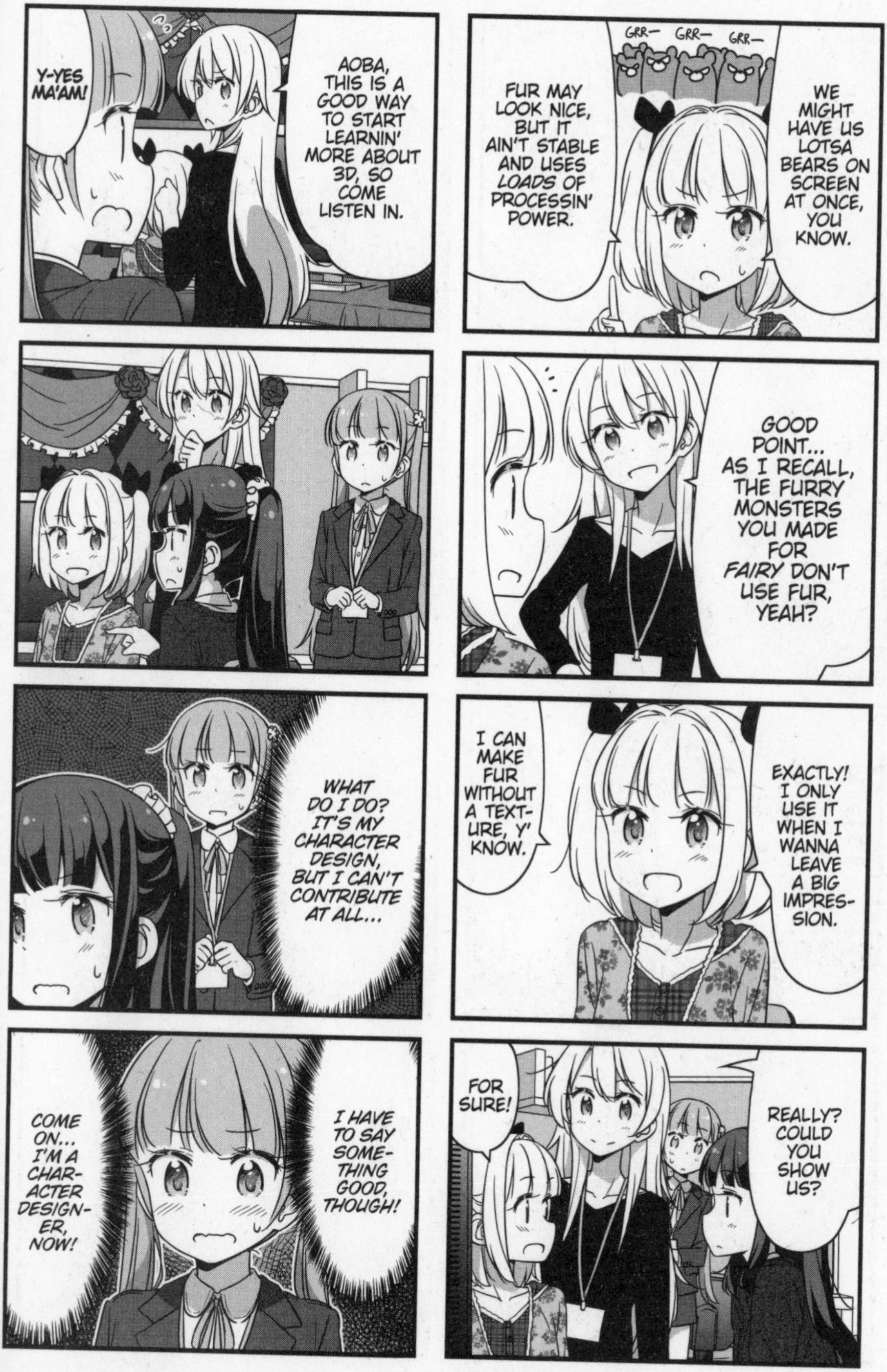
GRR— GRR— GRR—
WE MIGHT HAVE US LOTSA BEARS ON SCREEN AT ONCE, YOU KNOW.
FUR MAY LOOK NICE, BUT IT AIN'T STABLE AND USES *LOADS OF* PROCESSIN' POWER.
AOBA, THIS IS A GOOD WAY TO START LEARNIN' MORE ABOUT 3D, SO COME LISTEN IN.
Y-YES MA'AM!
GOOD POINT... AS I RECALL, THE FURRY MONSTERS YOU MADE FOR *FAIRY* DON'T USE FUR, YEAH?
EXACTLY! I ONLY USE IT WHEN I WANNA LEAVE A BIG IMPRES-SION.
I CAN MAKE FUR WITHOUT A TEXT-URE, Y' KNOW.
WHAT DO I DO? IT'S MY CHARACTER DESIGN, BUT I CAN'T CONTRIBUTE AT ALL...
REALLY? COULD YOU SHOW US?
FOR SURE!
I HAVE TO SAY SOME-THING GOOD, THOUGH!
COME ON... I'M A CHAR-ACTER DESIGN-ER, NOW!

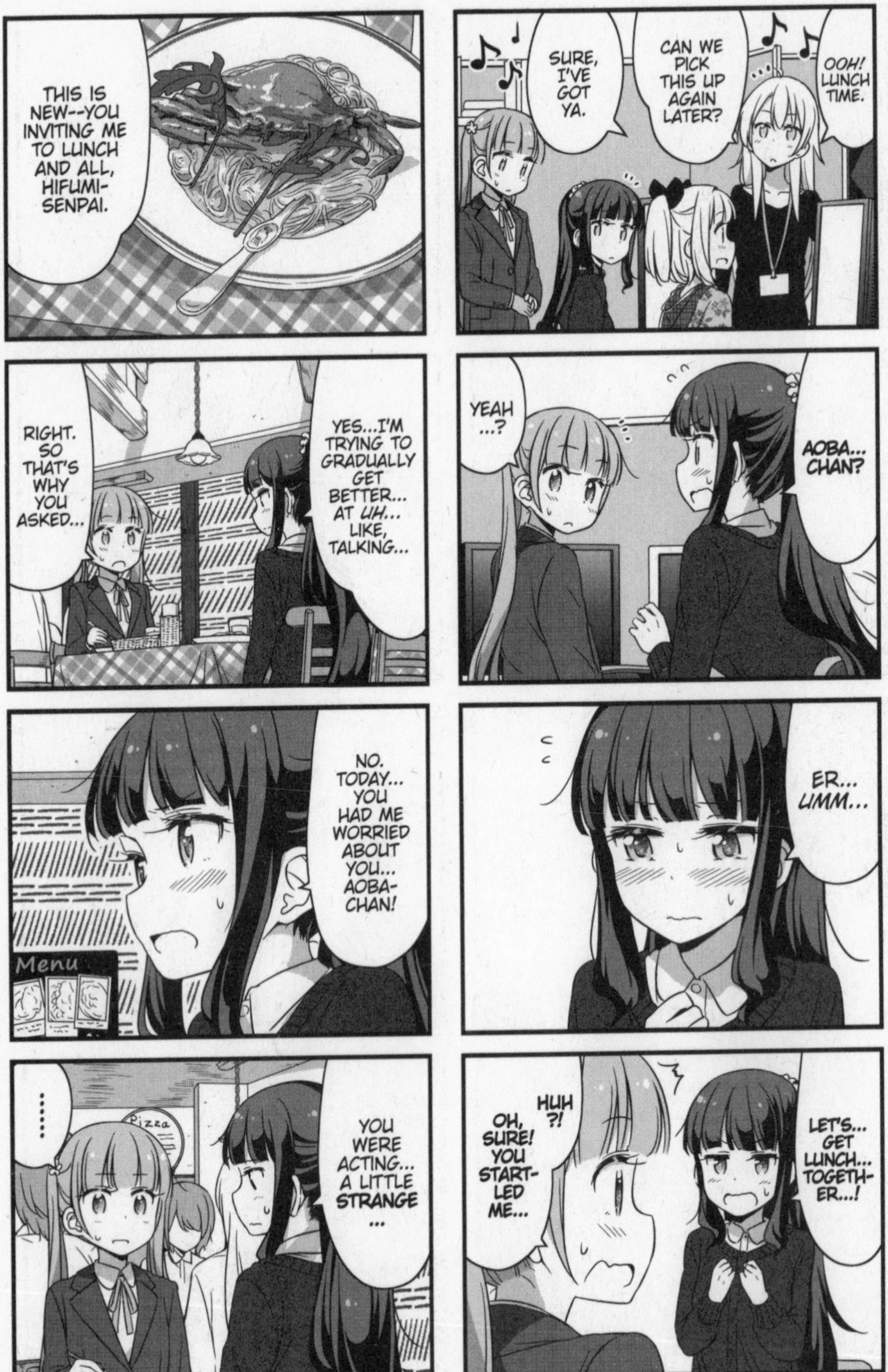
OOH! LUNCH TIME.
CAN WE PICK THIS UP AGAIN LATER?
SURE, I'VE GOT YA.
AOBA... CHAN?
YEAH ...?
ER... UMM...
LET'S... GET LUNCH... TOGETH-ER...!
HUH ?!
OH, SURE! YOU START-LED ME...
THIS IS NEW--YOU INVITING ME TO LUNCH AND ALL, HIFUMI-SENPAI.
YES...I'M TRYING TO GRADUALLY GET BETTER... AT UH... LIKE, TALKING...
RIGHT. SO THAT'S WHY YOU ASKED...
NO. TODAY... YOU HAD ME WORRIED ABOUT YOU... AOBA-CHAN!
Menu
YOU WERE ACTING... A LITTLE STRANGE ...
Pizza
......

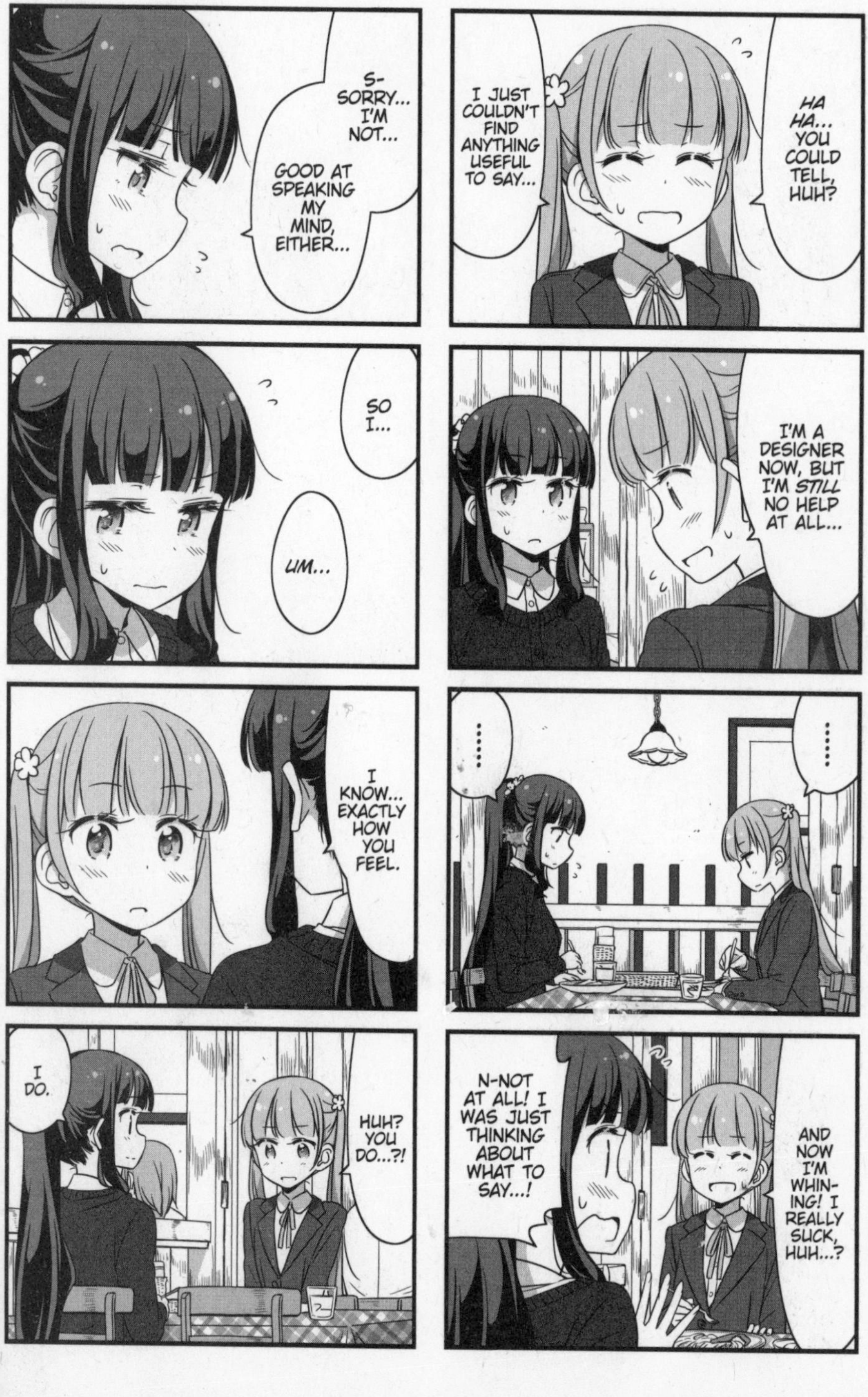
HA HA... YOU COULD TELL, HUH?
I JUST COULDN'T FIND ANYTHING USEFUL TO SAY...
S-SORRY... I'M NOT...
GOOD AT SPEAKING MY MIND, EITHER...
I'M A DESIGNER NOW, BUT I'M *STILL* NO HELP AT ALL...
SO I...
UM...
......
......
I KNOW... EXACTLY HOW YOU FEEL.
AND NOW I'M WHINING! I REALLY SUCK, HUH...?
N-NOT AT ALL! I WAS JUST THINKING ABOUT WHAT TO SAY...!
HUH? YOU DO...?!
I DO.

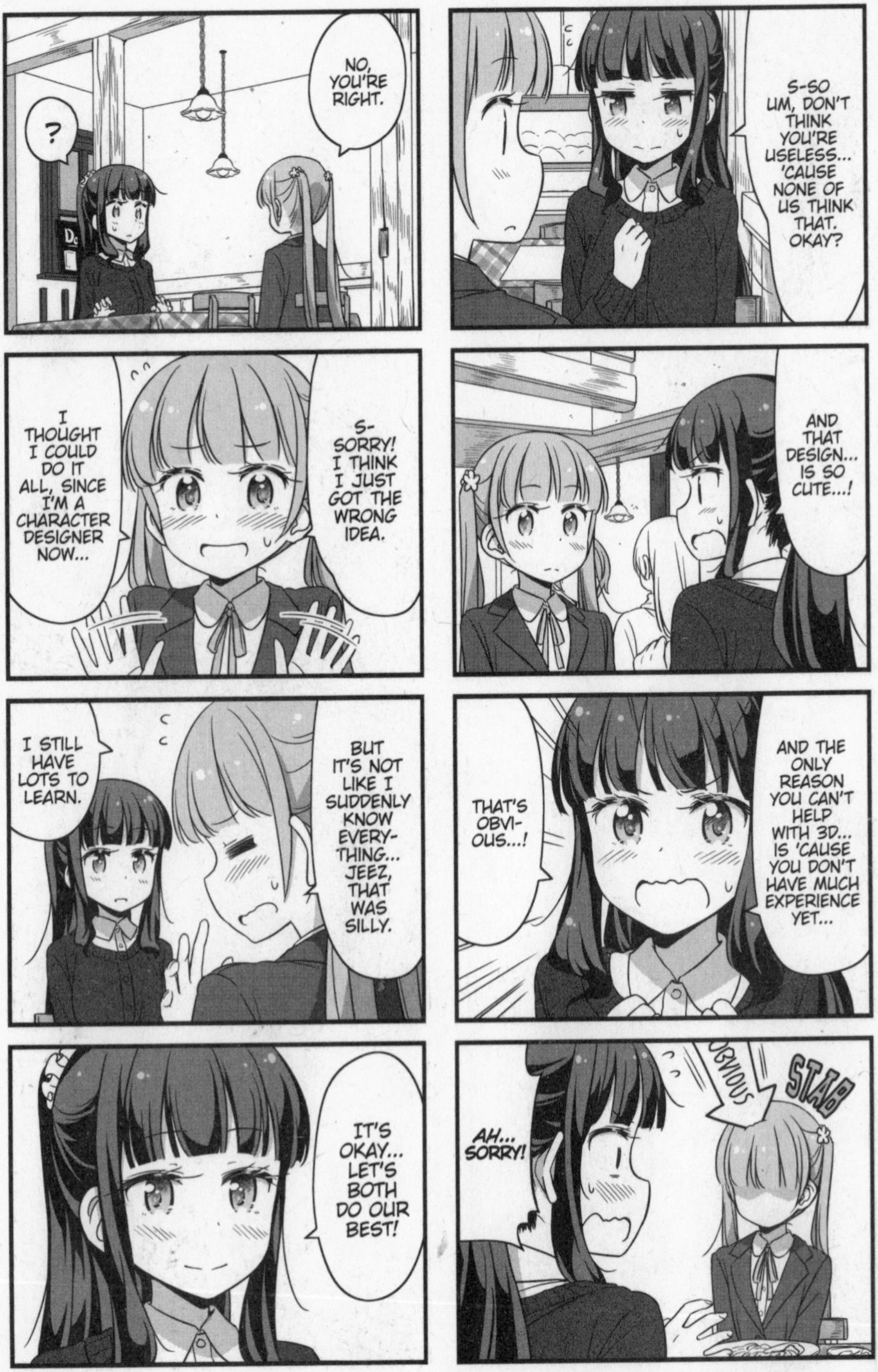
S-SO UM, DON'T THINK YOU'RE USELESS... 'CAUSE NONE OF US THINK THAT. OKAY?
AND THAT DESIGN... IS SO CUTE...!
AND THE ONLY REASON YOU CAN'T HELP WITH 3D... IS 'CAUSE YOU DON'T HAVE MUCH EXPERIENCE YET...
THAT'S OBVI-OUS...!
OBVIOUS
STAB
AH... SORRY!
NO, YOU'RE RIGHT.
?
S-SORRY! I THINK I JUST GOT THE WRONG IDEA.
I THOUGHT I COULD DO IT ALL, SINCE I'M A CHARACTER DESIGNER NOW...
BUT IT'S NOT LIKE I SUDDENLY KNOW EVERY-THING... JEEZ, THAT WAS SILLY.
I STILL HAVE LOTS TO LEARN.
IT'S OKAY... LET'S BOTH DO OUR BEST!

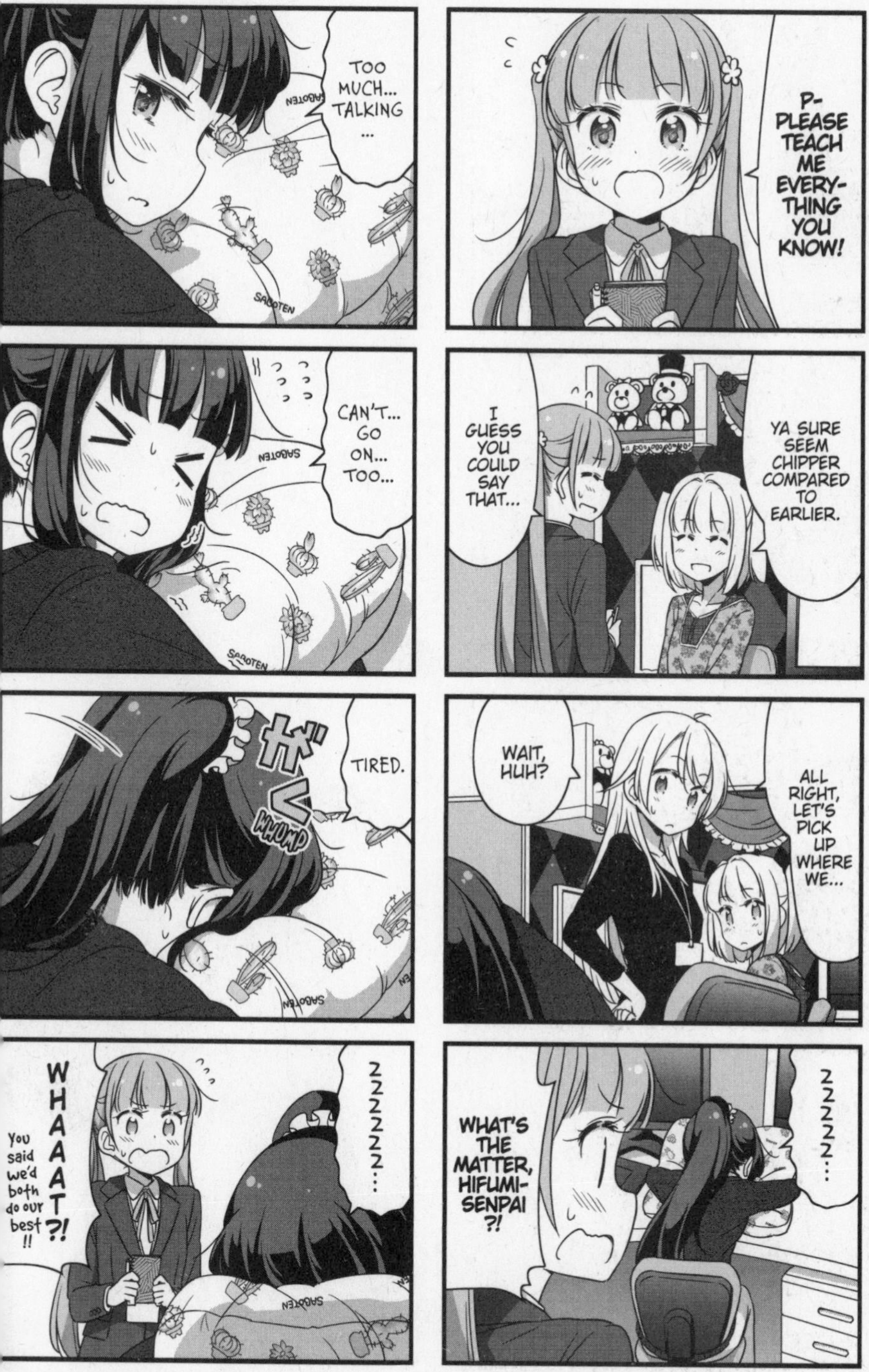
P-PLEASE TEACH ME EVERYTHING YOU KNOW!
TOO MUCH... TALKING ...
YA SURE SEEM CHIPPER COMPARED TO EARLIER.
I GUESS YOU COULD SAY THAT...
CAN'T... GO ON... TOO...
ALL RIGHT, LET'S PICK UP WHERE WE...
WAIT, HUH?
TIRED.
WHUMP
ZZZZZ...
WHAT'S THE MATTER, HIFUMI-SENPAI?!
ZZZZZ...
WHAAAAT?!
You said we'd both do our best!!

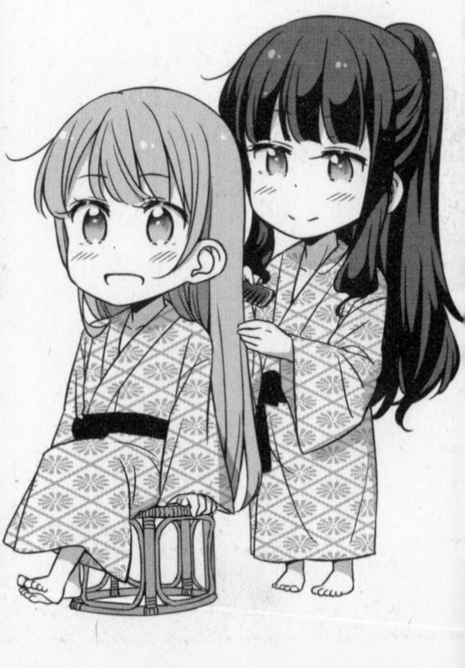

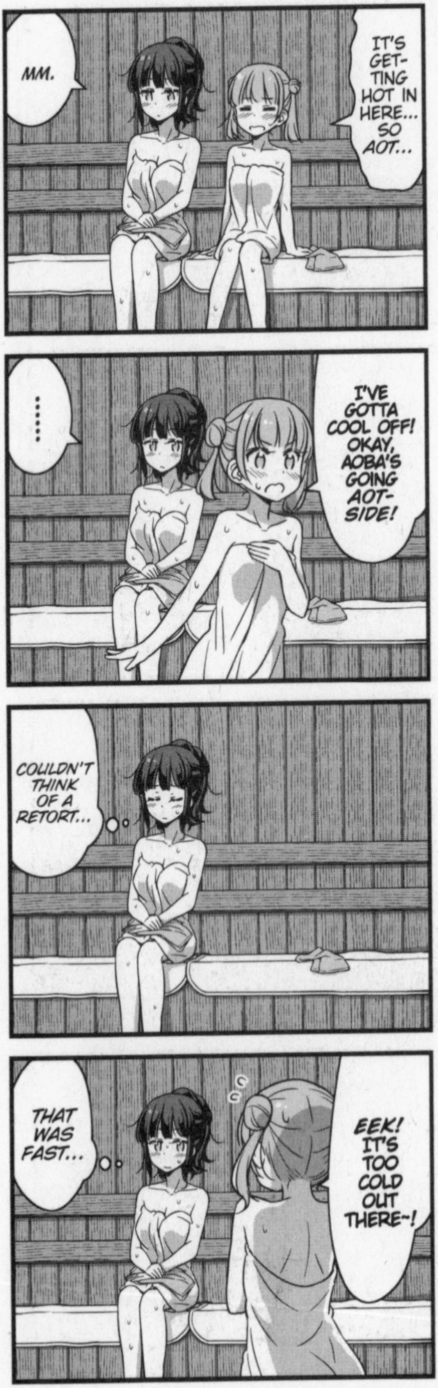
IT'S GET-TING HOT IN HERE... SO AOT...
MM.
I'VE GOTTA COOL OFF! OKAY, AOBA'S GOING AOT-SIDE!
......
COULDN'T THINK OF A RETORT...
EEK! IT'S TOO COLD OUT THERE~!
THAT WAS FAST...

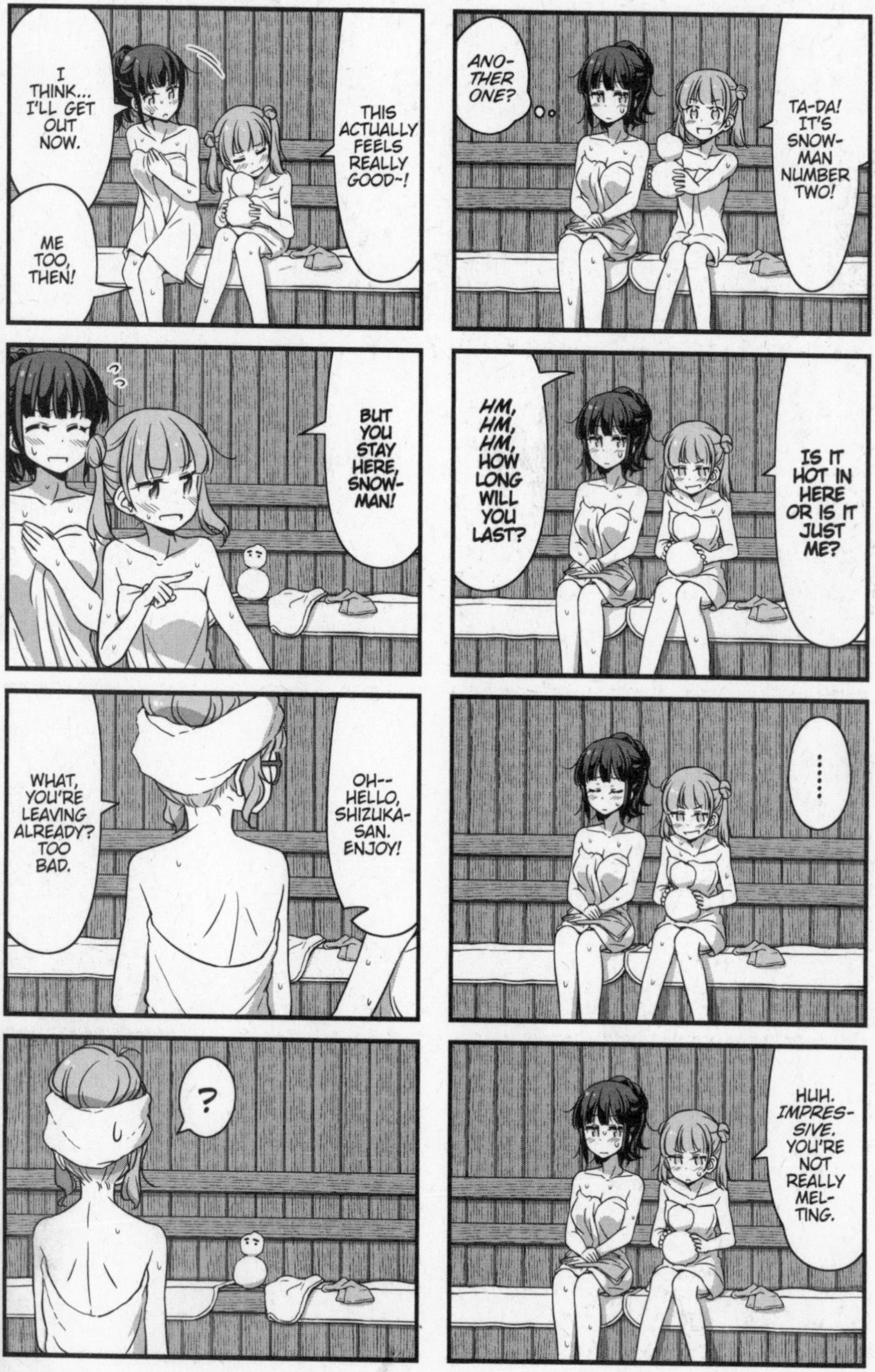
TA-DA! IT'S SNOW-MAN NUMBER TWO!
ANO-THER ONE?
IS IT HOT IN HERE OR IS IT JUST ME?
HM, HM, HM, HOW LONG WILL YOU LAST?
......
HUH. IMPRES-SIVE. YOU'RE NOT REALLY MEL-TING.
THIS ACTUALLY FEELS REALLY GOOD~!
I THINK... I'LL GET OUT NOW.
ME TOO, THEN!
BUT YOU STAY HERE, SNOW-MAN!
OH-- HELLO, SHIZUKA-SAN. ENJOY!
WHAT, YOU'RE LEAVING ALREADY? TOO BAD.
?

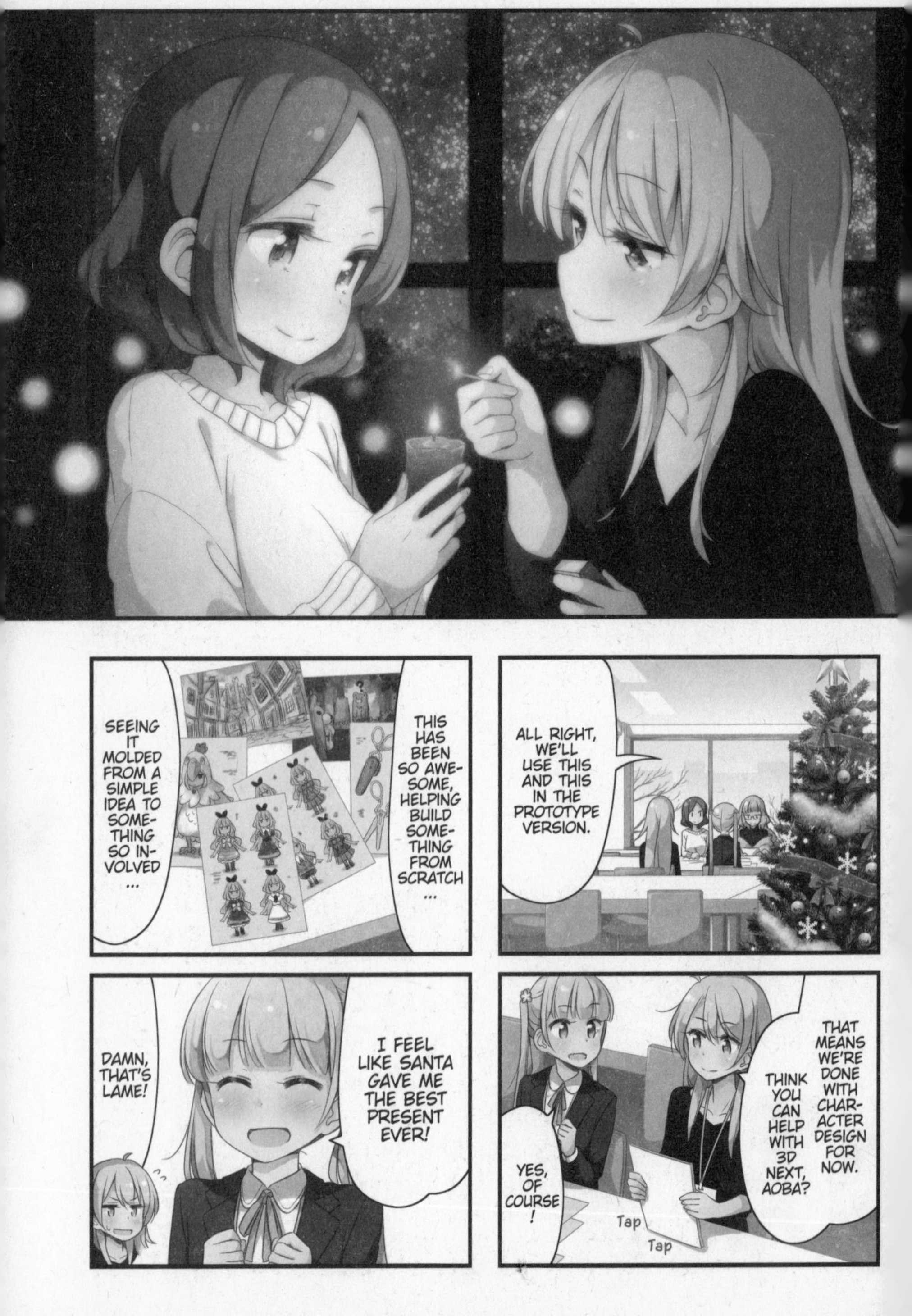
ALL RIGHT, WE'LL USE THIS AND THIS IN THE PROTOTYPE VERSION.
THIS HAS BEEN SO AWESOME, HELPING BUILD SOMETHING FROM SCRATCH...
SEEING IT MOLDED FROM A SIMPLE IDEA TO SOMETHING SO INVOLVED...
THAT MEANS WE'RE DONE WITH CHARACTER DESIGN FOR NOW.
THINK YOU CAN HELP WITH 3D NEXT, AOBA?
YES, OF COURSE!
Tap
Tap
I FEEL LIKE SANTA GAVE ME THE BEST PRESENT EVER!
DAMN, THAT'S LAME!

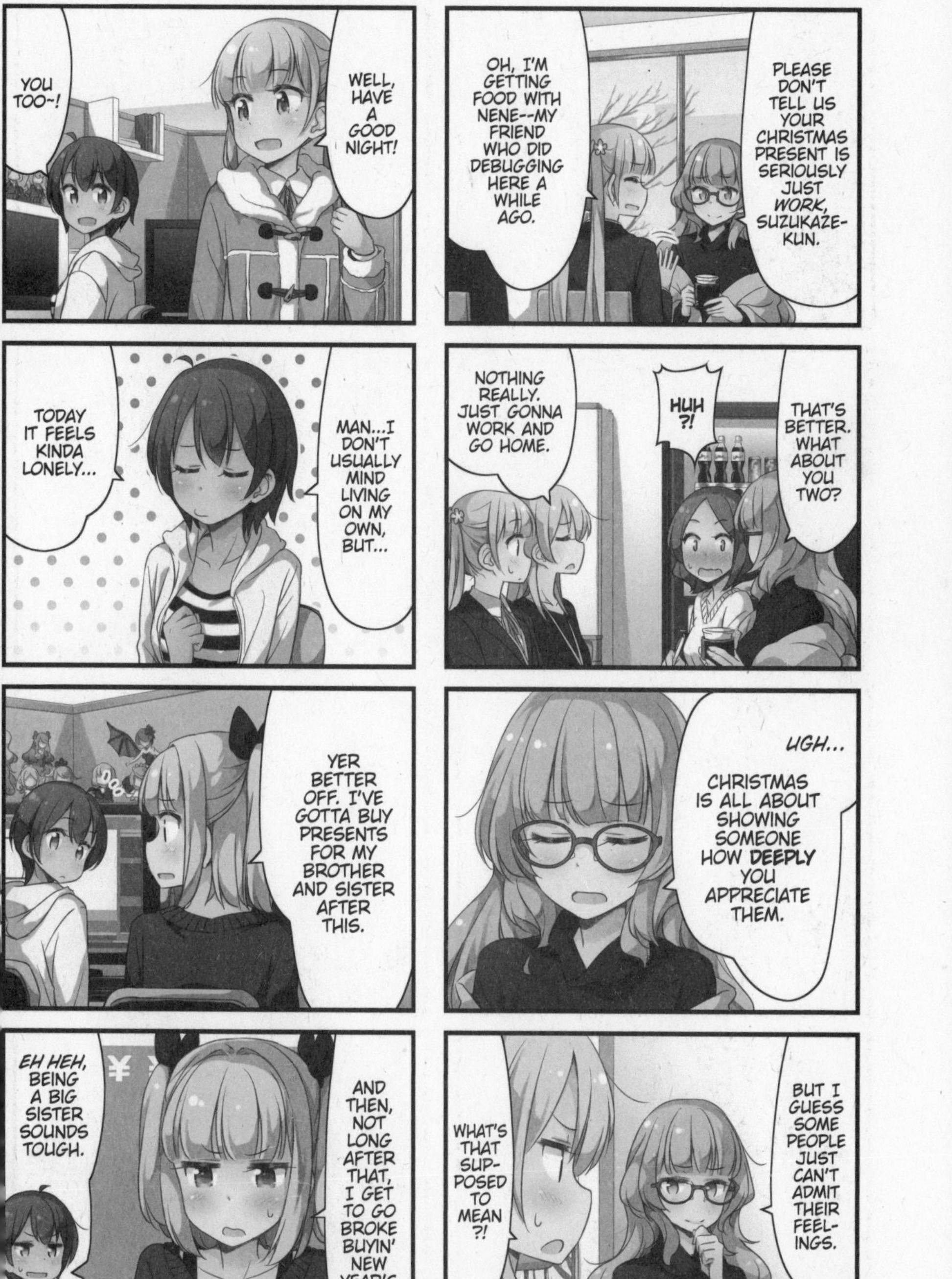
PLEASE DON'T TELL US YOUR CHRISTMAS PRESENT IS SERIOUSLY JUST *WORK*, SUZUKAZE-KUN.
OH, I'M GETTING FOOD WITH NENE--MY FRIEND WHO DID DEBUGGING HERE A WHILE AGO.
THAT'S BETTER. WHAT ABOUT YOU TWO?
HUH?!
NOTHING REALLY. JUST GONNA WORK AND GO HOME.
UGH...
CHRISTMAS IS ALL ABOUT SHOWING SOMEONE HOW **DEEPLY** YOU APPRECIATE THEM.
BUT I GUESS SOME PEOPLE JUST CAN'T ADMIT THEIR FEEL-INGS.
WHAT'S THAT SUP-POSED TO MEAN?!
WELL, HAVE A GOOD NIGHT!
YOU TOO~!
MAN...I DON'T USUALLY MIND LIVING ON MY OWN, BUT...
TODAY IT FEELS KINDA LONELY...
YER BETTER OFF. I'VE GOTTA BUY PRESENTS FOR MY BROTHER AND SISTER AFTER THIS.
AND THEN, NOT LONG AFTER THAT, I GET TO GO BROKE BUYIN' NEW YEAR'S GIFTS.
EH HEH, BEING A BIG SISTER SOUNDS TOUGH.

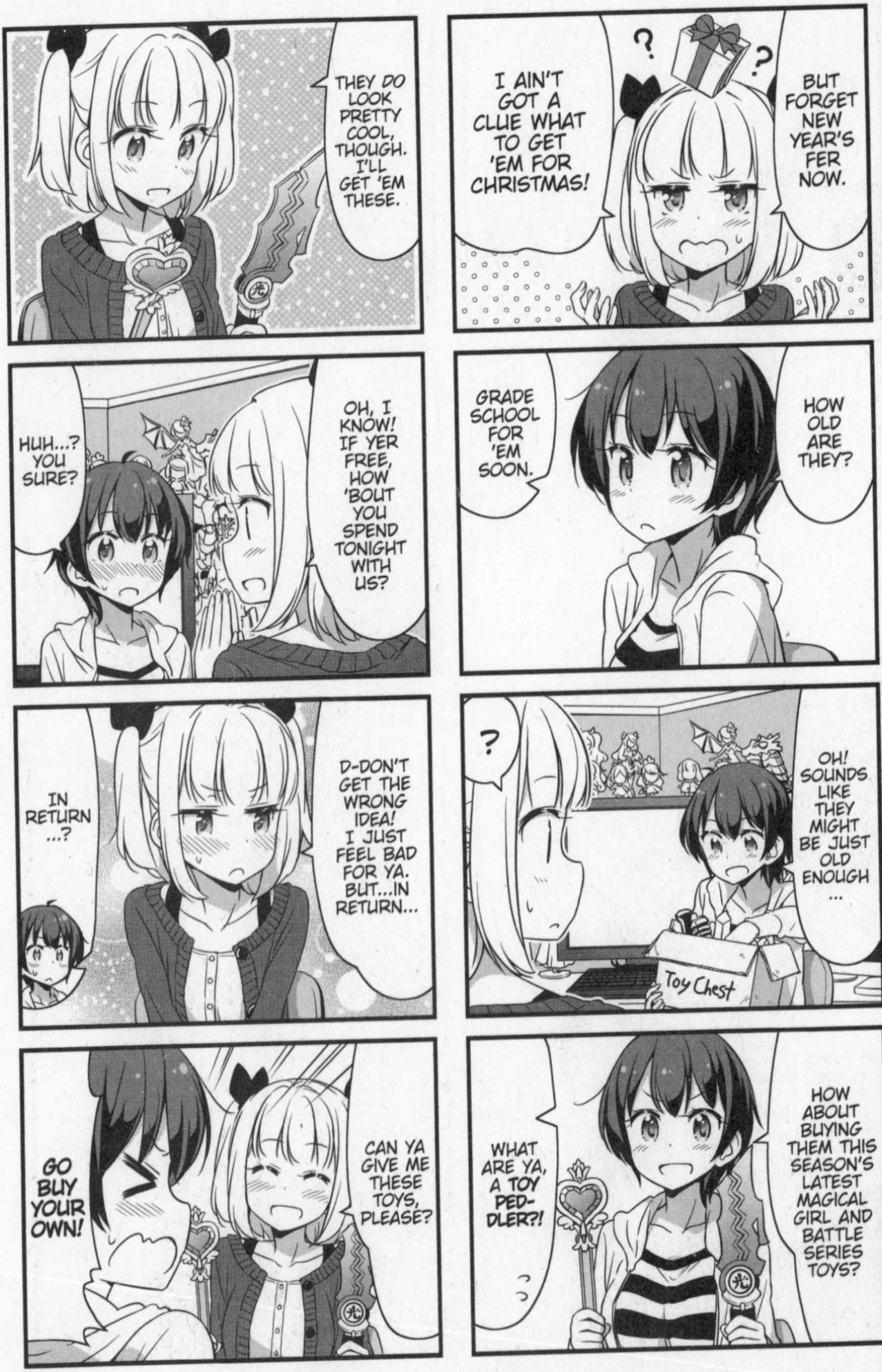
BUT FORGET NEW YEAR'S FER NOW.
I AIN'T GOT A CLUE WHAT TO GET 'EM FOR CHRISTMAS!
HOW OLD ARE THEY?
GRADE SCHOOL FOR 'EM SOON.
OH! SOUNDS LIKE THEY MIGHT BE JUST OLD ENOUGH ...
?
Toy Chest
HOW ABOUT BUYING THEM THIS SEASON'S LATEST MAGICAL GIRL AND BATTLE SERIES TOYS?
WHAT ARE YA, A TOY PED-DLER?!
THEY DO LOOK PRETTY COOL, THOUGH. I'LL GET 'EM THESE.
OH, I KNOW! IF YER FREE, HOW 'BOUT YOU SPEND TONIGHT WITH US?
HUH...? YOU SURE?
D-DON'T GET THE WRONG IDEA! I JUST FEEL BAD FOR YA. BUT...IN RETURN...
IN RETURN ...?
CAN YA GIVE ME THESE TOYS, PLEASE?
GO BUY YOUR OWN!

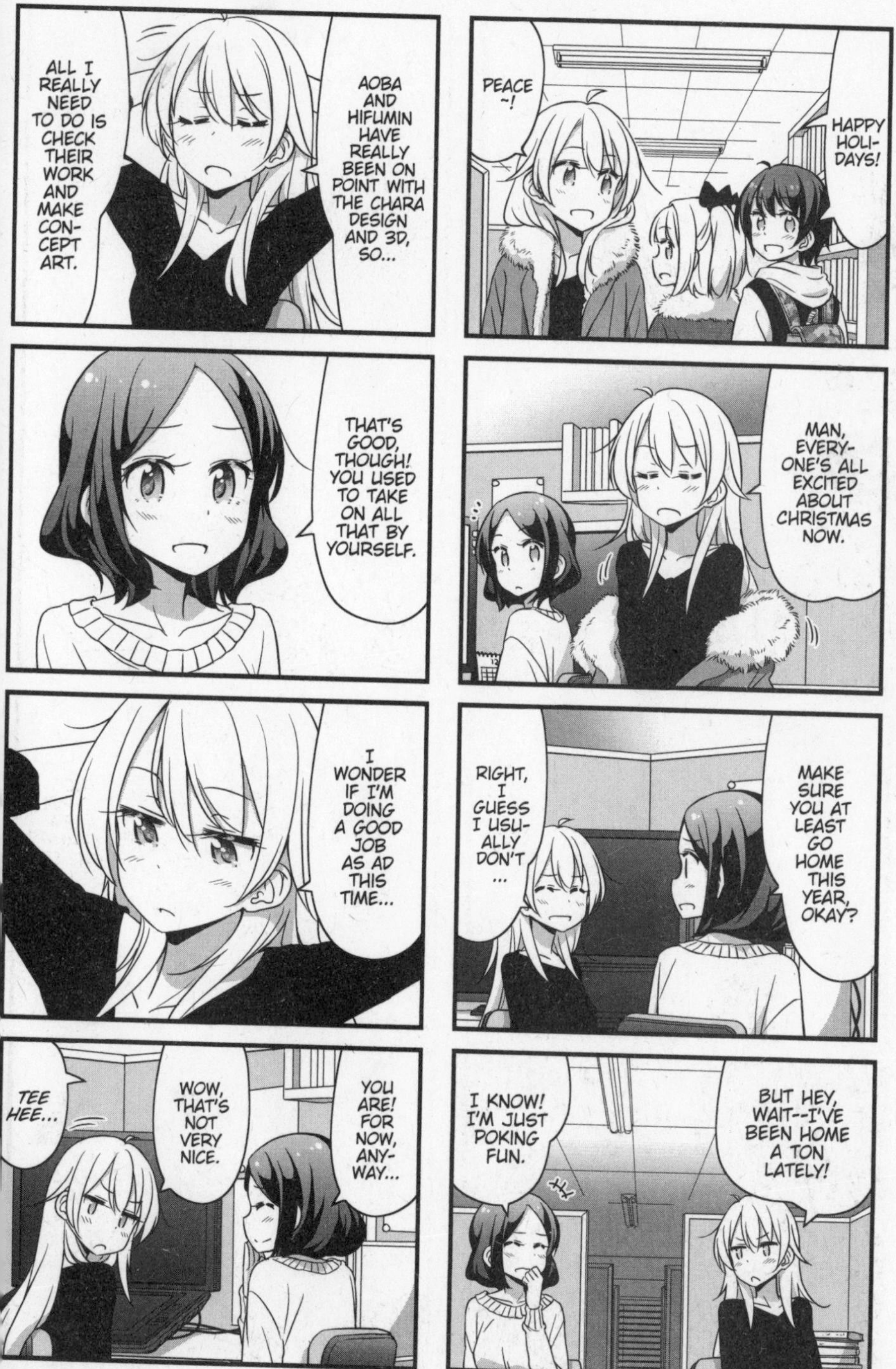
HAPPY HOLI-DAYS!
PEACE ~!
MAN, EVERY-ONE'S ALL EXCITED ABOUT CHRISTMAS NOW.
MAKE SURE YOU AT LEAST GO HOME THIS YEAR, OKAY?
RIGHT, I GUESS I USU-ALLY DON'T ...
BUT HEY, WAIT--I'VE BEEN HOME A TON LATELY!
I KNOW! I'M JUST POKING FUN.
AOBA AND HIFUMIN HAVE REALLY BEEN ON POINT WITH THE CHARA DESIGN AND 3D, SO...
ALL I REALLY NEED TO DO IS CHECK THEIR WORK AND MAKE CON-CEPT ART.
THAT'S GOOD, THOUGH! YOU USED TO TAKE ON ALL THAT BY YOURSELF.
I WONDER IF I'M DOING A GOOD JOB AS AD THIS TIME...
YOU ARE! FOR NOW, ANY-WAY...
WOW, THAT'S NOT VERY NICE.
TEE HEE...

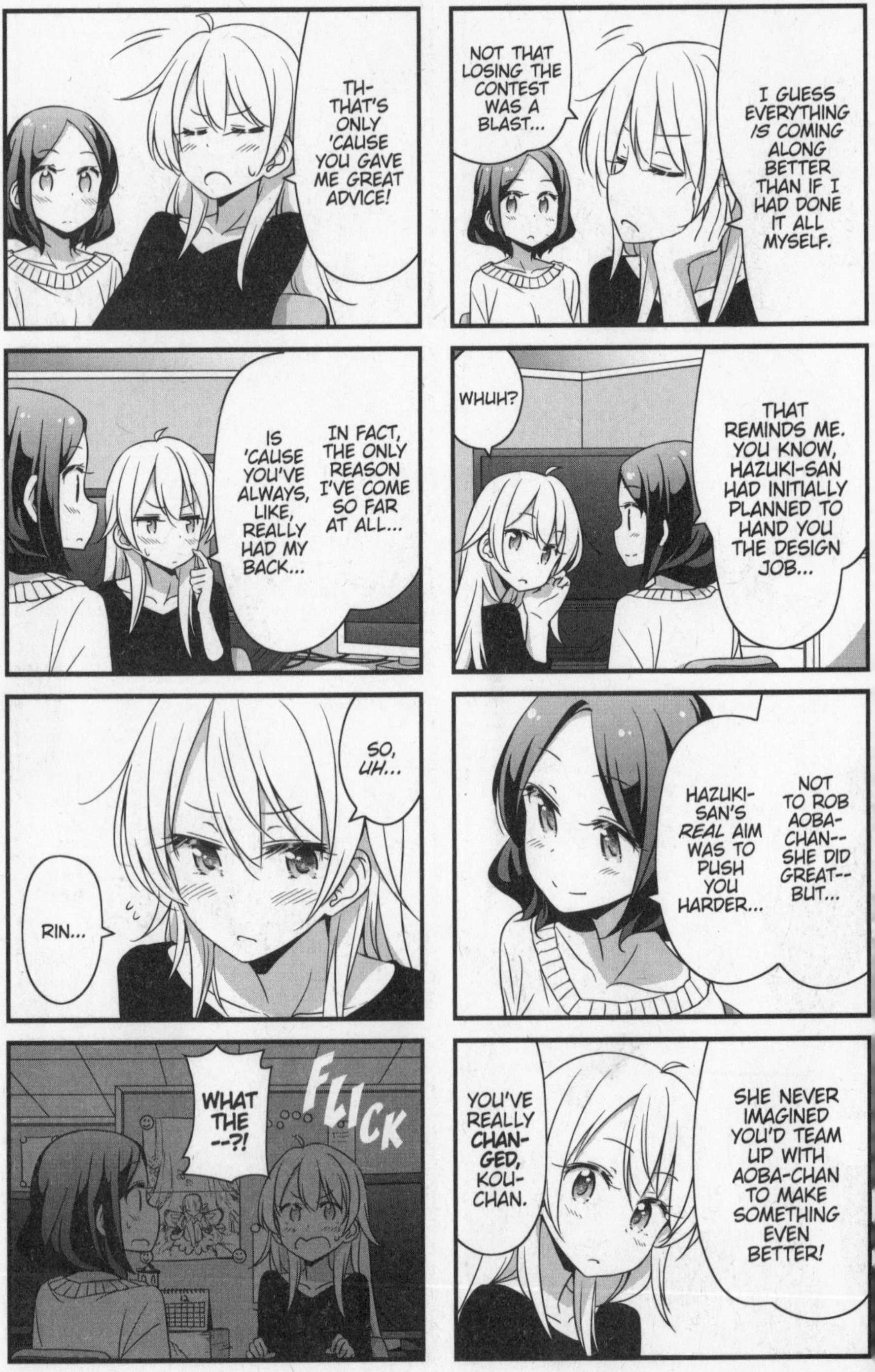
I GUESS EVERYTHING *IS* COMING ALONG BETTER THAN IF I HAD DONE IT ALL MYSELF.
NOT THAT LOSING THE CONTEST WAS A BLAST...
TH-THAT'S ONLY 'CAUSE YOU GAVE ME GREAT ADVICE!
THAT REMINDS ME. YOU KNOW, HAZUKI-SAN HAD INITIALLY PLANNED TO HAND YOU THE DESIGN JOB...
WHUH?
IN FACT, THE ONLY REASON I'VE COME SO FAR AT ALL...
IS 'CAUSE YOU'VE ALWAYS, LIKE, REALLY HAD MY BACK...
NOT TO ROB AOBA-CHAN--SHE DID GREAT--BUT...
HAZUKI-SAN'S *REAL* AIM WAS TO PUSH YOU HARDER...
SO, UH...
RIN...
SHE NEVER IMAGINED YOU'D TEAM UP WITH AOBA-CHAN TO MAKE SOMETHING EVEN BETTER!
YOU'VE REALLY CHANGED, KOU-CHAN.
FLICK
WHAT THE--?!

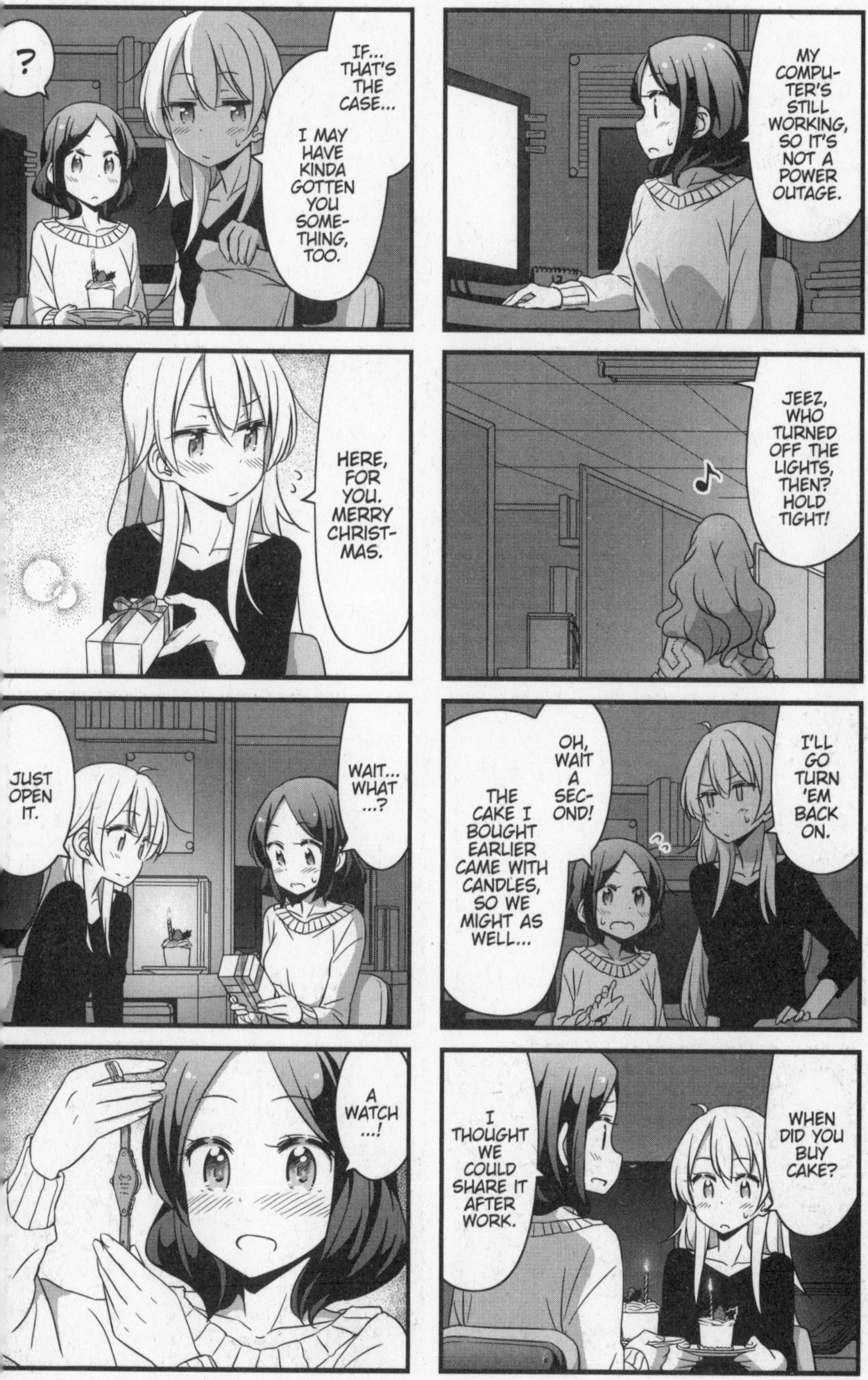
MY COMPUTER'S STILL WORKING, SO IT'S NOT A POWER OUTAGE.
JEEZ, WHO TURNED OFF THE LIGHTS, THEN? HOLD TIGHT!
I'LL GO TURN 'EM BACK ON.
OH, WAIT A SECOND!
THE CAKE I BOUGHT EARLIER CAME WITH CANDLES, SO WE MIGHT AS WELL...
WHEN DID YOU BUY CAKE?
I THOUGHT WE COULD SHARE IT AFTER WORK.
IF... THAT'S THE CASE...
I MAY HAVE KINDA GOTTEN YOU SOMETHING, TOO.
?
HERE, FOR YOU. MERRY CHRISTMAS.
WAIT... WHAT ...?
JUST OPEN IT.
A WATCH ...!

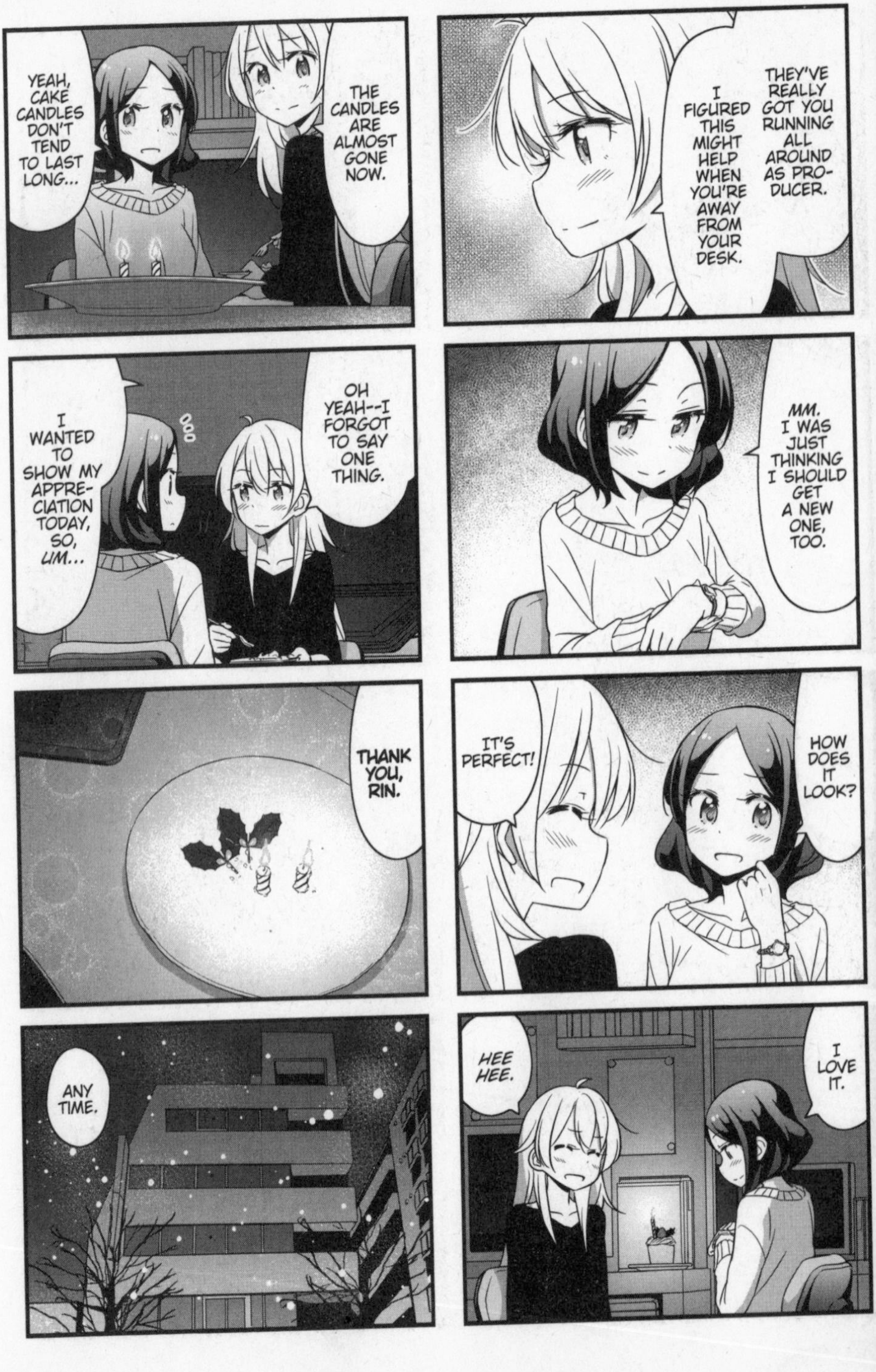
THEY'VE REALLY GOT YOU RUNNING ALL AROUND AS PRO-DUCER.
I FIGURED THIS MIGHT HELP WHEN YOU'RE AWAY FROM YOUR DESK.
MM. I WAS JUST THINKING I SHOULD GET A NEW ONE, TOO.
HOW DOES IT LOOK?
IT'S PERFECT!
I LOVE IT.
HEE HEE.
THE CANDLES ARE ALMOST GONE NOW.
YEAH, CAKE CANDLES DON'T TEND TO LAST LONG...
OH YEAH--I FORGOT TO SAY ONE THING.
I WANTED TO SHOW MY APPRECIATION TODAY, SO, UM...
THANK YOU, RIN.
ANY TIME.

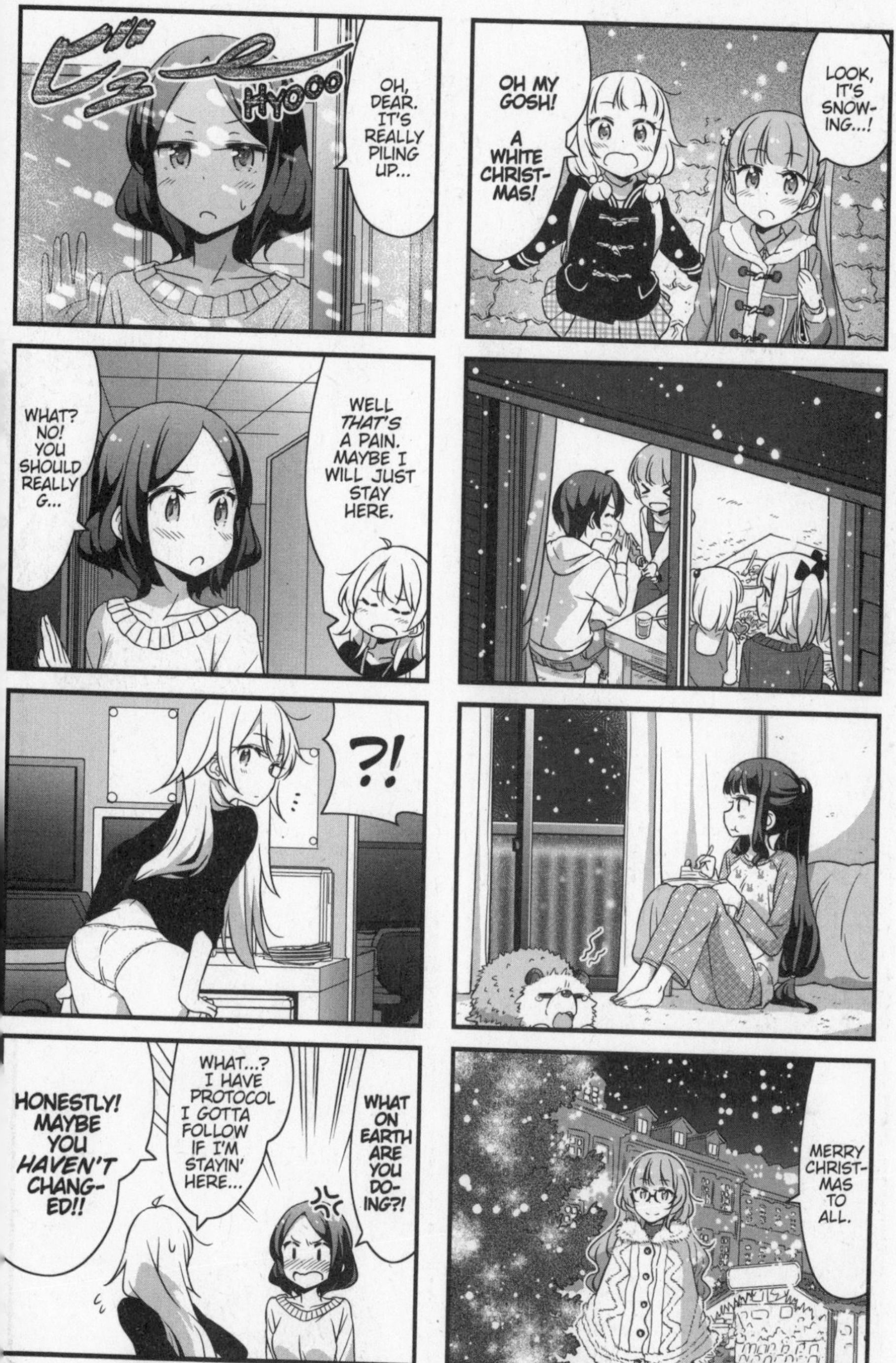
LOOK, IT'S SNOWING...!
OH MY GOSH!
A WHITE CHRISTMAS!
HYOOO
OH, DEAR. IT'S REALLY PILING UP...
WELL *THAT'S* A PAIN. MAYBE I WILL JUST STAY HERE.
WHAT? NO! YOU SHOULD REALLY G...
?!
MERRY CHRISTMAS TO ALL.
WHAT ON EARTH ARE YOU DOING?!
WHAT...? I HAVE PROTOCOL I GOTTA FOLLOW IF I'M STAYIN' HERE...
HONESTLY! MAYBE YOU *HAVEN'T* CHANGED!!

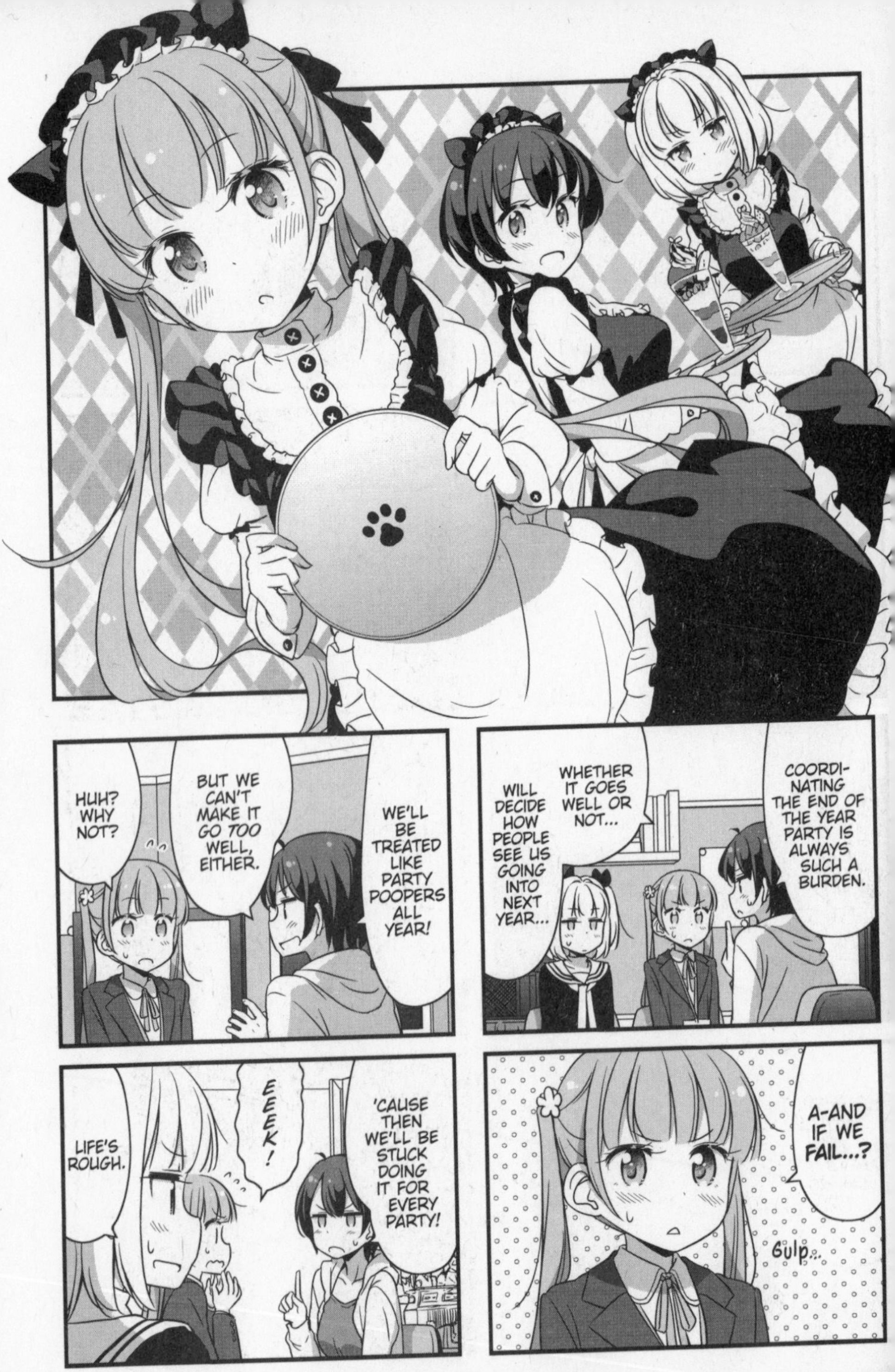
COORDI-NATING THE END OF THE YEAR PARTY IS ALWAYS SUCH A BURDEN.
WHETHER IT GOES WELL OR NOT...
WILL DECIDE HOW PEOPLE SEE US GOING INTO NEXT YEAR...
A-AND IF WE FAIL...?
Gulp...
WE'LL BE TREATED LIKE PARTY POOPERS ALL YEAR!
BUT WE CAN'T MAKE IT GO TOO WELL, EITHER.
HUH? WHY NOT?
'CAUSE THEN WE'LL BE STUCK DOING IT FOR EVERY PARTY!
EEEK!
LIFE'S ROUGH.

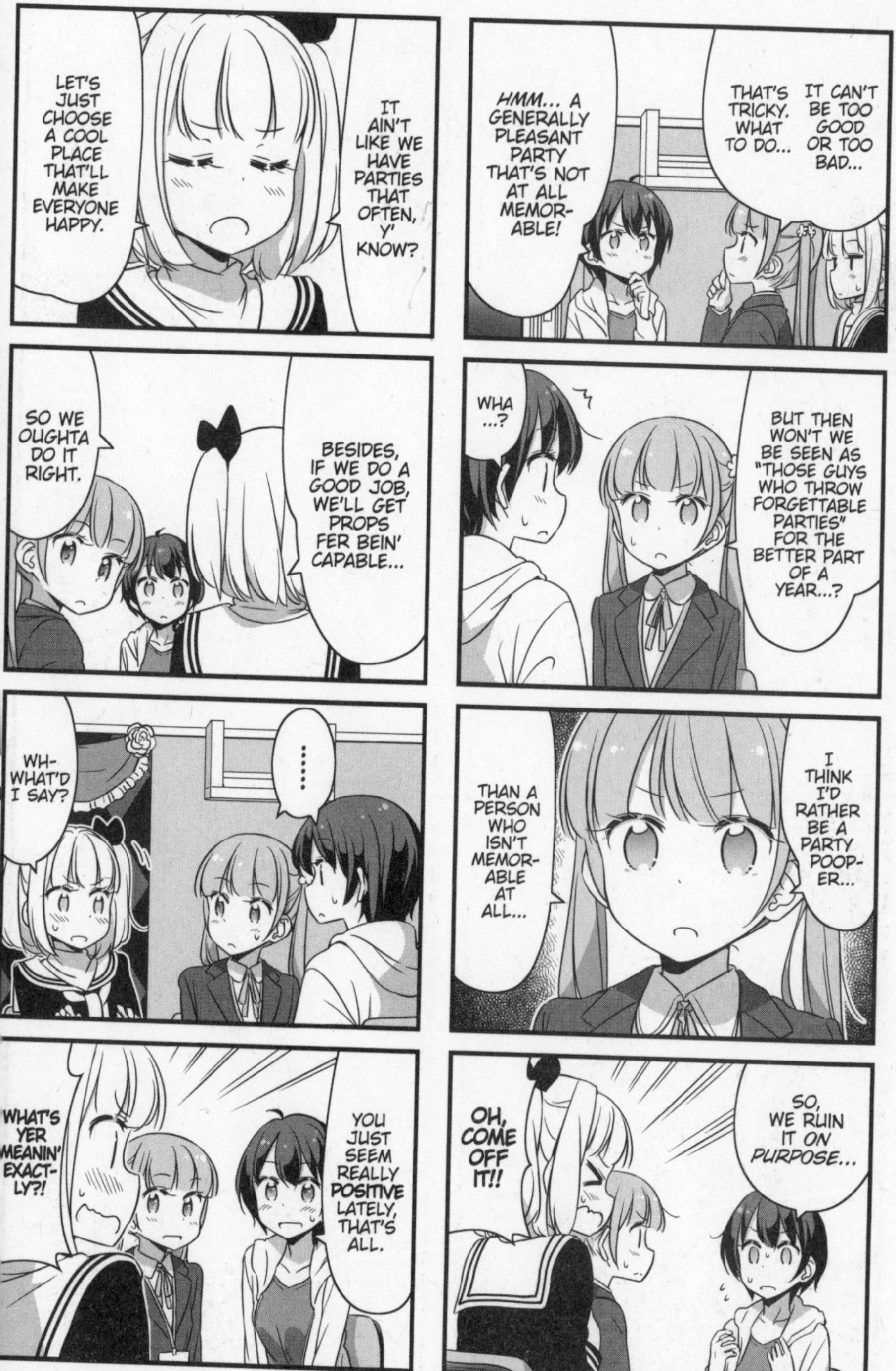
IT CAN'T BE TOO GOOD OR TOO BAD...
THAT'S TRICKY. WHAT TO DO...
HMM... A GENERALLY PLEASANT PARTY THAT'S NOT AT ALL MEMORABLE!
IT AIN'T LIKE WE HAVE PARTIES THAT OFTEN, Y' KNOW?
LET'S JUST CHOOSE A COOL PLACE THAT'LL MAKE EVERYONE HAPPY.
BUT THEN WON'T WE BE SEEN AS "THOSE GUYS WHO THROW FORGETTABLE PARTIES" FOR THE BETTER PART OF A YEAR...?
WHA ...?
BESIDES, IF WE DO A GOOD JOB, WE'LL GET PROPS FER BEIN' CAPABLE...
SO WE OUGHTA DO IT RIGHT.
I THINK I'D RATHER BE A PARTY POOPER...
THAN A PERSON WHO ISN'T MEMORABLE AT ALL...
......
WH- WHAT'D I SAY?
SO, WE RUIN IT *ON PURPOSE*...
OH, COME OFF IT!!
YOU JUST SEEM REALLY **POSITIVE** LATELY, THAT'S ALL.
WHAT'S YER MEANIN' EXACTLY?!

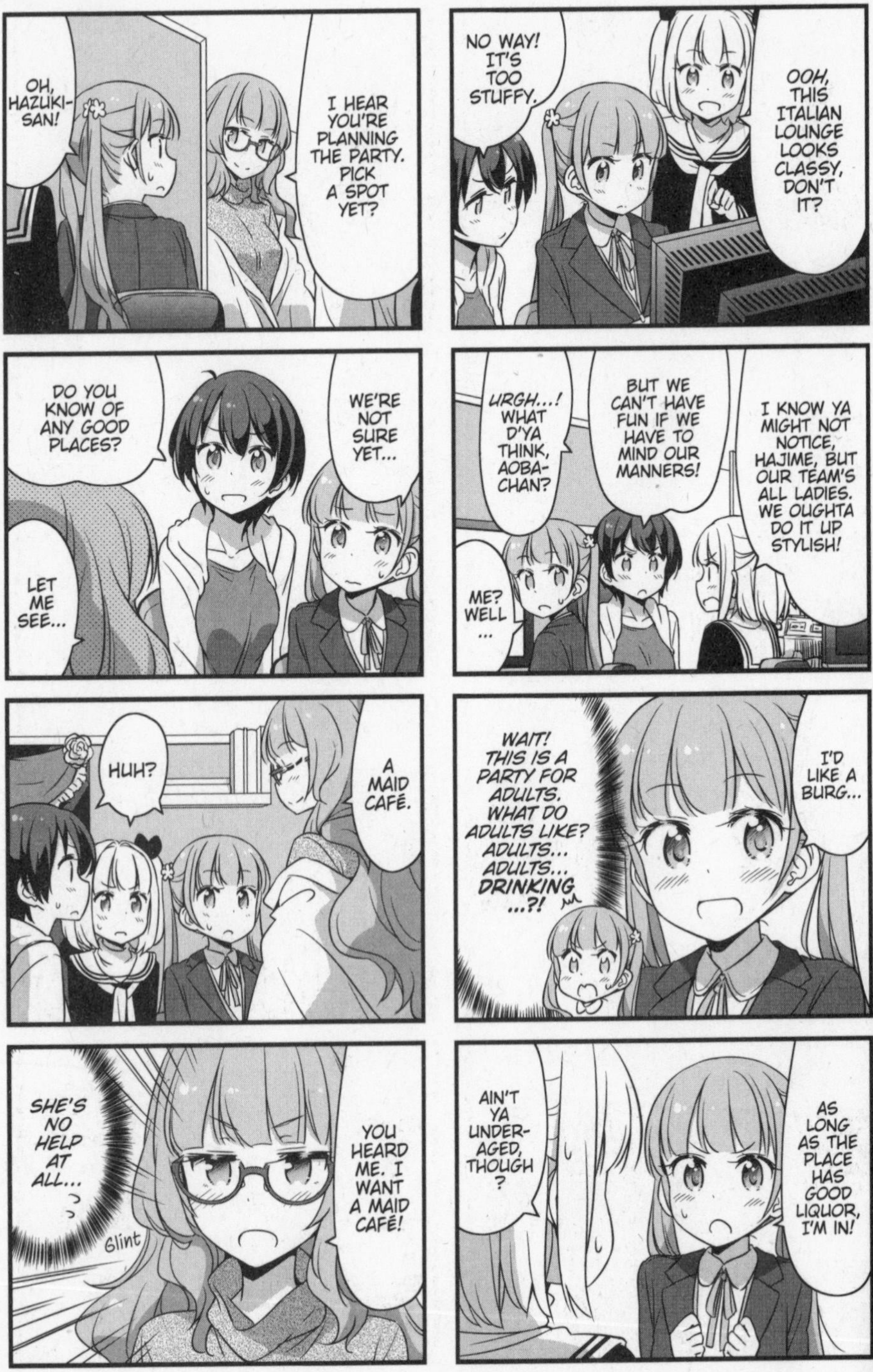
OOH, THIS ITALIAN LOUNGE LOOKS CLASSY, DON'T IT?
NO WAY! IT'S TOO STUFFY.
I HEAR YOU'RE PLANNING THE PARTY. PICK A SPOT YET?
OH, HAZUKI-SAN!
I KNOW YA MIGHT NOT NOTICE, HAJIME, BUT OUR TEAM'S ALL LADIES. WE OUGHTA DO IT UP STYLISH!
BUT WE CAN'T HAVE FUN IF WE HAVE TO MIND OUR MANNERS!
URGH...! WHAT D'YA THINK, AOBA-CHAN?
ME? WELL ...
WE'RE NOT SURE YET...
DO YOU KNOW OF ANY GOOD PLACES?
LET ME SEE...
I'D LIKE A BURG...
WAIT! THIS IS A PARTY FOR ADULTS. WHAT DO ADULTS LIKE? ADULTS... ADULTS... DRINKING ...?!
A MAID CAFÉ.
HUH?
AS LONG AS THE PLACE HAS GOOD LIQUOR, I'M IN!
AIN'T YA UNDER-AGED, THOUGH ?
YOU HEARD ME. I WANT A MAID CAFÉ!
SHE'S NO HELP AT ALL...
Glint

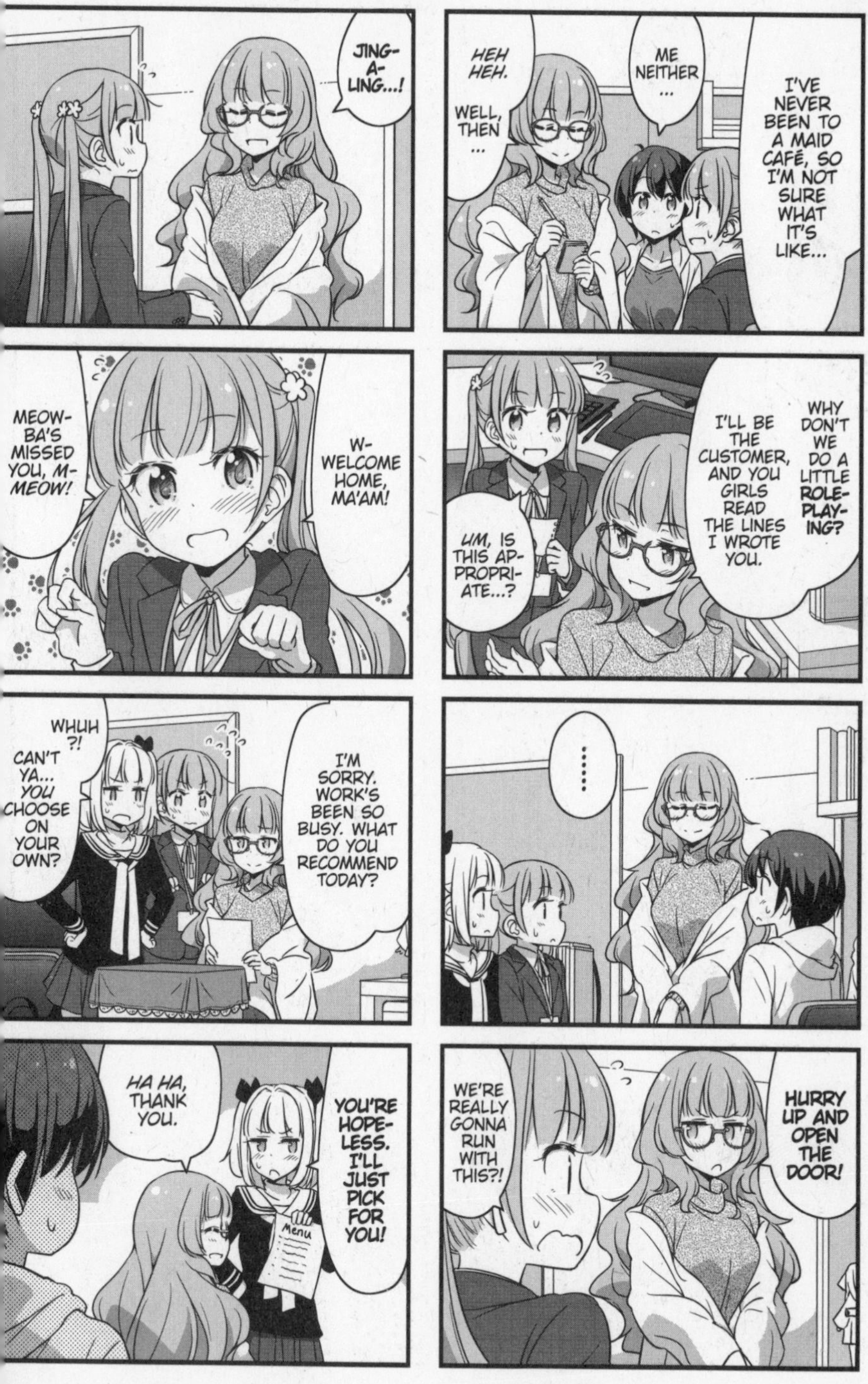
I'VE NEVER BEEN TO A MAID CAFÉ, SO I'M NOT SURE WHAT IT'S LIKE...
ME NEITHER...
HEH HEH.
WELL, THEN...
JING-A-LING...!
WHY DON'T WE DO A LITTLE ROLE-PLAYING?
I'LL BE THE CUSTOMER, AND YOU GIRLS READ THE LINES I WROTE YOU.
UM, IS THIS APPROPRIATE...?
W-WELCOME HOME, MA'AM!
MEOW-BA'S MISSED YOU, M-MEOW!
......
I'M SORRY. WORK'S BEEN SO BUSY. WHAT DO YOU RECOMMEND TODAY?
WHUH?!
CAN'T YA... YOU CHOOSE ON YOUR OWN?
HURRY UP AND OPEN THE DOOR!
WE'RE REALLY GONNA RUN WITH THIS?!
YOU'RE HOPELESS. I'LL JUST PICK FOR YOU!
Menu
HA HA, THANK YOU.

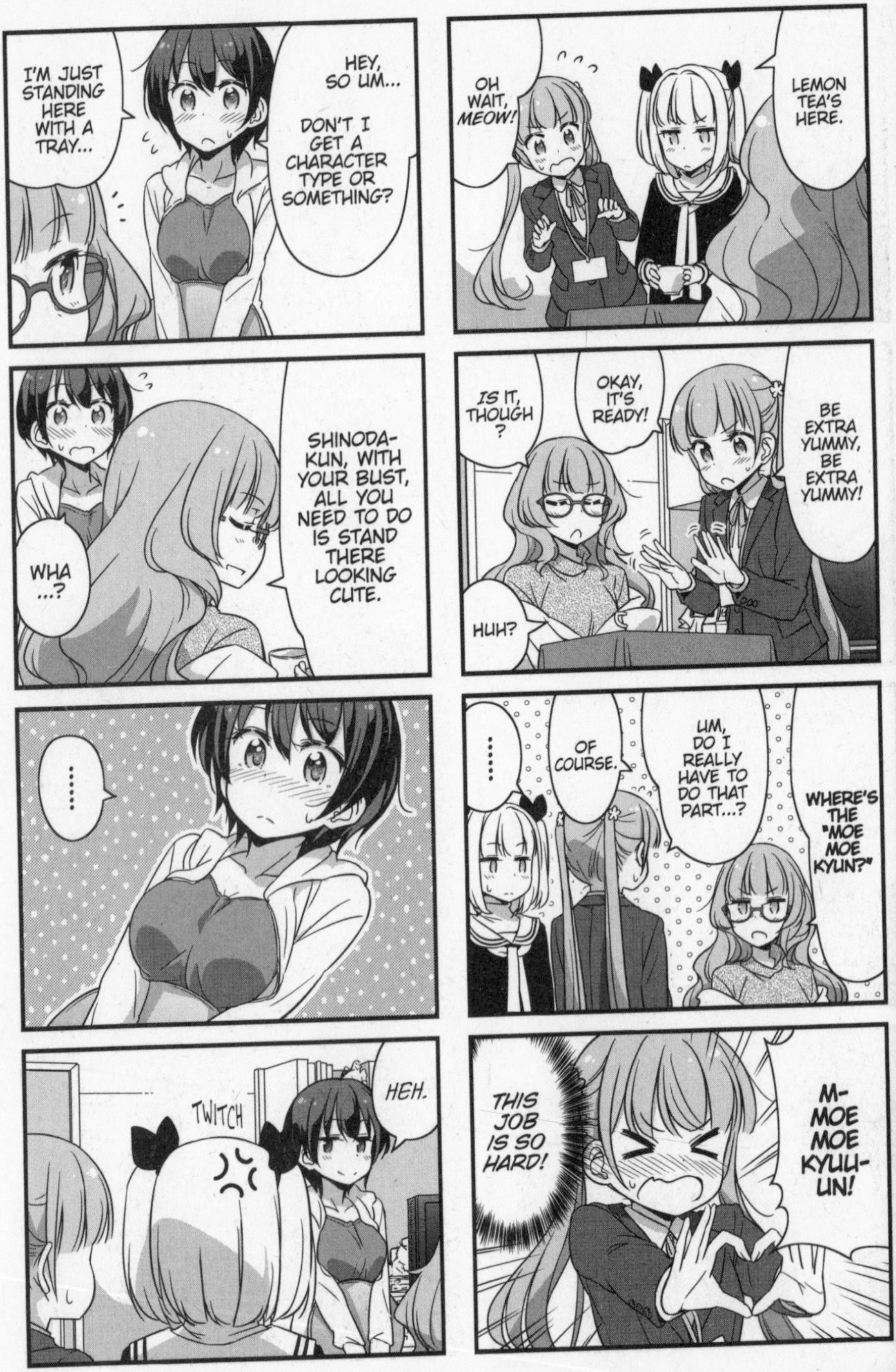
LEMON TEA'S HERE.
OH WAIT, MEOW!
BE EXTRA YUMMY, BE EXTRA YUMMY!
OKAY, IT'S READY!
IS IT, THOUGH?
HUH?
WHERE'S THE "MOE MOE KYUN?"
UM, DO I REALLY HAVE TO DO THAT PART...?
OF COURSE.
......
M-MOE MOE KYUU-UN!
THIS JOB IS SO HARD!
HEY, SO UM...
DON'T I GET A CHARACTER TYPE OR SOMETHING?
I'M JUST STANDING HERE WITH A TRAY...
SHINODA-KUN, WITH YOUR BUST, ALL YOU NEED TO DO IS STAND THERE LOOKING CUTE.
WHA...?
......
HEH.
TWITCH

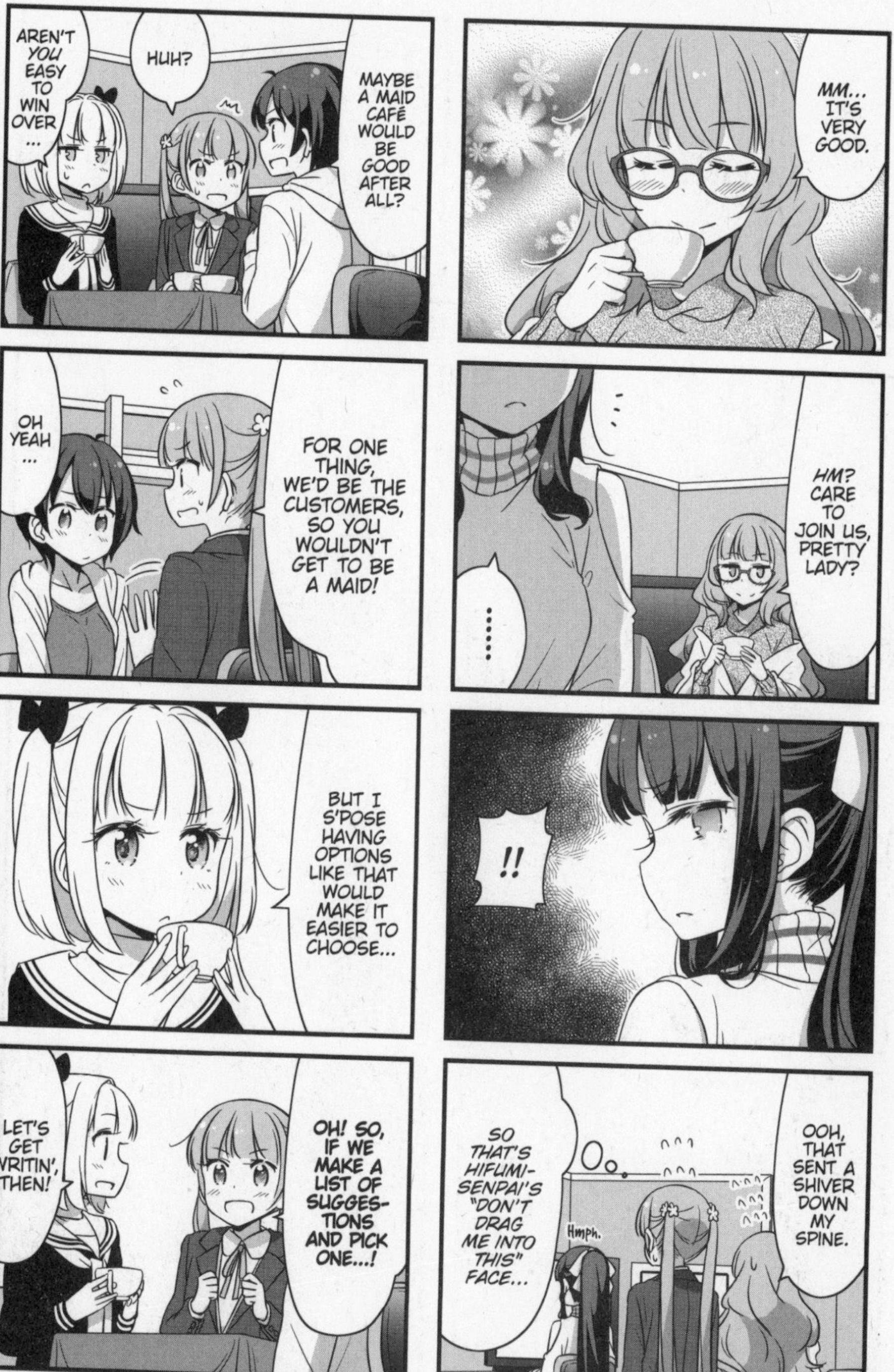
MM... IT'S VERY GOOD.
MAYBE A MAID CAFÉ WOULD BE GOOD AFTER ALL?
HUH?
AREN'T *YOU* EASY TO WIN OVER...
HM? CARE TO JOIN US, PRETTY LADY?
......
FOR ONE THING, WE'D BE THE CUSTOMERS, SO YOU WOULDN'T GET TO BE A MAID!
OH YEAH...
!!
BUT I S'POSE HAVING OPTIONS LIKE THAT WOULD MAKE IT EASIER TO CHOOSE...
OOH, THAT SENT A SHIVER DOWN MY SPINE.
SO THAT'S HIFUMI-SENPAI'S "DON'T DRAG ME INTO THIS" FACE...
Hmph.
OH! SO, IF WE MAKE A LIST OF SUGGES-TIONS AND PICK ONE...!
LET'S GET WRITIN', THEN!

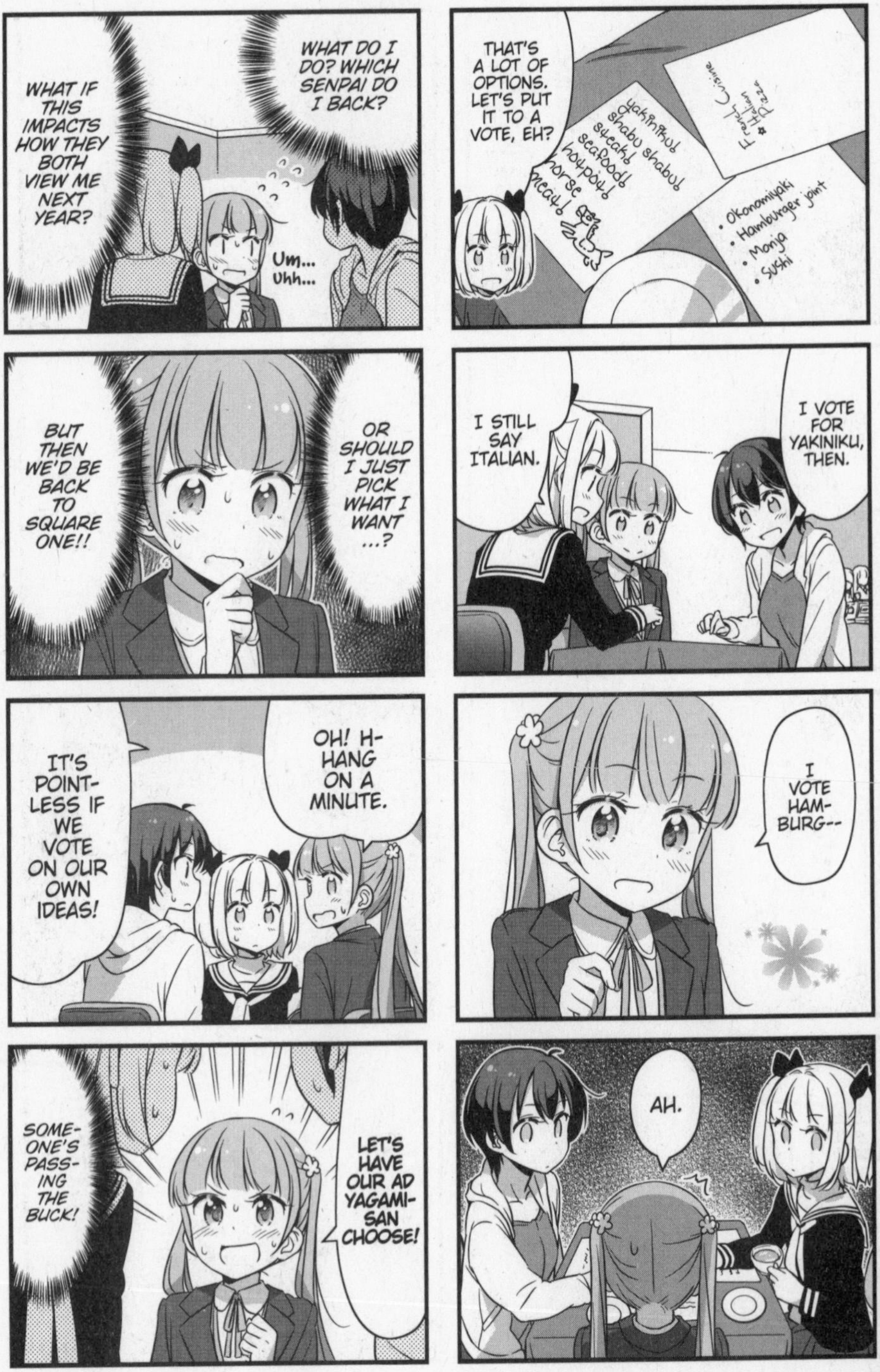
THAT'S A LOT OF OPTIONS. LET'S PUT IT TO A VOTE, EH?
French Cuisine
Italian
Pizza
yakiniku! shabu shabu! steak! seafood! hotpot! horse meat!
• Okonomiyaki
• Hamburger joint
• Monja
• Sushi
WHAT DO I DO? WHICH SENPAI DO I BACK?
WHAT IF THIS IMPACTS HOW THEY BOTH VIEW ME NEXT YEAR?
Um... Uhh...
I VOTE FOR YAKINIKU, THEN.
I STILL SAY ITALIAN.
OR SHOULD I JUST PICK WHAT I WANT ...?
BUT THEN WE'D BE BACK TO SQUARE ONE!!
I VOTE HAMBURG--
OH! H-HANG ON A MINUTE.
IT'S POINTLESS IF WE VOTE ON OUR OWN IDEAS!
AH.
LET'S HAVE OUR AD YAGAMI-SAN CHOOSE!
SOMEONE'S PASSING THE BUCK!

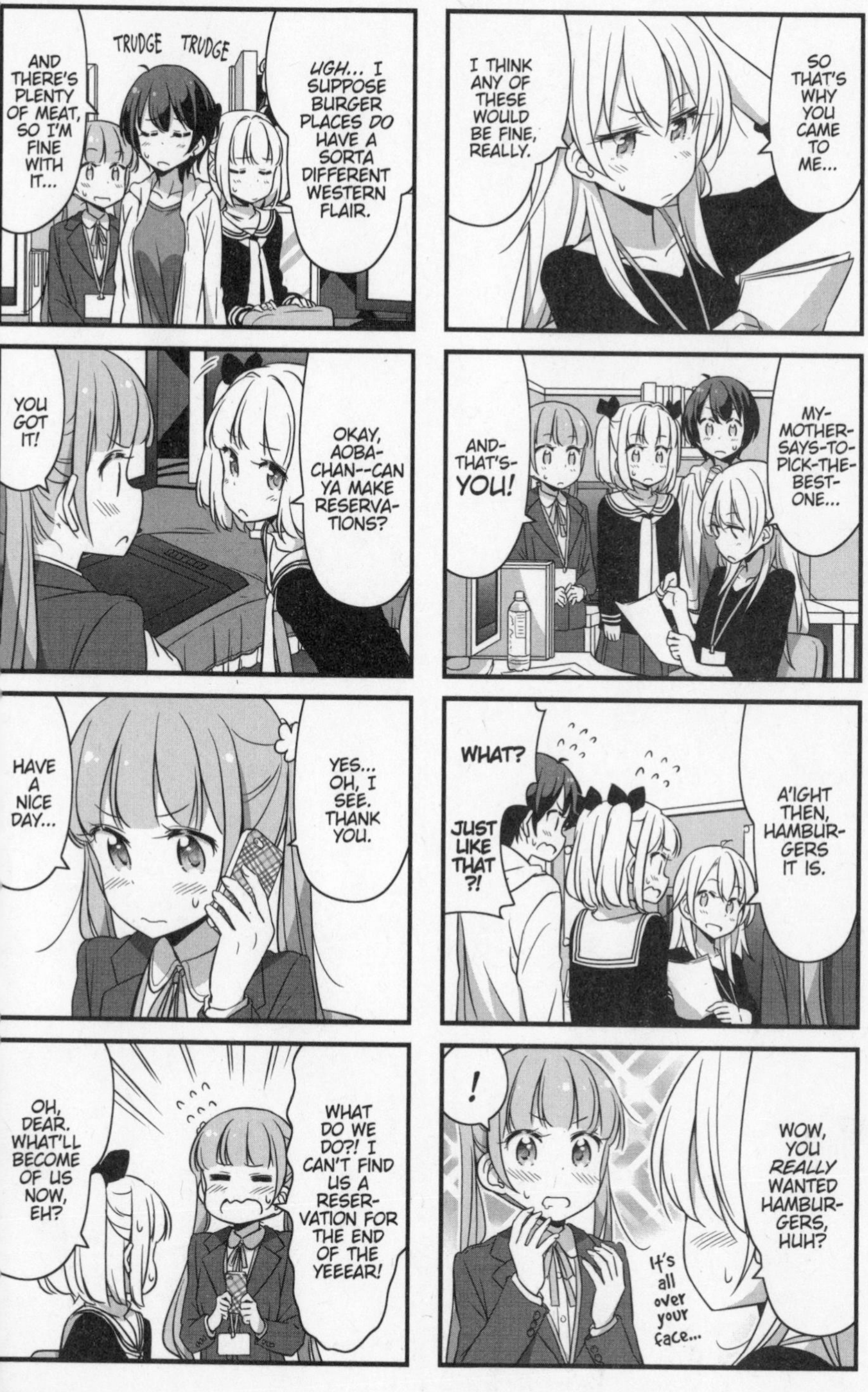
SO THAT'S WHY YOU CAME TO ME...
I THINK ANY OF THESE WOULD BE FINE, REALLY.
MY-MOTHER-SAYS-TO-PICK-THE-BEST-ONE...
AND-THAT'S-YOU!
A'IGHT THEN, HAMBURGERS IT IS.
WHAT?
JUST LIKE THAT?!
WOW, YOU *REALLY* WANTED HAMBURGERS, HUH?
!
It's all over your face...
TRUDGE TRUDGE
UGH... I SUPPOSE BURGER PLACES *DO* HAVE A SORTA DIFFERENT WESTERN FLAIR.
AND THERE'S PLENTY OF MEAT, SO I'M FINE WITH IT...
OKAY, AOBA-CHAN--CAN YA MAKE RESERVATIONS?
YOU GOT IT!
YES... OH, I SEE. THANK YOU.
HAVE A NICE DAY...
WHAT DO WE DO?! I CAN'T FIND US A RESERVATION FOR THE END OF THE YEEEAR!
OH, DEAR. WHAT'LL BECOME OF US NOW, EH?

nEW GAmE!

NEW GAME!

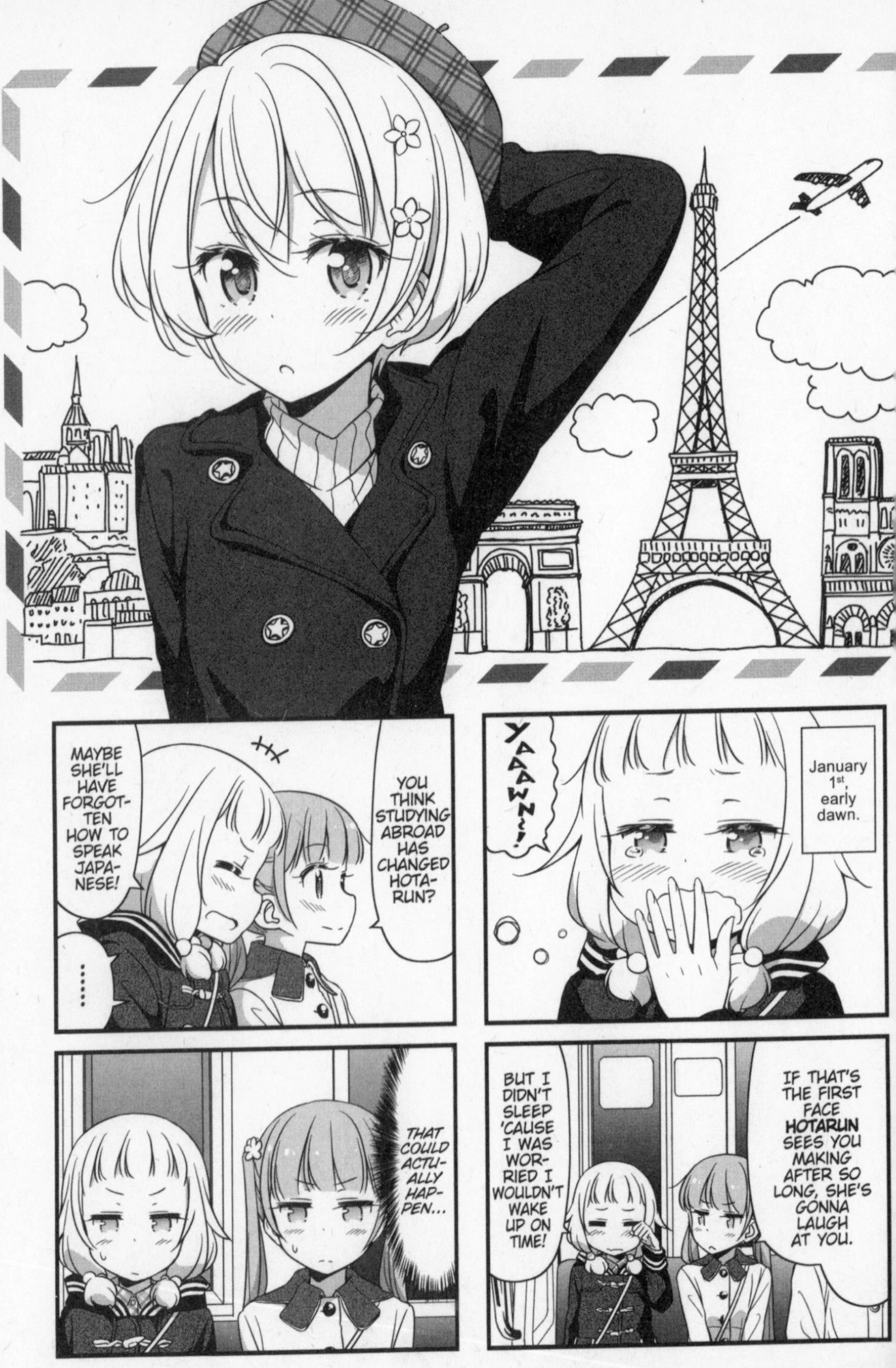

January 1st, early dawn.
YAAAWN~!
YOU THINK STUDYING ABROAD HAS CHANGED HOTARUN?
MAYBE SHE'LL HAVE FORGOTTEN HOW TO SPEAK JAPANESE!
......
IF THAT'S THE FIRST FACE **HOTARUN** SEES YOU MAKING AFTER SO LONG, SHE'S GONNA LAUGH AT YOU.
BUT I DIDN'T SLEEP 'CAUSE I WAS WORRIED I WOULDN'T WAKE UP ON TIME!
THAT COULD ACTUALLY HAPPEN...

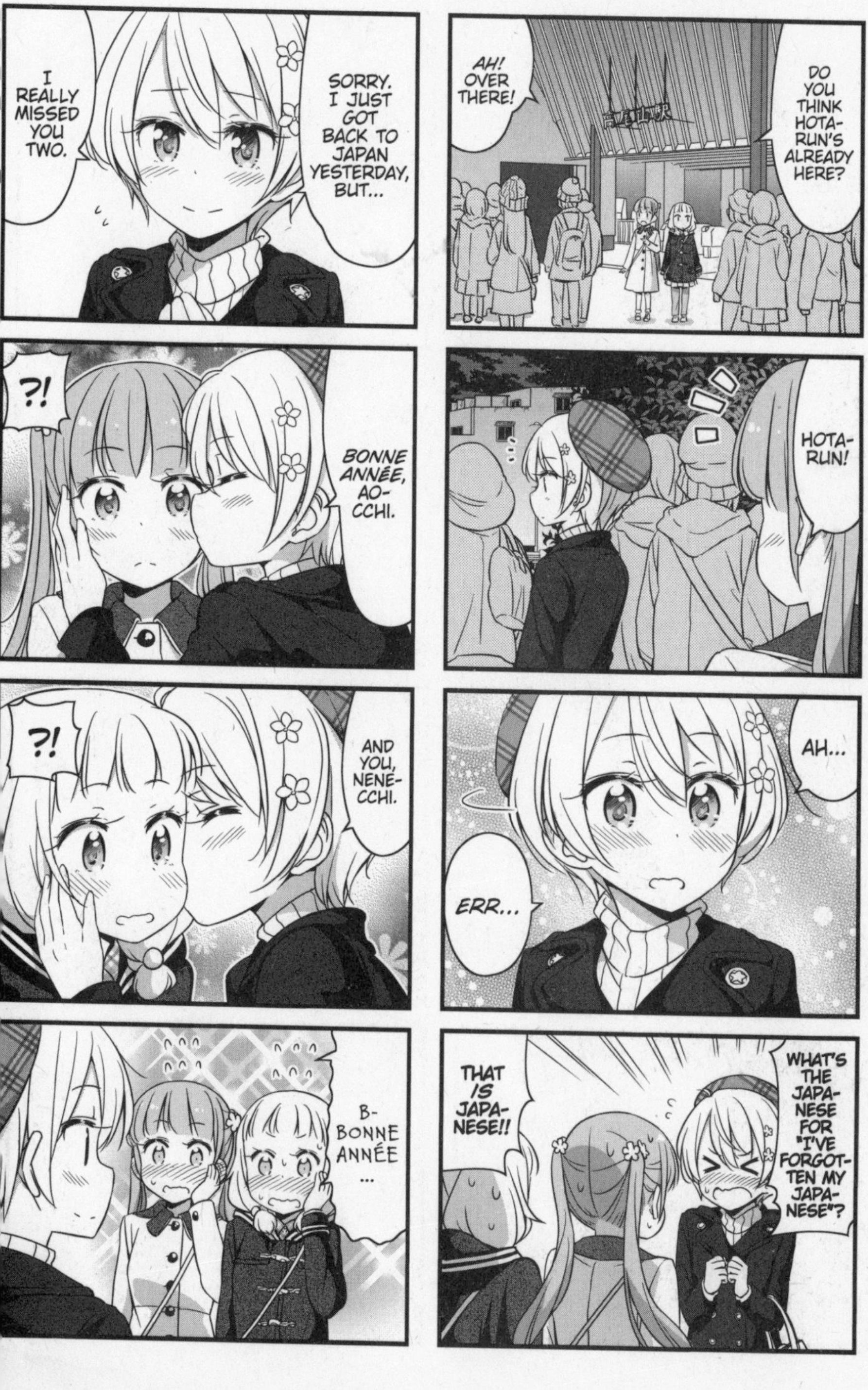
DO YOU THINK HOTA-RUN'S ALREADY HERE?
AH! OVER THERE!
SORRY. I JUST GOT BACK TO JAPAN YESTERDAY, BUT...
I REALLY MISSED YOU TWO.
HOTA-RUN!
BONNE ANNÉE, AO-CCHI.
?!
AH...
ERR...
AND YOU, NENE-CCHI.
?!
WHAT'S THE JAPANESE FOR "I'VE FORGOTTEN MY JAPANESE"?
THAT IS JAPANESE!!
B-BONNE ANNÉE...

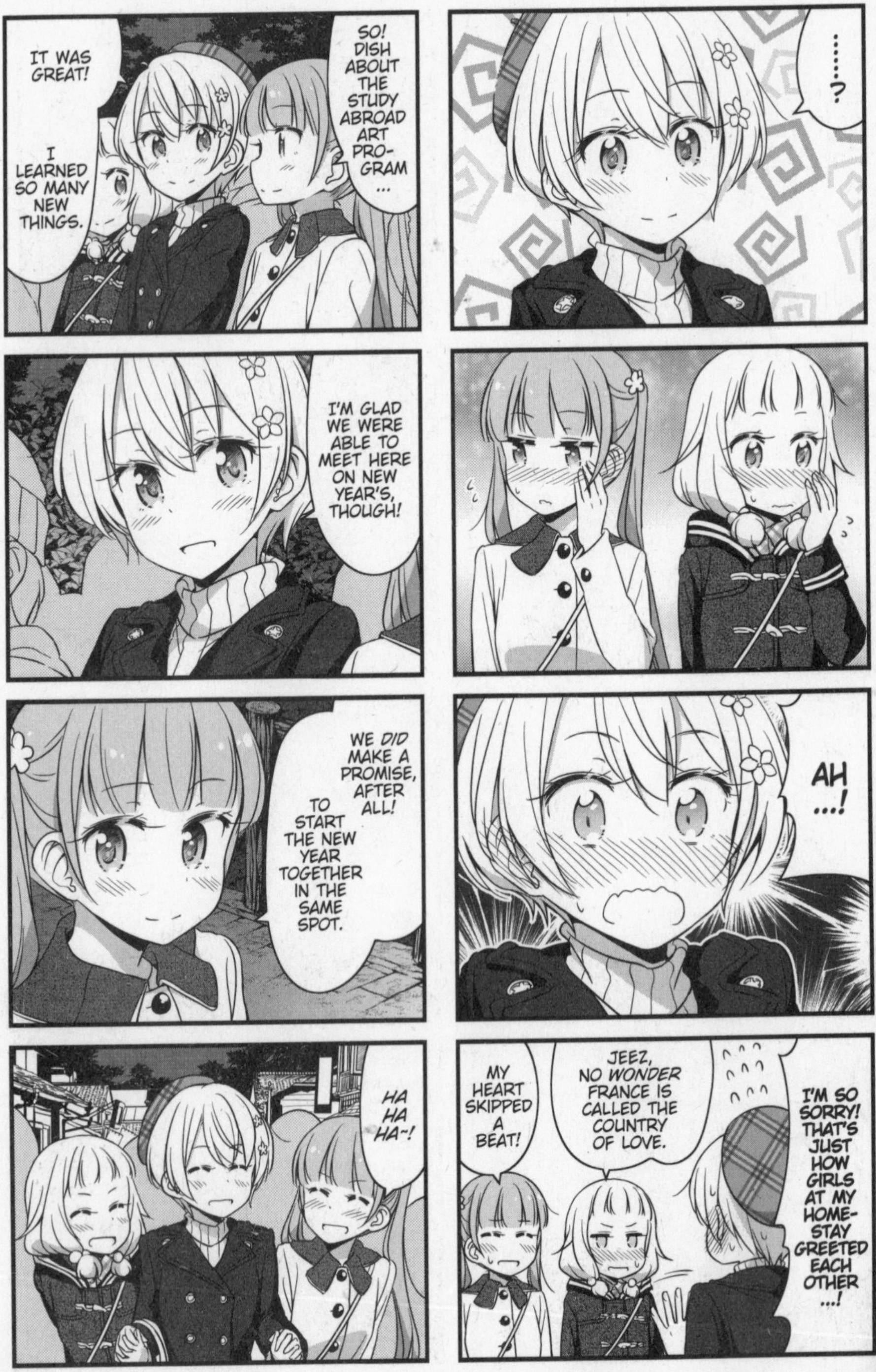
SO! DISH ABOUT THE STUDY ABROAD ART PROGRAM ...
IT WAS GREAT!
I LEARNED SO MANY NEW THINGS.
......?
I'M GLAD WE WERE ABLE TO MEET HERE ON NEW YEAR'S, THOUGH!
WE *DID* MAKE A PROMISE, AFTER ALL!
TO START THE NEW YEAR TOGETHER IN THE SAME SPOT.
AH ...!
HA HA HA~!
MY HEART SKIPPED A BEAT!
JEEZ, NO *WONDER* FRANCE IS CALLED THE COUNTRY OF LOVE.
I'M SO SORRY! THAT'S JUST HOW GIRLS AT MY HOMESTAY GREETED EACH OTHER ...!

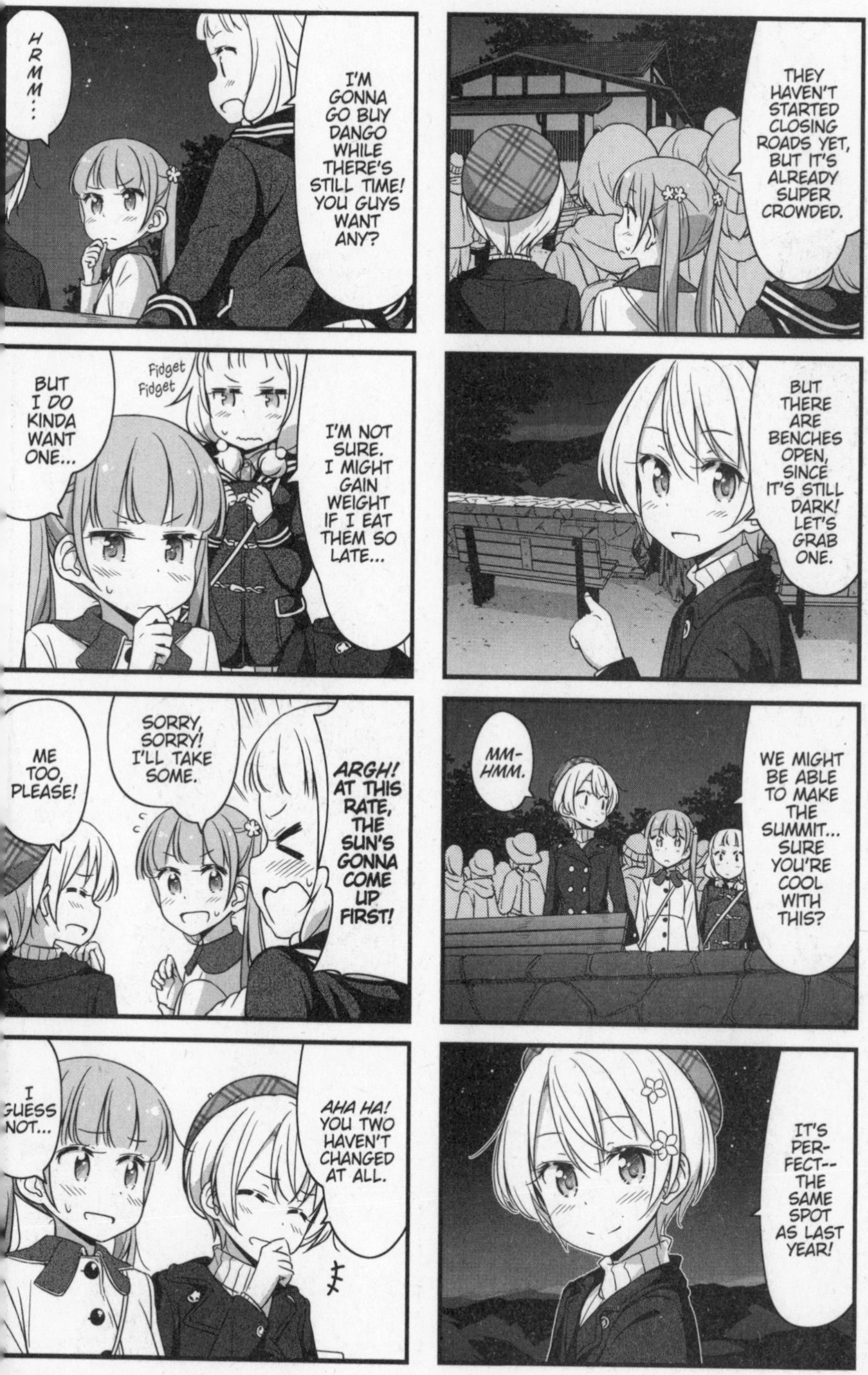
THEY HAVEN'T STARTED CLOSING ROADS YET, BUT IT'S ALREADY SUPER CROWDED.
I'M GONNA GO BUY DANGO WHILE THERE'S STILL TIME! YOU GUYS WANT ANY?
HRMM...
BUT THERE ARE BENCHES OPEN, SINCE IT'S STILL DARK! LET'S GRAB ONE.
I'M NOT SURE. I MIGHT GAIN WEIGHT IF I EAT THEM SO LATE...
Fidget Fidget
BUT I *DO* KINDA WANT ONE...
WE MIGHT BE ABLE TO MAKE THE SUMMIT... SURE YOU'RE COOL WITH THIS?
MM-HMM.
ARGH! AT THIS RATE, THE SUN'S GONNA COME UP FIRST!
SORRY, SORRY! I'LL TAKE SOME.
ME TOO, PLEASE!
IT'S PERFECT--THE SAME SPOT AS LAST YEAR!
AHA HA! YOU TWO HAVEN'T CHANGED AT ALL.
I GUESS NOT...

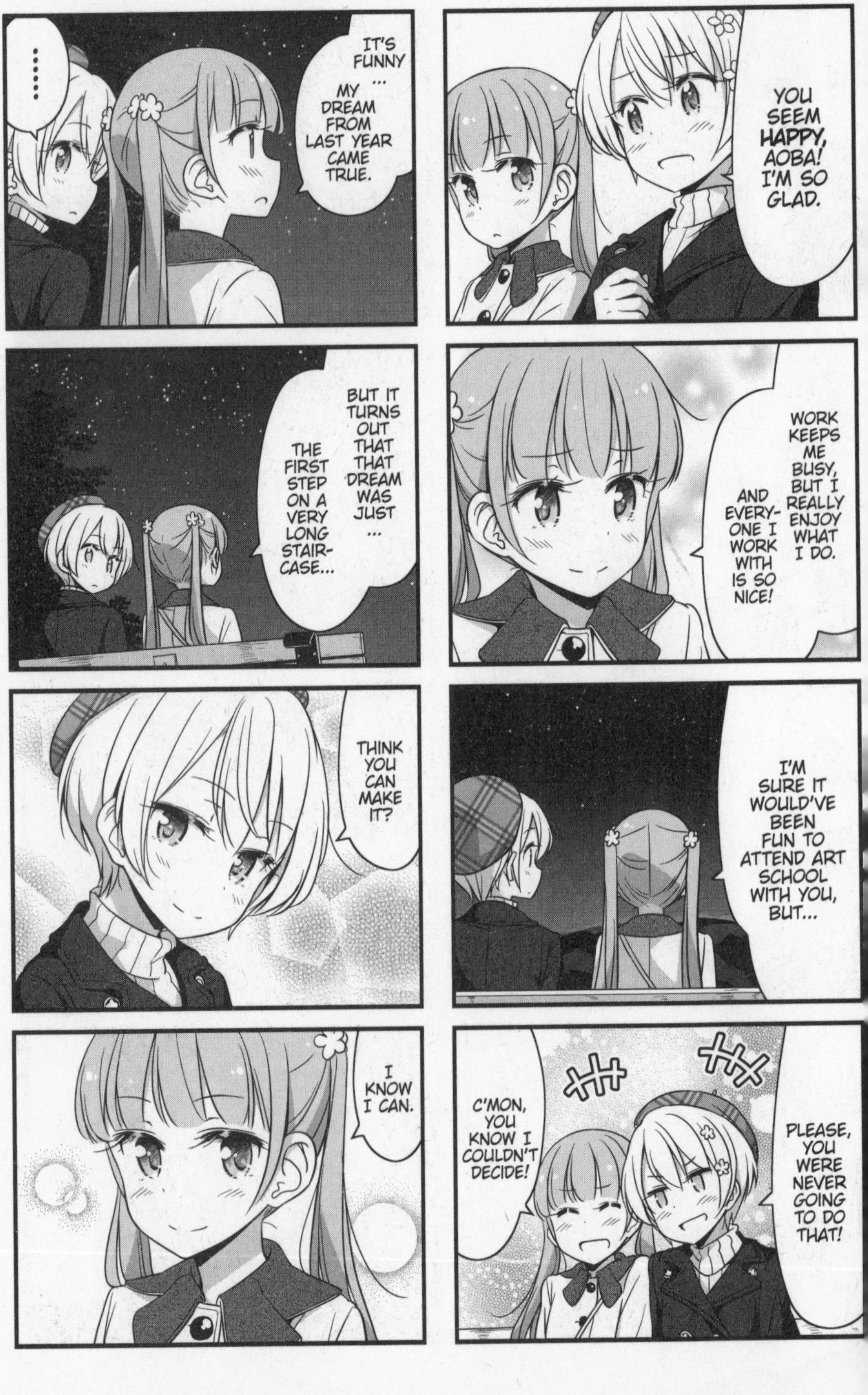
YOU SEEM HAPPY, AOBA! I'M SO GLAD.
IT'S FUNNY... MY DREAM FROM LAST YEAR CAME TRUE.
......
WORK KEEPS ME BUSY, BUT I REALLY ENJOY WHAT I DO.
AND EVERYONE I WORK WITH IS SO NICE!
BUT IT TURNS OUT THAT THAT DREAM WAS JUST...
THE FIRST STEP ON A VERY LONG STAIRCASE...
I'M SURE IT WOULD'VE BEEN FUN TO ATTEND ART SCHOOL WITH YOU, BUT...
THINK YOU CAN MAKE IT?
PLEASE, YOU WERE NEVER GOING TO DO THAT!
C'MON, YOU KNOW I COULDN'T DECIDE!
I KNOW I CAN.

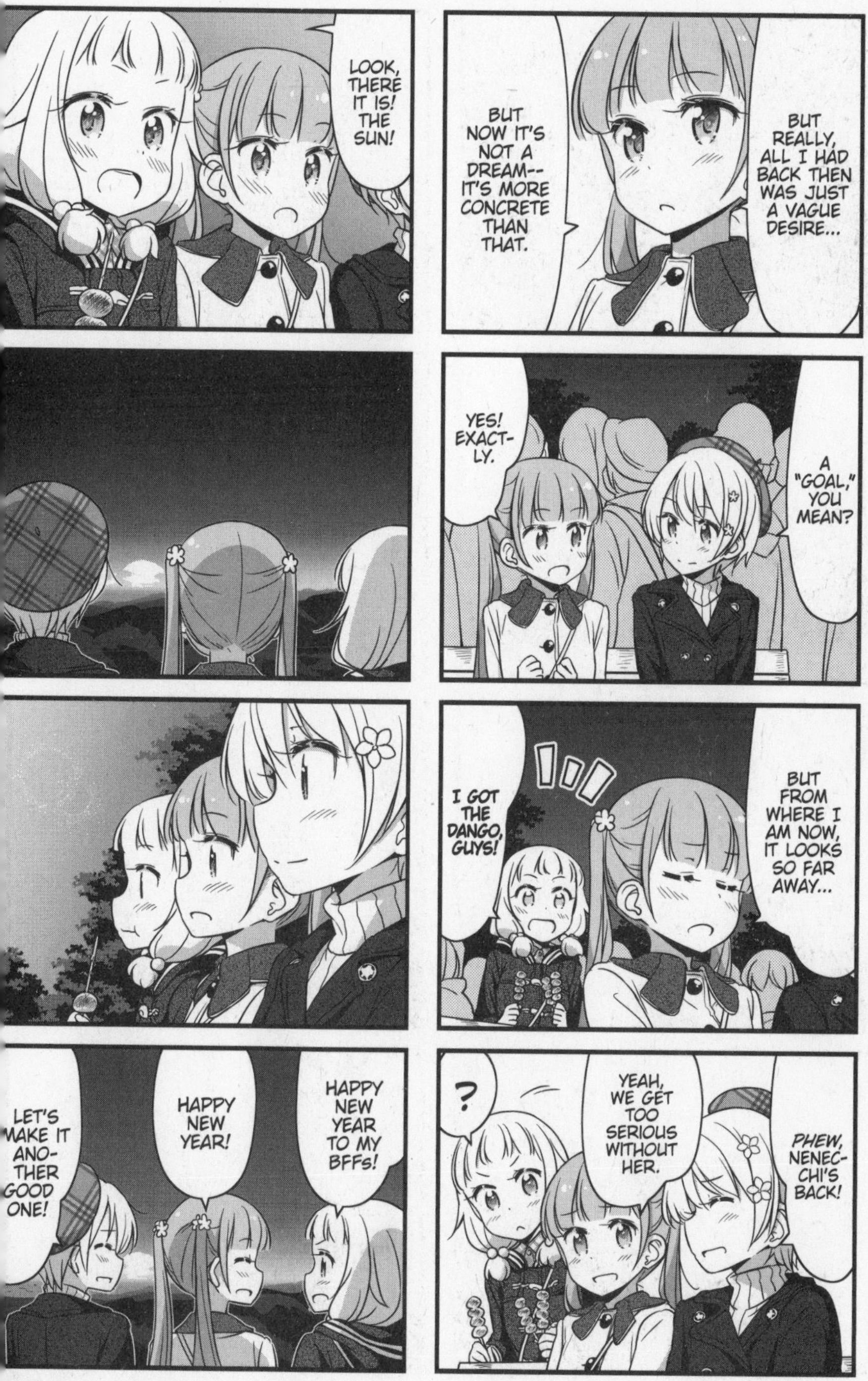
BUT REALLY, ALL I HAD BACK THEN WAS JUST A VAGUE DESIRE...
BUT NOW IT'S NOT A DREAM-- IT'S MORE CONCRETE THAN THAT.
LOOK, THERE IT IS! THE SUN!
A "GOAL," YOU MEAN?
YES! EXACT-LY.
BUT FROM WHERE I AM NOW, IT LOOKS SO FAR AWAY...
I GOT THE DANGO, GUYS!
PHEW, NENEC-CHI'S BACK!
YEAH, WE GET TOO SERIOUS WITHOUT HER.
?
HAPPY NEW YEAR TO MY BFFs!
HAPPY NEW YEAR!
LET'S MAKE IT ANO-THER GOOD ONE!

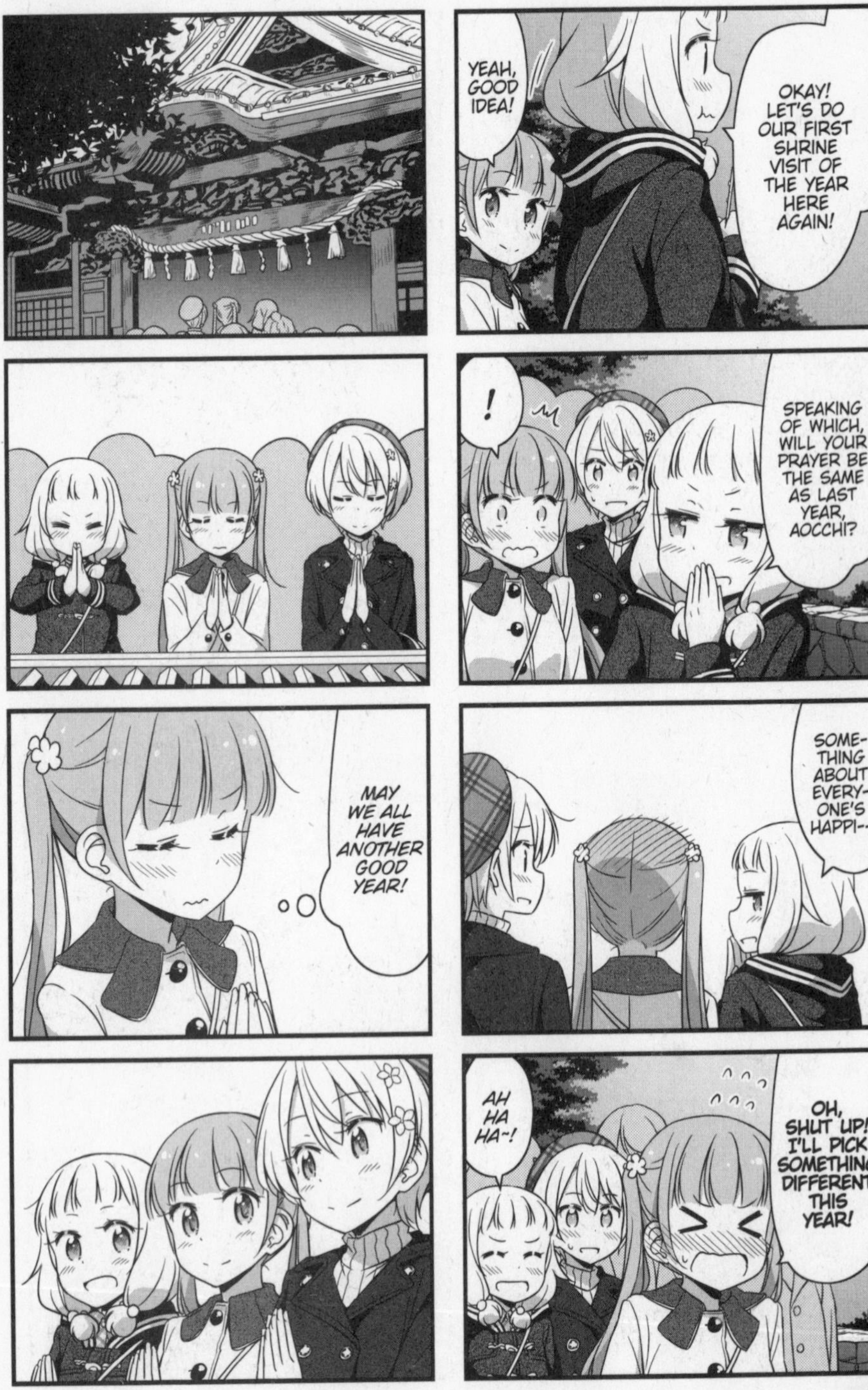
OKAY! LET'S DO OUR FIRST SHRINE VISIT OF THE YEAR HERE AGAIN!
YEAH, GOOD IDEA!
SPEAKING OF WHICH, WILL YOUR PRAYER BE THE SAME AS LAST YEAR, AOCCHI?
!
SOME-THING ABOUT EVERY-ONE'S HAPPI--
MAY WE ALL HAVE ANOTHER GOOD YEAR!
OH, SHUT UP! I'LL PICK SOMETHING DIFFERENT THIS YEAR!
AH HA HA~!

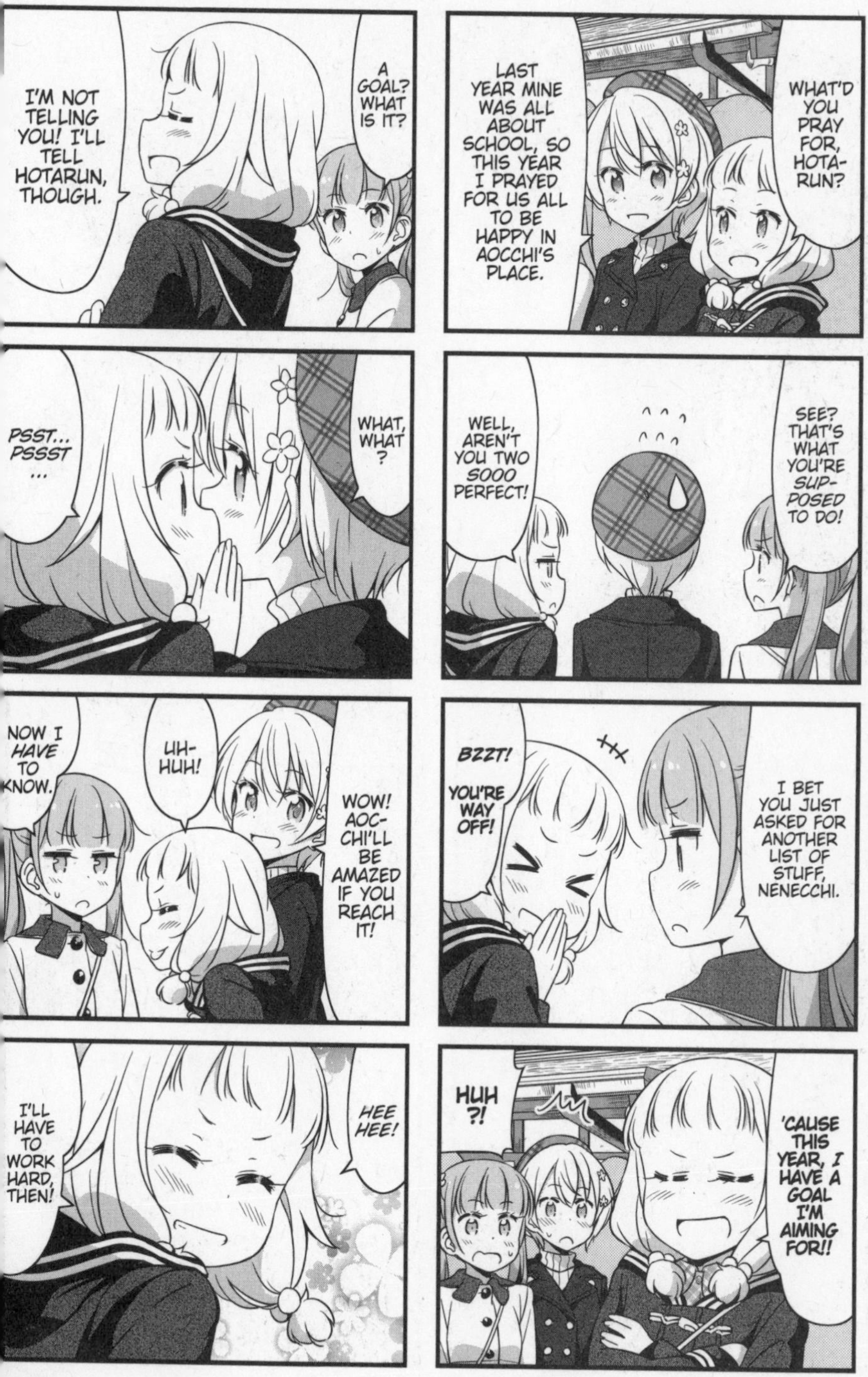
WHAT'D YOU PRAY FOR, HOTARUN?
LAST YEAR MINE WAS ALL ABOUT SCHOOL, SO THIS YEAR I PRAYED FOR US ALL TO BE HAPPY IN AOCCHI'S PLACE.
SEE? THAT'S WHAT YOU'RE SUPPOSED TO DO!
WELL, AREN'T YOU TWO SOOO PERFECT!
I BET YOU JUST ASKED FOR ANOTHER LIST OF STUFF, NENECCHI.
BZZT! YOU'RE WAY OFF!
'CAUSE THIS YEAR, I HAVE A GOAL I'M AIMING FOR!!
HUH?!
A GOAL? WHAT IS IT?
I'M NOT TELLING YOU! I'LL TELL HOTARUN, THOUGH.
WHAT, WHAT?
PSST... PSSST...
WOW! AOC-CHI'LL BE AMAZED IF YOU REACH IT!
UH-HUH!
NOW I HAVE TO KNOW.
HEE HEE!
I'LL HAVE TO WORK HARD, THEN!

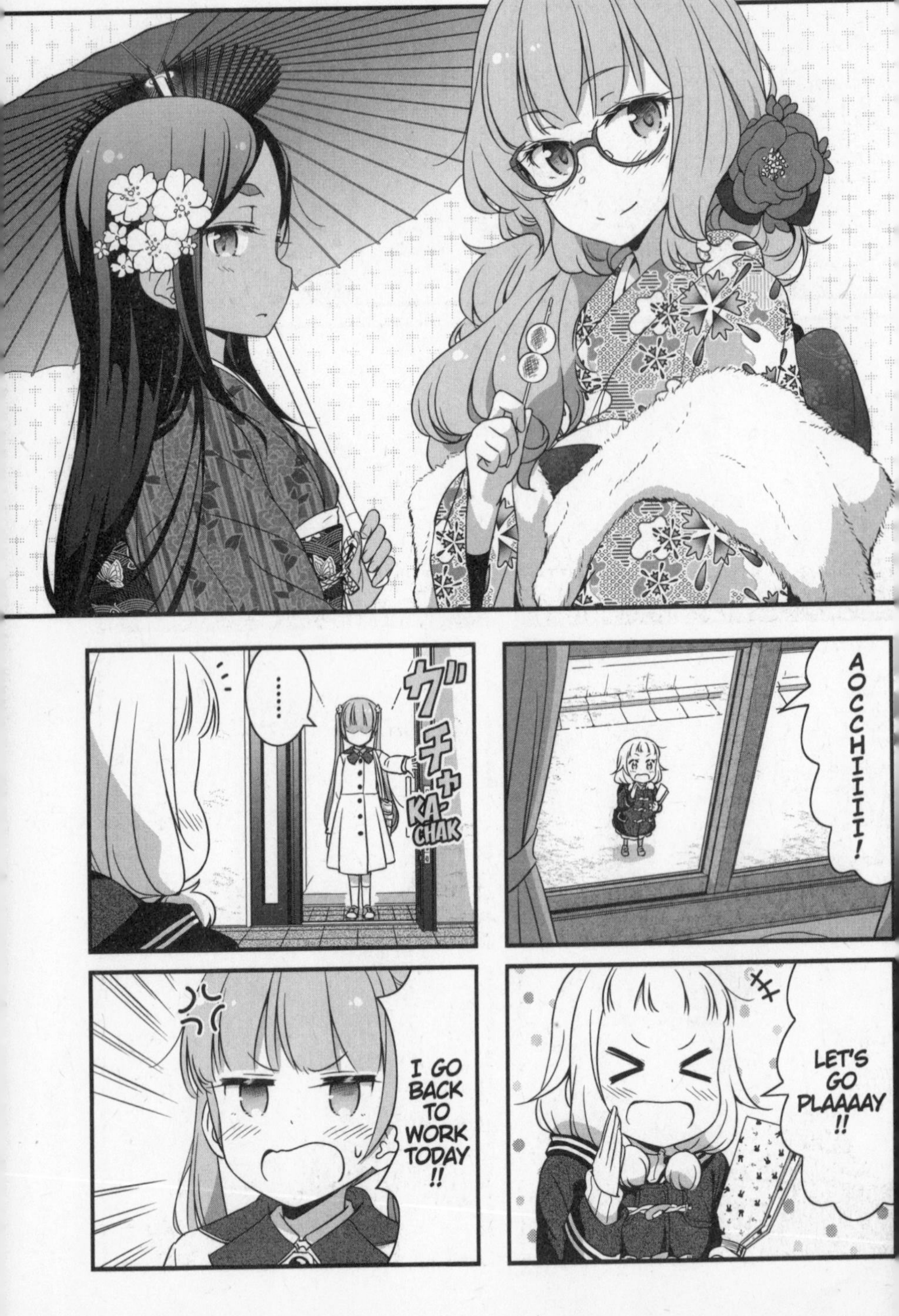
AOCCHIIIII!
……
KA-CHAK
LET'S GO PLAAAAY!!
I GO BACK TO WORK TODAY!!

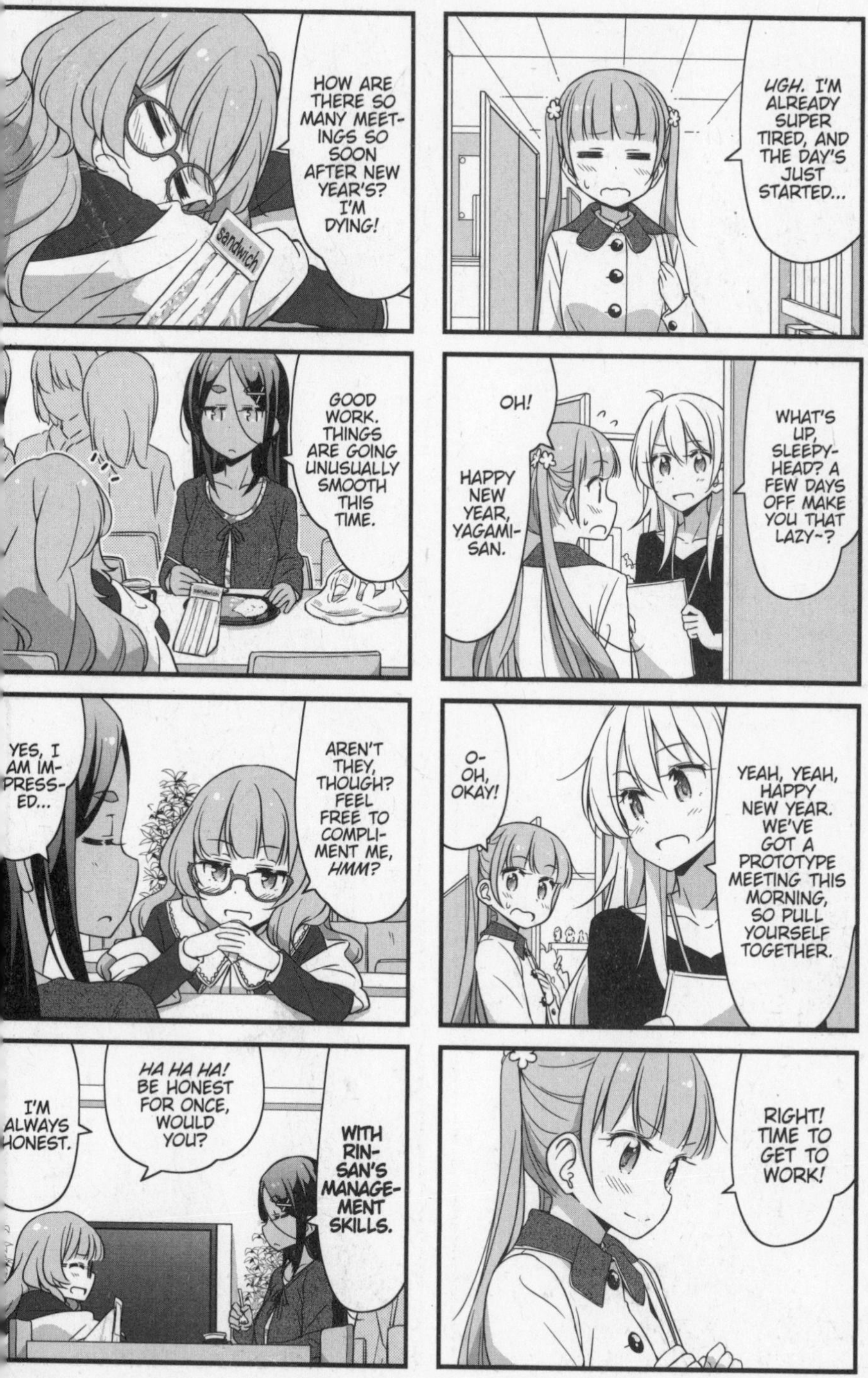
UGH. I'M ALREADY SUPER TIRED, AND THE DAY'S JUST STARTED...
WHAT'S UP, SLEEPY-HEAD? A FEW DAYS OFF MAKE YOU THAT LAZY~?
OH!
HAPPY NEW YEAR, YAGAMI-SAN.
YEAH, YEAH, HAPPY NEW YEAR. WE'VE GOT A PROTOTYPE MEETING THIS MORNING, SO PULL YOURSELF TOGETHER.
O-OH, OKAY!
RIGHT! TIME TO GET TO WORK!
HOW ARE THERE SO MANY MEETINGS SO SOON AFTER NEW YEAR'S? I'M DYING!
sandwich
GOOD WORK. THINGS ARE GOING UNUSUALLY SMOOTH THIS TIME.
AREN'T THEY, THOUGH? FEEL FREE TO COMPLIMENT ME, HMM?
YES, I AM IMPRESSED...
HA HA HA! BE HONEST FOR ONCE, WOULD YOU?
I'M ALWAYS HONEST.
WITH RIN-SAN'S MANAGEMENT SKILLS.

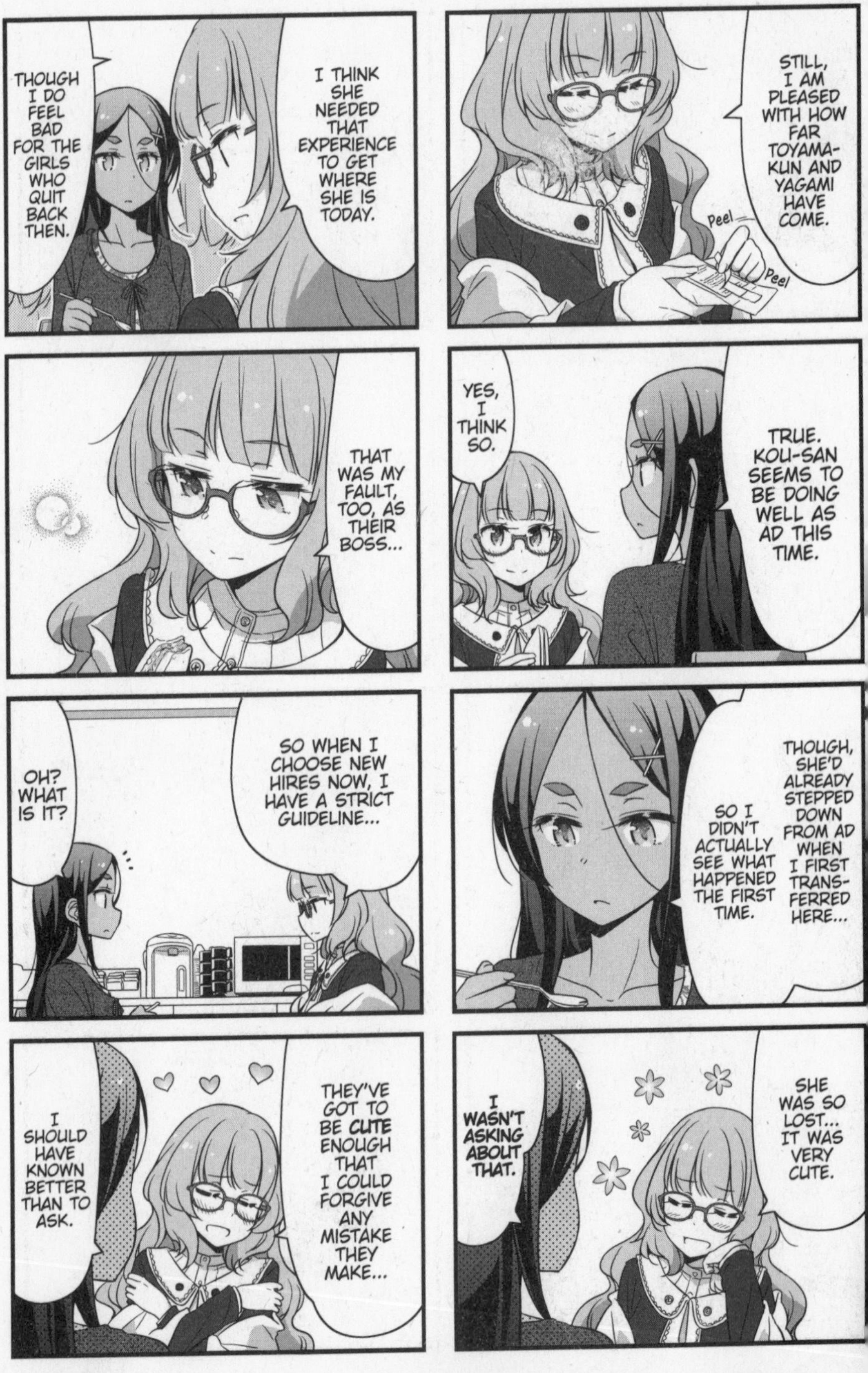
STILL, I AM PLEASED WITH HOW FAR TOYAMA-KUN AND YAGAMI HAVE COME.
Peel
Peel
I THINK SHE NEEDED THAT EXPERIENCE TO GET WHERE SHE IS TODAY.
THOUGH I DO FEEL BAD FOR THE GIRLS WHO QUIT BACK THEN.
TRUE. KOU-SAN SEEMS TO BE DOING WELL AS AD THIS TIME.
YES, I THINK SO.
THAT WAS MY FAULT, TOO, AS THEIR BOSS...
THOUGH, SHE'D ALREADY STEPPED DOWN FROM AD WHEN I FIRST TRANSFERRED HERE...
SO I DIDN'T ACTUALLY SEE WHAT HAPPENED THE FIRST TIME.
SO WHEN I CHOOSE NEW HIRES NOW, I HAVE A STRICT GUIDELINE...
OH? WHAT IS IT?
SHE WAS SO LOST... IT WAS VERY CUTE.
I WASN'T ASKING ABOUT THAT.
THEY'VE GOT TO BE **CUTE** ENOUGH THAT I COULD FORGIVE ANY MISTAKE THEY MAKE...
I SHOULD HAVE KNOWN BETTER THAN TO ASK.

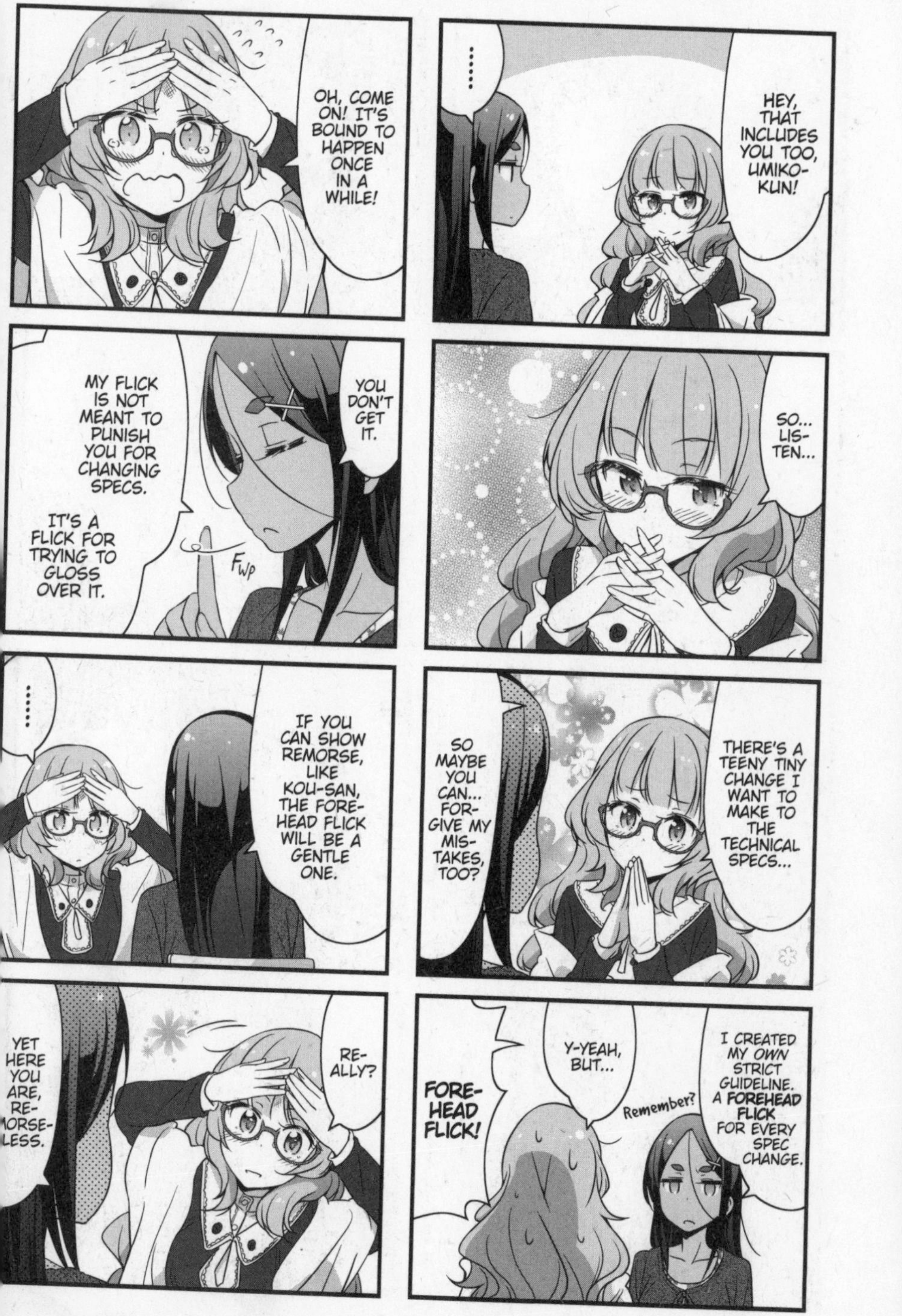
HEY, THAT INCLUDES YOU TOO, UMIKO-KUN!
……
SO... LIS-TEN...
THERE'S A TEENY TINY CHANGE I WANT TO MAKE TO THE TECHNICAL SPECS...
SO MAYBE YOU CAN... FOR-GIVE MY MIS-TAKES, TOO?
I CREATED MY OWN STRICT GUIDELINE. A FOREHEAD FLICK FOR EVERY SPEC CHANGE.
Remember?
Y-YEAH, BUT...
FORE-HEAD FLICK!
OH, COME ON! IT'S BOUND TO HAPPEN ONCE IN A WHILE!
YOU DON'T GET IT.
MY FLICK IS NOT MEANT TO PUNISH YOU FOR CHANGING SPECS.
IT'S A FLICK FOR TRYING TO GLOSS OVER IT.
FWP
IF YOU CAN SHOW REMORSE, LIKE KOU-SAN, THE FORE-HEAD FLICK WILL BE A GENTLE ONE.
……
RE-ALLY?
YET HERE YOU ARE, RE-MORSE-LESS.

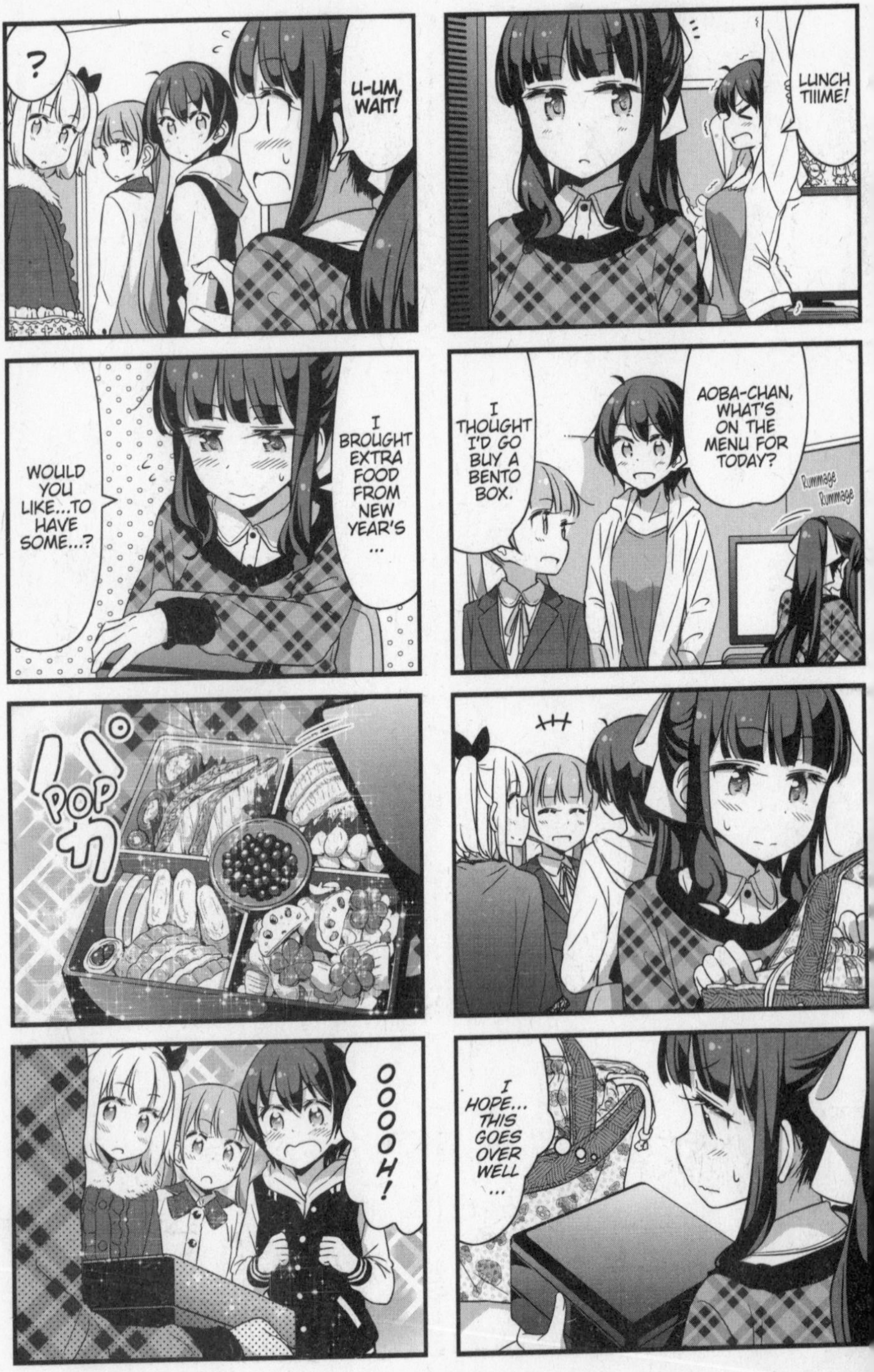
LUNCH TIIIME!
AOBA-CHAN, WHAT'S ON THE MENU FOR TODAY?
I THOUGHT I'D GO BUY A BENTO BOX.
...
Rummage Rummage
I HOPE... THIS GOES OVER WELL...
U-UM, WAIT!
?
I BROUGHT EXTRA FOOD FROM NEW YEAR'S...
WOULD YOU LIKE...TO HAVE SOME...?
パ POP カ
OOOOOH!

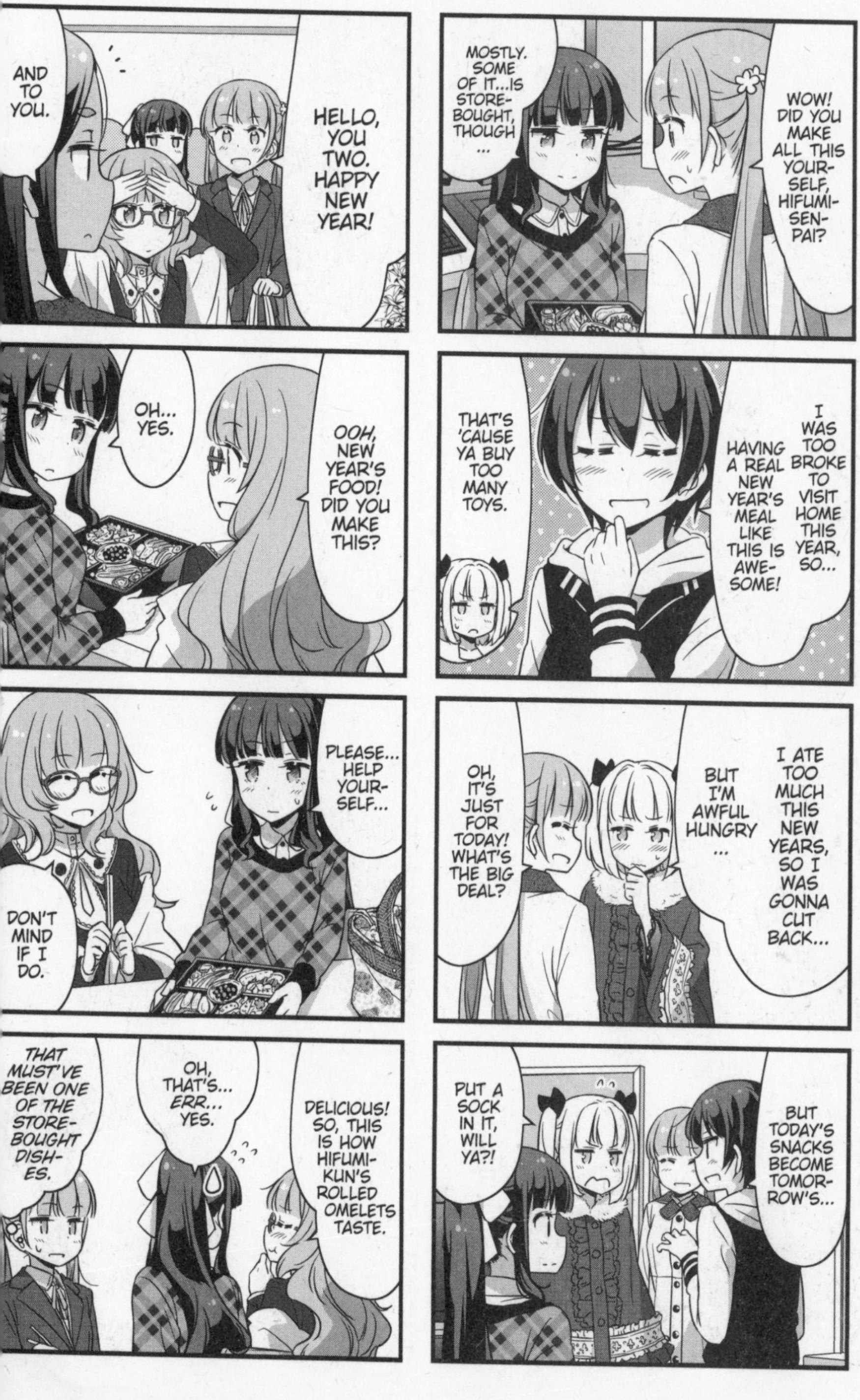
WOW! DID YOU MAKE ALL THIS YOURSELF, HIFUMI-SENPAI?
MOSTLY. SOME OF IT...IS STORE-BOUGHT, THOUGH...
HELLO, YOU TWO. HAPPY NEW YEAR!
AND TO YOU.
I WAS TOO BROKE TO VISIT HOME THIS YEAR, SO...
HAVING A REAL NEW YEAR'S MEAL LIKE THIS IS AWESOME!
THAT'S 'CAUSE YA BUY TOO MANY TOYS.
OOH, NEW YEAR'S FOOD! DID YOU MAKE THIS?
OH... YES.
I ATE TOO MUCH THIS NEW YEARS, SO I WAS GONNA CUT BACK...
BUT I'M AWFUL HUNGRY...
OH, IT'S JUST FOR TODAY! WHAT'S THE BIG DEAL?
PLEASE... HELP YOURSELF...
DON'T MIND IF I DO.
BUT TODAY'S SNACKS BECOME TOMORROW'S...
PUT A SOCK IN IT, WILL YA?!
DELICIOUS! SO, THIS IS HOW HIFUMI-KUN'S ROLLED OMELETS TASTE.
OH, THAT'S... ERR... YES.
THAT MUST'VE BEEN ONE OF THE STORE-BOUGHT DISHES.

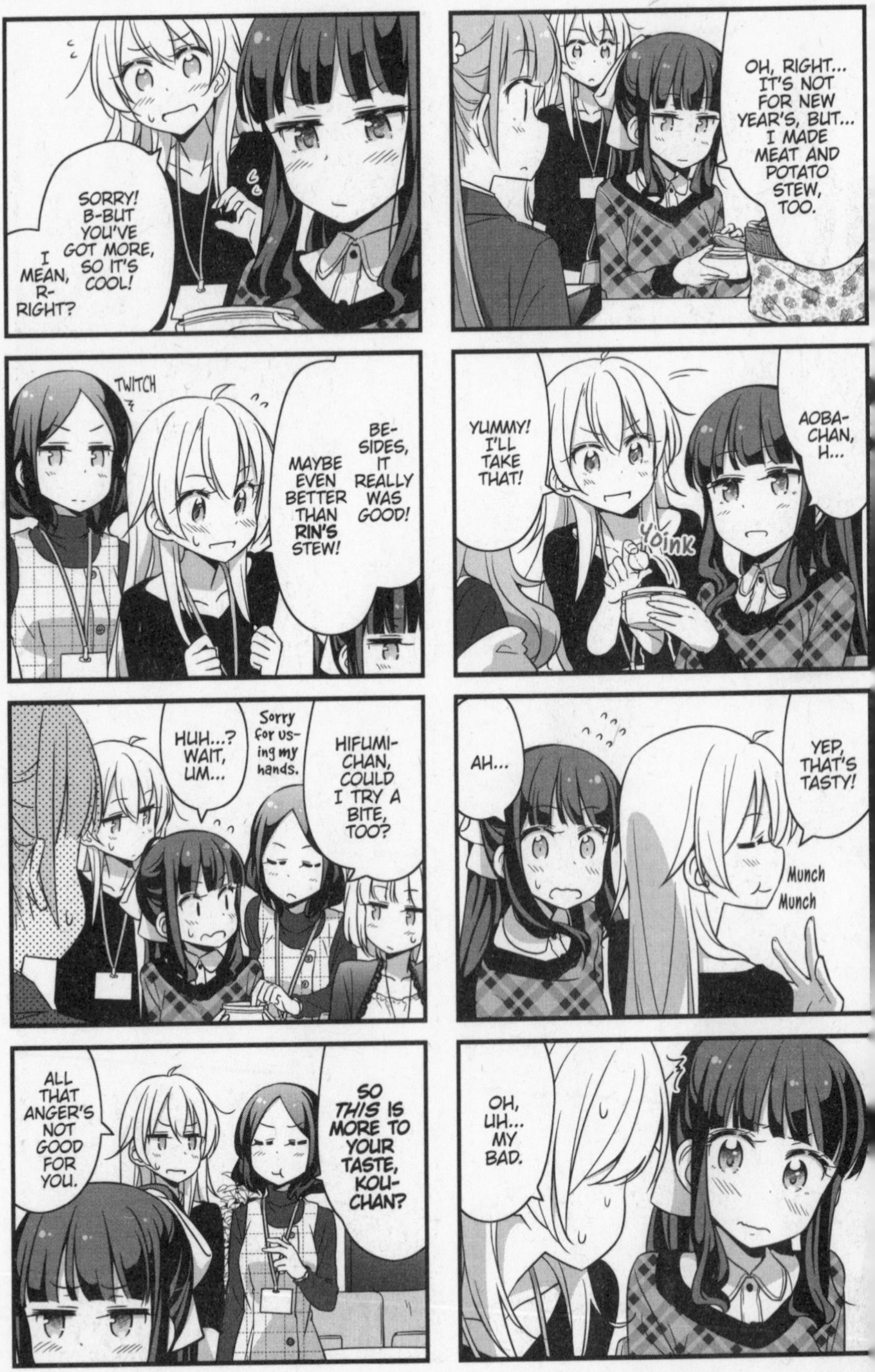
OH, RIGHT... IT'S NOT FOR NEW YEAR'S, BUT... I MADE MEAT AND POTATO STEW, TOO.
AOBA-CHAN, H...
YUMMY! I'LL TAKE THAT!
Yoink
YEP, THAT'S TASTY!
Munch Munch
AH...
OH, UH... MY BAD.
SORRY! B-BUT YOU'VE GOT MORE, SO IT'S COOL!
I MEAN, R-RIGHT?
BE-SIDES, IT REALLY WAS GOOD!
MAYBE EVEN BETTER THAN RIN'S STEW!
TWITCH
HIFUMI-CHAN, COULD I TRY A BITE, TOO?
Sorry for using my hands.
HUH...? WAIT, UM...
SO THIS IS MORE TO YOUR TASTE, KOU-CHAN?
ALL THAT ANGER'S NOT GOOD FOR YOU.

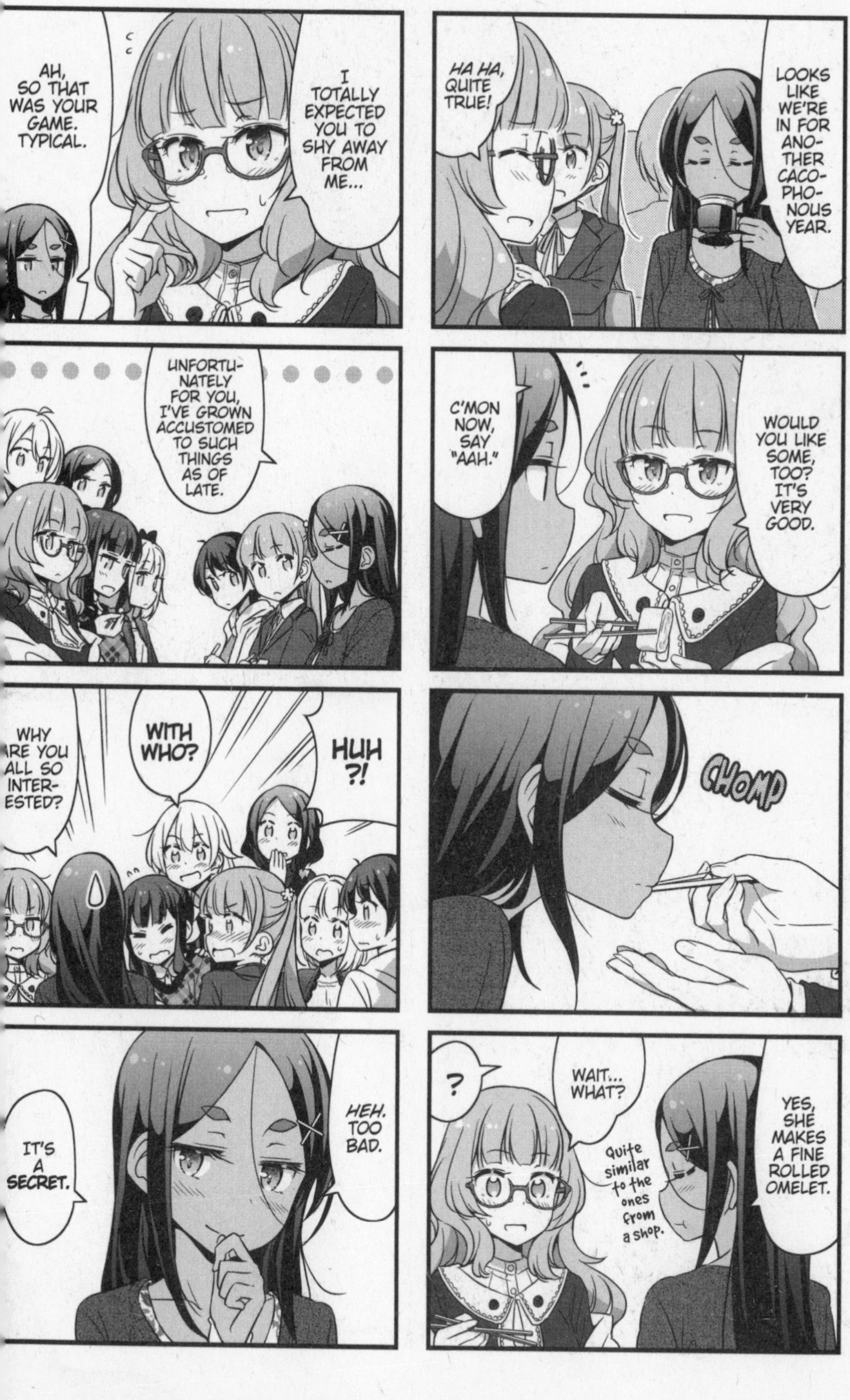
LOOKS LIKE WE'RE IN FOR ANOTHER CACOPHONOUS YEAR.
HA HA, QUITE TRUE!
WOULD YOU LIKE SOME, TOO? IT'S VERY GOOD.
C'MON NOW, SAY "AAH."
CHOMP
YES, SHE MAKES A FINE ROLLED OMELET.
WAIT... WHAT?
Quite similar to the ones from a shop.
?
I TOTALLY EXPECTED YOU TO SHY AWAY FROM ME...
AH, SO THAT WAS YOUR GAME. TYPICAL.
UNFORTUNATELY FOR YOU, I'VE GROWN ACCUSTOMED TO SUCH THINGS AS OF LATE.
HUH ?!
WITH WHO?
WHY ARE YOU ALL SO INTERESTED?
HEH. TOO BAD.
IT'S A SECRET.

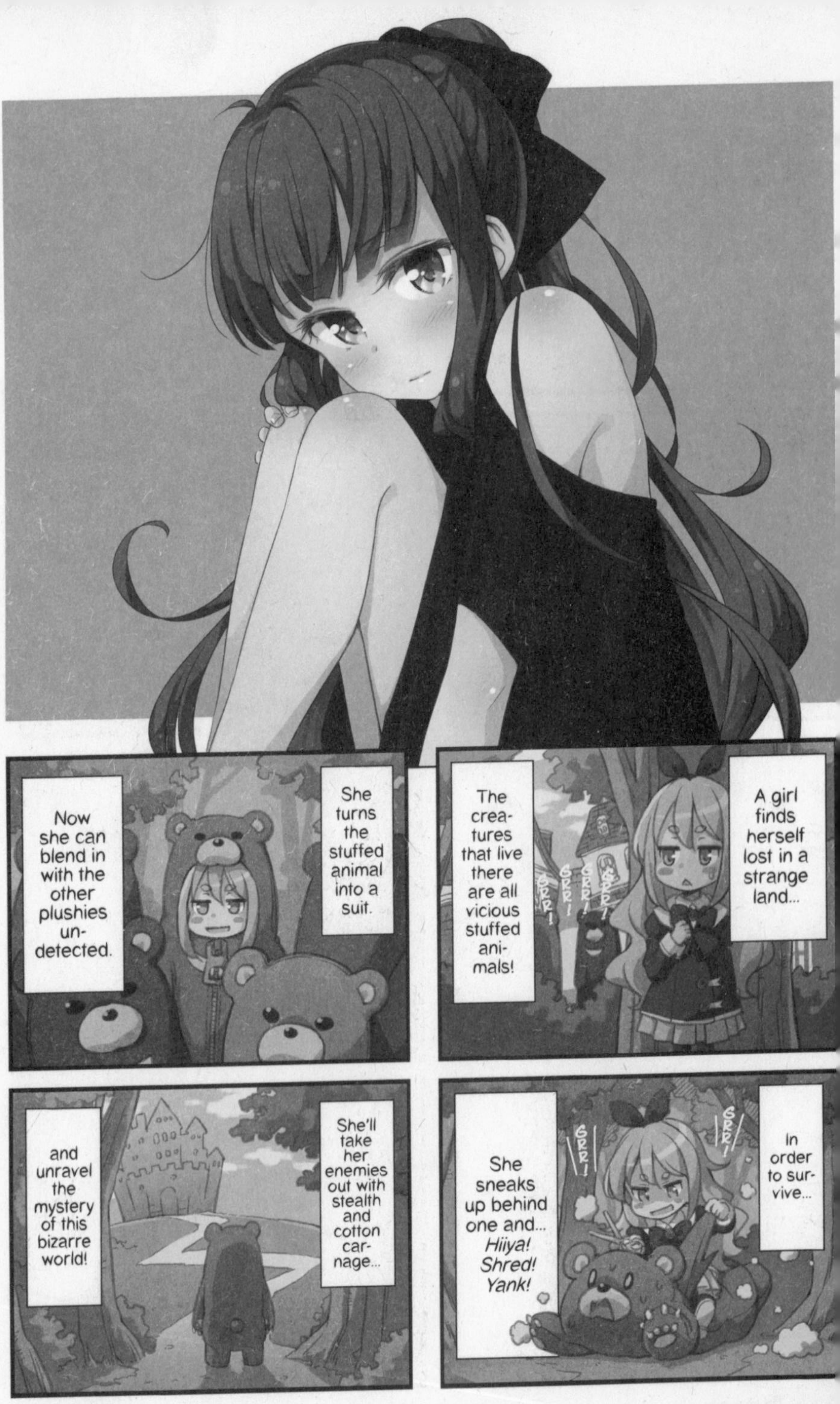
A girl finds herself lost in a strange land...
The creatures that live there are all vicious stuffed animals!
GRR!
GRR!
GRR!
In order to survive...
GRR!
GRR!
She sneaks up behind one and... Hiiya! Shred! Yank!
She turns the stuffed animal into a suit.
Now she can blend in with the other plushies undetected.
She'll take her enemies out with stealth and cotton carnage...
and unravel the mystery of this bizarre world!

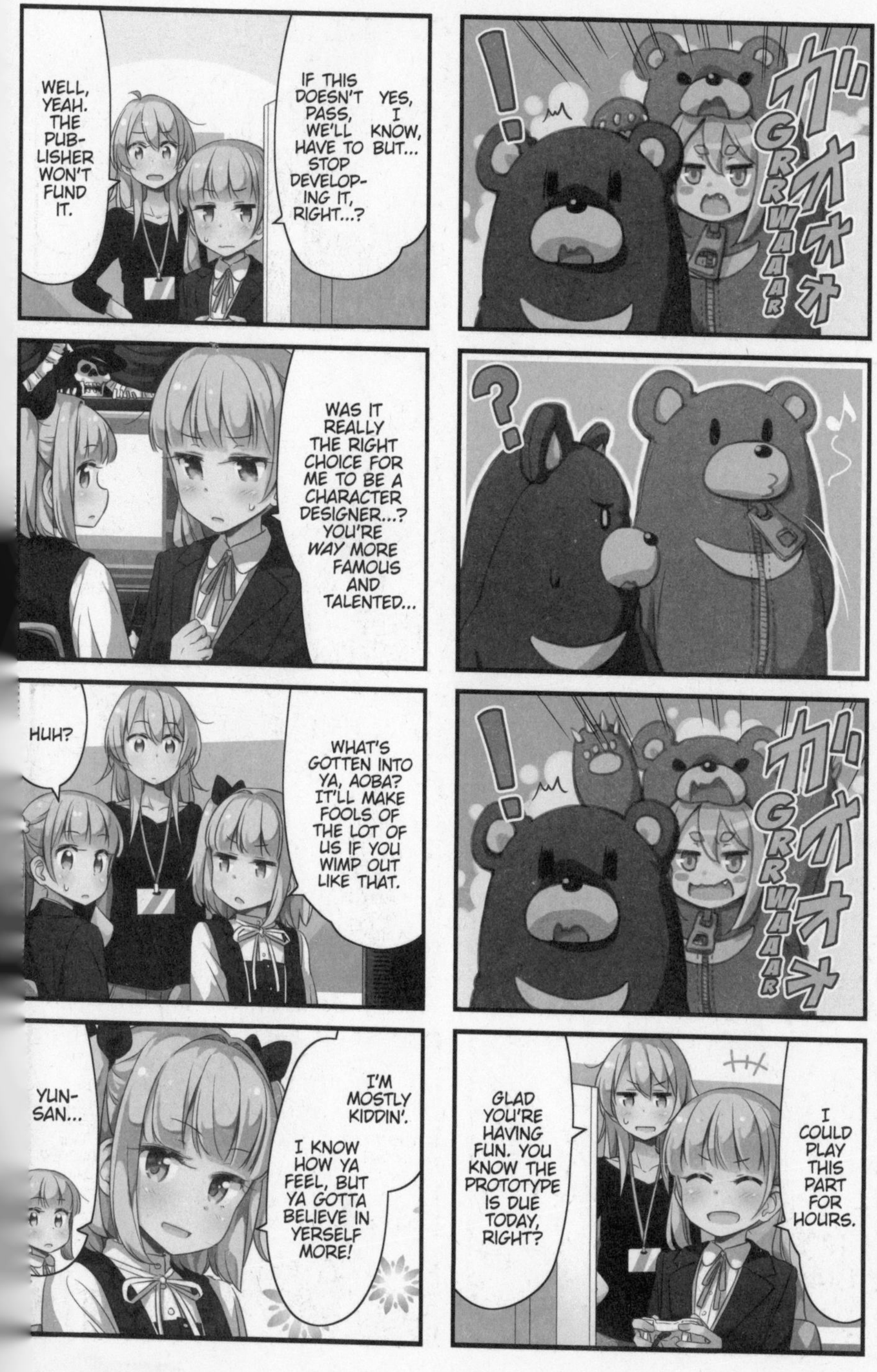
!
ガオオオ
GRRWAAAR
?
!
ガオオオ
GRRWAAAR
I COULD PLAY THIS PART FOR HOURS.
GLAD YOU'RE HAVING FUN. YOU KNOW THE PROTOTYPE IS DUE TODAY, RIGHT?
YES, I KNOW, BUT...
IF THIS DOESN'T PASS, WE'LL HAVE TO STOP DEVELOPING IT, RIGHT...?
WELL, YEAH. THE PUBLISHER WON'T FUND IT.
WAS IT REALLY THE RIGHT CHOICE FOR ME TO BE A CHARACTER DESIGNER...? YOU'RE *WAY* MORE FAMOUS AND TALENTED...
WHAT'S GOTTEN INTO YA, AOBA? IT'LL MAKE FOOLS OF THE LOT OF US IF YOU WIMP OUT LIKE THAT.
HUH?
I'M MOSTLY KIDDIN'.
I KNOW HOW YA FEEL, BUT YA GOTTA BELIEVE IN YERSELF MORE!
YUN-SAN...

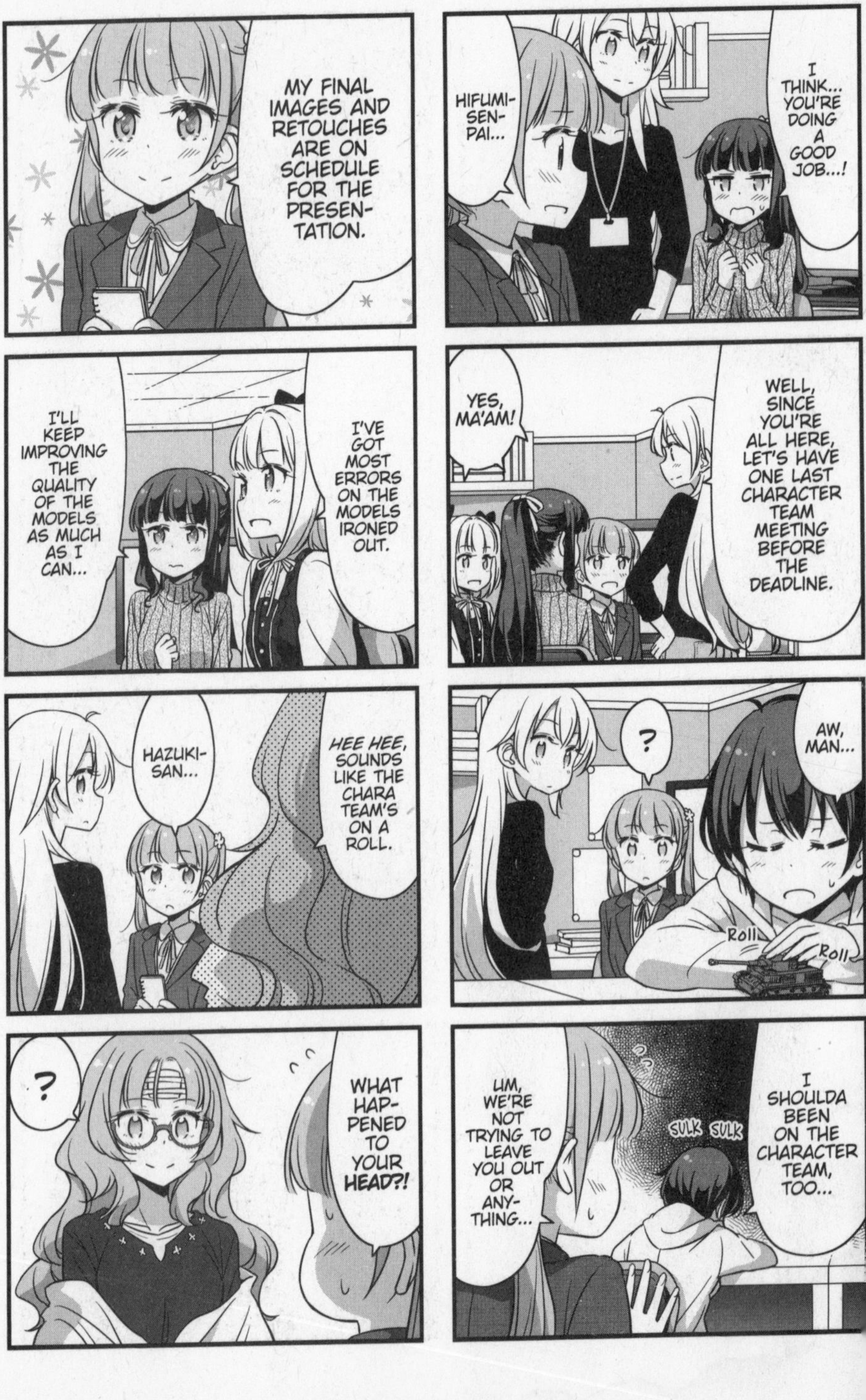
I THINK... YOU'RE DOING A GOOD JOB...!
HIFUMI-SEN-PAI...
WELL, SINCE YOU'RE ALL HERE, LET'S HAVE ONE LAST CHARACTER TEAM MEETING BEFORE THE DEADLINE.
YES, MA'AM!
AW, MAN...
?
Roll
Roll
I SHOULDA BEEN ON THE CHARACTER TEAM, TOO...
SULK SULK
UM, WE'RE NOT TRYING TO LEAVE YOU OUT OR ANY-THING...
MY FINAL IMAGES AND RETOUCHES ARE ON SCHEDULE FOR THE PRESEN-TATION.
I'VE GOT MOST ERRORS ON THE MODELS IRONED OUT.
I'LL KEEP IMPROVING THE QUALITY OF THE MODELS AS MUCH AS I CAN...
HEE HEE, SOUNDS LIKE THE CHARA TEAM'S ON A ROLL.
HAZUKI-SAN...
WHAT HAP-PENED TO YOUR **HEAD?!**
?

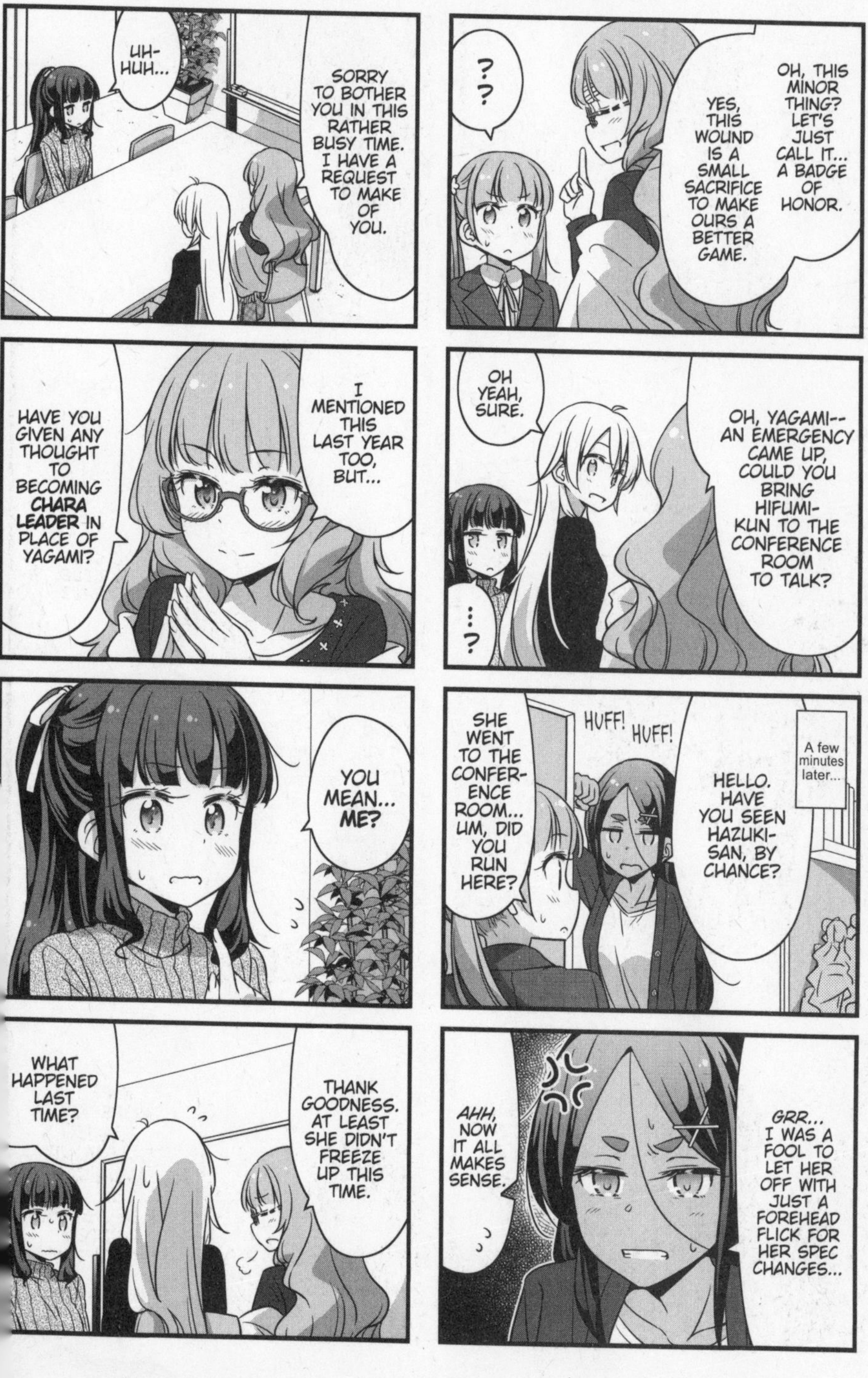
OH, THIS MINOR THING? LET'S JUST CALL IT... A BADGE OF HONOR.
YES, THIS WOUND IS A SMALL SACRIFICE TO MAKE OURS A BETTER GAME.
??
SORRY TO BOTHER YOU IN THIS RATHER BUSY TIME. I HAVE A REQUEST TO MAKE OF YOU.
UH-HUH...
OH, YAGAMI--AN EMERGENCY CAME UP, COULD YOU BRING HIFUMI-KUN TO THE CONFERENCE ROOM TO TALK?
OH YEAH, SURE.
...?
I MENTIONED THIS LAST YEAR TOO, BUT...
HAVE YOU GIVEN ANY THOUGHT TO BECOMING **CHARA LEADER** IN PLACE OF YAGAMI?
A few minutes later...
HELLO. HAVE YOU SEEN HAZUKI-SAN, BY CHANCE?
HUFF! HUFF!
SHE WENT TO THE CONFERENCE ROOM... UM, DID YOU RUN HERE?
YOU MEAN... **ME?**
GRR... I WAS A FOOL TO LET HER OFF WITH JUST A FOREHEAD FLICK FOR HER SPEC CHANGES...
AHH, NOW IT ALL MAKES SENSE.
THANK GOODNESS. AT LEAST SHE DIDN'T FREEZE UP THIS TIME.
WHAT HAPPENED LAST TIME?

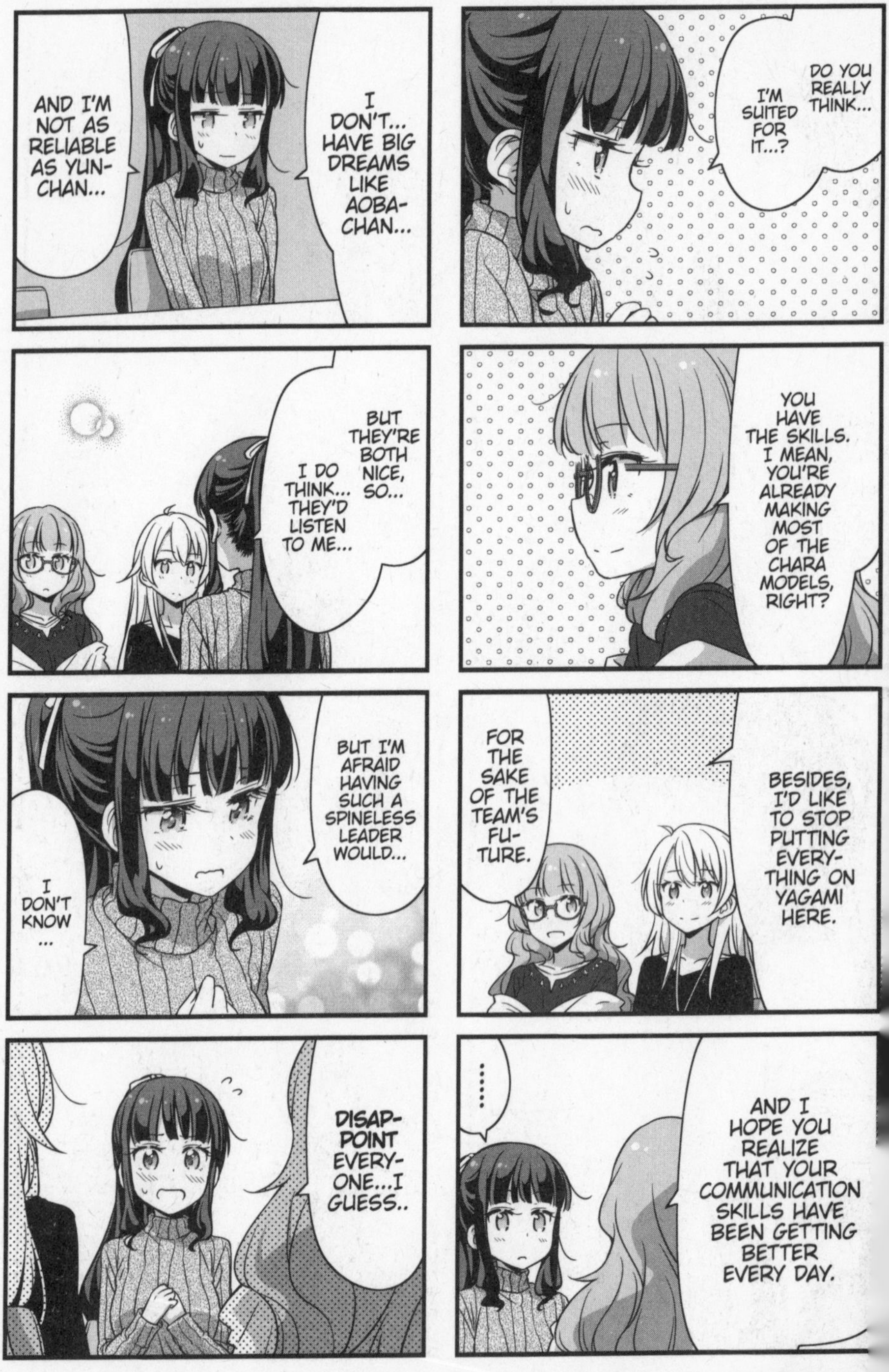
DO YOU REALLY THINK...
I'M SUITED FOR IT...?
I DON'T... HAVE BIG DREAMS LIKE AOBA-CHAN...
AND I'M NOT AS RELIABLE AS YUN-CHAN...
YOU HAVE THE SKILLS. I MEAN, YOU'RE ALREADY MAKING MOST OF THE CHARA MODELS, RIGHT?
BUT THEY'RE BOTH NICE, SO...
I DO THINK... THEY'D LISTEN TO ME...
BESIDES, I'D LIKE TO STOP PUTTING EVERYTHING ON YAGAMI HERE.
FOR THE SAKE OF THE TEAM'S FUTURE.
BUT I'M AFRAID HAVING SUCH A SPINELESS LEADER WOULD...
I DON'T KNOW ...
AND I HOPE YOU REALIZE THAT YOUR COMMUNICATION SKILLS HAVE BEEN GETTING BETTER EVERY DAY.
......
DISAPPOINT EVERYONE...I GUESS..

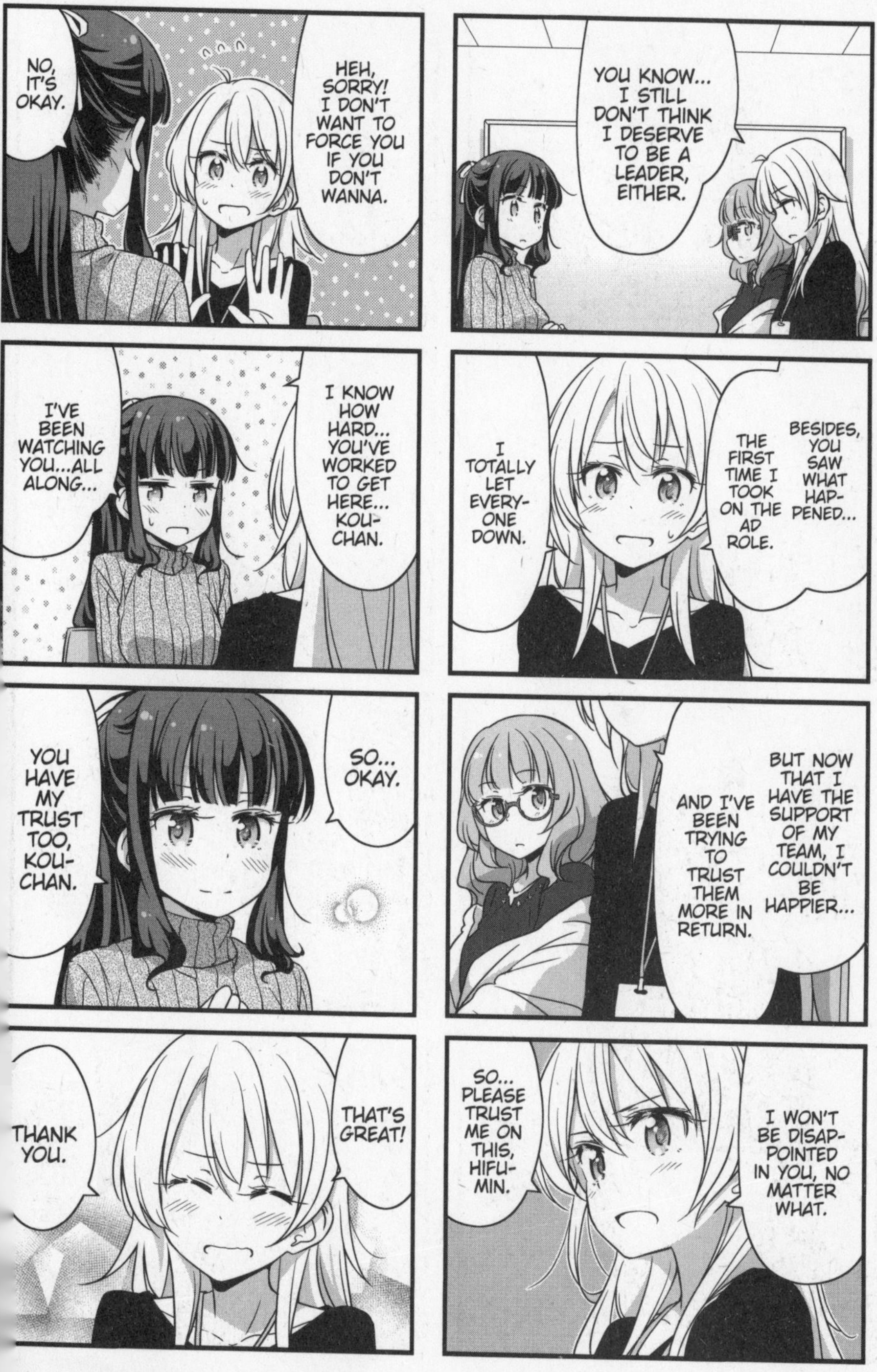
YOU KNOW... I STILL DON'T THINK I DESERVE TO BE A LEADER, EITHER.
HEH, SORRY! I DON'T WANT TO FORCE YOU IF YOU DON'T WANNA.
NO, IT'S OKAY.
BESIDES, YOU SAW WHAT HAPPENED...
THE FIRST TIME I TOOK ON THE AD ROLE.
I TOTALLY LET EVERYONE DOWN.
I KNOW HOW HARD... YOU'VE WORKED TO GET HERE... KOU-CHAN.
I'VE BEEN WATCHING YOU...ALL ALONG...
BUT NOW THAT I HAVE THE SUPPORT OF MY TEAM, I COULDN'T BE HAPPIER...
AND I'VE BEEN TRYING TO TRUST THEM MORE IN RETURN.
SO... OKAY.
YOU HAVE MY TRUST TOO, KOU-CHAN.
I WON'T BE DISAPPOINTED IN YOU, NO MATTER WHAT.
SO... PLEASE TRUST ME ON THIS, HIFUMIN.
THAT'S GREAT!
THANK YOU.

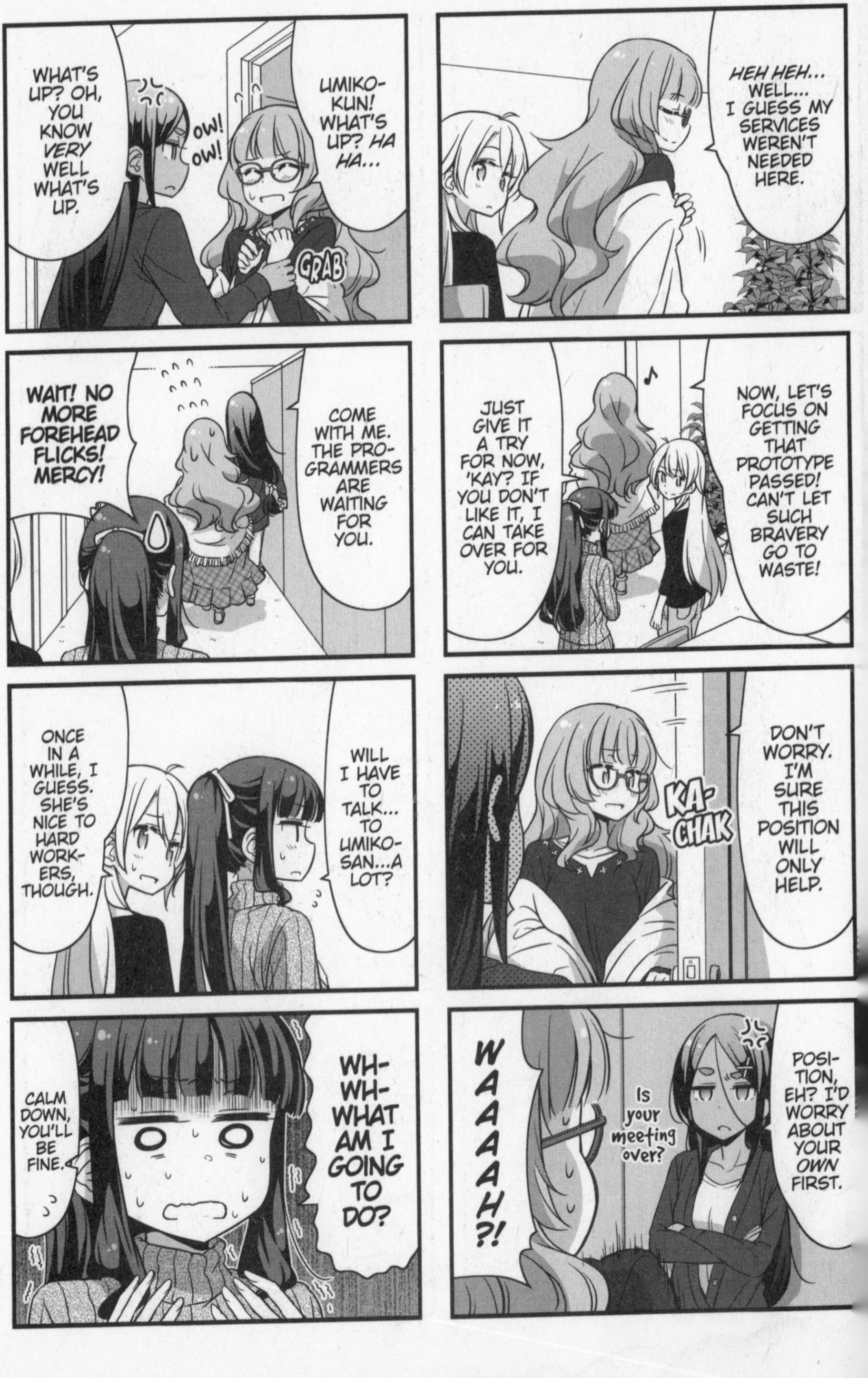
HEH HEH... WELL... I GUESS MY SERVICES WEREN'T NEEDED HERE.
UMIKO-KUN! WHAT'S UP? HA HA...
OW! OW!
WHAT'S UP? OH, YOU KNOW VERY WELL WHAT'S UP.
GRAB
NOW, LET'S FOCUS ON GETTING THAT PROTOTYPE PASSED! CAN'T LET SUCH BRAVERY GO TO WASTE!
JUST GIVE IT A TRY FOR NOW, 'KAY? IF YOU DON'T LIKE IT, I CAN TAKE OVER FOR YOU.
COME WITH ME. THE PRO-GRAMMERS ARE WAITING FOR YOU.
WAIT! NO MORE FOREHEAD FLICKS! MERCY!
DON'T WORRY. I'M SURE THIS POSITION WILL ONLY HELP.
KA-CHAK
WILL I HAVE TO TALK... TO UMIKO-SAN...A LOT?
ONCE IN A WHILE, I GUESS. SHE'S NICE TO HARD WORK-ERS, THOUGH.
POSI-TION, EH? I'D WORRY ABOUT YOUR OWN FIRST.
Is your meeting over?
WAAAAAH?!
WH-WH-WHAT AM I GOING TO DO?
CALM DOWN, YOU'LL BE FINE.

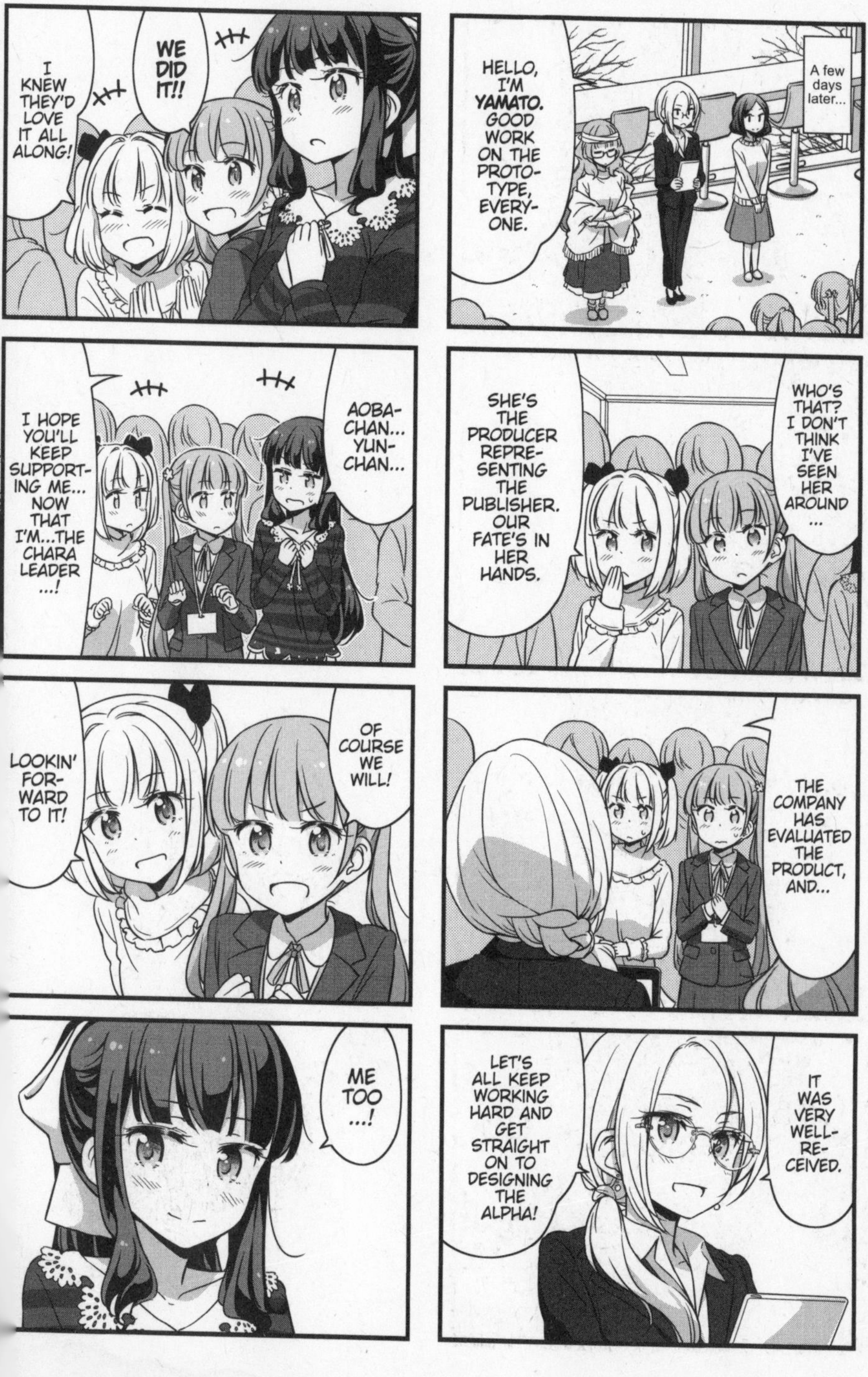
A few days later...
HELLO, I'M YAMATO. GOOD WORK ON THE PROTOTYPE, EVERYONE.
WHO'S THAT? I DON'T THINK I'VE SEEN HER AROUND...
SHE'S THE PRODUCER REPRESENTING THE PUBLISHER. OUR FATE'S IN HER HANDS.
THE COMPANY HAS EVALUATED THE PRODUCT, AND...
IT WAS VERY WELL-RECEIVED.
LET'S ALL KEEP WORKING HARD AND GET STRAIGHT ON TO DESIGNING THE ALPHA!
WE DID IT!!
I KNEW THEY'D LOVE IT ALL ALONG!
AOBA-CHAN... YUN-CHAN...
I HOPE YOU'LL KEEP SUPPORTING ME... NOW THAT I'M...THE CHARA LEADER...!
OF COURSE WE WILL!
LOOKIN' FORWARD TO IT!
ME TOO...!

YOU'VE GOT IT TOUGH TOO, MR. SNOWMAN.
I SAW HOW SUZU-KAZE-KUN WAS TOYING WITH YOU...
BUT YOU KNOW, HER DARK SIDE KINDA EXCITES ME...
I WOULDN'T MIND BEING IN YOUR SHOES... JUST KIDDING, HEE HEE...
SORRY, I FORGOT MY TOWEL!
KOFF KOFF... AHEM.
?

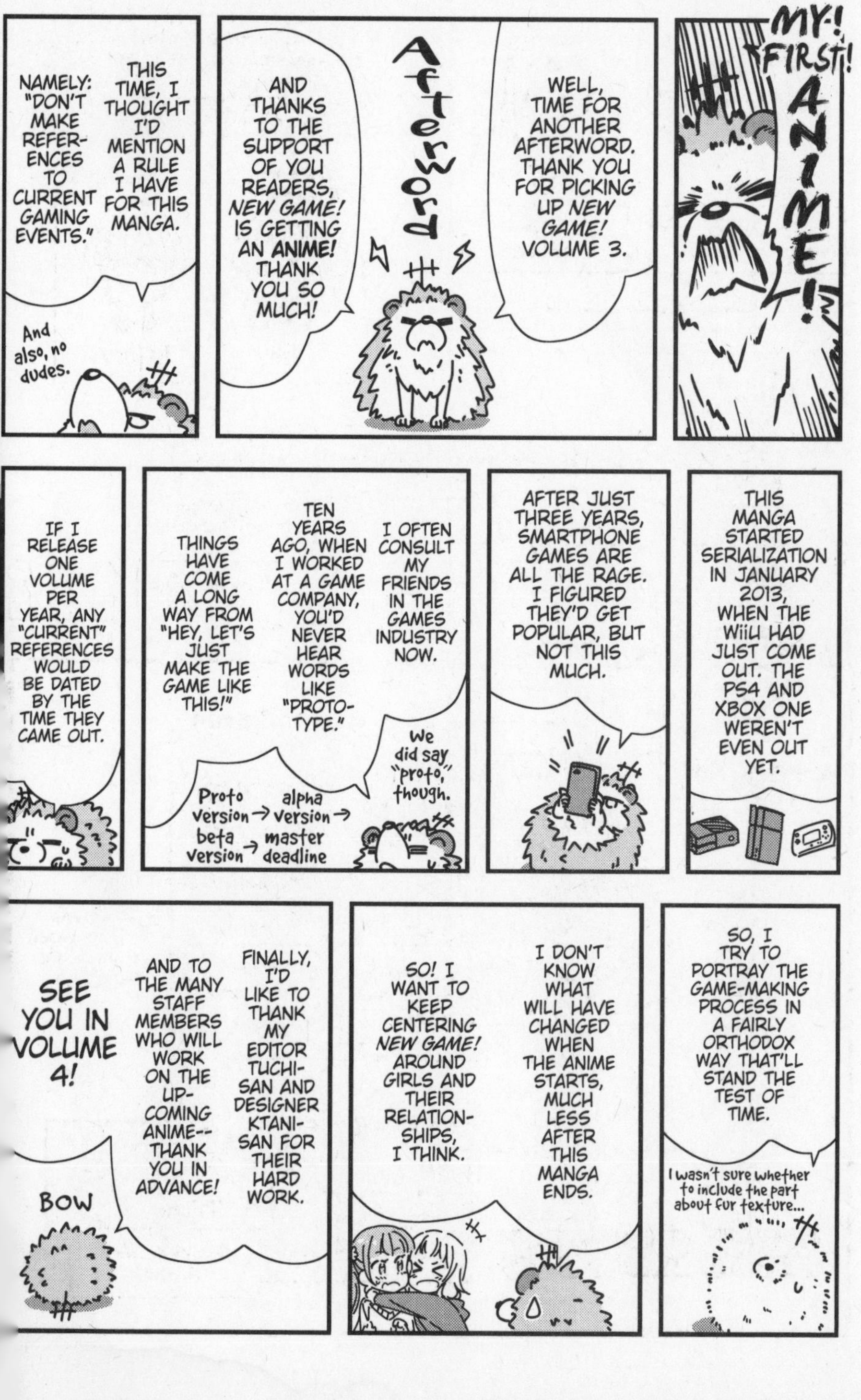
MY! FIRST! ANIME!
Afterword
WELL, TIME FOR ANOTHER AFTERWORD. THANK YOU FOR PICKING UP *NEW GAME!* VOLUME 3.
AND THANKS TO THE SUPPORT OF YOU READERS, *NEW GAME!* IS GETTING AN **ANIME!** THANK YOU SO MUCH!
THIS TIME, I THOUGHT I'D MENTION A RULE I HAVE FOR THIS MANGA.
NAMELY: "DON'T MAKE REFERENCES TO CURRENT GAMING EVENTS."
And also, no dudes.
THIS MANGA STARTED SERIALIZATION IN JANUARY 2013, WHEN THE WiiU HAD JUST COME OUT. THE PS4 AND XBOX ONE WEREN'T EVEN OUT YET.
AFTER JUST THREE YEARS, SMARTPHONE GAMES ARE ALL THE RAGE. I FIGURED THEY'D GET POPULAR, BUT NOT THIS MUCH.
I OFTEN CONSULT MY FRIENDS IN THE GAMES INDUSTRY NOW.
TEN YEARS AGO, WHEN I WORKED AT A GAME COMPANY, YOU'D NEVER HEAR WORDS LIKE "PROTOTYPE."
THINGS HAVE COME A LONG WAY FROM "HEY, LET'S JUST MAKE THE GAME LIKE THIS!"
We did say "proto," though.
Proto version → alpha version → beta version → master deadline
IF I RELEASE ONE VOLUME PER YEAR, ANY "CURRENT" REFERENCES WOULD BE DATED BY THE TIME THEY CAME OUT.
SO, I TRY TO PORTRAY THE GAME-MAKING PROCESS IN A FAIRLY ORTHODOX WAY THAT'LL STAND THE TEST OF TIME.
I wasn't sure whether to include the part about fur texture...
I DON'T KNOW WHAT WILL HAVE CHANGED WHEN THE ANIME STARTS, MUCH LESS AFTER THIS MANGA ENDS.
SO! I WANT TO KEEP CENTERING *NEW GAME!* AROUND GIRLS AND THEIR RELATIONSHIPS, I THINK.
FINALLY, I'D LIKE TO THANK MY EDITOR TUCHI-SAN AND DESIGNER KTANI-SAN FOR THEIR HARD WORK.
AND TO THE MANY STAFF MEMBERS WHO WILL WORK ON THE UPCOMING ANIME--THANK YOU IN ADVANCE!
SEE YOU IN VOLUME 4!
BOW

The day before the company trip (2)

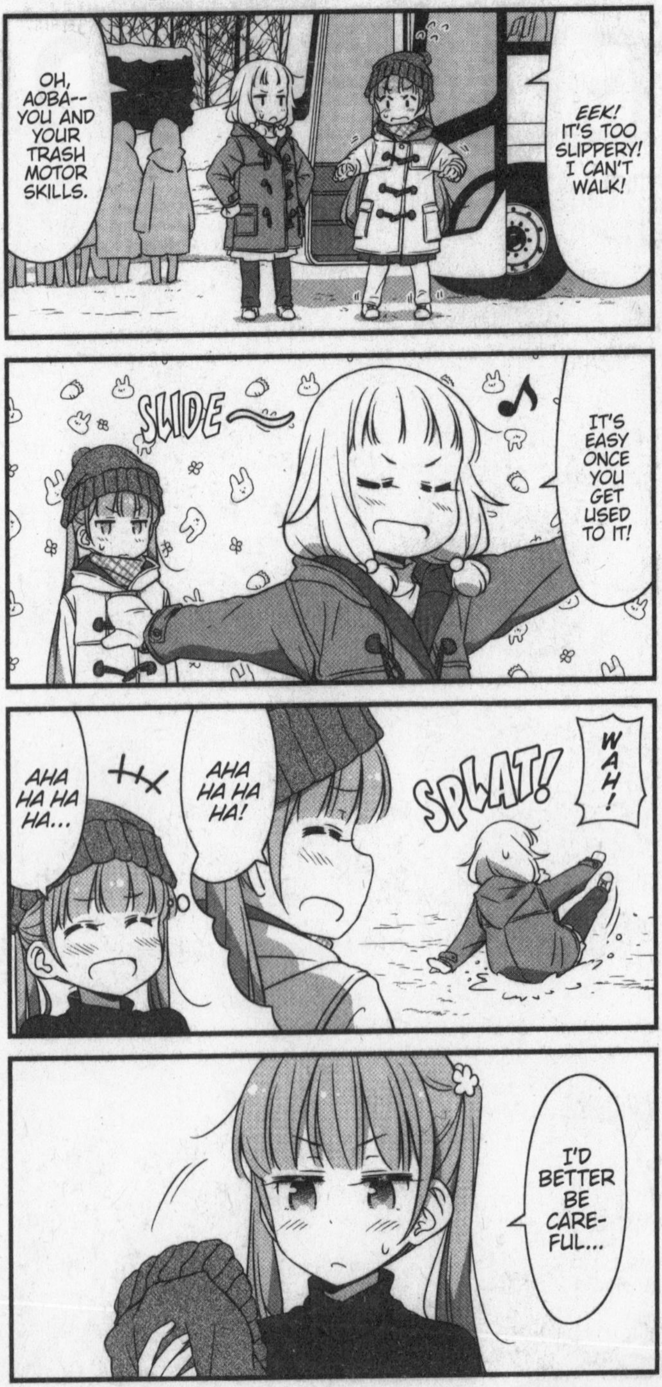
EEK! IT'S TOO SLIPPERY! I CAN'T WALK!
OH, AOBA-- YOU AND YOUR TRASH MOTOR SKILLS.
IT'S EASY ONCE YOU GET USED TO IT!
SLIDE
WAH!
SPLAT!
AHA HA HA HA!
AHA HA HA HA...
I'D BETTER BE CARE-FUL...

SEVEN SEAS ENTERTAINMENT PRESENTS

VOLUME 3

WITHDRAWN

TRANSLATION
Jenny McKeon

ADAPTATION
Jamal Joseph Jr.

LETTERING AND RETOUCH
Courtney Williams

COVER DESIGN
Nicky Lim

PROOFREADER
Danielle King
Dayna Abel

EDITOR
Jenn Grunigen

PRODUCTION ASSISTANT
CK Russell

PRODUCTION MANAGER
Lissa Pattillo

EDITOR-IN-CHIEF
Adam Arnold

PUBLISHER
Jason DeAngelis

NEW GAME! VOLUME 3
© Shotaro Tokuno 2016
First published in 2016 by Houbunsha Co., LTD. Tokyo, Japan.
English translation rights arranged with Houbunsha Co., TLD.

ISBN: 978-1-626929-00-5

Printed in Canada

First Printing: September 2018

10 9 8 7 6 5 4 3 2 1

FOLLOW US ONLINE: www.sevenseasentertainment.com

READING DIRECTIONS

This book reads from *right to left*, Japanese style. If
this is your first time reading manga, you start
reading from the top right panel on each page and
take it from there. If you get lost, just follow the
numbered diagram here. It may seem backwards at
first, but you'll get the hang of it! Have fun!!

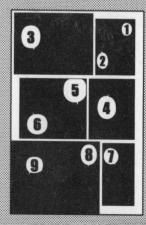

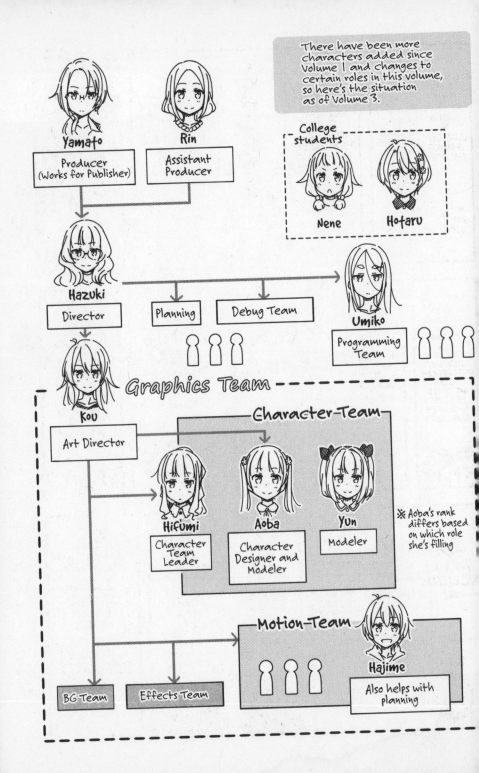

There have been more characters added since Volume 1 and changes to certain roles in this volume, so here's the situation as of Volume 3.

Yamato — Producer (Works for Publisher)

Rin — Assistant Producer

College students

Nene

Hotaru

Hazuki — Director

Planning

Debug Team

Umiko — Programming Team

Graphics Team

Kou — Art Director

Character Team

Hifumi — Character Team Leader

Aoba — Character Designer and Modeler

Yun — Modeler

※ Aoba's rank differs based on which role she's filling

Motion Team

Hajime — Also helps with planning

BG Team

Effects Team

The day before the company trip (1)

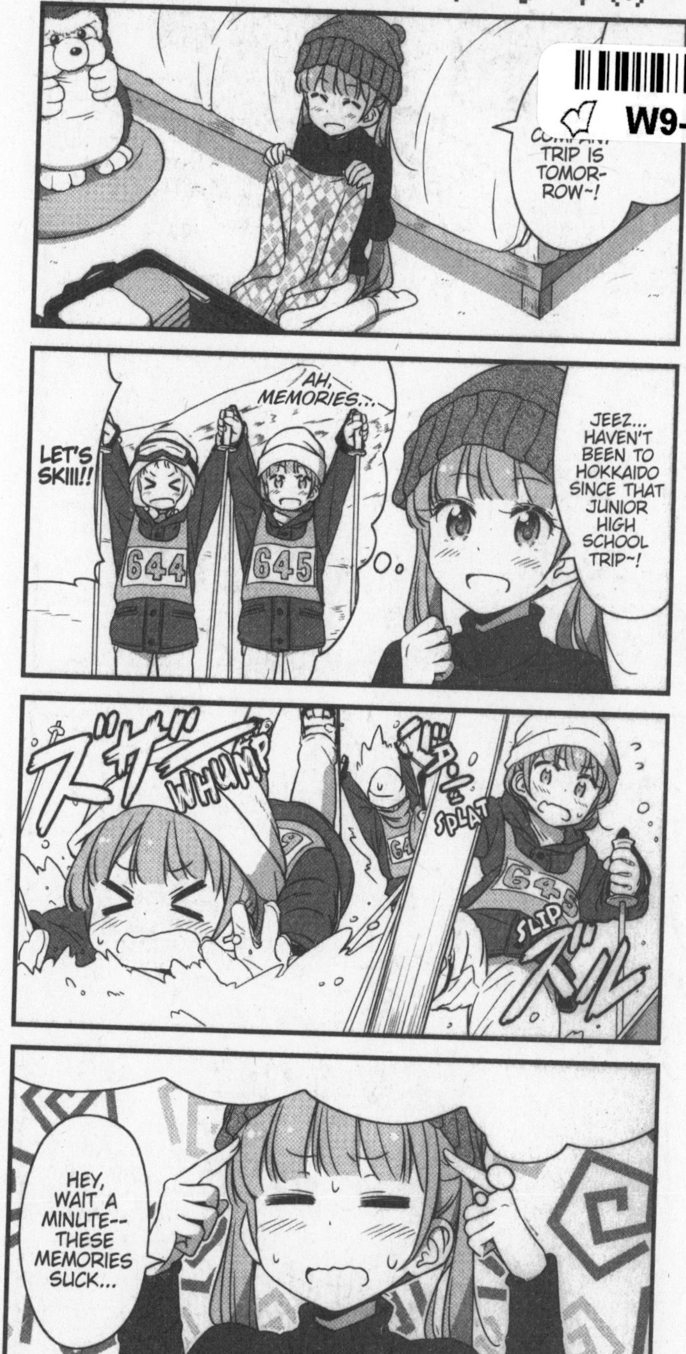
COMPANY TRIP IS TOMORROW~!
JEEZ... HAVEN'T BEEN TO HOKKAIDO SINCE THAT JUNIOR HIGH SCHOOL TRIP~!
AH, MEMORIES...
LET'S SKIII!!
SPLAT
SLIP
WHUMP
HEY, WAIT A MINUTE-- THESE MEMORIES SUCK...